SATAN'S BECKONING

by

Michael K Foster

Typeset in Bembo Std

Editing, design, typesetting and publishing by UK Book Publishing

UK Book Publishing is a trading name of Consilience Media

www.ukbookpublishing.com

ISBN: 978-1-910223-78-9

Cover images:

Human Skull © Benjamin Earwicker – freeimages.com
Penshaw Monument © Mark Bryant – freeimages.com

In memory of Robert Ducker

By **MICHAEL K FOSTER**

DCI Mason & David Carlisle series:

THE WHARF BUTCHER

SATAN'S BECKONING

Acknowledgements

As all my DCI Mason and David Carlisle novels are works of fiction based in the North East of England, there are so many people without whose help and support it would have been difficult, if not impossible, to write with any sense of authenticity. Suffering from dyslexia as I do, my grateful thanks go out to the late Rita Day and my dear wife Pauline, whose belief and inspiration has never waned.

I am indebted to Detective Constable Maurice Waugh, a former member of the Yorkshire Ripper Squad, and Ken Stewart, a former member of South Shields CID, whose technical assistance in the aspects of how the police tackle crime has allowed me a better understanding of what actually takes place. Their efforts have helped me enormously.

To single out a few other names in particular who helped make the difference to this book, I would like to thank Paul Foster and Lynn Oakes for their encouragement and unqualified support in developing the initial cover graphics. Last but not least I would express my heartfelt appreciation to the Beta reader team: Jan Duffy, Mark Duffy, Daniel Inman, and Brenda Forster, without whose help this book would never have made the bookshelf.

Preface

Eyes glued to the computer screen, he licked his lips in anticipation as another wave of excitement washed over him. His throat tightened, and he could barely breathe. The room was 'T' shaped, a cold, damp claustrophobic structure completely isolated from the rest of the building. It was dark inside, only a flickering candle-light. Rotating the focus adjustment, a familiar emptiness returned to the pit of his stomach.

He breathed in her fear. This one was another looker, long legs, slim waist, small firm breasts and neat rounded buttocks. He liked them like that, and he knew how to hurt.

Ever so slowly he zoomed in on camera one.

Where are you, bitch!

Chapter One

January, 2013

Barry Steel was barely alive when they pulled him from the cab of his blue Ford Transit van that night. This was no accident, nor was it suicide. Somewhere beneath the layers of twisted metal, along with a dead woman's body now trapped in the front passenger seat of the little red Volkswagen Polo, lay the truth. It would take all night before accident investigators would get to the bottom of it – they were in no hurry.

Jack Mason waved his warrant card under the young Constable's nose, signed his name in the crime scene entry log sheet, and braced himself against the elements. Not usually the sort of job for a Detective Chief Inspector at ten minutes to midnight, he thought. As if he didn't have enough problems already. Feeling like shit, his head was pounding and the back of his throat felt like coarse sandpaper. He'd read somewhere that oestrogen gave women a stronger immune system, and more resistance to respiratory illnesses compared to their testosterone-filled counterparts.

Bullshit, he cursed.

Mason heard the ambulance radio crackle into life, then saw the blue emergency warning lights spinning. Seconds later, he watched as four burly firemen prepared to lift the heavily sedated van driver into the back of the waiting ambulance. Overseeing the proceedings, a young female trauma-team doctor was holding up an IV bag, whilst giving out instructions to a male paramedic on the other end of the drip line. It was then that he spotted the large recovery truck. It was facing downhill, its engine switched off and cab windows heavily frosted over. Closer to home, not far from the crash scene, he caught his first glimpse of the Fire and Rescue Appliance. Nearby a group of road traffic officers stood huddled around the back of their police BMW X5 Traffic vehicles. Picked out in the floodlights, their distinct yellow hi-vis jackets reminded him of a nineties skiing jacket his father once made him wear.

'Not the best of nights, Jack.'

Mason turned sharply to confront the Crime Scene Manager. Early fifties, with an unruly shock of jet black hair, Stan Johnson had a touch of the eccentricity about him. He bred budgerigars for show and was honorary president of his local Morris Dancers' Society, whatever that meant. Amidst bouts of coughing, he watched as Johnson glanced across at the crumpled wreckage and raised his black thickset bushy eyebrows as if about to speak.

'Do we have an ID on the casualty?' Mason asked.

'His name's Barry Steel, he works for the local water authority.'

'Not his lucky night!'

Johnson's frown lines corrugated. 'He was on his way to an emergency callout when the accident happened.'

'Has he said anything?'

'Not yet he hasn't, he's still unconscious.'

Mason hunched his shoulders and dug his hands deep into his coat pockets. When he spoke, his warm breath condensed into tiny water vapour droplets sending out thick clouds of white fog. He wasn't a conspicuously tall man, five-nine, stocky, with strong powerful shoulders and short cropped hair. His nose had been broken a few times, and stuck back on a face that had seen more than its fair share of trouble. Barely six weeks into his new role with the Serious Crime Squad, Mason was out to impress – or that was his intention.

Cursing man flu, his whole body was aching and he clearly lacked energy. Now turned forty-five, his twenty-seven years with the Metropolitan police had taught him many things. Above all, never take anything for granted.

'What do we know about the red Volkswagen Polo?' he asked.

'It's registered to a Miss Caroline Harper,' Johnson replied.

'And the young woman still trapped inside of it?'

'No ID as yet, but she's already been pronounced dead.'

'Ouch! Bad start for someone's New Year.'

'I'm afraid so,' Johnson acknowledged.

Mason did a quick mental check. He'd taken the call shortly after crawling into bed that night. Head on collision, they'd said. The driver was missing and uniforms were out searching. This sort of thing happened regularly in Gateshead; late night revellers out of control. Mason hated uncertainty. The not knowing what was coming next. Ducking below the police cordon tape, he pulled his collar up and made towards the crash scene.

Out of all the police doctors who could have been on duty that night, it had to be Henry Hindson. The man exuded arrogance from every pore of his body, and he wasn't liked either. Well, Mason cursed, might as well get it over with.

'What do we have, Henry?'

'Young woman, slightly built, around thirtyish,' Hindson mumbled.

'Died on impact?'

'You need to look closer, Jack.'

Hindson's reply was abrupt, and Mason had picked up on it. Seething with anger, he struggled to stay in control. His whole body was aching and his legs felt as though they had lead weights attached to them. To make matters worse, every few milliseconds the dead woman's face was illuminated by the ambulance's blue flashing spinner lights. Eyes glazed over, mouth frozen open in a cry of revulsion, she was staring back at him through the mangled passenger door. Not your usual drunken driver head-on collision, he thought. This one felt different – sinister, more controlled.

Mason stepped back a pace, his voice sounding croakier by the minute.

'Estimated time of death?'

The doctor stood for a moment, removed his wool beanie hat, and ran his fingers through silky white hair. 'It's difficult to be exact. Not more than four hours, I'd say.'

'Four hours!'

'She didn't die here if that's what you're thinking, this one was murdered.'

Mason flinched as the SOC's camera flash bounced off the dead woman's wax-like features. From where he now stood, only the rear half of the Polo was visible. The air reeked of diesel fumes, and the temporary floodlighting was casting ominous shadows over the entire crash scene. It was then he noticed the water authority's van roof had been cut away. There was blood over the driver's seat, oil on the floor, and the steering wheel had been removed by the emergency services.

'What makes you say that?' Mason asked.

'Take your pick: there's bruising to the neck and severe blunt force traumas to the back of the skull. No doubt a detailed post-mortem examination will tell us more.'

Mason tried not to dwell on it.

'Strangled?'

The doctor nodded. 'There's oil stains on her dress but very little blood, which you'd anticipate finding from such extensive head trauma injuries.'

'Murdered elsewhere, well I'll be damned!'

From what he could see, Coldwell Lane ran a good half mile to the crossroads with Windy Nook. Judging by the impact damage, speed was the overriding factor here.

Stepping from the shadows he was met by Sergeant Morrison, an old school copper now nearing retirement. The sergeant removed his peaked cap and peered in through a small jagged opening at the rear of the Volkswagen Polo. What Morrison didn't know about RTC's wasn't worth discussing.

'What do you think, old-timer?' Mason asked.

'It looks like the driver's done a runner, boss.'

Mason stared at him quizzically.

'TWOC, do you think?'

'We'll need to check whether the vehicle was in gear before it collided,' the sergeant confirmed. 'At least that should tell us how it arrived here.'

'Who would jump ship with a dead woman sat beside you?'

'Some scumbag did.'

Mason peered into the well of the vehicle again. There was glass everywhere, a strong smell of engine oil and the metallic clicking sound of cooling metal. Fingerprints found on the steering wheel might uncover something. There again, it had probably been wiped clean. He stared at the dead woman's face. She was a pretty thing, with long wavy brown hair, high cheekbones, and incredibly long eyelashes. She looked so innocent, he thought.

He flashed his torch beam ahead of them. Some crime scenes spoke volumes to him, but not this one. This one felt different, as though he'd stepped through an open door not knowing what was on the other side. What had started off as a routine road traffic accident was now a full-blown murder investigation.

As he walked back towards the recovery vehicle, he suddenly stopped dead in his tracks. Hold on a minute!

Ch*pter
Two

Jack Mason rolled out of bed in a sweat. It was eight thirty, and he'd not slept a wink. He showered, got dressed and went downstairs and made himself a mug of coffee before settling down into his favourite chair. Breakfast television was already playing out on last night's fatal road traffic accident, which somehow looked different in broad daylight. Diversions in place, a local news presenter was reporting havoc to the early morning rush hour traffic. As police officers continued with their investigations, Coldwell Lane and the surrounding districts were still closed to the general public. With no mention of murder, Mason felt somewhat relieved. At least he had a head start on the press.

It was late morning when he finally reached Gateshead Police Station. Part of the Northumbria Police's Central Area Command, these past few weeks had been hectic. His new office furniture had arrived, but he still had mountains of paperwork to file away. Sited on the third floor with views overlooking the car park, Matalan and Gateshead Magistrates' Court, his office was rectangular in shape. It had a low ceiling, cream coloured walls, and was fitted out in heavy duty brown carpet tiles. Not exactly his choice of colour either. He would have preferred green, as it was much more soothing to the eye.

Logging onto his computer, he ran back over the overnight serials. A hit and run in Felling, a street brawl outside The Gloucester public house in Gateshead High West Street; all seemed to add for another regular night. When he came to the Alpaca thefts though, he paused in reflection for a second. This was the third such incident in as many weeks, and all within a ten mile radius of each other. Having gained the attention of Acting Superintendent Francis Sutherland, Mason was taking no chances. His new boss had a fixation that NAFIS, the National Automated Fingerprint Identification System, was the be-all and end-all to solving every crime. If that wasn't bad enough, just how he was going catch Alpaca thieves using a fingerprint recognition system was beyond him. But just in case, and as a precautionary measure, he would need to think of something.

Never a dull moment, he cursed.

'A quick word in your ear, if I may,' Sergeant Holt said, poking his head in round the open office door.

'Yes, George.'

'An update on last night's RTC, if I may.'

'Good man, what's happening?'

'Coldwell Lane has finally reopened, boss.' The Sergeant's bottom jaw tightened slightly. 'Mind, it took emergency teams the best part of an hour to release the dead woman from the vehicle. She'd been strangled, apparently.'

'Not exactly an accident then?'

'It would appear not—'

'What about her vehicle?'

'Ah, yes, the ignition keys,' Holt dithered. 'They were turned to the unlock position, and the vehicle was in neutral on impact. According to Road Traffic, it looks like it was free-wheeled down into Coldwell Lane.'

'Nasty!'

'Which means the transit van driver didn't stand a bloody chance.'

'What about the VIN?

'It checks out – the vehicle belongs to a Miss Caroline Harper,' Holt replied.

Did anyone witness anything, Mason wondered? It was eleven o'clock, nearing closing time – surely somebody must have heard or seen something suspicious on their way home from the pub that night. There again, Felling wasn't exactly a police friendly area and he certainly wasn't pinning his hopes on anyone coming forward with information. No, whoever had murdered this young woman certainly knew what they were doing.

'What news on the van driver's condition?'

'According to the QE, there's been a slight improvement.' There was hesitation in the sergeant's voice, a checking of notes. 'He's still in a coma, apparently.'

Mason knew his next question was pointless, but he still felt the need to ask it.

'What news on the Volkswagen's driver?'

'Still nothing,' the sergeant said, his voice trailing off.

Mason's frustrations were interrupted by another coughing fit.

'Any news on the dead woman's ID?'

'We've recovered a black purse. It was found wedged down the front passenger seat of the vehicle.'

'A purse—'

'Yes, it's currently with forensics.'

'Anything in it?' asked Mason, lifting his head in interest.

'A young woman's driver's licence, a couple of payment receipts, and—'

'Forensics you say?'

'Yes. Tom Hedley's dealing with it. And before you ask, it will take him at least twenty-four hours to sift through the detail.' The Sergeant's face looked sheepishly across at him. 'He'll let you know the results as and when they come in.'

Mason considered the facts. There were more questions than answers. Even though DNA and dental records were a more reliable source of identification, the prospect of waiting another twenty-four hours didn't exactly excite him. Besides, the minute the press found out she'd been murdered all hell would be let loose. News travelled fast, and walls had ears. No, he thought, he would need to find another way round it. There again, if the driving licence photograph matched that of the dead woman now lying in the mortuary, there was a slim chance he might be able to pull something off.

Despite a heavy chest cough, at least his headache had cleared.

'What news on last night's break-ins, George?'

'Nothing yet, boss. No doubt they were drugs related.'

Mason nodded his agreement.

'Is that all?'

'Just one more thing,' the sergeant said. 'A couple of newspaper reporters have been hanging around in reception. They're obviously looking for a statement on last night's RTC.'

'Any mention of murder?'

'No, fingers crossed. No doubt they'll be sniffing around the Coroner's office once a post-mortem has been carried out,' the sergeant replied.

Mason was about to say something when he broke into another coughing fit.

'That chest of yours sounds bloody awful, boss.'

'It's nothing a stiff whisky won't put right, George.'

With that the sergeant took off.

His mind running amok, Mason picked up the office telephone and rang forensics. Within minutes the image of a young woman's driving licence flashed across his computer screen. The first thing he checked was the date of issue. From what he could see, Caroline Harper was an attractive young woman. Thirtyish, slightly built with long shoulder length hair. She had a pale complexion and high cheekbones. He didn't know this young woman, but she was far too young to have fallen into some monster's hands. There again, murder came in all forms and guises, and it certainly wasn't selective.

Mason jotted down the address, *Prince Consort Road, Gateshead*, and closed his notebook. He knew the area well. There were a couple of decent pubs there, so it was probably worth a visit. Pleased with his findings, he answered a few e-mails, sifted through his mail, and tidied a few more files away. Things were looking up, and if the dead woman now lying in a Gateshead mortuary was Caroline Harper, then it wasn't going to be an overly complex case to solve.

It had started to rain by the time he'd reached the car park.

He wasn't impressed.

Chapter Three

Armed with the latest information, earlier that morning DCI Mason had contacted Dr Gillian King, the Senior Anatomical Pathology Technician at Gateshead Coroner's Office. Things were coming along nicely and after revisiting Coldwell Lane, he decided to call in at the mortuary. Situated close to the main hospital entrance, from the outside the coroner's office looked just like any other building in the street. Inside was a totally different matter of course. Still suffering from man-flu, his head had cleared somewhat. Even so, his nostrils weren't immune to the putrid smells now permeating throughout the building. Mason hated mortuaries at the best of times. No matter how much disinfectant they used, the place still reeked of death.

Wearing a blue gown, green plastic apron and white boots, Dr Gillian King was a florid, corpulent woman. Married with two teenage sons, she had a matronly appearance which was surprisingly the opposite of what Mason had anticipated finding in such morose surroundings.

'You're early, Jack,' said King. 'Is someone coming to make a formal identification?'

'Not that I'm aware of.'

'Well,' replied King, 'the post-mortem examination isn't due to start until three o'clock this afternoon. How can I help?'

Mason cursed his luck as he reached into a pocket and pulled out a small brown envelope. The ink barely dry, he noted, as he handed King a copy of Caroline Harper's driving licence.

'Would this be the same young woman who was brought here during the early hours of this morning?' he asked.

'How did you come by this information?' asked King.

'It was wedged down the front passenger seat of the victim's vehicle.'

'Not in her handbag?'

'No, she wasn't carrying one.'

King raised her heavily pencilled bushy eyebrows and stared at the woman's driving licence. 'Caroline Harper,' she whispered. 'I take it you're looking for some kind of informal identification?'

'It would be useful, yes.'

'It's difficult to tell, Jack. Perhaps you might care to take a look for yourself.'

The minute he stepped into the post-mortem suite, Mason felt his stomach lurch. This was the last place he wanted to be right now. Detached from the rest of the building, the room was cold, windowless, and felt distinctly creepy. The walls, light grey in colour and blue speckled floor tiles, were overshadowed by a long bank of steel fronted fridges running along the entire length of one wall. Three stainless-steel post-mortem tables dominated the central ground. None of them were occupied. Void of feeling, the room had that all too familiar morbid finality about it that Mason detested. The people who came here usually didn't have very much to say for themselves.

He watched as a middle-aged Anatomical Technician wheeled a blue hydraulic body trolley towards one of the fridge doors, opened it, and dropped one of the stainless-steel body trays down onto the trolley. The first thing he noticed after she slid the cover back to reveal the dead woman's upper torso was her eyes. They were wide open and staring back at him just as they had done earlier that morning. He took a deep breath. King pointed out the blunt force trauma to the back of the young woman's skull. There were also two noticeable lacerations running diagonally across the right cheek bone, as though freshly cut with a surgical knife. Moving closer, he could see distinct evidence of bruising to the nape of the neck. Consistent with concentrated thumb pressure, he also noted there was noticeable bruising to the ankles and wrists. Mason paused in reflection for a moment – a gathering of thoughts.

Dr King, meanwhile, had picked up a small digital camera from a nearby stainless-steel workbench and connected it to her laptop. After taking several close-up images of the young woman's facial features, she deftly aligned them with the photograph he'd given her.

'This isn't an exact science, you do realise that. However, the position of the eyes, nose and jaw line, all align.' The Home Office Pathologist pointed to the computer screen and made a little sweeping gesture. 'There are two distinct moles, one here on the left maxilla – the other above the left brow ridge.'

As if to record the time, King habitually glanced up at the large white wall clock. She checked herself, and then said, 'I would undoubtedly say it's the same person, but please don't quote me on that. Not until a formal identification has been carried out.'

'I'm grateful,' Mason nodded.

The Home Office Pathologist frowned. 'Is something wrong?' she asked.

'It's this place,' Mason shuddered. 'It always gives me the creeps.'

'I would have thought you were used to it by now, Jack.' King smiled. 'There again, after thirteen years of working here I suppose you become immune to it.'

'I've never liked mortuaries,' Mason admitted. 'It's not the living that concerns me, it's your clients. They spook the living shit out of me.'

King's face showed concern.

'There's something else you should know,' she said, leaning

back against the stainless steel workbench. 'The severe bruising to the young woman's ankles and wrists, it's consistent with being constrained at some point. What's more, she's missing both her middle and ring fingers from her left hand. They were removed at mid-point closest to the palm.'

Her gaze held his.

'What, during the accident?'

'No. Prior,' King replied bluntly.

'Her left hand,' Mason said thoughtfully. 'That's odd.'

'It's strange you should mention that. Some years ago, I was asked to carry out a similar post-mortem on a young woman in Durham. She too was early thirties, and attractive as I remember. It was one of those cases that leave an everlasting impression on your mind. I'll never forget it. She was found in a rubbish skip having suffered a severe blunt traumatic episode to the back of her skull. She too had died from manual strangulation. Why I remember the case is that she was missing both her middle and ring fingers from her left hand.'

Mason stepped back a pace, taken aback by King's equivocal remark. Feeling a right prat dressed in his blue gown and overshoes, he tried to focus his mind.

'When did this take place?'

'It would be six years ago, near Seaham harbour as I remember.'

'A rubbish skip—'

King's eyes narrowed. 'Two young females both murdered under very similar circumstances, both missing fingers on the same hand.'

Pen poised at the ready, Mason shuffled awkwardly again.

'Any other injuries I should know about?'

'I'm not a detective, Jack, but something to bear in mind is the Seaham woman was a drug addict as I recall.'

'What are the chances of the killer not being the same person?' Mason sighed.

'That's more your department, I'm afraid.'

Mason, now hanging on Dr King's every word, chewed the end

of his pen. 'Tell me, what did he use to saw off the victim's fingers?'

'They were cut not sawn.'

'Before or after she was strangled?'

'Let's wait for the post-mortem results before we go jumping to conclusions.'

Mason cocked his head to one side. 'Off the record—'

'This is another drugs related case in my opinion,' King replied.

'It's not looking good, is it?'

'It's funny how some cases stick in your mind,' said King shaking her head. 'I somehow get the impression that this wasn't an afterthought. I seem to remember he used a rather crude implement on the Seaham woman. There again, please don't quote me on that. Not until I've read the case files again.'

'Could he have used heavy duty secateurs?'

'Who knows?' King shrugged. 'I wouldn't rule anything out at this stage.'

Mason glanced down at the young woman's body again, his mind all over the place. 'Anything of the sexual element involved?' he asked.

'Don't push it, Jack. I don't have my crystal ball with me. Perhaps we'll know more after we've carried out the post-mortem examination later this afternoon.' King turned sharply to face him. 'In the meantime I'll dig out my reports on the young Seaham woman. Maybe we can make some comparisons.'

Mason stood for a while, still taking in the detail. Thankfully, this didn't sound like another sexually craved killer at work. If these murders were linked, then what connected them? And why did he carry out the little ritual of removing his victim's fingers?

'There's more to this than—' Mason's voice tailed off.

'I'm sorry Jack, but that's as much as I can tell you at this stage.'

'You've been more than helpful,' Mason said appreciatively.

'Let's not rush into it. We can talk about it after the post-mortem examination has been carried out. No doubt you'll be in attendance?'

Mason shook his head. 'No, DS Williams is standing in for me on this one. No doubt he'll keep me informed of any new developments.'

'I don't envy your task,' said King. The Home Office Pathologist suddenly stopped in her tracks, as if she'd remembered something else. 'It may be prudent to give David Carlisle a quick call. He's a criminal profiler, and runs a private investigation practice in South Shields. I'll give you his details. I'm sure he'll be able to assist you in this.'

'Thanks for the advice. I've worked with him before.'

'One thing is for sure,' said King closing down the lid of her laptop computer. 'You'll need to get that chest of yours checked out. You're beginning to sound like my clients.'

Who said that the dead don't talk, Mason cursed.

Chapter Four

Earlier that morning

David Carlisle gazed up at the underbelly of his beloved Rover P4 100 and shook his head in utter disbelief. Typical, he cursed. For weeks now he'd been intending to fix that loud grating noise coming from underneath the bonnet. He hadn't, and now things had got out of hand. He should never have driven to Gateshead in the first place. Stuck in the middle of rush hour traffic for two hours and waiting for the recovery truck to arrive, he'd felt uncomfortable. Not the best of places to break down either. Just before the Tyne Bridge and after the traffic lights, he'd caused major tailbacks as far back as Gateshead High Street. Had it not been for a friendly passing police officer bailing him out, then things could have turned ugly.

'It's your gearbox, mate,' the mechanic yelled from beneath the jack lift. 'It's shagged.'

'What are we looking at?'

There was only a second's pause, enough to send a shiver down the private investigator's spine.

'I'll need to strip her down,' the mechanic replied.

Carlisle caught the mechanic's glances and the look of concern.

'What does that entail?'

'Well,' the mechanic replied, thrusting his greasy hands deep inside his overall pockets. 'This here's a 1963 model. It has a six cylinder engine which they borrowed from Land Rover if I'm not wrong. What's more, they're bastards to fix.'

Carlisle stared up at the underbelly of the car in bewilderment.

'How long will that take to fix?'

'It's the spare parts; they're a bloody nightmare to get hold of.'

'Someone must stock them, surely?'

The mechanic kicked the side of the car hoist with the toecap of his safety boot. He was giving very little away. 'The problem is they've stopped making spare parts for these years ago.'

'What about eBay?'

'It's a waste of time.'

'So that's it?'

'I can try a pal of mine. He may be able to help.'

'Anything's worth a try,' Carlisle said dejectedly.

The mechanic wiped his greasy hands down the front of overalls that looked as though they could have done with an oil change. Wonderful, he thought. This was all he needed right now. The thought of going another single day without his beloved Rover just didn't bear thinking about. He felt he was losing a friend, and a best one at that. He watched as the mechanic flopped back into a battered old computer chair, and made the dreaded call.

Carlisle wasn't an expert on cars, but he knew enough to know that things were pretty desperate. Then, quite unexpectedly, the mechanic swung to face him.

'How does four-hundred quid sound?'

Carlisle gave him a cursory thumb up.

'Leave it with me,' the mechanic replied.

Carlisle thrust his business card into the outstretched greasy hand, and watched the mechanic's eyes as they narrowed a fraction.

'Private Investigator, what the hell is that all about?'

'What it says on the card.'

'You don't work for the government by any chance?'

'No. Why?'

'It's just—' the mechanic's voice suddenly tailed off.

'Is there a problem?'

There could be, mate.'

There was suspicion in the mechanic's glances – mistrust, unease. Carlisle took a step back and steadied himself and said, 'I'm not a snivelling taxman if that's what you're thinking. I run my own business, I'm a Private Investigator.'

The mechanic gave him a quizzical look. 'Sort of like, MI5.'

'You could say that, yes.'

Carlisle leaned back against the garage wall and thought about it. After years spent studying behavioural psychology at Bristol University, he'd joined the Metropolitan police ending up as a criminal psychologist on the Murder Investigation Team (MIT). What a great period in his life that had been, hunting down psychopaths, serial killers and the occasional terrorist who threatened National Security. It was rewarding work. Then, after his transfer to the Northumbria Police, it had all started to go downhill. Policing wasn't the same anymore. Endless hours spent chasing a petty criminal wasn't exactly his idea of policing. It was soul destroying work, and he hated every minute of it. When the chance of redundancy finally came along, he had jumped at the opportunity. God, he thought, that was seven years ago.

'Cool,' the mechanic grinned. 'I thought you were an undercover informant.'

The bell on the garage wall sent the mechanic scurrying into a back room, as another secret conversation took precedence. How anyone could work in such appalling conditions was beyond him. Still popular with the punters, though, the sign above the door read: REPAIRS AS CHEAP AS CHIPS

Then the backroom door opened again.

'Leave it with me,' the mechanic said. 'I'll have her fixed in no time.'

Good news at last, thought Carlisle. At least something was going to plan.

★

By the time David Carlisle reached Laygate it had started to rain.
Now at the mercy of the elements, he'd not felt this exposed in
a long time. It was 11:30am when he finally reached his office in
Fowler Street, and he was soaked to the skin. There were three
messages on his answering machine, but none of them grabbed his
attention. Sometimes it felt as if the criminal world had gone into
winter hibernation. There again, maybe not. There was never a dull
moment in South Shields, especially after Christmas when money
was tight and the black market was awash with stolen goods.

Earlier that morning he'd phoned Willem de Kooning, a 55 year-
old antique dealer whose business partner had recently walked out
on him. The case was complex, and the fact that he'd driven off in a
stolen Mercedes-Benz C-Class carrying a large amount of antique
silverware in the boot of the car made life difficult. Normally he
would have declined the case, but money was tight and their business
was desperately in need of a cash injection.

'What do you think?' his business partner asked.

'Think?' he replied.

'How do you like my new shoes?'

Carlisle gave her a look that said – *cool.*

Jane Collins liked unexpected surprises, and as she performed
yet another graceful pirouette, she reminded him of a five year old
child attending her first birthday party. She was a strikingly attractive
woman, late thirties, with long blonde hair and deep blue eyes that
could melt snow in an Arctic blizzard. But there was a darker side,
unexplained, that Carlisle had never quite got to the bottom of.
He'd often quizzed her about it, but she always shied away from the
subject.

'Like them or not?' Jane flirted.

'They certainly complement your legs.'

'I was asking about my new shoes,' she huffed, 'not my figure.

Which reminds me, did you remember to contact Willem de
Kooning this morning?'

'Ah-hah, and I—'

'And what did he have to say to you?'

'Not a lot. When I finally caught up with him he was on his
way to another antiques auction. If you ask me the man's a bloody
nightmare to track down.'

Jane slid her slender frame onto the small adjoining window sill
and peered down on the street below. It had stopped raining, and
everywhere puddles hung around the pavements.

Carlisle's iPhone rang.

The anything for nothing brigade. He switched the thing off.

One of the major drawbacks of being a private investigator
was the amount of lowlife scroungers who fished for free advice.
There were any amount of them, petty criminals who proudly wore
their electronic monitoring tags as if it was a badge of honour. It
was moments like these, and there had been many over the years,
when he wished he'd stuck to behavioural psychology. Nothing was
straightforward anymore. If it wasn't one thing it was another.

Annoyed with himself, he sucked in the air and pocketed his
iPhone again.

'That reminds me,' said Jane, peering down at her desk diary. 'You
asked me to remind you about your five o'clock appointment with
Mr Smallman.'

'Shit! I'd almost forgotten about him.'

He watched as Jane tucked an annoying strand of hair behind her
ear, and turned to face him again. 'Is Mr Smallman's partner really
having an affair with the chairman of the local parish squash club?'

'I very much doubt it. Why?'

'He seems such a sweet old gentleman,' Jane replied.

'You wouldn't say that if he sat you on his knee.'

'*David!*'

He studied Jane's reactions, and hadn't realised just how much she reminded him of Jackie. Her normally calm and pleasant demeanour, her face contorting in an all-consuming anger, lips pouting, eyes flashing, and mouth quivering. How time heals wounds, he thought. It had been almost eighteen months since his wife had died in a tragic ferryboat accident in India. He thought he'd come to terms with it, but he hadn't. It was the little things in life that plagued him most. Sometimes he wondered if he would ever survive without her. Life seemed cruel, and it wasn't selective by any stretch of the imagination.

He shuffled a few files around on an untidy desk, and then said, 'Mr Smallman's a frustrated ninety-five year old bachelor who lives in his own little fantasy world. Besides, this so-called partner of his isn't exactly a spring chicken either. She's ninety-two, and not a day younger. How in hell's name he believes she's having it off with a twenty-three year old fitness instructor, beggars belief.'

'Bless him,' Jane smiled.

He refrained from answering, knowing full well what Jane was thinking.

'Before I forget,' she said. 'DCI Jack Mason rang.'

'Mason! What the hell does he want?'

'He's found a new watering hole in Benton and wants you to meet him there.'

'Does he indeed, and did he say why?'

'No, but he certainly seems to be enjoying himself in his new role. He never stopped talking about it, from the minute I picked the phone up.'

Carlisle leaned back in his chair and thought about it. Jack Mason wasn't exactly a socialising beast, far from it. Mason was a moron, and socialising wasn't part of nature.

Then the penny dropped.

Chapter Five

It had just turned nine o'clock when David Carlisle strolled into the little backstreet garage in Laygate, South Shields. True to his word, the mechanic had done a fantastic job in fixing his gearbox. He was half expecting it to blow up in his face. It didn't, and as if by magic that all too familiar grating noise that had driven him mad for weeks now, had finally disappeared.

Concerned about a young female offender who couldn't keep her hands off other people's property, he dropped by at the Probation Offices in Gateshead. It could be heavy-going at times, and past experience had taught him that a good stiff talking to usually did the trick. Not all cases were straightforward, of course. It was the young offenders who fell through the cracks who troubled him most. Lowlifes addicted to petty-crime, who went on to be the real criminals. Not surprisingly his visit turned out to be a total waste of time, the young offender having absconded. These things happened. There was always an element of risk about them, but there was nothing anyone could do about it.

Feeling let down, Carlisle sped north towards Benton. He normally enjoyed driving, but traffic jams and heavy congestion annoyed him intensely. Four Lane Ends had a different character this time of day; even the Ship Inn wasn't overly busy. Apart from a few diehards sat aimlessly staring at a flat-screen television, the pub resembled a funeral parlour.

Sure enough he found Jack Mason standing at the corner of the bar. Pint in hand, head buried deep inside the morning papers, the Detective Chief Inspector seemed a million miles away. He reminded him of his father in some ways. He too could be a bit of a grumpy old sod at times. The trouble was, and there was no getting away from it, Mason liked his drink. A creature of habit, there was never a day went by when he didn't fancy a pint. And that was the thing; besides having a fantastic reputation, the Ship Inn had a great atmosphere and at weekends sported live bands. Not a good sign, he thought.

'How's business nowadays?' Mason asked without bothering to lift his head.

'It couldn't be better.'

Mason leaned back against the bar rail and regarded him quizzically. Having recently transferred to Northumbria Police Serious Crime Squad, he was obviously out to impress. Wearing a blue pin-stripe suit, white shirt and silk navy-blue tie, if nothing else he certainly looked the part. Not everything in the garden was rosy, of course. Mason's recent handling of a dangerous psychopath, hell-bent on tearing the streets of Newcastle apart, had clearly dented his ego. Hauled in front of the Independent Police Complaints Commission for the excessive use of firearms, he'd always sworn the suspect was armed. Everyone knew he wasn't, of course, but that was Mason's way of doing things. Had it not been for the Area Commander standing by some questionable decisions, then things could have turned out very different.

'I'm not having much luck lately,' Mason said despondently.

'So I've heard.'

Their eyes met.

'I'm not talking about that IPCC's stuff. I was referring to the sale of my old house.'

Carlisle drew back, confused. 'Oh, what's happened?'

'Someone dropped out of the chain at the eleventh hour, and I lost my buyer.' Mason made a non-committal gesture as if unsure he wanted the subject to progress. 'As it turns out, one of my mates is a local estate agent and has managed to rent it out on a short term agreement.'

'Someone you know?'

The DCI thoughtfully stared over the top of his pint glass. 'No, he's a neurologist. Works for the local NHS, and comes from Bombay so I'm told. He has a wife and three kids and he's a regular guy by all accounts.'

'Born in India, was he?'

'I haven't a clue. There are an awful lot of immigrants moving into the area at the moment, and it's pushing up the house prices.'

'No wonder the property market is buoyant down south, it's—'

'Don't believe everything you read in the papers.' Mason puffed out his cheeks and shuffled awkwardly on his feet. 'It all depends on where you want to live, and whether you can afford the extortionate charges that some of the estate agents are asking.'

They chatted a while, catching up on old times.

'How's the new job?' Carlisle asked casually.

'It's not bad. I seem to have fallen on my feet this time.'

'Keeping you busy?'

'You could say that. I'm currently heading up a new murder enquiry.'

'What, local?'

'Yes. A young woman from Gateshead; you may have heard about it.' Mason's face darkened. 'This one's a bit of a puzzler, though. We've searched her house and found nothing up to now.'

Carlisle paused, his beer glass inches from his lips. 'Wasn't she involved in a car accident and the driver did a runner?'

'That's the one, but there's a lot more to it than the press are letting on.'

'It sounds pretty straightforward to me. Find the driver, and you find her killer.'

'I wish—'

Mason went on to explain in a little more detail, and the more Carlisle heard the more intrigued he became. It wasn't a clear-cut case. It had a darker side, but he was damned if he was going to let on about it. Not at the moment he wasn't.

'What's your new team like?'

'They're not bad actually. A few of the old hands have joined me, but there are still an awful lot of new faces around.' Mason looked at him quizzically. 'You know me. If they don't make the grade they're off the team.'

Nothing changed there, Carlisle thought.

There was a hint of sarcasm in Mason's tone, which Carlisle had picked up on. The DCI was tight lipped, vague, and seemed reluctant to give anything away. Being a profiler had its advantages, but he was damned if he was going to share his information freely. Not unless he was paid for it.

'You seem to be enjoying yourself.'

'There's never a dull moment when you're working on a murder inquiry, my friend.'

'No. I suppose not.'

'So, what are you up to nowadays?'

Carlisle forced a smile. 'There are plenty of miscreants in South Shields to keep me busy, Jack. The damn place is full of them.'

'Speaking of miscreants, I'm rather curious as to why someone would want to cut off his victim's fingers? What the hell is all that about?'

'A trophy hunter perhaps—'

'No, not when drugs are involved.'

'Which fingers?' he asked, trying his best not to sound too overly enthusiastic.

'Left hand, middle and ring fingers.'

'And the other victim, this Seaham woman you talked about?'

'Same hand, same two fingers.'

Carlisle eyed him for a moment. 'This latest victim, was she involved in drugs?'

'Nope, I can't say that she was.'

'But she could have been a pusher?'

'Not that I'm aware of, she wasn't.'

Carlisle held his left hand up in front of Mason's face, stretched his fingers out and bent the middle and ring fingers down until they touched the palm of his hand.

'What does this tell you?'

Mason's expression remained vacant. 'Bugger all. Why?'

'What if she wore expensive diamond rings on her fingers?' Carlisle paused to let his words sink in. 'Good enough reason to kill, don't you think?'

'Nice thought, but we've already been over that ground.'

'What about sexual—'

Mason cut him short. 'No, this one's definitely drugs related. Someone is sending out a warning signal. I've seen it before; it's the way these people operate.'

Carlisle took another swig of his beer while he considered this. 'The bruising to the latest victim's ankles and wrists – he could have held her captive at some stage.'

Mason shook his head. 'Yeah, but why wait six years between murders. It's a hell of a long time.'

'It is if you're suffering a psychological disorder.'

Mason almost choked on his beer.

Still pondering over his friend's hidden agenda; Carlisle's eye's toured the room. The trouble was he'd already guessed what was going on inside Mason's head – *what if the killer had committed further atrocities during the six year cooling-off period?*

Anything was possible. Two shattered families, a whole lot of unanswered questions, and the press loving every minute of it. Still, it didn't mean they were looking for a serial killer. Not yet, they weren't. There again, solving some crimes was like walking across a bomb site – you trod carefully or got yourself blown to pieces in the process.

'There could be darker forces at work here, Jack.'

Mason banged his empty glass on the bar top in a show of contempt.

'Christ, you don't pull any punches.'

'But you ask a lot of questions.'

'And you don't answer them.'

There was silence between them, and he sensed his friend's frustrations.

'It's awkward without seeing the case files.'

'Let's hope we're not dealing with another head-the-ball,' Mason replied.

Suddenly the general conversation was over, and Carlisle could feel the intensity in Mason's voice. It was time to cut to the chase.

'It's the bruising to her ankles and wrists that are the giveaway. One such case that springs to mind involved a middle aged male who suffered a delusional crisis. He knew who he wanted to be, but never quite knew how to get there. Sadly, six women lost their lives before they finally caught up with him. Even then I doubt he knew who his true identity was. The trouble was, he was running a sex club – chains, whips, leather masks, you name it he was into it. When they finally caught up with him, his mind was so fucked up with sexual fantasy that he hung himself in his prison cell.'

'Dabbling with the occult can be a dangerous business, my friend.'

'I couldn't agree more,' Carlisle replied.

Mason's look was confused, as if the seeds of doubt had already been sown.

'Where to start,' the DCI sighed. 'Tom Hedley of Forensics is convinced the killer knows a thing or two about police forensic procedures. He's thorough with it, quick about his business, and leaves us few clues behind. I get the distinct impression these murders were planned. They're certainly not spontaneous killings like any of the others I've dealt with in the past.'

'It doesn't sound good.'

Mason managed a weak smile, as he always did in troubled times. Now wasn't the time to tout for business, but neither was he willing to talk bullshit anymore. Carlisle knew exactly what was going on inside the Detective Chief Inspector's head, and it wasn't worth the paper it was written on. No, he thought, to be tormented by a killer who liked nothing more than to play tricks with other people's minds was one thing, stopping them another. It was a sickening game of chess, and there could only be the one outcome – *checkmate!*

Carlisle leaned back on the bar rail and looked into the bottom of his glass. Business was about timing, about feeling the right vibes. Not all police cases were straightforward, but this one certainly intrigued him. The trouble was, and it had been niggling away at him ever since leaving South Shields that morning: *Would Mason offer him another contract?*

Patience, he would need plenty of that. Finding it was the problem.

'How's the daughter nowadays?' he said, deciding to change the subject.

'She's fine. Couldn't be better in fact.' Mason shuffled awkwardly, another bad sign. 'Mind, I'm finding it difficult in getting time off work these days.'

His mind now elsewhere, when Mason had finished the rest of his story – about the difficulties he was facing, police cutbacks, and the grief he was getting from his ex-wife – Carlisle sensed a potential business opportunity opening up. Then, just as he was about to exploit it, Mason beat him to it.

'I hate to admit it, but I'm a bit short on lateral thinkers. This is my first big assignment, and I'm naturally out to impress. The trouble is this case feels totally different from the rest. More complex, more controlled. If I'm brutally honest with myself we'll need to think outside the box on this one.'

Could his old workmate be mellowing with age? There again,

two murders, both intrinsically linked, didn't bode well on anyone's books. But that was the nature of the beast; murder came in all guises and none of it clear-cut.

Mason had finished his pint, but he wasn't having another.

'Anything I can do to help?'

'What if I were to offer you the same terms and conditions as the last time?'

Carlisle could hardly believe his ears.

'Is that a firm offer?'

Mason dutifully stroked his chin, the copper inside him surfacing. 'Yeah, but I'll need to run it past my new boss first.'

New boss, Carlisle thought. What new boss!

Chapter Six

Now bathed in a low wintery sun; the rugged North East coastline looked magnificent against a fiery orange backdrop. This time of year South Shields promenade was never overly busy. Besides, the weather was too unpredictable nowadays, as if the seasons had been turned upside down.

Lowering his side window, Carlisle drew in the stiff sea breeze. It felt good, the cool air wafting against his flushed cheeks. Now popular with middle-aged born again bikers, the little roadside café that he and Jackie used to frequent when they were courting was now crammed with expensive motorbikes. Having reached an age of maturity where every spare penny of disposable income could be channelled into powerful road machines, these people were living the dream.

On reaching the next junction, he turned left and up into Beach Road. Today, like any other day of the week, Marine Park was full of mums and toddlers out feeding the ducks. The little narrow-gauge steam train that tirelessly ran pleasure rides around the park's boating lake during the long summer months was nowhere to be seen. It was mid-January, and in a few months' time the whole area would be swarming with tourists again. Carlisle loved South Shields, and everything it stood for. Thank God for the small mercies in life, he mused.

All the parking spaces at the back of the office were taken, so he parked on a piece of waste ground opposite William Street. Still deep in thought, Carlisle was having second thoughts about Jack Mason's half-cocked proposal. The timing felt wrong, and yet the killer's MO seemed to be drawing him ever closer towards the eternal trapdoor of darkness. There was never a dull moment these days. One minute his desktop was empty, the next all hell was being let loose.

In some respects these murders bore all the hallmarks of a psychopathic killing, and whoever was responsible was well organised. The massive blow to the victim's head and the fact that she was knocked unconscious before he strangled her, told him that. The reasons to kill were complex, and at times mind boggling. But this case felt different, as if the killer had held a personal grudge against these women. And yes, there were plenty of bad guys out there only too willing to exploit their weaknesses.

Then, in a moment of unbroken contemplation, he thought about the bruising to the latest victim's ankles and wrists. Maybe these murders weren't related after all – a drugs deal gone wrong? And another thing, why run the risks of detection by displaying his victim's broken bodies as pantomime? What was all that about?

Suddenly his head was awash with all kinds of notions and none of them made sense anymore. To him this was the stuff of horror movies – mindless killings of pure evil. What if this really was the work of devil worshipers? People spreading their evil practices on the streets of Newcastle? He'd witnessed this before, vile people who'd gone the extra mile and all in the name of Satan. Their victims, usually prostitutes, rapists and perverts, had all fallen through the cracks. Misfits who were easy prey for some unsuspecting social predator with nothing but blood on their hands.

Superstitious to the core, Carlisle tried to push these notions to the back of his mind. He'd been here before, many times. Devil worshipers or not, this case had all the hallmarks of something more sinister and the urge to accept too great. His mind already made up, it was time to give Jack Mason his answer.

Chapter Seven

Still in the early stages of his investigation, Jack Mason was quietly confident of an early breakthrough. Nothing of any significance had shown up from their visit to the Nova Hotel at York. A few loose ends had been tied up, including a couple of witness statements and some grainy CCTV footage recovered from the hotel reception lobby. Earlier that morning, having contacted the West Yorkshire police regarding the dead woman's driving licence, he was beginning to feel upbeat again. The mechanics of a murder investigation could be quite overwhelming at times, but the minute the desk sergeant at Morley Town Police Station announced they'd spoken with Caroline Harper's elder sister, he was on to it like a flash.

Accompanied by DC Carrington, a twenty-nine year old budding young detective and newly appointed member to his team, they journeyed south together. Nowadays, once the newspapers and TV had picked up on the story it was difficult to breathe, let alone carry out a full blown murder enquiry. As far as he knew, the news of Caroline Harper's murder still hadn't reached this far south. Not yet it hadn't, but he was still keeping an open mind about it all the same. Shit happened, and fresh leads had a nasty habit of quickly turning cold on him. It was always the same with policing. You had to stay focused to keep ahead of the game.

Five miles south of Leeds, just off the M62, the iconic clock tower of Morley's Town Hall suddenly sprang into view. He'd never been here before; this was his first time. His initial impressions were favourable, and the long rows of stone terraced houses that graced the town looked Victorian. To the west, behind stone built cottages, open pastureland ran all the way down into Dewsbury Road. He'd read somewhere the town was famous for its textile industry. The mills had long gone, but the old "Shoddy" industry as it was known, had left an indelible mark on the landscape. On a dull January morning, West Yorkshire had unquestionably left its quirky character on Mason's mind, but what other dark secrets lay in store he had no idea.

Mason stood for a moment before giving the doorknocker a sharp authoritative rap. He heard the security chain rattle and watched as the door drew open a couple of inches. Then, through the gloom, a face appeared in the gap.

'Ms Harper?'

'Aye luv, that's me.'

Wendy Harper wasn't a tall woman, more fragile looking with a slight stoop. Wearing an old pink jumper and a pair of baggy blue jeans, she looked early forties.

'I'm DCI Mason, and this is Detective Constable Carrington,' Mason explained. 'Can we have a word?'

Confused, the occupant glanced inquisitively down at his warrant card and frowned. Like most police officers he knew, Mason felt uncomfortable about breaking bad news, especially where death was involved. There again, most interviews would have normally been carried out by Detective Constables or Detective Sergeants. Once a police officer had reached the rank of Inspector, they invariably favoured a desk job. Not Jack Mason, it wasn't his style. He preferred working at street level, in amongst the bad guys.

'We're here in connection with a fatal road traffic accident,' Mason said, sounding as sympathetic as he could manage. 'May we come in please?'

'Yes of course, my luv.'

Mason had been dreading this moment ever since leaving Gateshead Police Station that morning. He hated delivering bad news. Apart from the emotional stress involved, it was the faces of the deceased that haunted him more than anything else.

He stood for a moment taking in the detail.

'I appreciate this may have come as a bit of a shock to you, but there are some important questions that need to be asked.'

Ms Harper's face clouded. 'Like what, Detective Chief Inspector?'

Mason pulled out a copy of Caroline Harper's driving licence, and held it up for her to see. The woman looked puzzled, taken aback as if not quite believing. Unsteady on her feet, Ms Harper carried a knurled Malacca walking cane in her left hand, which she used to her best advantage. Outwardly she appeared reserved, but distant in communication. It was her eyes that were the giveaway. Whatever it was she was suffering from, it had certainly taken its toll. Her complexion was pasty, her personality flat and her body movements were rhythmically beyond her control.

Then it twigged: perhaps she was living with Parkinson's disease.

'Tell me, Ms Harper. Do you recognise this young lady?'

The moment he said it, Mason felt a bad premonition come over him.

'Yes luv,' she replied barely giving it a glance. 'Just as I told the two young police officers this morning, that's ma sister—'

'I see.'

'Is summat up with the poor lass?'

'I'm sorry to inform you, Ms Harper,' Mason said, and hating every minute of it, 'but we have every reason to believe that your sister may have been involved in a fatal road traffic accident late on Thursday night.'

Ms Harper's eyes filled. 'How can you be sure it was Caroline?'

'No one can say for certain the dead girl is Caroline,' DC Carrington said softly, 'not until the body has been formally identified.'

Ms Harper pushed back and hugged herself. 'I could never do that, not to my own sister.'

'I'm so sorry.' DC Carrington attempted to put a comforting arm around her shoulder, but she determinedly flinched away. 'You and Caroline were close, I take it?'

'She's ma sister, luv.'

'Yes, we know,' DC Carrington acknowledged.

'This is terrible,' Ms Harper gasped, letting slip her broad Yorkshire accent.

Mason drew breath. 'I realise this must be difficult for you; perhaps you might like to take a few moments.'

Ms Harper stared inquisitively across at him, as if still unsure.

'I'll make us a cuppa,' she said, shuffling awkwardly towards the rear of the building.

'Yes, of course.'

Mason bit his lip as his eyes toured the room. The property was small, scantily furnished, uncluttered. There were no children's toys scattered about the place, or family photographs come to think of it. Unlike her younger sister, Wendy Harper lived a frugal lifestyle. Minutes later she returned bearing a tray of drinks, which she set down on a small coffee table in front of a gas fire.

There followed another awkward silence between them.

'Why don't you tell us about Caroline,' DC Carrington said demurely.

'Where do I begin?'

'Why not start when you were younger.'

'When we were younger,' Ms Harper softly repeated.

'Yes. Where did the two of you grow up?'

Suddenly looking like a small lost child, Ms Harper stared into her tea cup. After pouring out her heart, she sat bemused for a while. Somewhere between the sentences the tears started to flow, but she somehow managed to compose herself. Then, quite unexpectedly, another story began to unfold.

Mason, sitting quietly, began to take notes.

His first impressions of Caroline Harper were that of a bright young spark, a typical teenager who'd hung around with friends discussing music and fashion. Brought up on a large council estate in Middlesbrough, she'd always liked to experiment with her hair. It was a different colour every week, and a different style. After leaving school, she'd worked as a young trainee Estate Agent for a large property business. Well-liked, according to Ms Harper, her younger sister really enjoyed her new job.

Ms Harper went on, 'Like most young women, Caroline had her moments of course. You only have to look at her photographs to see what a very attractive young woman she is. And that was the trouble. I don't want you to take this the wrong way, but around this period Caroline had unknowingly fallen in with all the wrong people. Having moved to London with her so-called fancy new boyfriend, that's when it all started to go wrong.'

'What kind of people?'

An expression of pain passed over Ms Harper's face. She paused momentarily, long enough to regain her composure again. 'Caroline worked as a hostess in one of Soho's nightclubs. She spent most of her time there, drinking and socialising. The place had an awful reputation by all accounts. Not that I know much about these things, but from what I could gather she'd been subjected to terrible sexual abuse and practically forced into slave prostitution.'

Mason raised an eyebrow. 'So what happened to her?'

'Had it not been for close family and friends rallying round, God knows where she would have ended up.'

'I take it someone got her out of there?'

'Yes, it was our uncle George. He was an ex-guardsman as I remember. One thing for sure, he certainly knew how to handle himself. At the time, a couple of his mates went down to London with him. They were big lads, pitmen, not the sort of people you'd want to get involved with.'

'And what happened to this Uncle George?'

'He died, poor chap.'

'He died!'

'Cancer,' she sighed.

Ms Harper sat back and gave a resentful shake of the head. She had sharp facial features, high cheekbones and a prominent chin, not unlike her sister's driving licence photograph. After a while, the intervals between the sobs grew longer and it was then the bitterness began to surface. Not only had the tone of her voice changed, her resentment towards society in general had too. Throughout, Mason sat copiously taking down notes. Human trafficking was rife in the capital; he knew that, having witnessed the evil first hand. Living on the edge, as Caroline apparently had, there was little wonder she'd fallen prey to unsavoury sex predators, pimps and the more scrupulous drug dealers who dealt in the sex trade. It was then he recalled his conversation with David Carlisle and their discussions surrounding the satanic cult.

Unless he could come up with an alternative solution, then he would need to ask Ms Harper to make a formal identification of the dead women.

He thought a moment. 'When Caroline returned back to Middleborough, how long was it before she became involved in another relationship?'

Ms Harper hesitated, a confused look.

'She married Richard Sloane if that's what you mean.'

Mason's eyes met with Detective Carrington's.

'Married, you say?'

'I thought you people were already aware of that, Inspector. It was her husband who reported her missing to you people.'

Mason drew back as if the living room floor had suddenly opened up in front of him and he was staring down into a bottomless black abyss. Of course, he reasoned, having run away from her husband she'd obviously reverted back to her maiden name. How could they have missed that? It was elementary police work, basic stuff.

Mason took another deep breath. 'Tell me,' he said. 'Did she ever make any further contact with her husband, a telephone call perhaps? Something the police weren't aware of?'

'No. Not to my knowledge.'

Carrington stared at Mason as he tried to curtail his anger. Having failed to uncover the obvious, someone had screwed up big time. That would come later, he told himself.

Feeling like a real idiot, he leaned over and took another sip of his tea.

'I presume Caroline's husband still lives at the same address?'

'Yes, he does. Why?'

'You wouldn't happen to have his contact details handy?'

Ms Harper fumbled in her handbag, and retrieved a well-thumbed address book.

'I don't wish to sound intrusive,' Mason said leaning heavily on the sympathy. 'It's just that your sister's driver's licence is currently made out to her maiden name and not to her married name as one would expect. Is there a reason for that, perhaps?'

'It's quite simple, Inspector. Her husband isn't a very nice man and Caroline was desperate to get away from him.'

Mason looked at Carrington.

'And what makes you say that?'

She told them more, but Mason's suspicions were already aroused. His next question, when it came, was more direct and more to the point. 'How would you best describe Richard Sloane?'

'He's an arrogant old sod, why?'

'Arrogant!'

'Yes, he thinks he's a class above everyone else.'

'Looks down at you, does he?'

Ms Harper gave a mock shudder. 'Indeed.'

The atmosphere was strained, and from what Mason could gather Caroline's husband cared more about his business ventures than he did any wife. Ms Harper was scathing about him and, according to her, it seemed that nobody had a good word for Richard Sloane. But was she telling him the truth, or had the breaking news affected her sense of reasoning? Yes, her sister was a highly strung young woman, a party animal who liked nothing more than to mix with people her own age. And yet, when he thought about it, she'd married a man almost twice her age. Things had obviously gone wrong, and he needed to get to the bottom of it.

'What line of business is your sister's husband currently in?'

'He owns *'Clothes-2-Day'*, Inspector, and he's a very wealthy man.' Ms Harper shuffled awkwardly in her armchair. Her voice barely a whisper, she pointed a finger at the two of them. 'I'm told he has dozens of clothing outlets in Hong Kong, and that's where he spends his time apparently.'

'Hong Kong—'

'Yes. Kowloon.'

'It must have been an extremely difficult time for your sister,' Mason said, still not entirely sure where their conversation was heading. 'Did Caroline ever mention anything about her overseas trips to Hong Kong with you at all?'

'No. Not to me she didn't,' Ms Harper replied bluntly.

'But she would have accompanied her husband there no doubt.'

'What makes you say that?'

'Not everyone gets the opportunity to see the Far East, Ms Harper.'

'That may well be,' Ms Harper interrupted, 'but as far as I know she never ever went there.'

Ms Harper glared at him through bloodshot eyes. Something was wrong, and the deeper he dug the bigger the hole he seemed to be making for himself.

'Tell me,' Mason said. 'When was the last time *you* saw Caroline?'

'Why do you ask, Inspector?'

'Well, her husband had reported her missing eight weeks ago.'

Ms Harper reddened. 'What if I was to tell you that I was out with her last Wednesday?'

'*Last Wednesday!*'

'That's right, Inspector.'

'Well,' Mason said, pen poised at the ready. 'Perhaps you'd better explain to me what the two of you were up to that day.'

Looking at each of them in turn, an entirely different story began to emerge, and one involving a shopping trip to York city centre. Mason, who was sitting silent as a stone, frantically scribbled down the details. The two sisters had lunched together at a little café near the Shambles. The rest was women's talk, uninteresting, but all documented down nevertheless.

'And that was the last time you saw your sister?'

Ms Harper burst into tears again. 'Yes, it would have been.'

Mason closed his notebook and made a mental note of it. 'Tell me,' he said. 'Did Caroline ever mention anything to you about stopping at the Nova Hotel that night?'

Ms Harper looked surprised.

'No she didn't. I thought she'd driven home to Gateshead that afternoon.'

'And would that be, Prince Consort Road?'

He watched as Ms Harper cupped her hands to her face, and mumbled something inaudible. In no mood for sentiments, within minutes of his phoning Gateshead Police Station the case had taken on another dimension. He tried ringing David Carlisle, but his iPhone went straight to answering service.

Cursing his luck, he left a voice message.

Mason stood to leave.

'You've been most helpful, Ms Harper,' Mason said. 'Before we go, I must inform you that a Police Coroner's Officer may shortly contact you and arrange for you or another person who knew the deceased well, and in their company view the body for the purpose of identification.'

'What about her husband, Richard Sloane?'

Mason looked down at her sympathetically. 'I'll see what I can do.'

'Thank you, Inspector. I'm sure there are others.'

Mason glanced at his watch and did a quick mental calculation. The fact that Ms Harper had gone shopping with her sister that day, had turned everything on its head. It was the breakthrough they'd been looking for, and another vital gap in the victim's timeline had been plugged. The question was, and he wasn't treating it lightly, having returned to the Nova Hotel after seeing her older sister off from York railway station that afternoon, where had she dined that evening?

As DC Carrington pulled away from the kerb, Mason fastened his seatbelt. Things were moving at a pace, and he had to pinch himself to come to terms with it. Still keeping an open mind, he rang the Coroner's Office on the off chance that a formal identification had been made. Not that he was expecting one, but it would have been a nice addition all the same. There were all sorts of rumours doing the rounds, and far too many false leads flying about if he was honest. There again, why on earth would Caroline Harper spend another night in York if she wasn't meeting up with someone?

It was then he remembered her credit card details. Having checked her bank statements, there had been no further transactions that day. So unless she'd paid for her meals by cash, then someone else must have picked up the tab that night.

As usual the A1M was a nightmare, mile upon mile of roadwork's and not a single workman in site. Still trying to get comfortable, his iPhone pinged in his pocket. It was forensics.

There'd been a new development.

Chapter Eight

The journey from South Shields had taken David Carlisle a little under thirty-five minutes that morning. Now running late, he'd intended to call in at the Magistrates' Court but there wasn't the time. Besides, his client, a young Spanish woman involved in drugs trafficking who couldn't speak a word of English, had failed to show for her court hearing. As was usually the case, her interpreter, a smooth talking wannabe chat show host, was furious. Welcome to the real world, Carlisle smiled. Opportunist criminals seldom risked facing a long prison sentence, especially if they thought they could get away with it.

But on a fine morning like this, the first thing that struck him the moment he climbed out of his car was the lack of any police presence. Apart from a SOC van and a couple of unmarked police cars, there was little to suggest that this was now a major crime scene. He stood for a moment staring aimlessly at the police cordon tape marked: CRIME SCENE DO NOT CROSS.

Met by the duty Crime Scene Manager, he was quickly brought up to speed on the latest unfolding events. Things were coming on nicely and apart from a few glitches, forensics was systematically going about their business with a new sense of purpose.

The day Caroline Harper was murdered; neighbours reported seeing a tall, dark, stranger hanging around in the vicinity. The details were sketchy and inconsistent, but at least it had given uniforms something to get their teeth into. As a rule Carlisle normally felt relaxed when sifting through a murder victim's property, as all too often it would reveal another painful chapter in a person's life. He'd read somewhere the victim had once been a budding ballet dancer, but it was pure speculation of course. It's what sold newspapers, underhand journalism gone mad.

Feeling upbeat, he entered the victim's flat convinced in the knowledge the connection lay hidden in Caroline Harper's past. Clearly disliked, if not despised by many of her associates, she had most certainly placed herself in a very vulnerable position. Had her killer sought revenge for some wrongdoing done to him in his past life, or was it simply her outspoken personality itself? Whatever dark secrets this young woman had been hiding, Carlisle was determined to uncover them.

'We're all but done here,' the senior forensic scientist said, adjusting his face mask.

'Is it ok to move around?'

'Apart from the kitchen, but that shouldn't take long.'

Still looking for that vital piece of inspiration, Carlisle poked his head in round the living room door. Getting inside the killer's head was like a drug to him, and it was moments like these he loved most about his job. For as long as evil existed, there would always be those who were willing to combat it.

The flat was unquestionably bijou, cramped, and decked out in cheap second-hand furniture. With barely enough room to swing a cat let alone accommodate a full blown murder team, he was beginning to have second thoughts. Somewhere in another room, he heard the distinct whirr of a SOC camera lens opening up, and caught the flash in the hallway mirror. For some unknown reason, he was suddenly overcome by uncertainty.

Not as he'd expected to find, the only person missing that morning was Jack Mason. Perhaps the DCI's progress-review meeting with his new boss was more involved than he'd anticipated. No doubt defending his corner, Mason would be in his element. That's what he did best, badger people into submission.

'Find anything of interest?' Carlisle asked.

Tom Hedley scratched the side of his head as if looking for divine intervention. 'Nothing's turned up yet,' the senior forensic scientist said. 'Being a murder victim appears to be the last thing on this young woman's mind.'

'A professional cover-up, do you think?'

'I wouldn't go so far as to say that. There again, this place doesn't look as though it's been lived in for weeks.'

Carlisle watched as Hedley stepped aside to allow a young forensic officer to squeeze past him. Whatever it was the young woman was looking for, she seemed determined to find it. Crawling on hands and knees beside her, a second officer, much older, was scrutinising the input cables. Then the penny dropped. They were checking out the TV programme recording dates. Clever, he thought. Nothing was left to chance; if the killer had left any clues behind then these were the people to find them. Apart from the obvious white fingerprint dust scattered about the place, the room was remarkably tidy. It was then he spotted the glossy cover of a *Vogue* fashion magazine placed on a side table in a moment of haste. One of its pages had been turned back and used as a book mark.

He checked the date, and made a mental note of it.

There were two upstairs bedrooms; the larger reeked of perfume. It wasn't a large room, narrow, with a clear view overlooking the main road. To one corner stood a large rickety old wardrobe, crammed full of expensive designer clothes. Many of them carried well-known designer labels. Beneath the small bay window was an old walnut dressing table. Its top, covered in perfumes bottles, gave it a feminine feel. Distracted, his eye caught the bottle of Chanel No 5, identical in size to the one he'd always bought Jackie at Christmas. A memory tugged him – a romantic weekend in Scotland – Inveraray, a small town on the western shore of Loch Fyne and the gateway to Argyll. There were lots of things to see and do, mountains to climb, and breath-taking places to explore. Sometimes he felt dragged down by his past, as it was never far from his mind.

'Jack Mason is on his way over,' an unfamiliar voice called out.

Startled, Carlisle spun sharply to face a burly, broad-shouldered detective who now ascended the stairs. Pleasantries exchanged, it wasn't long before Detective Sergeant Holt got down to the real business in hand.

'I hear you're joining us?' Holt said, in a broad Geordie accent.

'That's right. I've read through the case files, and thought I'd get my head around it all,' he replied.

'Not a good start, I'm afraid. There again, murder is never pleasant at any time. Whatever this young woman had done, she certainly didn't deserve to die as she did. Tell me,' the sergeant said thoughtfully, 'what sort of monster are we up against?'

'This type of case is never straightforward, I'm afraid, as there's always an element of unpredictability about these people's actions. It can be very unnerving at times.'

'Yeah, but it's this place that gives me the creeps,' the sergeant shuddered. 'It's like walking into a morgue when you're having one of your off days.'

'Fear of the dead?'

'It's the not knowing that always drives me nuts,' the sergeant admitted.

Carlisle nodded. 'It's the way their minds work. They leave us few clues behind, and yet they offer up their victims as if they were sacrificial gifts. You always know when you're up against a professional killer.'

'Tell me about it,' Holt sighed.

Carlisle waited for the detective sergeant to drift back downstairs again. He needed some thinking time, no interruptions, that's how he liked to deal with these matters. All the signs were there, the little idiosyncrasies and warning signals that he'd come to recognise. There was no forced entry, no sign of a struggle ever taking place, and no cross-contamination to be found. Stripped of all personality, the room felt cold, detached. In all probability the killer had a key to the place. If not, then how else could he have possibly removed so much vital evidence?

Then he remembered the photograph that Tom Hedley had faxed him earlier that morning. There were no house keys attached to the dead woman's key ring, which was unusual to say the least as most people he knew always kept their house and car keys together – on the same key ring.

He stood for a while, convinced in the knowledge that Caroline Harper had been a high maintenance roller. The expensive clothes she wore, the elite social circles she'd moved around in, they were all part and parcel of her high-octane lifestyle. From what he could gather hers seemed a materialistic existence, selfish and uncompromising. What's more, she probably hadn't given a damn how old or ugly her husband was, just that he had money.

Well that's how he saw it, and the evidence seemed to be pointing to that. But that wasn't all. There was something else, a darker side full of jealousy and hate. The solution to some crimes more often than not lay in the victim's character. And that was the giveaway. He knew from experience that this kind of marriage seldom lasted long. Once the novelty had worn off that's when the serious problems manifested themselves. Scorned women were deadly predators, but cutting off a high maintenance woman's money supply was like severing the life blood in her veins. But why turn her back on such a wealthy lifestyle, only to live in a hovel such as this? It just didn't add up. None of it did. There again, he thought, what if she'd fallen in with the wrong crowd again?

He shone his torch in the bathroom.

Forensic dust everywhere, shelves, skirting boards and ledges, but not a scrap of evidence to suggest she'd once lived here. Had they overlooked something, a small piece of detail perhaps?

'Where are you?' Mason's voice boomed out.

'I'm up here, Jack.'

Mason's eyes toured the room on entry. 'Not exactly Buckingham Palace, is it?'

'I'm afraid not,' Carlisle responded glumly.

'So why leave a luxury penthouse for this dump.' Mason ran his hand over the top of the bathroom cabinet and brushed the white forensic powder from his fingers. 'He must have left something behind for us.'

'I doubt she was murdered here,' Carlisle replied. 'It looks like she'd been using this place as a bolt hole.'

Mason was quiet for a moment. 'Somewhere to lay low until the dust settled, eh?'

'It looks that way.'

'Do you think her husband could be involved?'

'It's difficult to say, but he's certainly a suspect.'

'His name's Richard Sloane. He's a sixty-four year old clothing tycoon and owns *Clothes-2-Day.*' Mason took a deep breath. 'According to Caroline's elder sister, he's a nasty piece of work to deal with.'

'Job done,' Carlisle grinned.

'You wish!'

There are always two sides to a story, Carlisle thought. But this one seemed to have dozens. He gave a little rolling motion with his hand. 'Whatever it was that this young woman was running away from, she'd certainly met an untimely ending. Find her reason for leaving, and we'll probably find her killer.'

Mason paused in thought.

'Two days before Caroline was murdered she was out shopping with her elder sister in York. We know she stopped at the local Nova Hotel that night, then drove north the following morning. Who she was with, we have no idea, but thirty-six hours later she was dead. If she didn't come here after leaving York, where the hell did she go?'

Carlisle's mind suddenly went blank.

Chapter Nine

He hit the play button, but still hadn't quite got the hang of the new system. Fifteen monitor screens, six different images, and all playing at once. Best piece of kit so far, he thought, best by a long chalk. Even though the pictures were a little fuzzy, it still sent a cold shiver down his spine. Then, from another part of the room he heard the crackle of the police radio. Another call, another place, their problems were spreading like a tumour. They were looking in all the wrong places again, just as they had done for years. It was time to set the record straight – ruffle a few more feathers in the process.

There was always the profiler, of course.

Inside the dimly lit room that reeked of sweat and takeaway food, he sat huddled over the monitor controls. He preferred to operate like this. Windows shut, no light peeping through the window blinds, and all the doors firmly locked. The people around here minded their own business. Good as gold, he thought. They never had much to say for themselves, not to him they didn't. He preferred the peace and quiet. It allowed him to focus his mind on the real business in hand – the more important issues.

He turned his head instinctively as he flicked the control button with his index finger. Some days he found it hard to motivate himself let alone concentrate. Not today though. Never once did he take his eyes off the monitor screens. Never once did he think of anything else but the task in hand. Then, as a new image flashed across the top bank of monitor screens, he reached over and fiddled with the brightness control.

A little more contrast, he thought – perfect.

It couldn't have worked out better had he tried. This one was a looker, petite, slim waist, and the way he liked them to look. Two whole years and never once had she seen what was coming to her, never once.

You're not laughing now, greedy bitch!

Then, switching to the central bank of monitor screens he uploaded a recording from the latest news feed. This time he chose Sky. Not much in the way of close up dead bodies on the other news channels. It was getting ridiculous, an utter waste of time.

Trembling with excitement, he watched as the news cameraman panned in on the accident scene. It was just starting to get light, and Coldwell Lane looked a gloomier place than ever that morning – the incline even steeper. As his dark, predatory eyes began to settle on the shattered blue Ford Transit van, the news presenter's story began to unfold. She was a plump, pompous, condescending bitch, whom he took an instant disliking to. Her mouth moved like a fish out of water – snatching at the air between sentences. Turning, she pointed towards the open van driver's cab door.

Idiot, he screamed, *you're concentrating on the wrong vehicle.*

Disappointment gripped him, as that all too familiar knot in his stomach tightened again. As his fist thumped the control table yet another resounding blow, the anger inside him was boiling over. It was all getting out of hand. This greedy bitch had deserved to die, surely they must have known that much.

Then, just when he thought that he'd seen enough, the cameraman panned in on another part of the crash scene. Much more interesting, he thought.

Excitement gripped him, and he licked his lips in anticipation. There, on the top bank of monitor screens a new image appeared.

It was perfect, absolutely perfect!

Chapter Ten

Shortly after 10.15am, Jack Mason returned to Gateshead Police Station. Still unable to shift the heavy chest cold, earlier that morning he'd dropped by at the local medical centre to pick up a course of antibiotics. Now a full blown murder investigation, his first team briefing of *Operation Marco Polo* – the name given to the Coldwell Lane murder investigation – had been moved to his new office. He'd intended to use the regular briefing suite that day, but that was being renovated. The only other suitable room, if he could call it that, was a large training suite regularly used by the Counter Terrorist Unit. Not a good option, he thought, as it was far too big.

From the evidence gathered so far, Mason had planned to keep his ops team small. Having selected some of his more experienced police officers available to him, he was hoping for a quick breakthrough. Not all cases had as much information as this. Running a murder enquiry was like panning for gold: you had to sift through the minute detail in order to get your rewards. Central to his investigations was the little black purse found wedged down the front passenger seat of the victim's car. Not to be snubbed at, he was more than aware just how easy it was to overcomplicate things. Over the years he'd learnt never to take anything for granted. Nothing was straightforward, and reality was all too often a pipedream. There again, overlook some vital piece of evidence and everything else would fade into insignificance.

Mason stood for a moment, both hands deep inside his trouser pockets and chewed over the facts. The victim had driven south that morning, to York. Caught on CCTV cameras checking into the Nova Hotel, she had with her a small weekend case, laptop, and a large handbag slung loosely over her left shoulder. Why she was there, and who she had met apart from her sister, he hadn't a clue. One thing for sure, the victim certainly had expensive tastes. Ninety-four pounds spent on a skimpy little green top was more than his dear old mother received from her weekly state pension. Not the cheapest of boutique shops either. The prices they charged were outrageous.

Dr Gillian King, the Home Office pathologist, had revealed little about the victim's attacker. According to King, the contents of the victim's stomach revealed she'd eaten a Carbonara Pizza the night she was murdered. Where, they had no idea, as none of the restaurants within a ten mile radius of Gateshead had reported seeing anything. Even forensics was baffled as to the lack of DNA left at the crime scene. There were no witness statements, no fingerprints, and very little in the way of trace evidence found on Caroline Harper's clothing. These things took time, he realised that, but the public's insatiable demand for answers was beginning to get to him.

Opening the case files, Mason glanced once more at the SOC photographs taken at the crash scene. It wasn't exactly pleasant viewing, either. Trapped in the front passenger seat of her vehicle, the young woman's facial features looked ghastly. It was Friday, close to the weekend, and the small assembled team now sitting in front of him were in unusually good spirits that morning.

All that was about to change, he guessed.

'Harry, what do we know about the RTC?' Mason asked.

Harry Manley annoyingly popped another Humbug into his mouth, and grinned. A muscular man, early forties, with a bushy mop of jet-black hair that sat on top of a narrow oblong face, the Detective Constable was undoubtedly the joker in the pack.

'According to the forensic vehicle examiners' report, the Volkswagen Polo was centrally positioned at the top of Windy Nook bank when it was sent coasting down into Coldwell Lane. There were no skid marks, the tyre kind that is, and the impact speed is estimated in excess of sixty miles per hour.'

'And the blue transit van?' Mason asked. 'What do we know about that?'

'It was travelling in the opposite direction at thirty miles per hour, boss.' Manley paused to re-examine his notes again. 'It states the Volkswagen's lights hadn't been switched on, and the ignition key was in the unlock position.'

'Ouch!' Mason shrugged. 'As I recall, Coldwell Lane was full of parked cars around the time of the incident.'

'Which means the transit driver didn't stand a bloody chance,' Manley acknowledged.

A mobile warbled in the office, and Mason was quick to pick up on it.

'Sorry, Jack,' said DS Holt. 'I forgot to—'

The lecherous grin on the sergeant's face told him the caller was probably Holt's new found girlfriend. Another costly mistake, Mason thought.

'You were saying, Harry?'

'Why fasten the seatbelt to the dead woman's body, boss?'

'I've no idea.'

'Unless, of course, that's where he strangled her.'

Mason gestured towards Dr Colin Brown, a lean, long-backed, medium-built, balding man, with a stern flushed face and thick bushy sideburns.

'What's your take on it, Colin?'

The room fell silent as the police doctor opened a thick green folder in front of him and took out his report. He adjusted his spectacles, and stared thoughtfully across at Harry Manley. 'That's a bloody good question,' the doctor replied. 'I'm sure you're aware that only up to the first six hours of death, can lividity be altered by moving the body. After that, lividity is fixed as the blood vessels begin to break down within the body. That said, shortly after Caroline Harper was strangled, the Home Office pathologist's report confirms the victim had lain on her back for several hours.'

'So, she was killed elsewhere,' said DS Holt.

'Yes, she was.'

'Which means she was dead when he positioned her into the front passenger seat of her vehicle?'

'That's right, George.'

'The bastard,' Manley gasped.

Rob Savage, a dapper Detective Sergeant in his late thirties and former boxing champion, raised a hand to speak. A tall man, around six-foot one, he was a good four inches taller than Jack Mason. 'It's just an observation, boss. Looking at the impact photographs it appears the emergency teams had one hell of a job freeing her from the vehicle that night. In which case, the whole crime scene would have been heavily contaminated.'

The doctor lifted his horn rimmed spectacles onto his brow, and sighed. 'We're talking body contamination here, Rob. There is a subtle difference, of course.'

'Like what?' Savage grunted as if unable to conceal his oversight.

'Well, for one, there was no trace evidence under the victim's fingernails, which means she never put up a fight. What's more, after leaving York to the time the emergency crews recovered her body from the crash scene, we know she wore different clothes.'

'She could have changed them anywhere,' said Savage.

'It's possible, Rob, but the lack of trace evidence suggests the front passenger seat may have been covered with some sort of plastic sheeting before he positioned her into the vehicle.'

'Surely that's one for the Technicians to decide?'

'I'm just raising a point, that's all.'

'Even so,' said Savage. 'He still had to lift her into the vehicle, so how could he possibly do that without cross contamination?'

'He could have worn rubber gloves and a protective apron, of course.'

Mason interrupted. 'Rob raises a good point, Colin.'

The doctor collected his thoughts and narrowed his eyes towards the detective sergeant. 'What if he wore protective coveralls similar to the ones you and I use to protect a crime scene?'

The room fell silent.

'You're not suggesting he's a copper by any chance?' Manley said.

'Far from it, but our killer seems to know an awful lot about forensics.'

Mason leaned forward in his seat. 'OK. Let's not jump to conclusions at this stage. Which reminds me, where's Peter Davenport, the regular SOC photographer, nowadays?'

Rob Savage explained. 'He suffered a nasty skiing accident in Scotland, badly fractured his leg in two places. Rumour has it he's making a remarkable recovery and expects to be back to work in a couple of weeks.'

Mason made a note of it. 'Do you have anything further to add, Colin?'

'Yes, I do,' the doctor replied. 'The specimens sent for Systematic Toxicology Analysis showed negative for drugs and other substances. Apart from small traces of analgesics which are most likely to be Paracetamol, the victim was clean.' Dr Brown's narrow facial features twitched in thought. 'Something else to bear in mind is the skin discolouration to her ankles and wrists. To me, that suggests she may have been restrained at some point.'

Mason checked his notes.

'What about her mobile phone, George?'

'No trace of it so far, boss,' said Holt. 'Whatever system she was using, it wasn't registered in either her married or maiden name. We're still waiting for the National Phone Crime Unit to get back to us. Hopefully they'll throw some light on the situation.'

'I take it that's a no?'

'Yes, but we haven't given up on it yet,' Holt replied.

Rob Savage shook his head. 'It's beginning to sound like she never existed.'

The noise levels heightened.

'Right then,' said Mason. 'Let's be clear on one thing here, whoever killed her carried out his crime within thirty-six hours of her leaving the Nova Hotel in York. There are too many gaps in her timeline for my liking. Where did she go that day, where did she eat, and who was she with? In other words, we need to concentrate more effort on the victim's last known movements.'

Mason braced himself. This was one of those little moments he disliked, the clutching at straws. Deep down he was desperately trying to conjure up a game plan, but right now couldn't think of one. All that he knew for definite, was that from the time she left York to the time her body was recovered from Coldwell Lane the victim was wearing different clothes. What's more, further discussions with Dr Gillian King had confirmed that the first victim, Cheryl Sawyer, had died under very similar circumstances.

'It's a heck of a large area to cover,' the doctor replied.

'Yes, I realise that.'

'If she didn't put up a struggle,' said DS Savage, shaking his head. 'It sounds suspicious to me.'

'Hold on a minute!' Mason said. 'If her wrists and ankles were bound, how could she have put up a fight?

Savage looked puzzled. 'So why the theatrical re-enactment of staging an elaborate accident in the first place, unless—' Everyone held their breath in anticipation. 'Nah, forget it.'

Mason's face dropped.

'More to the point,' the doctor questioned. 'Why cut off two of her fingers?'

'Maybe he tried to nick her rings, like he did with the last one,' Manley jested.

Mason was now on the edge of his seat. This was the last thing he wanted to hear right now. Besides, the physiological aspects were more David Carlisle's field, and the profiler was currently giving evidence at Leeds Crown Court. One thing was for sure: whoever killed Caroline Harper certainly knew what he was doing.

'Good point, Harry,' Mason nodded. 'We know these women wore expensive rings, so if drugs were involved it could have been his motive for killing them.'

'What about the local pawnshops, boss?'

'More likely to have been sold in a pub, don't you think?'

'What, twenty-thousand nickers worth of diamonds?' DS Holt cut in.

Gasps all round.

'OK,' Mason said. 'Let's run a check on all the local pawn shops.'

'I'll put my feelers out,' said Manley, dutifully popping another humbug into his mouth. 'I know a few scumbags who owe me a few favours.'

Mason wasn't sure why, but he suddenly sensed they were onto something. He shook his head in approval. 'The removal of the victim's fingers needs to be kept under wraps for the time being. The last thing we need is the media getting hold of it. If this is the killer's signature, and God forbid he strikes again, at least we'll know it's him when he does.'

'That could be difficult, Jack,' said Dr Brown.

'And why?'

'I've heard the press are already sniffing around the Coroner's office.'

Mason knew where this could be heading, but there was little he could do about it. News travelled fast, and the press were quick about their business.

'That certainly changes things.'

'Do you want me to have a word, Jack?' said Dr Brown.

'No, leave that with me,' Mason sighed. 'I'll speak to Gillian King after the meeting.'

'What's happening about witness statements on the RTC?' asked DS Holt. 'Anyone come forward with any more information?'

'No, none that I'm aware of,' Mason replied. 'And there's certainly nothing on the files, George.'

'Perhaps we should revisit the collision scene, get uniforms to carry out a door to door.' Holt pulled a face. 'As I remember, there are a couple of decent pubs at the top of the Felling High Street worth a visit. Maybe we should talk to those customers who were drinking in the area that night.'

'I thought we'd already done that,' Mason said.

'We have, but people tend to forget things. Punters talk, especially after a few drinks.'

Savage turned to Holt. 'That's true, which makes every punter in the pub that night either a witness or a possible suspect.'

The drinks tray arrived, and everyone made a bee-line for the plate of chocolate biscuits. Just as Mason was about to lean over to grab one, his desk phone rang. Checking out the caller display, he raised his hand as he reached over and grabbed it.

'Yes, ma'am. We have it covered. There's an all-night stakeout operation in place for tonight. Let's hope they strike again. If they do, we'll be ready and waiting for them.'

With that he hung up.

'What's the Super after now?' Manley chuckled, wiping the biscuit crumbs from his chin.

'Bloody Alpacas,' Mason replied. 'The woman has a fixation we can catch the thieves red-handed. Doesn't she know we're in the middle of a murder investigation down here?'

Manley was quick off the mark. 'Maybe she has plans to open up an Alpaca delicatessen, boss.'

The team fell about laughing.

Mason leaned over to grab a chocolate biscuit. There weren't any.

'That's it,' he said slamming the flat of his hand on the top of the desk. 'You lot can bring your own sodding biscuits the next time.'

A loud hiss rang out around the room.

It was the joker in the pack who spoke first. 'Actually they're quite moreish,' Manley grinned. 'Not much good for dunking in your coffee though, the chocolate runs.'

Mason made a little sweeping gesture with his hand, as he saw the funnier side.

'Joking aside, lads, has anyone bothered their arses to find out how the transit van driver is doing?'

'He's out of intensive,' Savage replied.

'Has he given us a statement yet?'

'Yes, and no, boss. The trouble is he doesn't remember a bloody thing about what happened that night. All he recalls is leaving home to pick up his van from the works yard; the rest is a blank.'

Mason leaned over as if resigned to the fact.

'Pity, and yet I was half-expecting that would happen.' The DCI scratched the side of his head. 'Mind, he looked in pretty bad shape when they lifted him into the back of the ambulance, he's lucky to be alive I suppose.'

'It's nice to hear he's making a good recovery,' said Holt.

Mason checked his watch; ten-thirty and they still hadn't started on the Seaham murder case files. God what a mess, he thought. It was Sod's law that a Water Board van happened to be travelling in the opposite direction that night. Had it not, then things might have turned out differently. A lot different, he cursed.

Twenty minutes later, with fresh plans in place, the meeting drew to a close. Much to George Holt's disgust, the moment he was told he would be heading up the overnight Alpaca surveillance operation, his face dropped. The weather forecast wasn't looking good either; heavy snow was forecast that night.

More importantly, thought Mason, was the raid on his biscuit stash.

Chapter
Eleven

David Carlisle could not remember the last time he'd drunk his way through a bottle of champagne. It was one he'd been keeping as a celebration drink in case Jackie fell pregnant. Staring down at the empty bottle the memories came flooding back. Knowing and loving Ireland as Jackie did, it was only natural they'd visited the place as often as they had. His wife always believed her visits to Strabane inspired her sense of well-being. It was like a second homecoming to her. During the winter months they'd spend hours walking the banks of the River Mourne together, taking in the wildlife and admiring the foothills of the Sperrin Mountains and beyond. Somehow they'd always end up at Jackie's favourite restaurant bar, Murphy's on the Green, just off Market Street in Strabane. The place had a great atmosphere, besides serving really good food. Sometimes he was amazed at just how many of Jackie's old school mates would frequent the bar. People she'd grown up with long before moving to university in Newcastle. That was all behind him now, nothing but a distant memory.

Nothing had prepared him for what happened that fateful day. One minute Jackie was alive, the next she'd been torn away from him in a sea of utter panic. All he could remember as the ferry rolled over and onto its side, was the look of utter disbelief on her face. First the sound of breaking glass, followed by loud rumbling noises as people and vehicles were thrown into the river. No one stood a chance, and no one saw it coming. Waking up in a hospital bed to be told that your wife was listed amongst the casualties wasn't exactly the best day of Carlisle's life. He was devastated.

Legs like jelly, Carlisle staggered into the kitchen and made another cup of strong black coffee. Feeling like shit, his head was pounding and he swore never to move his eyeballs again. God, he felt awful. Slumped in his favourite chair, he sat mesmerised watching the steam vapour vanish from his coffee. Trying to get his head around the rest of the day's plans was like trying to hit a hole-in-one in golf. Nothing seemed to function anymore. He tried moving his legs, but the champagne was clouding his brain and his feet were refusing to budge. He should never have opened the bottle in the first place. It was pure self-indulgence, sheer greed. Furious with himself, he showered, got dressed and prepared for the day ahead.

The early morning chill had finally given way to a watery sun when he walked the short distance to the little village square. Although the rest of the world had a spring in its step, he felt he was treading on eggshells. He thought he was going to throw up, but he didn't. Instead he pushed on regardless.

'What a bloody state,' Carrington said, staring back at him from the driver's seat of the undercover pool car.

'Please don't shout.'

'Get in,' she insisted.

Sliding into the front passenger seat, Carlisle quietly closed the door behind him and buckled up his safety belt. 'I could do with a little sympathy, Sue.'

'Like hell,' Carrington huffed. 'We have a long day ahead of us, and you look like shit!'

Exiting Whitburn village, the young detective drove west towards Gateshead. They didn't get far. The rush hour traffic on reaching Heworth roundabout was now at a standstill. Fast living up to its reputation as Gateshead's largest permanent car park, horns blaring, engines revving, no wonder his head was in bits.

Carrington eyed him with suspicion.

'Jack Mason wants us to take a fresh look at Caroline Harper's flat.'

'Does he now?'

'Yes. He wants you to try and get your head round what's been going on in there.' The young detective stared across at him as if not quite believing. 'There's little chance of that happening by the looks of things. God! What a bloody state.'

'I'm fine,' he said in an effort to brush her comments aside.

'You're joking!'

Sometimes it was easier to say nothing. His head was pounding, his tongue felt like coarse sandpaper, and he could sorely have done with a drink of water. Not the best start to his day, he cursed.

'What's the latest feedback from uniforms?' he asked.

The young detective flicked an annoying strand of hair from her eyes. 'We're still carrying out a house-to-house sweep of the area, but I'm not pinning any hopes on it.'

'What about neighbours?'

'Nobody's willing to talk.'

'Tittle-tattle, gossip more like.'

She stared at him, but said nothing.

Carlisle didn't do theory, it wasn't his style. His was more about understanding the psychological aspects of the crime – what made a killer tick. If Caroline Harper wasn't stalked, and her killer wasn't an opportunist, then surely he must have been known to her.

From the outside the property looked deserted. All the curtains were drawn, and there was blue and white police cordon tape still attached to the front door. Carrington said nothing, but the look on her face told him he was still in her bad books.

'It's not looking good, is it,' she said fiddling with the car radio.

'Given the circumstances I suppose that's understandable.'

Carrington stared blankly out through the windscreen again. 'Let's get some fresh air. It certainly looks like you could do with some.'

'And do what,' he groaned.

'Familiarise ourselves with the area.'

'Do you have anywhere in mind?'

'There are a couple of pubs I think we should visit.'

The thought of the smell of stale beer made Carlisle retch. Drink was the last thing on his mind right now. If only she knew how bad he felt, then maybe she wouldn't have suggested it.

He leaned in closer, his voice barely a whisper. 'He didn't kill her here, Sue.'

'Oh, and what makes you say that?'

'He's grooming them, winning them over before he strangles them.'

'You haven't said that before.'

'No. Not yet I haven't.'

'Damn you,' Carrington huffed. 'Don't tell me that inquisitive mind of yours has suddenly started to function again.'

'It's just that—'

Her eyes demanded attention.

'The way I see it, Coldwell Lane is barely a stone's throw from here and this place fits the bill perfectly.'

'I'm not sure about that either,' Carlisle shrugged. 'We need to wind the clock back a couple of weeks, think this through logically. Caroline Harper was strangled sometime between the hours of eight and nine-thirty, which gave her killer plenty of time to carry out his dirty work. Think about it: there must be dozens of outlying districts where he could have performed his vile deeds before driving here.'

'So what are you proposing we do?'

'We need to look further afield, spread our tentacles out.'

Detective Carrington said nothing, and walked on regardless. Bensham and Saltwell estates were largely a legacy of the rapid growth that Gateshead underwent following the Industrial Revolution. The houses, a mix of terraced, semis and elegant villas were in sharp contrast to the visual anarchy of Gateshead's town centre, where a planning wedge had been firmly driven between the sublime and ridiculous. Nevertheless, Saltwell Park was one of Britain's finest examples of a Victorian Park and part of Gateshead's heritage, which at least offered the local community some respite from the urban sprawl of the city.

Having checked out a dozen pubs that morning, all within a few miles radius of the victim's flat, they finally entered the Gold Medal on Chowdene Bank. In what was now a well-practised routine, DC Carrington flashed her warrant card under the young barman's nose and held up Caroline's Harper's photograph in front of him.

'Recognise this woman?'

The barman screwed his face up, and barely focused his attention. 'Yeah, she comes here now and again. Why do you ask?'

'When was the last time you saw her?'

'About a week ago,' the barman replied.

'Can you be sure it was her?'

'Yeah, of course I'm sure.'

'Is she a regular in here?'

'Nah.' The barman pulled another pint as he went about his business serving another customer. 'She's a looker that one, and likes to flaunt it with the men. That's how I recognised her.'

Carrington paused in reflection for a moment and thought about it.

'What's your name?' she demanded.

The barman's face had turned a jaundiced colour, and he averted his eyes before answering. 'Jess,' he muttered.

'Jess, what?'

'Allan,' he replied. 'Listen, I'm not into drugs if that's what you're thinking.'

'I never mentioned anything about drugs,' Carrington

insisted, pen poised at the ready. 'But I may do later!'

The young detective's answer had the desired effect.

'She normally comes in with her fella. A tall skinny guy, with long, swept-back black hair. If you ask me, some guys have all the frigging luck.'

'What else can you tell me about him?' Carrington insisted.

'He's loaded with money, that's for sure.'

'What do you mean – loaded?'

'The flashy car he drives, and the expensive clothes he wears, he's—'

Carrington's blue eyes widened. 'What type of car is it?'

'It's silver, and before you ask I haven't a frigging clue what make it is.'

Full of contradictions, Carlisle guessed he was mid-thirties, scrawny looking with a pockmarked face and shifty eyes. His main disability, if that's what he could call it, was a bad attitude problem. Everything about him was a chore, as if the end of the shift couldn't come fast enough.

'Tell me,' Carrington said, her voice switching back into police mode again, 'how do you know it was silver?'

The barman puckered his lips and huffed. 'I was taking a smoke break when they pulled into the pub car park that night. You could tell he had money, the moment he stepped onto the tarmac. His car was expensive looking, silver, with alloy wheels and big white flashy bucket seats.' The barman's dark mouse-like eyes were all over the place again, as if trying to escape from her questioning. 'If you must know, she reminded me of one of those chat show hosts – large as life with a big bubbly personality. Not him, he's an arrogant sod, very demanding and always talks down at you when he speaks.'

'And they always come here together?'

The barman stared at them with suspicion. 'So what's your interest in these people?'

Carlisle felt they were onto something. If he drove an expensive car, there was every chance of tracing it. He gestured towards the back of the building. 'Does the pub car park have CCTV coverage?'

'No, mate, the patrons leave their cars here at their own risk.'

'This boyfriend, is he from these parts?'

'No, he has a funny sort of Yorkshire twang. Well I think it is Yorkshire, or maybe he's from Lancashire.' The barman almost laughed. 'I can never tell the difference between those two accents, they both sound the frigging same to me. One things for sure, he's definitely not a Geordie.'

Carrington's eyes met with Carlisle's.

'And they've never set foot in here since?' she said.

'Not when I've been around.'

What do you think?' Carlisle said, moving to the one side of the bar.

'Flash cars, expensive clothes, they'd stand out a mile around these parts,' Carrington replied. 'Someone on Prince Consort Road must have noticed something.'

'You'd have thought so,' Carlisle agreed.

'I'll get Uniform Branch to carry out a discreet check.'

Feeling peckish, Carlisle's attention was suddenly drawn to the bar menu board. The prices seemed reasonable, and the place was obviously popular – mainly pensioners and young women with kids. But what about night-time, he wondered. Like most pubs nowadays they'd learnt to reinvent themselves in the evenings. Theme nights, karaoke, live bands, you name it; they'd thought of just about everything to pull in the punters. Not that he objected. Carlisle's main grudge was the extortionate prices they were charging for drinks – it was daylight robbery.

'It's sorted,' said Carrington, returning her mobile to her handbag.

'God, that was quick.'

'No point in hanging around,' she smiled. 'I've asked uniforms to check out the local garages for CCTV footage. Let's see if it throws anything up.'

'That could be useful—'

Carrington stared at him unable to contain her enthusiasm. 'What are your initial thoughts?' she asked.

'Two murders both connected. It's not looking good, is it? One thing's for sure, his victims certainly liked the rich trappings of wealthy men.'

'That's a typical sexist remark.'

'Not really, Sue. There's a small minority of devious young women out there whose sole purpose in life is to ensnare rich partners. They're called Piranha Women, and they're looking for a cushy lifestyle. If they do happen to fall out of favour, then all the better as they will exploit their target through a legal loophole in the courts. Their solicitors know the score, and are out for every penny they can get their hands on.'

'How can you say that, because none of my friends are like that?'

'Like I say, it's a very small minority.'

'What! Like a high class hooker?'

'You could say that, yes. Those women are always on the lookout for an easy meal-ticket. Besides, it's a man's thing, Sue. It's what men are born to do, eye up the talent.'

'So you think Caroline Harper may have been one of these so called—'

'It's possible, and we need to look at every avenue.'

There was devilment in Carrington's eyes. 'I hope you don't consider me in that light.'

'Not when you're on duty, Miss Carrington,' he grinned. 'Besides, I'm not loaded with money and you're no man-eater.'

She giggled but said nothing.

They spent the next fifteen minutes running back over the possibilities.

'These so called – Piranha Women,' Carrington said as she stared at the tall building opposite. 'It makes sense. I hate to admit, but I think you could be onto something here.'

'If not, then why would an attractive young woman marry a sixty-four year old ugly man, if it wasn't for his money?'

He caught the sudden change in her glances.

'What about her husband, do you think he could be implicated?'

'That's a matter for the police,' he replied.

Carrington frowned. 'According to DCI Mason we know they didn't get on well together. Besides, Richard Sloane is still out in Hong Kong and we've not been able to contact him. We know he's stinking rich, and has massive business interests out in China. Apart from that, there's not an awful lot more we know about him.'

'Having second thoughts?'

Carrington turned sharply to face him. 'This Hong Kong thing is far too convenient in my opinion. Besides, he must have known what type of woman he was marrying and yet he still went ahead and married her.'

Nice to have a woman's viewpoint, he thought.

Carlisle felt the need to explain. 'Caroline Harper was a highly strung young woman who liked nothing more than to party into the early hours of the morning.' He fell silent for a moment. 'Drugs, rock and roll and sex, the three go hand in hand but not necessarily in that order.'

'Perhaps that's why she chose this area to run away to, because of the nightlife around here.' The young detective eyes widened. 'There again, she wasn't into drugs so we can rule that one out.'

'Let's hope there isn't a darker side attached to all of this.'

'Do you know what?' Carrington replied. 'I'd never thought about that.'

'She's done it before, Sue.'

'Yes I know. What about sex predators?'

Carlisle suddenly felt the knot in his stomach tighten.

'These women were targeted for reasons known only to the killer, and that's the problem.'

She stared at him looking puzzled. 'So why cut off their fingers?'

'I have my own thoughts about that too.'

'The rest of the team believe it was their rings he was after. Twenty thousand quid's worth of diamonds is not to be sniffed at by anybody's standards.'

'Who knows?' he replied. 'Let's hope it's not his calling card.'

'Really—'

His iPhone pinged – withheld number. He looked at the display.

Having a fun day?

Who could that be? He wondered.

Chapter
Twelve

The eleven-o'clock briefing trumped up all the usual suspects that morning. As always there was a mad scramble for seats. Six straight-backed chairs laid out in a single row in front of Jack Mason's desk were as many as they could muster. The rest of the team were standing shoulder to shoulder at the back of the room in amongst the new filing cabinets. Apart from breaking every health and safety regulation in the book, there wasn't enough room to swing a cat let alone hold a full-blown team meeting. Carlisle should have realised Mason's commitment was unparalleled, but his approach to changing situations was ambiguous to say the least. It was Friday, and his weekend fishing trip with his ageing father was fast slipping away from him. The team were clutching at straws, and if ever they were going to catch the killer they'd need to come up with a plan. At least it made sense.

'Tell me, said Mason. 'What makes you think she knew her killer?'

Carlisle shook his head in bemusement. This was the third time the DCI had posed that question that morning, and each time differently. If Jack Mason did have a plan, he wasn't letting on about it.

Every ear in the room tuned in, the profiler dug in deep. 'There was no forced entry, no signs of a struggle, and very little found in the way of trace evidence.'

'And that's what you're basing your assumptions on?' Mason

asked.

'That and the fact she was found dead in the front passenger seat of her car.'

'He could have had a key to her flat, of course.'

'He probably did,' Carlisle replied bluntly.

'What about the Seaham victim, Cheryl Sawyer?' Mason remarked. 'Out on the town that night, beaten over the head and strangled before he dumped her in a rubbish skip. He doesn't hang about, does he?'

Carlisle adjusted his glasses. 'I agree, but I doubt his intention was to dispose of her body.'

'So he's an exhibitionist.'

'No. But he does pick and choose his moments,' Carlisle acknowledged.

'In which case Cheryl Sawyer's murder was spontaneous.'

'No. This was planned, and she never saw it coming.'

Mason took a deep breath. 'Two murders, six years separating them. If he's not an opportunist or an exhibitionist, then who the hell are we looking for?'

'If nothing else, it proves he's mobile and the drop zone isn't always the kill zone. The fact that these women ran away from home made them easy targets for a psychopathic predator.'

'So he *is* selective?'

'Yes, and that's why I believe these murders were planned,' Carlisle thoughtfully replied. 'Something in his past has angered him and whatever it was, it triggered him to kill again.'

Mason continued to stare out of the office window, his mood far from relaxed. 'I'm still not convinced. These women were hunted down like wounded animals and plucked off the streets. If he did have a key to Caroline Harper's flat, then he had all the time in the world to pick up a fresh set of clothes and remove any vital evidence he felt necessary.'

'True,' Tom Hedley cut in, 'but the lack of trace evidence doesn't support that.'

Mason shot Hedley a sideways glance. 'So what about these reports of a stranger seen in the vicinity of her flat that night?' Mason waited for the noise levels to die down before continuing. 'He's described as a white male, around six-foot two and lean in stature.'

'It could have been anyone,' Rob Savage cut in.

'I'm not convinced of that either.' Mason argued. 'According to the Autopsy report, and I quote: "*The victim was manually asphyxiated by a male whose approximate height was six-foot-two*". Doesn't that ring any alarm bells with any of you?'

Carlisle took another swig of his coffee, and pondered over Mason's heady statement. Like a bull in a china shop, the Detective Chief Inspector was recklessly jumping at conclusions again. Feet first and straight into the deep end as usual. As far as he was concerned, six years was an awful long time between murders. The newspapers were full of it and whoever had murdered these women certainly knew how to gain maximum attention. The question was, and it had been eating away at him ever since leaving home that morning, how many more women had he killed?

'Should we go public on this one, boss?' DS Holt asked.

Mason continued to stare out of the office window. 'No, George. Not until we've spoken with Harper's husband.'

'What do we know about Richard Sloane?' Hedley asked.

'As far I'm aware he's flying back from Hong Kong and is booked on the first domestic flight out of Heathrow tomorrow morning to Newcastle.' Mason made a little sweeping hand gesture. 'I want you to accompany me on this one, David. Let's see what he has to say for himself.'

'Is Sloane aware of his wife's death?' Hedley asked.

'Probably not, but I've set up a formal identification with the Home Office pathologist.'

Hedley shook his head as if to make a point. 'Is that wise, Jack?'

'Maybe not, but the least he knows the better at this stage.'

Mason sat down at his desk again, his mind already elsewhere.

'What's the latest on the pizza investigations, George?'

DS Holt nervously cleared his throat and gave Mason a thin wintery smile. 'We've checked all the local takeaway and fast food outlets in the area, but nobody remembers seeing her.'

'If she didn't eat in her flat that night, then where did she eat?'

'I've no idea!' Holt replied, shaking his head.

'What about the northbound service stations?' Mason pointed out.

'Her last known movements are pretty ambiguous, boss.' Holt explained. 'It was eight thirty-five when she was last seen approaching Catterick. She was heading north and—'

'Is that where the new motorway improvements are taking place?'

'Yes,' DC Blanch cut in. 'Her car was picked up by the average speed cameras.'

'Was anyone in with her?'

'Not as far as we know, boss.'

'And after that, where did she go?'

'She disappeared off the radar,' Blanch sheepishly replied.

Mason picked up his notebook. 'No more sightings after Catterick then. What about marked patrol cars? Were any operating that stretch of motorway that morning?'

The room fell silent again.

DC Blanch was early twenties, and a good few years younger than Carlisle. He wasn't a particularly tall man, lean in stature with short cropped blond hair and sharp pointed chin. Not long out of training by his clean-cut appearance, he was immaculately turned out in a blue pinstripe suit, white shirt and red silk tie. Blanch was the up and coming new star on the team. Someone to keep an eye on, Carlisle guessed.

'OK. What do we know about Gateshead?' Mason said pointing to the wall map. 'There's plenty of CCTV coverage in and around the town centre. There's a one way system, controlled bus lanes, so we must have something on her movements?'

'I doubt she got that far, Jack,' Tom Hedley remarked.

Mason annoyingly brushed Hedley's comment aside.

'Any other possible sightings we know of?'

'No, boss,' DC Blanch replied glumly.

'Right, then,' said Mason. 'We need to concentrate our efforts north of Durham. We know she liked the nightlife, so it's my guess she was heading for Newcastle's Quayside.'

DC Blanch bit his lip. 'What exactly are we looking for, boss?'

'I want a check run on all the local bars and restaurants in the vicinity, and gather what CCTV footage is available. I'm looking for eyewitness accounts, nightclub doormen statements, and anyone who saw anything suspicious. What was she up to that night, and who was she with. Let's keep it simple.'

DS Miller raised his hand as if to speak. 'Yes, Vic.'

'What about this new partner of hers?'

'I was coming to that, Vic.' Mason fiddled with his computer cable. 'Sue, what did you find out from yesterday's trawl of the Bensham area?'

The young detective had managed to squeeze into the last available seat that morning. Dressed more for comfort than appearance, her make-up was immaculate.

'There's a couple of new leads, boss. The barman at the Gold Medal on Chowdene Bank described her boyfriend as a tall, skinny chap, swarthy looking, with long, swept-back black hair. From what we could gather, he's thirtyish, a middle class professional who isn't short of a bob or two.'

'Local?'

Carrington rolled her eyes as if to emphasise the fact. 'No, but he does drive an expensive car and likes to dress flashy.'

Mason shot her a glance. 'What type of car?'

'It was silver with alloy wheels and had fancy white bucket interior seats.'

'Did he say what make it was?'

'No,' Carrington replied. 'The barman was a bit of a dick-head if I'm totally honest.'

Laughter broke out.

'What about CCTV coverage?'

'There isn't any. Cars are left in the pub car park at the owners' own risk.'

Mason waited for another outburst, but it never came.

'What's the latest feedback from uniforms?' Mason asked.

'Not a lot.' Carrington managed a thin smile. 'There's been dozens of sightings of a red Volkswagen Polo seen in the vicinity, but that's it I'm afraid.'

'We need to get Road Traffic involved on this one.' Mason made a quick note, and then turned to Carrington again. 'What else did this barman tell you?'

'He gave a rather conflicting description about her boyfriend's accent. It's either Yorkshire or Lancastrian, but he's definitely not a Geordie—'

'Hang about!' Mason's stare hardened. 'Her sister lives in Yorkshire, doesn't she?'

'Yes, she does.'

'And we know the two of them regularly met up in York.' Mason's face showed concern as he leaned over and closed the lid of his laptop computer. 'Apart from her sister, who else did she meet up with in York that day?'

Harry Manley scratched his brow as though the serious side was about to surface. 'I'd put my money on this so called new boyfriend she was seeing. Let's face it, people from Middlesbrough do tend to have a bit of a Yorkshire twang. We may need to get the Cleveland Police involved on this one, boss.'

It took Mason a few seconds to digest what Manley had said. 'You're right, Harry. We know both victims came from Middlesbrough, and the last sighting of Caroline Harper was just north of Catterick.

What if she diverted to Teesside that morning?'

'There is the A66 turn off just before Scotch Corner,' Carlisle added.

Mason shot him a glance. 'That's a bloody good point.'

'Perhaps it's her car movements we should be looking at and not the occupant.'

Mason put his pen against his lips and thought about it. 'There's bound to be plenty of CCTV coverage at our disposal. We need to check it out.'

A new enthusiasm swept the room.

'Should we go public on this one?' Rob Savage suggested.

'Not yet,' Mason replied.

Carlisle didn't warm to Savage's knee-jerk reaction. It was too risky, far too open- ended in his opinion. Besides, the killer, whoever he was, would be watching their every movement. Spook him and he would simply go to ground. They needed a more subtle approach, but right now he couldn't think of one.

Mason checked his watch.

'One thing's for sure, this new development needs to be kept low key.'

Harry Manley raised a hand again. 'Why not extend our enquiries further north of the river instead of concentrating solely on Newcastle's Quayside?'

Mason looked up. The dismissive expression on his face said it all.

'Why the hell would we want to do that, Harry?

'Well. If we're talking of an hour's driving distance from Coldwell Lane,' Manley explained, 'he could be operating north of the River Tyne.'

What made this case so vastly different was the suspect's uncanny knowledge of the area. Whoever he was, he certainly moved around a lot. As usual, Mason had unsurprisingly warmed to the idea. Now as he sat tapping the end of a chewed pen on the back of his notepad, Carlisle could almost hear the cogs ticking away inside the

Detective Chief Inspector's head. There were so many choices, so many possibilities. It was a large catchment area and a lot of new ground to be covered.

Before leaving, Carlisle picked up the Cheryl Sawyer case files. Things were moving at a pace, but not fast enough in his mind. Besides, there was always the possibility the killer might strike again, and that possibility didn't bear thinking about.

Chapter
Thirteen

A steady drizzle had settled in when David Carlisle pulled his Rover P4 100 into the designated police parking bay at Newcastle Airport. Located on the north side of the airport's main arrivals terminal, it was ideally situated. Twenty minutes later, Jack Mason arrived. Wearing a scruffy pair of Nike trainers, black leather bomber jacket and faded jeans, he looked anything like a man in charge of a murder investigation. Not that it concerned him, it probably didn't, but at least it brought a wry smile to Carlisle's face.

He watched as the Detective Chief Inspector sauntered off back towards the busy information desk. Hands in pockets, shoulders hunched, he appeared in no hurry. According to the arrivals board the inbound flight from Heathrow was already running fifty-minutes late. Not a good sign, he thought. Carlisle hated uncertainty, and always found it difficult to apply himself in those situations.

Met by the Head of Security, they exchanged pleasantries before moving into the rear of the building. Immaculately turned out in a grey pinstripe suit, blue tie and expensive brogue shoes, Derek Chalmers exuded authority from every pore in his skin. When the call to duty would arise, no doubt Chalmers would deal with it as only he knew how to. Security was tight. It had to be. There was any amount of unscrupulous villains out there only too willing to ply their illicit trade in the country. These were dangerous times, and some people wouldn't think twice about blowing your brains out, even if it meant facing a lengthy prison sentence.

Ushered into a small back room normally set aside for Border Control, they were offered coffee and left to their own devices. The room was small, claustrophobic, with three plastic chairs and a cheap Formica table screwed to the floor. The walls, covered with information posters setting out people's rights, gave the place a totalitarian feel. Not the most inspiring of rooms, it felt more like an interrogation cell where the formal goal was eliciting useful information out of people.

Having caught the first available domestic flight out of Heathrow that morning, the moment Richard Sloane stepped out onto the stair from the plane, he was whisked through Border Control and into the back of the building. Following brief introductions, Mason waved his warrant card under the entrepreneur's nose and immediately took centre stage. What kind of interview technique he had in mind was anyone's guess. After all, he was the man in charge of a murder enquiry. Leads had a habit of vanishing and the Detective Chief Inspector seemed determined to quickly get to the bottom of it. Even so, they'd still managed to pick up enough information about their suspect's background to feel relaxed about it. Nothing much, it was mainly business stuff, but still interesting nevertheless.

There were times, Carlisle had to admit, when he took an instant dislike to someone. What's more, the person they were about to interview was the husband of the wife who'd been brutally murdered under very suspicious circumstances. Having amassed a personal fortune through his wildly successful e-commerce site, *Clothes-2-Day,* Richard Sloane's clothing empire was one of the fastest growing children's clothing outlets in Europe. Not bad for a man who ten years previously had been on the bones of his arse.

Mason lifted his eyebrows a fraction.

'I'm DCI Mason and this is David Carlisle. Please take a seat.'

Sloane was quick to protest.

'What the hell is going on, Inspector?'

'I can assure you it won't take long. Coffee?' said Mason.

Sloane nodded, but said nothing.'

'Milk... sugar?'

'Neither,' the clothing entrepreneur mumbled.

Sloane was everything that Carlisle imagined him to be. He was lean, a little over six-foot with a rugged, well-travelled face. His hair, streaked with grey, gave him that distinguished appearance that only age could provide. But was he mentally up to it?

They were about to find out.

'Just a couple of routine questions,' Mason said settling back in his seat.

'Regarding?'

'It's your wife, Mr Sloane. When was the last time you saw her?'

'I'm surprised, Inspector. I thought you people would have known the answer to that.'

There was a hint of arrogance in Sloane's voice, which Mason picked up on. 'I'm aware of your wife's disappearance, Mr Sloane, but that wasn't the question I asked you.'

'In which case,' said Sloane, 'that would have been a fortnight before I reported her missing to you people.'

'I see. And you've never made contact since?'

'No. Why?'

Mason frowned as he reached into his jacket to pull out a notebook. Flipping through the pages until reaching the desired place, he paused in reflection for a moment. 'Does the name Caroline Harper mean anything to you at all?'

Sloane hesitated with just the faintest hint of concern in his face. 'Yes, of course. Harper was my wife's maiden name.'

'And does she have an older sister who lives in Morley?'

'Yes, she does. Is that what this is all about?'

Mason managed a faint smile. 'How well would you say you know the sister, Ms Harper?'

'We've met at family gatherings, weddings, christenings, that sort of thing. Other than that we've spoken only briefly.'

'Family gatherings, I presume?'

Sloane's face showed concern. 'Can I ask what this is all about, Inspector?'

'Why did your wife leave home, Mr Sloane?'

'That's rather a stupid question to ask. You already know why I—'

Mason stopped him short by putting his hand up.

'Remind me. How long had she been gone before you reported her missing?'

'Two weeks. Why?'

Carlisle cringed as Mason handed Sloane a copy of Caroline Harper's driving licence, and then said, 'Is this the same lady in question?'

'Yes, that's Caroline. Where did you get this from?'

Carlisle's heart sank.

'In which case,' Mason began, 'I'm sorry to inform you that your wife was tragically killed in a road traffic accident on the night of January tenth.' Mason sat quietly for a few a minutes as Sloane stared pensively back at them. 'Perhaps there is something you care to ask me, Mr Sloane?'

'Where did this happen, Inspector?' said Sloane, barely breaking out of his shell.

'At a place called Coldwell Lane. It's close to Felling Square in Gateshead. Are you at all familiar with the area?'

'No, I'm not,' said Sloane. 'May I ask what happened?'

'Yes, of course. At around 11.30pm on Thursday the tenth of January, your wife's car was involved in a head-on collision with a Ford Transit van. That's as much as I can tell you at this stage.'

'Can you be certain it was her?'

'I'm sorry, Mr Sloane, but until a formal identification has been carried out I'm unable to disclose any further details.'

Some people thought Sloane's wife was a fun-loving woman, others not. And that was the nub of the matter. Sloane's wife had a darker side, a side that even Carlisle found difficult to comprehend. Sometimes he felt sympathy towards the victim, but this case was far from straightforward. Caroline Harper couldn't have cared less about her husband's personal welfare, just that he had money. In many ways, there was little wonder she'd fallen in with the wrong crowd. Even so, why had someone gone to all the trouble of staging her murder as if it were a pantomime?

Unless of course—

Mason was standing now, aimlessly staring down at the floor. 'I realise that this may have come as a bit of a shock to you, but it would be in everyone's interests if you would assist us in making a formal identification. It will only take a few minutes, Mr Sloane.'

Carlisle caught the sudden shift in the entrepreneur's body language.

'Can't it wait, Inspector?'

Mason's jaw dropped. 'And why would you want to do that, for heaven's sake?'

'Having travelled half-way round the world, I'm extremely tired. What's more, the internal flight was running an hour late, and I have some very important business appointments to keep.'

Mason thought for a moment.

'And when would you consider convenient?'

'This has all come as a terrible shock to me. Besides, I don't think I could face a formal identification right now.'

Like hell! Carlisle thought. Having slept most of his journey in the luxury of first class, Sloane looked as fresh as a daisy. What was he playing at?

'Fair enough,' Mason replied, as if to make a point. 'But I must warn you that this is now a murder investigation, and anything you say could be used against you in—'

Sloane sat bolt upright.

'Wait a minute! You never mentioned anything about *murder*. Had you have done so then I doubt we'd still be sitting here.'

'Well, there you have it,' Mason shrugged.

'I obviously need to speak to my lawyers. This isn't right.'

'Isn't right?' Mason repeated. 'This is a murder investigation, goddammit.'

'I know my legal rights, Inspector. Surely you don't think I'm a killer?'

Mason shifted uneasily, having dropped himself in it.

'Everyone's a suspect, Mr Sloane.'

'That's your concern, Inspector, not mine.'

Sloane punched a number into his iPhone, and listened to the ringtone. Bad move, Carlisle thought. Mason had already taken umbrage.

'The crux of the matter is this,' Mason went on. 'I've asked you politely to make a formal identification and you've bluntly refused. You seem to forget, Mr Sloane, I'm here to uphold the letter of the law. I'm not here to waste taxpayer's valuable time and money.'

'Like hell, Inspector. First you inform me it was a road traffic accident, and now you're telling me this is a murder investigation.'

Carlisle chose his moment. 'Think about it, Mr Sloane. Even you must appreciate the sensitivity of the situation. The police are only trying to protect the deceased's family, and that's why they've asked you to carry out a formal identification. It will only take a few minutes.'

Sloane recoiled in his seat. His feathers had been ruffled and the blood had drained from his face. 'Had you people told me that in the first place, I would have reacted very differently.'

'I take it that's a yes?' Mason grunted.

Sloane took a deep breath. 'Let's see what my lawyer's make of it all, Inspector.'

'It's Detective Chief Inspector actually,' Mason replied sternly.

'And what difference does that make?'

Things had got out of hand, and Mason's tactless performance had caused another major setback. Once Sloane's lawyers were involved, the case would take on a whole new dimension. Sloane looked down on people. He was arrogant, and demanded people's attention and nothing less. The only positive, if Carlisle could call it that, was that Mason had exposed Sloane's weaker side. There again, he thought, what if Sloane had contracted someone else to carry out his dirty work for him? Money wasn't a problem here, and there were plenty of unscrupulous people only too willing to kill for it.

There was much to think about and the possibilities seemed endless. And another thing, why had Sloane's wife run off in the first place? She'd obviously planned her own escape; if not, then why had she taken off with shedloads of her husband's money and reverted back to her maiden name? One thing was for sure, they would need to keep an eye on Richard Sloane.

A sharp rap on the interview room door caused Carlisle to flinch.

'Sorry to interrupt, gentlemen,' the Head of Security said. 'We've finally managed to clear Mr Sloane's luggage through customs.'

Carlisle caught the nervous twitch in Sloane's left eye, and wondered what other dark secrets were lurking inside the wealthy entrepreneur's luggage.

He made a mental note of it.

Chapter
Fourteen

All was not as it appeared, thought Carlisle. Not that he was critical of the way in which Durham Constabulary had handled Cheryl Sawyer's murder case, it was more the manner in which the victim had been brutally murdered that concerned him more than anything. If ever he was going to solve this case, he would need to unravel the deadliest secrets of the killer's mind. What made him tick? Once he understood that, the rest would fall into place, or that was the theory at least.

It was late-morning when David Carlisle finally pulled into the car park overlooking Seaham harbour. In the cold light of day it wasn't much to look at. This once thriving mining community had changed very little over the years, and North Road looked just as it had done twenty years ago. Further north the long stretches of golden sands were now shrouded in mist. On a clear day you could see for miles; not today you couldn't. The steely North Sea was angry, and the honey coloured limestone cliffs that hugged the rugged North-East coastline had an all too familiar, ominous look about them.

What to do next?

When he was younger he often came here on school holidays. Most of his spare time was spent crabbing with friends, in amongst the pool rocks that embraced the beautiful shoreline. Here the shelter of the harbour basin gave added protection; it was ideal. The world had changed dramatically since then. The young eyes that once looked out on the streets of Seaham were now but distant memories.

Turning his collar against a stiff easterly breeze, Carlisle gathered his bearings. Having sat up half the night reading through case files, it was ironic to think the killer had chosen this particular area, of all places. According to the coroner's report, the twenty-seven year old woman had died from compression of the neck. Not an uncommon ending, but at least the killer's modus operandi had remained consistent throughout. Although he'd always felt some sympathy towards the victims, hidden beneath the detail there was always a darker side to emerge. Sometimes it was a troubled past, others, purely a physical attraction. The selection process of some killers was either specific or nonspecific; they rarely deviated from the norm.

From where he now stood, fifteen miles separated both crime scenes. Coldwell Lane, a journey of some twenty five minutes by car, suddenly seemed a million miles away. Even so, geographic profiling was still a very useful tool. Although the method often relied on a crime-analysis program called Rigel to track down serial offenders, numerous police forces up and down the country had used it with an element of success. This case was different, though, more complex owing to a six year lapse between murders. Had the killer changed jobs, or simply moved house? Anything was possible, and it was a dilemma he'd been wrestling with for the best part of that weekend.

Deep in thought, from an inside jacket pocket he pulled out an envelope containing a series of SOC photographs. Taken at the crime scene six years ago, there was still plenty to go on. Not a tall woman, Cheryl Sawyer was a bit on the skinny side, he thought. Dumped in the back of a rubbish skip and from what he could see her clothes had been partially removed, no attempt had been made to cover up her body. On closer inspection there was extensive bruising at the nape of her neck, and blunt force trauma to the back of her skull. The more he thought about it the more convinced he was that they were dealing with the same killer. The commission of murder was swift, incisive, and directed towards accomplishing the same goal – that of killing the victim quickly.

But why Seaham, why here?

He tried to picture the scene, putting himself in the killer's shoes. It had been raining that night, plenty of cloud cover and not many people about. Close to midnight and smacked out of her mind on drugs, the young woman wouldn't be saying much either. The heroin would be doing its stuff, so there was little or nothing she could do about it. Besides, the killer's mind would have already been made up and the anger inside him had probably reached boiling point – all the while the pitter-patter of rain globules would be striking his protective coveralls. It was then he would step back and deliver a massive blow to the back of her skull. Motionless, and lying in a crumpled heap on the ground, there would be no need to check for hidden cameras. There weren't any. He'd already checked that angle out – weeks ago. Almost home and dry, his hands would wrap mercilessly round her tiny neck, as he would finally finish her off.

Well, it may have happened like that. At least that's what the SOC's photographs were telling him. The trouble with being a profiler was his mind had been trained to think that way. That's how he dealt with these things, unravelling the dark secrets of a serial killer's mind. Sometimes the act was all too predictable, and trying to understand a psychopath's psychological and emotional needs was like a drug to him.

The more he thought about it, the more convinced he was that's how it had happened. Nothing complicated: simple yet effective. The night Cheryl Sawyer was murdered she'd been captured on the town's CCTV cameras. High on drugs and moving from bar to bar along with hundreds of other young revellers, she would have been easy pickings for any social predator that happened to chance his arm that night. That's how these things panned out – drugs, rock and roll and sex. Not necessary in that order, but often ending with the same tragic consequences. This wasn't the easiest of crimes to solve, disturbing yes, sinister most definitely. The thing was, and this was the interesting bit, she probably knew her killer.

But why had Cheryl Sawyer met such an untimely ending, and was this a drugs related crime? From the drug barons at the top, to the street pushers at the bottom, far too many people were involved. On the face of it each had an important role to play, as each was heavily dependent on the other to keep a tight grip on things. To renege on a drug deal or break a dealer's sacrosanct rule would be asking for serious trouble.

Well, those were the facts. Now he had to deal with it.

'Got a light, mister?'

Startled, Carlisle swung to confront him.

He was young, barely ten – definitely no more.

'I stopped smoking years ago, son.'

'Frightened of cancer, mister?'

'Yeah, I suppose I was at the time. But that didn't stop me from smoking.'

'What did then?'

'Money, I guess.'

'I nicked this from my ma,' the young lad said proudly. 'It cost us nowt.'

'You stole from your mother?'

The young lad shrugged as if it was a natural thing to do. 'You're not from round these parts are you, mister?'

'No I'm not.'

'Tell me,' the young lad said, wiping his nose with the sleeve of his jumper. 'What is it you're looking for?'

'What makes you think I'm looking for something?' Carlisle answered sharply.

The young lad petulantly kicked the ground with the toe of his muddy trainers, looking like a lost soul. 'Cos,' he sighed, 'I've been watching you, and you've been hanging around this car park for ages now.'

'Have I?'

'Yeah, ages and ages.'

'If you must know, I'm chasing shadows, son.' Carlisle winked. 'But don't tell anyone, because I'm keeping it a secret.'

'That's what me ma always tells us when I ask what she's doing. If you must know, she will say, I'm chasing shadows. Be off with you now and don't come back till I'm finished around here.'

'Good advice son,' Carlisle smiled. 'Best be off then, eh.'

He watched as the young lad skipped off towards the cliff tops, turning from time to time. A hundred yards on, after crossing the main road, he disappeared from view into a haven of back streets. Sometimes Carlisle would get lucky when visiting a crime scene; unlock a vital piece of detail that allowed him to unravel the answers. Today he was having a bad day.

Not the prettiest of places, Seaham was one of the largest towns on the Durham coastline. For generations the town had a strong belief in its mining industry as its main source of income. When the coal mines finally closed and the region went into decline, that's when the lowlifes moved in. It was a vicious cycle, and one that Carlisle had little time for. He loved this stretch of coastline, and always felt in harmony with it. To him, this was God's country and the people who lived here were the very salt of the earth. Not all were angels, of course. Cheryl Sawyer's untimely death had proved that. But the fact that she was murdered and tested positive for amphetamines had clearly put a different slant on the proceedings.

"A drugs deal gone wrong," as someone had so kindly marked her police files.

Who would want her dead, he thought, and why theatrically pose her broken body in the back of a rubbish skip? Apart from a clear set of footprints found at the crime scene, even the police were baffled. There'd been no forced entry into her flat, and no signs of a struggle having taken place.

So, he asked, what had attracted her killer to Seaham? These murders had been orchestrated. They were far too controlled to be anything else. The speed and ferocity of the kill was frightening. One minute they were alive, the next they were fighting to stave off the inevitable. It was always a contentious issue, but were they dealing with a potential serial killer here? Two unsolved murders, both intrinsically linked, didn't bode well in anyone's books. What if these weren't spontaneous killings after all? What if they'd been planned all along? One thing was for sure, the killer's modus operandi had remained unbroken throughout. Whatever was eating away inside the killer's head was escalating out of control. Snuffing out another person's life without the slightest hint of remorse, took a certain kind of mentality. It was a vile, inhuman act. Not for the faint-hearted. There again, he argued, what if he'd been holding his victim captive and dehumanising her as an object for his own gratification?

Not the best of starts, he thought; maybe he should have had a better plan.

Chapter
Fifteen

Kurt Gillespie wasn't a tall man by any means. He had chiselled features and a long pointed nose that sat squarely beneath narrow slit eyes. A notorious villain, Gillespie wasn't the kind of man you'd want to tangle with. Not at any cost. The truth was, he'd made a shed load of money from selling drugs, most of which he'd blown at the dog track and entertaining loose women. But those days were behind him now – or so he would have everyone believe. That was Gillespie's way of doing things; the man was a born loser.

The light beginning to fade; it had just turned four when David Carlisle finally stepped into the little café just off North Terrace, close to Seaham shopping precinct. He knew a few of the customers there, local miscreants he'd dealt with in the not too distant past. There were times when being a private investigator had its downsides and it could be heavy going at times. Popular with lowlifes, the cosy warm interior had a menacing feel. It wasn't particularly flash either. Hard backed seats, matching pine tables, and a handful of trouble thrown in. The good thing about the place, if there was such a thing – he knew where to find his contact.

Just as Carlisle pushed past a tall, muscular man, with an arm full of tattoos and bearing a smile that was far from sincere, it was then he spotted his contact. He was sat in a corner seat, staring aimlessly out through the café window.

'Mind if I join you?' Carlisle said, already pulling up a seat.

Kurt Gillespie checked his watch as if time was at a premium.

'Carlisle, what brings you to this neck of the woods?' the drug dealer asked.

'Business—'

Gillespie hesitated. 'What kind of business?'

'I'm looking for someone.'

Carlisle leaned forward and glanced around. Cheryl Sawyer's murder would have been big locally – not much went on in Seaham without the press getting hold of it. Rumours would abound, and whole communities would close ranks if they thought they were threatened. If there was anything suspicious surrounding this young woman's murder, then Kurt Gillespie would have known about it.

Dressed in a black button down silk shirt, snappy powder blue suit and white loafer shoes, the drugs dealer oozed attention.

'So,' said Gillespie dismissively, 'who are you looking for?'

'No smoke without fire, eh!'

Both men smiled.

'You're right,' Gillespie replied. 'Everything has a price these days.'

'What can you tell me about Cheryl Sawyer?'

Gillespie shook his head. 'God, that was a few years ago. Wasn't she found in a skip over by the harbour?'

'That's the young woman,' Carlisle nodded.

'A bit of looker was our Cheryl. Mind, she could be difficult to make out at times.'

'I take it you knew her?'

Gillespie stared at him, eyes still full of suspicion. 'Yeah, you could say that. Never short of a bob of two was our Cheryl. Bonny lass, liked the nightlife, and certainly knew how to flaunt it.'

They sat for a while, engaged in small talk, each refusing to yield ground. It was then he noticed the signal. It was the eyes that were the giveaway. He couldn't be certain, but he thought he was in the middle of a drugs drop.

'Was she a customer of yours?' Carlisle asked.

'I've never liked the word customer. Users yes, but not customers.'
Gillespie shifted awkwardly. 'She wasn't one of your regular smack-
heads. She preferred the more sophisticated stuff, especially at
weekends. But hey, who am I to go round spouting my mouth off
about other people's lifestyles.'

Oblivious of her surroundings, the young girl behind the glass
counter continued to work her iPhone. She reeked of resentment, as
if the rest of the world owed her a massive favour or two. Her skirt,
frayed at the edges, was ridiculously short and her make-up was
all over the place. Not that Carlisle knew anything about the latest
teen fashions – he didn't. He'd lost all track of what the younger
generation was up to these days, a sure sign of getting old.

'I take it she was a friend of yours?'

'I'd like to think so,' Gillespie grinned. 'There was never a dull
moment when our Cheryl was around. She could be difficult at
times – never liked to be tied down.'

'Did she ever fall foul of anyone?'

Suddenly he had the drug dealer's attention. His eyes widened, as
if he knew far more than he was letting on. 'Not that I'm aware of,
she didn't. She wasn't like the rest, always scratching around to pay
for their next fix. Cheryl had money. It was never a problem to her.'

'What about friends?'

Gillespie scooted his chair closer, and Carlisle caught a repulsive
whiff of cheap aftershave. Suddenly he felt a nervous tremor wash
him. Not a good sign, he thought. He watched as the drug dealer's
dark bushy eyebrows raised a fraction and the corner of his mouth
twitched. Never one to miss a trick, nothing got under Gillespie's
radar.

'Ah! Cheryl's friends,' the drug dealer grinned, showing off a set
of white teeth that would have done any Seaham dentist proud.
'Wealthy people mainly, not your usual dregs from around these
parts. Mind, most of them were knob-heads as I remember. But you
know me, never one to look a gift horse in the mouth.'

'From around these parts, were they?'

'Nah, these were mainly high-rollers, city people.'

'Sunderland—'

'Nah, Middlesbrough.'

'Why choose this neck of the woods?' Carlisle asked.

Gillespie checked his surroundings before answering. 'Seaham is a busy place, especially at weekends. It can get very lively at times.'

The drug dealer's eyes suddenly darted across the room, reminding Carlisle of a cat on the prowl. Something was afoot, and whatever it was he suddenly felt part of it. These were dangerous times. What with hidden microphones, CCTV, and undercover detectives, the police were using every tool in their armoury in their fight against the drugs barons. He watched as Gillespie licked the froth from the end of his spoon and stared out of the window again.

Carlisle caught the sleight of hand as the man on the next table dropped something into another customer's carrier bag – business was brisk.

'Here's the deal. I'm—'

Gillespie stopped him mid-sentence. 'How much do you know about Cheryl?'

The drugs dealer was testing him out – looking for flaws in his story.

'Six years ago, she walked out on her husband, a rich investment banker from Manchester. A guy called Bertram Sawyer.' Carlisle let out a long sigh, and stretched his feet under the table. 'They lived out by Redcar somewhere, a big house, horses, and bags of open countryside to ride around in. According to the Cleveland police his wife had planned her escape from the start. Besides reverting back to her maiden name, she'd transferred huge sums of her husband's money into her own private bank account. A few weeks later she disappeared, and that was the last her husband saw of her.'

'That sounds about right.' Gillespie smiled. 'How much do the police know about this?'

'Not a lot. I suspect the case files are buried deep in a back room somewhere.'

Gillespie chewed on the end of his straw, with a smile that said everything.

'I always thought Cheryl was a bit of dark horse, and now I know why. So that's how she was able to flash her money about.'

'It takes all sorts, I suppose.'

Gillespie stroked his chin in contemplation. 'What you've just told me, I wouldn't be surprised if her husband hadn't got something to do with it.'

'Apparently not,' Carlisle replied. 'He was cleared of all involvement six years ago.'

'That's odd!'

'Think about it. Smacked out of her head on drugs, four wraps of high quality cocaine found in her back pocket, it's not hard to see why they believed her death was drugs related.'

'It doesn't sound right,' Gillespie said shaking his head. 'Everything gets blamed on drugs. Even you know that, Carlisle.'

'You're probably right, but it's not my call unfortunately.'

'The crafty little sod, no wonder she was always smartly turned out.' Gillespie's eyes narrowed a fraction. 'Just out of curiosity, how much money did she nick from her hubby?'

'Two hundred grand according to his bank manager,' Carlisle replied.

Gillespie blew through his teeth.

'If that was my wife I'd have wrung her fucking neck.'

'Someone did, and it wasn't a pretty sight apparently.' Carlisle changed tack. 'Tell me, was Cheryl ever involved with any of the other dealers around town?'

Gillespie glared at him. 'Meaning—'

'Did anyone else supply her?'

'It doesn't work like that, not around here it doesn't.'

The drug dealer's face had remained expressionless throughout, but his eyes displayed a mean look. Gillespie was on edge, fighting it, annoyed over his last remarks. For the first time in weeks Carlisle felt he was finally on to something. Not all was the truth, of course, but most of it was and that's what he was clinging to.

'Somebody strangled her, Kurt.'

'Yeah, and it caused an awful big stink around town.' Gillespie looked him in the eye. 'What if I was to tell you her death came as no surprise to everyone?'

'Oh!'

'There are those who believe she had what was coming to her.' Gillespie tapped the side of his nose. 'People who flash money about in a place like Seaham are bound to get noticed. It's not the done thing. Not around these parts it ain't.'

'You're not suggesting she was murdered for her money?'

'No!' Gillespie snapped. 'But her death wasn't drugs related. Had it have been, then I would have been the first to have known about it.'

'So why was she killed?'

Gillespie ordered himself another Banana Split milk shake, and the young girl playing her iPhone swung into action again. Hers was a well-practised routine – mindlessly orchestrated, decidedly robotic, with little or no job satisfaction thrown in.

Carlisle's iPhone pinged.

It was Jack Mason. Something urgent had cropped up.

'I need a quick favour, Kurt,' Carlisle said, now desperate to get going.

'It all depends.'

'I need to know who Cheryl hung around with at the time of her murder.'

'Why would you want to know that?'

'I need names,' Carlisle insisted.

Gillespie gave him a suspicious look. 'That's a big ask, Carlisle, especially when the police don't even know the answers to that. Like

I say, people around here talk. They see things differently. It unsettles them and they quickly become suspicious.'

'Name your price.'

'Nah,' Gillespie shrugged. 'I already owe you too many favours.'

They exchanged pleasantries, chatted some more.

'The man who killed Cheryl Sawyer must be stopped, Kurt. He's a dangerous predator, and needs to be taken off the streets.'

The drug dealer almost laughed as he stirred the fresh milkshake with a long silver spoon. 'That's drugs for you. It always attracts the dregs from the bottom of the barrel.'

Trying to get Gillespie to cooperate was like trying to sell snow to the Eskimos: impossible. Besides, six years was a heck of a long time between murders. He realised that, but a lot of water had passed under the bridge since then.

'What do you know about Wingate?' Carlisle asked.

'It's a village, not far from here. Why?'

'That's where Cheryl Sawyer was holed up after she went missing. According to the local estate agents she'd rented a three bedroom property there. It was close to the village pub, I'm told.'

'Yeah, I knew all about it,' Gillespie grinned.

'Who else did?'

Gillespie's eyes were all over the place, as if another drugs drop was imminent. Drug dealers were shrewd. They needed to be, and that's why they kept a close point of contact. What Gillespie didn't know, or maybe he did, was whom Cheryl Sawyer was mixing with at the time.

The drug dealer continued. 'Just about everyone in the land knew where Cheryl was holed up. She could be a loose cannon at times – liked to be the centre of attention. Late night parties, disco clubs, you name it, she was into it. Mind, who doesn't like to let their hair down from time to time?'

Carlisle chose his moment.

'Am I right in thinking there was a darker side attached to

Cheryl's nocturnal activities?'

Gillespie lowered his glass as if taken aback by his statement.

'Let's cut to the chase, Carlisle. What is it you're after?'

'Whoever murdered Cheryl was probably close to her. He was never in the limelight, and always sat on the side lines.'

'Involved with drugs, was he?'

'Probably not, but Cheryl would undoubtedly have befriended him. That's how the cunning bastard operates. He's sly with it, and needs to be stopped.'

'Anything else I should know?'

'He's probably a loner, someone who keeps to himself.'

Gillespie bristled. 'He sounds like the frigging Scarlet Pimpernel to me.'

'Exactly!' said Carlisle. 'Shortly after Cheryl was murdered he would have vanished into thin air. Someone out there must have noticed he'd gone missing.'

Gillespie fiddled with the end of his straw, and then said, 'I'll put my feelers out, ask around.'

Gillespie could be trusted. He wasn't the type of person to go spouting his mouth off, not like some of the drug dealers Carlisle knew. Even so, he still felt uncomfortable in his presence. Carlisle's chair made a scraping noise and the man sat opposite shot him a glance. Whatever it was that had spooked him, it had certainly caused him to flinch.

There followed an awkward silence, a sharpening of claws.

'There's something else you should know.'

'Like what?' Gillespie replied.

'I have it on good authority the police are watching you, so you'll need to be on your toes.'

'Don't fuck with me, Carlisle. I'd know if someone was following me?'

'So how do you think I found you here?'

Gillespie glared at him with suspicion. He was angry, and Carlisle had picked up on it. Oh shit, he thought. He could have really done without this!

'If you're trying to pull the wool over my eyes,' Gillespie whispered through gritted teeth, 'you're treading on very thin ice.'

'Play it your way, but remember whose side I'm on.'

Suddenly they were lifelong friends again. As if nothing had ever happened. God forbid if a police undercover team were watching them. Kurt Gillespie was the last person he'd want to be seen hanging around with. Keep it simple, Carlisle told himself. There again, make a mistake and Gillespie's men would hunt him down wherever he hid.

'Leave it with me,' the drug dealer smiled.

They talked a while, straightened a few more things out before it was time to leave.

Carlisle's iPhone pinged and he checked the new text message.

Never liked Seaham myself!

Someone was following him. If not they were tracking his iPhone with a spy app.

But who would do that? He thought.

He suddenly felt vulnerable.

Chapter Sixteen

Carlisle woke with a start. It was three in the morning and someone was banging on his front door. Then his iPhone buzzed on the bedside table. Half asleep, he stumbled out of bed and slid back the bedroom curtains. Nobody there! Whatever had roused him in the middle of the night was nowhere to be seen.

He checked the text message display.

Let the fun begin!

His heart sank – number withheld.

Annoyed, Carlisle hurried downstairs and made a mug of black coffee. It was then he noticed the small brown paper package innocently lying on the doormat. Curious, he bent down to pick it up. There was nothing to suggest who it was from, or what was inside for that matter. He gave it a quick shake. It felt light, and nothing inside rattled. Returning to the kitchen he grabbed a knife from the cutlery drawer and slid the blade under the sealed flap. Curious, he tentatively shook the contents onto the kitchen table.

A SEVERED FINGER!

Not wishing to touch it, panic gripped him. And yes, the North-East was full of pranksters only too keen to demonstrate the executioner's controlling power, but this felt totally different. It was dark outside, and as the rest of the world slept easy in their beds that morning, his worst nightmare was only just beginning.

The next time someone banged on his front door, it was Jack

Mason. Bleary eyed, the Detective Chief Inspector stifled a yawn and made a point of checking his watch.

'It's three-forty-two, my friend. Let's hope this isn't a wind-up?'

Still trying to come to terms with the situation, it was then Tom Hedley appeared in the doorway. The man looked pale, as well he might, Carlisle thought. Get a grip, he cursed. You're a profiler, you're supposed to deal with these things and not fall apart like a ten year-old child.

One by one, the three of them made their way into the back of the house. No one spoke. It was then Carlisle pointed towards the kitchen table.

'This arrived through my letterbox forty-minutes ago,' he said.

Mason drew back. 'What the fuck—'

'Well I'll be damned,' said Hedley calmly.

'I know,' Carlisle replied. 'Life is full of nasty little surprises, it seems.'

'May I ask who delivered it?' Hedley enquired.

'I've no idea, Tom. They certainly didn't hang around long enough for me to find out.'

His posture unruffled, Hedley slipped on a pair of rubber gloves and took a closer inspection. 'It's human all right,' the Senior Forensic Scientist said as he turned the severed finger over with the end of his pen. There was a moment's hesitation, just enough to build the tension again. 'Undoubtedly female, middle finger, I suspect. I'll need to run a few tests, but it's unquestionably human.'

'The bastard,' Mason cursed.

'Before we go jumping to conclusions,' Hedley said calmly, 'let's see what the forensic results throw up.'

Mason looked at each of them in turn. 'What about the packaging, Tom?'

Hedley stepped back a pace as if a blow had struck him. He had an owl shaped face, with a strong defined jawline. His hair was naturally curly, unkempt, light brown and powdered in white.

'Pretty bog standard wrapping paper, I'd say. No doubt your fingerprints are all over it, David.'

'What about the underside of the package sealing tape?' Mason asked.

'I'm sure we'll find something on it.'

'Let's hope the sick bastard has made his first big mistake.'

'Well it's definitely human.'

'But whose, Tom?'

Hedley's eye's slid first to the packaging, then back to the severed finger again. 'Fortunately this isn't a regular occurrence. There again, it's strange why someone should single you out.' The forensic scientist stretched his joints and gathered his composure as if his mind were already made up. 'What puzzles me is these people normally like to send this type of package to the media, as it gives them maximum exposure.'

'It could be just a sick prank?' Carlisle shrugged.

'I doubt it, it's definitely genuine.'

He watched as Hedley carefully slid the evidence into a small plastic bag. Sealing it shut, he held it up against the kitchen light. 'It's probably been packed in ice, as it looks well preserved.'

'It felt cold, Tom, I—'

Mason cut him short. 'What's in the text message?'

Still shaken, Carlisle checked his iPhone and read it out to them.

'It's probably a pay as you go phone,' Mason said, a tad grumpily. 'That's what most petty criminals are using nowadays. They're difficult to trace. Whoever he is, he certainly knew where to find you, my friend.'

Mason unfolded his arms, and made a few notes.

'Coffee, gentlemen?' said Carlisle.

'Luv a cup,' Mason replied.

Hedley looked at him sheepishly. 'Do you have tea?' he asked.

'Yes, Tom. I'll make a fresh pot.'

The three of them sat huddled around the kitchen table, piecing together the possibilities. Whoever had delivered the package in the early hours of the morning had certainly chosen their moment. If their sole intention had been to stir up a whole lot of trouble, they'd unquestionably succeeded in that.

Mason's eyes scanned the room.

'What about CCTV?'

'There's only the burglar alarm,' Carlisle replied.

'What about neighbours?'

'I've absolutely no idea.'

Mason turned to face him, and Carlisle felt the back of his neck prickle.

'I don't want to sound alarmist here, but if this is the killer's handiwork then he certainly knows where to find you. If it's fear he's trying to spread, he certainly knows how to do that.'

'It's probably a wind-up.'

'I doubt it,' Hedley said, shaking his head.

'He's obviously looking for some sort of knee-jerk reaction in my opinion. There again—' Mason stopped himself short.

Carlisle felt a sudden adrenaline rush. 'What if it is his signature? These people are notorious attention seekers. They like nothing more than to bolster their own personal egos.'

'Let's not go there,' Mason shrugged.

'Maybe we've ruffled his feathers and he's trying to hit back at us.'

'Anything is possible.'

Hedley drew breath. 'How will he react if we don't play to his games?'

'Badly, I suspect,' Carlisle replied.

'I thought as much.'

Carlisle pointed to the severed finger again. 'These people are prone to violating the rules of society.' A memory tugged him. 'A psychiatrist friend of mine once told me, never get into an argument with a psychopath as they always see themselves smarter than you and will react violently.'

'It doesn't sound good,' Mason shrugged, 'and this bastard's certainly off his rocker.'

'That's presuming it was the killer's doing,' said Hedley. 'Before we go running around like headless chickens, let's see what the lab results throw up.'

'I'm a profiler, Tom,' said Carlisle. 'I know how these things work. When the fox hears a chicken scream, it doesn't come running to help. It comes to kill.'

Mason squinted across at them both. 'So what do you need from us?'

Carlisle thought about it, but only for a second.

'Right now I could do with some thinking time.'

'In which case I suggest we carry on as normal,' Hedley shrugged.

Carlisle had thought about that too. Still shaken from his ordeal, he stretched back in his seat and let out a deep drawn out sigh. Hedley was right. They were both overreacting and not thinking it through logically. There again, he'd never been in this kind of situation before, but it unquestionably felt damn uncomfortable. He'd always dealt with other people's problems, never his own. There was a big difference, of course.

Carlisle's brow corrugated.

'One thing's for sure, you must never let the darkness creep into your mind. There are holes in the floor of the night, big enough for us to fall through.'

'Enough of all that baloney,' said Mason, pacing the floor and pointing a finger at him. 'If he does have access to classified police information, which is highly unlikely, he's bound to trip up at some stage. Besides, most criminals tend to forget they're dealing with experienced police officers here.'

Carlisle saw a rare flash of humanity in Mason's face, but refused to be drawn in. There again, neither of them were on the receiving end of the killer's mind games. Nor his actions come to think of it.

'Try keeping this simple,' Hedley pointed out. 'Let's talk it over with Acting Superintendent Sutherland. In the meantime, we keep it between the three of us.'

Mason stared into the bottom of his empty mug, as if his mind was already made up.

'*An inner circle,* I rather like the sound of that, Tom.'

No one spoke, each preferring to turn inwardly on their own private thoughts. It was still early days, and nothing was cast in stone. There again, everyone knew what the outcome would be. It was only a matter of time.

Chapter Seventeen

Sleep did not come easy.

It was 8:15am, and starting to get light when David Carlisle finally strolled up the main entrance ramp and into Gateshead Police Station. Over the years, he'd learnt never to underestimate the power of a killer's determination, as it would always come back to haunt you. These people were ruthless manipulators, masters at disguising their emotions and thoughts. He knew in his own mind what he wanted to do, but others were now making those decisions for him. Inwardly he felt vulnerable, almost isolated from the rest of the team. Now wasn't the time for cossetting, now was a time for reflection. In a way he was pleased that Acting Superintendent Sutherland had taken back control of the case. At least she would bring some stability to the team. More importantly, at least to him, was the fact he'd finally worked it out. Not that he had all the answers, of course. He didn't, but at least he now had a sense of direction.

Thinking back, the victim's severed finger pushed through his letter box would have triggered off an unstoppable chain reaction amongst the senior backroom staff. At least Tom Hedley had done his homework. Tom was old school, thorough, besides being level headed. This was a particularly nasty misogynistic reign of terror, aimed at vulnerable women. Carlisle also knew that geographically stable serial killers usually killed their victims in familiar surroundings. It was all about location, and locality was an integral part of geographical profiling. Most serial killers preferred to work within their comfort zones, familiar territory and usually close to home. Understanding why a psychopath crossed the line to commit murder in the first place was a key to unlocking what went on inside their heads. There again, logic had told him the killer probably lived south of the River Tyne, somewhere between Gateshead and Cleveland. It was a large catchment area, and one that was putting undue strain on Mason's overstretched resources.

'Not the best way to start your Monday morning,' Mason grunted, as he stared out of the office window. 'Sutherland's spoiling for a fight, and Tom Hedley's been in with her for the past forty minutes.'

'Do we know what this is all about?'

'God knows,' Mason shrugged. 'No doubt it has something to do with this severed finger incident. Apart from your grubby little fingerprints contaminating the packaging, little else has shown up. It had been kept on ice apparently, and perfectly preserved.'

'So it was him?'

'It would appear so.'

Carlisle took off his glasses and rubbed sore eyes.

'Has Sutherland discussed it with you at all?'

'No, and unless I hear otherwise our meeting is still set for nine o'clock.'

Mason looked physically drained, as did the rest of the team that morning. The weekend had come and gone. New developments had a nasty habit of throwing up a whole raft of challenges, and he could soon find he was out of a job.

'There is some good news. We've managed to triangulate a fix on his latest batch of text messages,' Mason pulled a face. 'They were genuine alright, and sent from Caroline Harper's iPhone.'

'He's probably ditched it by now?'

'No surprises there!'

'What about CCTV coverage?'

Mason nodded. 'The little corner shop, the one nearest your house, we've managed to recover some footage. The quality's crap, but at least it gives us an indication of the suspect's physical appearance.'

'What about age?'

Mason gave him an assuring glance. 'He's thirtyish, white, medium build, approximately six feet tall.'

'Any distinguishing features?'

'No, he was wearing a hoody at the time.'

'So he prefers to move around incognito?'

'He's a sly bastard,' Mason shrugged. 'Let's hope he becomes complacent at some point.'

Carlisle caught the urgency in Mason's tone, as if he had more important issues on his mind. Drinks arrived on a tray, brought in by a young female detective who looked fresh out of prep school. Mason had obviously remembered he took his coffee black, the stronger the better as far as Carlisle was concerned.

'At least he's declared his intentions, Jack.'

'The bastard's got some nerve if you ask me.' Mason spread his hands out on the desktop in front of him as if contemplating his next statement. 'At least Sutherland warmed to the idea of an inner circle, so we must be doing something right.'

Ah! *The inner circle,* thought Carlisle. He'd almost forgotten about that.

'Has she said anything else?'

'Not a lot. She's a bit of a dark horse when it comes to giving information away.'

The Detective Chief Inspector looked as Carlisle felt: demoralised. The weekend had come and gone, and now was the start of another week. Even though he was only there in an advisory capacity, he still felt sucked in by it all. This was his first real meeting with the Acting Superintendent, and he wasn't looking forward to it.

'What are her thoughts on someone leaking internal information?'

Mason took another swig of his coffee. 'It's not exactly rocket science, is it? Tell me, who else would have known you were working on the case unless they weren't working on it themselves?'

'That's true,' Carlisle said, dejectedly.

Mason's face had darkened. 'The trouble is, Sutherland demands answers and right now we know the square root of bog all.'

Carlisle gazed at the collection of horrendous photographs pinned to Mason's office walls. Death came in different guises, none of them reassuring.

'What's she like as a person?'

Mason slumped back in his chair, and ran his fingers across a few days' stubble. 'She's a high flyer, just like her father was. One thing's for sure, she doesn't take crap for an answer.'

'What's her background?'

Mason was starting to look old, and late night boozing sessions were beginning to catch up on him. Anxious, the DCI shuffled a few papers around on a cluttered desk and drew in a long intake of air. 'Unmarried; like many, she's married to the police force. I heard that before moving to the HM Inspectorate of Constabulary she sailed through her police exams. Not bad for a woman – she's an astute cookie by all accounts. A former pupil of Hexham's Queen Elizabeth High School, she joined the Cumbria police force as a young Constable back in 1986. Sutherland's a grafter, and isn't frightened of getting her hands dirty. Some say she's an interfering old bitch, but they're in the minority, I guess.' Once Mason had signed off a witness report he was checking, he continued, 'Whereas with some senior police officers you talk to you know for a fact they're scanning the room for something more interesting to say. You don't get that with Sutherland. She's approachable, and actually listens to you. Mind, she can be quite an obstinate bitch at times.'

Mason's was a typical sexist remark, Carlisle thought, but he didn't press the matter further. An image formed in his head. It was Sutherland and she was standing in a graveyard and holding a revolver to his head. A low swirling mist hung in the background, giving her a ghostlike appearance. Sometimes Carlisle thought he was losing it, as if he'd witnessed too much violence in his time.

'She obviously knows a thing or two about serious crime,' he said.

'Sutherland's been around the block a few times, if that's what you mean. Some say she was handpicked for her current position, but don't quote me on that.'

'Family contacts—'

'I doubt it. The people at her last place spoke very highly of her.'

They talked a while, Mason bringing Carlisle up to speed on the latest weekend's developments. Why someone would want to stir up a whole lot of trouble continually text messaging him beggared belief. But they had, and it didn't make sense. Unless, of course...

'So what's her problem?'

'Sutherland's worried about your safety, my friend. It seems this latest incident isn't helping any either. If you want my advice, you need to take a hard look at the people around you.' Mason put his empty mug back on the drinks tray and turned to face him. 'Mind, I'm still not convinced the killer is one of us. He's external in my opinion, someone with access to inside information.'

Another change of mind – Carlisle smelt a rat.

'Have you any ideas who?'

'Hey!' Mason said, raising his hands as in surrender. 'Who the hell am I in the grand scheme of things around here?'

'So what does Sutherland intend to do about me?'

'I haven't a clue. One thing's for sure, she's treating this latest incident very seriously.'

Carlisle caught the look of concern on Mason's face.

'Don't tell me she's considering pulling the plug on me?'

'God knows what she's thinking. Sutherland has a mind of her own.' Mason made a little sweeping hand gesture and groaned. 'She likes to keep you guessing; it's her way of dealing with it, I'm afraid.'

'I don't like the sound of it, Jack.'

'Me neither, if I'm brutally honest.'

Mason nodded. 'Yours isn't the easiest of posts to fill; at least you've got something going for you. Her biggest concern right now is your safety.' The DCI eyed him warily. 'Having said that, she believes it could be one of your clients – someone holding a personal grudge against you.'

'Highly unlikely, do you think?'

'But is it?'

'Well she's wrong.'

Carlisle mulled over the facts. It was a no brainer in his opinion, but now that Sutherland had singled him out, he suddenly felt vulnerable. What's more, there was something quite disturbing in all of this. Something he couldn't quite put his finger on. If someone on the inside was leaking confidential information to the wrong people, they had to be close to the action.

Mason checked his watch.

'No doubt Hedley's fighting your corner, so let's see what develops.'

'What about the day to day handling of the case?'

'That still remains with me – unless I hear otherwise. The less people who know about this latest incident, the better chance we have of catching him.' Mason slid his finger across his throat. 'God help him if he ever turns out to be a copper.'

'I'm still not convinced—'

'Well, if Richard Sloane didn't kill his wife, then who did?'

'I doubt it was Sloane.'

'What if he paid someone else to do his dirty work for him?'

Typical Mason, thought Carlisle. Turn it on its head and throw something else into the melting pot. The theory of a hired assassin was an irrational notion. Besides, it didn't take into account the first victim. Mason was clutching at straws, and whoever had killed these young women had simply gone to ground. And another thing: establishing Caroline Harper's last known movements was like looking for a needle in a haystack. *Maybe Sutherland's involvement wasn't bad after all.* At least it would bring a fresh pair of eyes to the case.

'What's the latest from the Missing Person Bureau?' Carlisle asked.

'There are far too many internet search engines for any investigation to be effective. Let's hope she doesn't come up with fingerprinting.'

Mason's desk phone rang. He checked the digital display, lifted the receiver and then said. 'Yes, ma'am. We're on our way up.'

Sutherland, Carlisle mouthed.

Mason nodded as he placed the receiver onto its cradle.

'When her majesty says jump, we jump.'

This wasn't his style. Mason was a creature of habit. He was impulsive, and liked to react to changing situations with spur of the moment decisions. Trying to pin Mason down with endless meetings was like keeping a dangerous animal locked in a cage. When you finally opened the door, you would need to stand well clear.

Chapter Eighteen

'Well, Jack,' said Sutherland, flicking an annoying strand of hair from her face. 'Who are your most likely candidates?'

Mason stared down at his notebook and then back at the Acting Superintendent. There was no getting away from it, his boss had thrown the book at him and he hated every minute of it. Even so, Mason did what he always did in times of trouble – he fought back. That's how hardened coppers survived when their backs were to the wall. But Sutherland was refusing to budge, and whoever said she was an easy touch had clearly misunderstood her resolve. Ruthless in approach, deadly in delivery, she was slowly tearing the Detective Chief Inspector apart.

'So, Jack. What are our latest crime stats?' she asked.

Mason cleared his throat, and stared across at Tom Hedley who'd sat quietly throughout. 'One murder investigation, six house break-ins, an overnight hit and run in Birtley, and not forgetting the Alpaca thefts.'

'I thought we'd resolved the Alpaca problem?'

'It would appear not, ma'am.'

'So how many have gone missing this time?'

'Four according to the latest incident report. As far I'm aware they were all taken from the same area.'

'Four! That's ten this week, Jack.'

'Yes, ma'am, but we're keeping a close eye on the situation. Every restaurant and pub in the county is now under scrutiny. Whoever has stolen these animals will certainly find it extremely difficult to dispose of them.'

'Surely people don't eat them?'

'I've absolutely no idea,' Mason replied.

Carlisle could hardly contain himself. For one brief moment he thought the Detective Chief Inspector was going to burst out laughing. He didn't; instead he spent the next fifteen minutes trying to explain his way out of another tight corner.

'So,' Sutherland said, still looking somewhat bemused, 'do we still believe our suspect has access to classified police information?'

'It's difficult to say at—'

'Backroom staff or outsider, Jack,' she interrupted firmly. 'What's it to be?'

Carlisle sat silent as stone, mentally preparing himself for the inevitable onslaught. Any hope of Jack Mason getting off lightly was fast slipping away. Sutherland's determination was unquestionable, but pointing a finger at a fellow police officer was a taboo that even he found difficulty in coming to terms with. Undoubtedly Mason had his suspicions, but he wasn't letting on about it. Had someone let their tongue slip – a loose comment or sly remark perhaps? Shit happened and things were getting out of hand. It was time to come to his friend's rescue.

'It feels like we're walking into a trap, ma'am,' Carlisle cut in.

'A trap, what trap?' Sutherland abruptly replied.

'Psychopaths are grandiose, and their world is all about them. Whenever a serial killer feels challenged they'll always revert to control.'

'Who mentioned anything about a serial killer?'

'I was merely raising a point, ma'am.'

Sutherland gave Carlisle a withering look. 'Which is?'

'It's my view the killer is trying to unsettle us, and wants us to react to it.'

Her face darkened. 'Don't tell me he's playing – *mind games?*'

'I believe he is, ma'am.'

The tone in her voice had softened somewhat. 'What are your thoughts on someone accessing the missing person files, Tom?'

'It's a difficult one,' Hedley replied stoically. 'But the killer does seem to have an uncanny knowledge of how the forensic system works.'

Mason shook his head. 'Anyone with half a brain can read about it on the internet.'

Sutherland looked at Mason, and then back to Tom Hedley. 'An outsider with inside knowledge, do you think?'

'It's possible,' Hedley agreed.

Sutherland narrowed her eyes a fraction. 'This new boyfriend Caroline Harper was last seen with, have we made any further progress in finding him?'

'No, not yet we haven't,' Mason admitted. 'There's an awful lot of confusion as to what's well-off and what's not.'

'But I thought he drove expensive cars?'

'He does, and that's exactly my point, ma'am. Apart from the barman at the Gold Medal, no one else has seen anything untoward in the pub car park—'

'But he's your main witness,' Sutherland replied sharply.

Carlisle sat quietly as the focus of attention slowly shifted back towards Caroline Harper's husband. His business in free-fall, was Richard Sloane capable of murder? Despite the confusion, there seemed to be a distinct pattern to the killer's selection criteria – attractive young women, early thirties, who had married wealthy men much older than them.

Taking a momentary break, Sutherland moved towards the back of the office and removed a thick leather bound book from a glass fronted bookcase. She looked mid-forties, Carlisle thought. Not unattractive with a slim waist, dark blues eyes, and short straight brown hair. It was then he noticed her shoes: she was wearing six-inch stiletto heels.

'These latest threats,' she suddenly announced. 'It seems odd why he should single you out at such an early stage in the proceedings. It normally doesn't happen like that.'

All eyes were on him.

'I would agree,' Carlisle nodded.

Sutherland returned to her seat carrying the book under her arm. 'Let's face it, these people are usually sensation seekers, they like nothing more than to get the media involved. People with psychopathic personalities normally like to demonstrate how clever they are; it gives them a sense of dominance. That's why they prefer to use knives to kill their quarry. Guns are too quick; they can't savour their victim's emotions. Tell me,' she said. 'Is that how you see it?'

God, she was good. Extremely good, Carlisle thought.

'You're right, ma'am. These people are inter-species predators. When you take them into an interview room, you quickly become their prey. Besides constantly watching over you they're reading you better than you're reading them.' Carlisle steadied himself. 'I personally find them extremely condescending individuals to deal with, and their powers of observation are remarkable. It's as if they want to take over the interview themselves.'

'That is interesting,' said Sutherland. 'What about motive?'

'Whoever he is, he's determined to make his point. What triggers him to kill is difficult to say, but six years between murders proves that he has a certain amount of control over his emotional feelings.'

'And these recent threats, what do you make of them?'

'He probably sees me as an obstacle in his path – someone spoiling his fun.'

'Trying to gain the upper hand, is he?' Sutherland smiled.

'You could say that. If not, he's sending out a warning message.'

'Is he hedonistic, do you think?'

'He's certainly not lust-based,' Carlisle replied, 'nor does he kill for the thrill of it. No, I'd say his actions are more anger based.'

'So these are reprisal killings.'

'More likely than not, but I wouldn't rule out retribution at this stage.'

Sutherland looked down at her notes. 'What makes you say that?'

'I'm convinced he's punishing his victims for the wrongdoing that someone else has done to him in his past. It's his way of dealing with it, and he probably sees it as a moral response – a justification for killing these women.'

Sutherland flicked through the pages of the book and stopped at the desired place. 'It's strange you should say that. It states here that retribution owes its etymology to the Latin *retribuo* – I pay back. Could this be his driving force?'

Carlisle got the feeling that Sutherland was concentrating more on the logic than the argument. Unlike Jack Mason whose style he was all too familiar with, hers was a methodical approach, more subtle. In fact he got the distinct impression she'd had a strict religious upbringing in her past, where Sundays always meant church. No doubt her father's strict upbringing would have been an overriding factor. An ex-guardsman and stern disciplinarian, much of it had obviously rubbed off on his daughter. He watched as the Acting Superintendent picked up Tom Hedley's draft forensic report and placed it on the table in front of her.

'Why would he keep a severed finger packed in ice, I wonder?'

Mason shuffled awkwardly. 'A trophy perhaps?'

'No, Jack,' Sutherland replied. 'He intended to preserve it all along. Not as a trophy, but more as a calling card. This was planned, don't you think?'

Carlisle bit his lip. God she was quick; how had he missed that one?

Sutherland looked at Mason, and then said, 'The autopsy report also mentions the possible use of rose secateurs being used to cut off his victim's fingers. Unless I'm mistaken, he'd obviously intended to steal these women's rings all along.'

'Well he's certainly no medical practitioner,' Mason replied smugly.

'Time, Jack. This was no afterthought.' Sutherland stared at her meeting notes before turning to face Carlisle again. 'Picking up on your earlier remarks, could his actions have satanic undertones?'

'I presume you're referring to *the sign of the horns?*' Carlisle replied. Sutherland tilted her head back thoughtfully. 'Yes, I am.'

'Six years between murders, and yet he still performs the same ritual – removing both the ring and middle fingers from his victim's left hand. Some say it's a salute to the devil, which is formed by extending the index and little fingers whilst holding down the middle and ring fingers with the thumb.'

Carlisle held his hand up in front of Sutherland's stern face in order to gain the desired effect.

'It's a bit over the top, don't you think?' There followed an awkward silence, a gathering of thoughts. 'Tell me,' Sutherland continued. 'How would you best sum him up?'

Carlisle put his notebook down, and thought about it.

'He's a white male, highly intelligent, and probably holds down a professional position. We know he's mobile, so he's more likely to be single. He's organised, charming, and yet he has no emotional attachment towards these women. Organised killers are very difficult to apprehend as they will go to inordinate lengths to cover their tracks. We know he's forensically savvy, having witnessed at first-hand his ability to clean up a crime scene. What's important to him, at least, is that his victim types are at their most vulnerable after they have moved out of stable environments. To me this demonstrates his cunning, and a desire to win over their trust before killing them.'

'And his method of killing, does that tell us anything?'

'He's consistent in his behaviour across the majority of the crime scene. It's this, his behavioural trademark that will eventually lead us to his detection. The trouble is, and I don't say this lightly, he's incorporating new skills and growing in confidence over time.' Carlisle paused in reflection, his audience transfixed. 'What intrigues me most about him is his post offence behaviour and a willingness to contact the police after a murder has been committed. In other words, he's either trying to fuel his own egotistic fantasies, or it is part of a ritualistic behavioural pattern. Either way, it proves he's egotistically driven.'

'Do you know what,' Sutherland said, 'I've not given much thought to that before?'

'The man's deluded,' Mason interrupted.

Sutherland was quick to react. 'Let's hope for your sake he doesn't hear voices, Jack.'

The Acting Superintendent looked at her watch, and snapped her laptop computer shut. In Carlisle's mind's eye, the truth was gravely simple. He was now a burden to the rest of the team, and Sutherland had undoubtedly picked up on the fact.

'How would you feel if we took you off the case?' she said coldly.

'With all due respect, I think that would be playing into the killer's hands. That's what he wants you to do. He needs to feel in control; it's important to him.'

'What about his threats?'

Carlisle swallowed hard. 'I realise the risks I could be taking, but allowing me to continue may throw him off balance.'

'He could turn aggressive, of course.'

'It's possible, but highly unlikely,' Carlisle replied. 'There again, all that is necessary for evil to triumph is that good people do nothing.'

'What's your take on it, Jack?'

Mason drew in a long intake of air.

'We could certainly do with a lateral thinker on the team, ma'am.'

'I agree. If we're ever going to resolve this case, we'll certainly need to think outside of the box. ' Sutherland paused momentarily to open a thick blue folder that had sat in front of her throughout the whole of the meeting that morning. Her look was stern. 'In which case you'll need some sort of police protection. After some careful consideration, I've decided to assign DC Carrington to act as your personal shadow protection officer. You've worked well together in the past, so I don't see there being a problem.' Sutherland closed the file, and studied their faces. 'What do you think, gentlemen?'

Mason managed a weak smile. 'Carrington's an excellent choice, ma'am. Having only recently completed a Close Protection training course, she'll blend in perfectly. There is, of course, the—'

The Acting Superintendent raised a hand to intervene. 'There will be no armed response of any kind on my watch, Jack. I want our suspect brought in to stand trial, no matter what it takes. Do I make myself clear on that?'

Everyone knew what Sutherland was referring to. Jack Mason had been hauled over the coals for the use of excessive force on his last assignment. The Wharf Butcher was undoubtedly a dangerous psychopath, but the DCI's methods of ending it hadn't gone unnoticed amongst many of the senior ranks.

Hedley cut through the tension.

'Shouldn't we reconsider including DC Carrington in our – *inner circle*?'

There was a brief moment of reflection, and then Sutherland said, 'Ah, yes, the inner circle. I'd almost forgotten about that. Not at this stage, Tom. I'm sure we can find a more suitable excuse as to why Carrington is working alongside a criminal profiler.'

'Leave that with me,' Mason insisted. 'I'll concoct something up.'

'There is one other thing,' said Sutherland. 'With all this new evidence at our disposal, let's see if we can't establish a positive link between the two murder victims. That's one for DC Carrington and David to pick up on. Perhaps a discreet word with the Cleveland Police might not go amiss at this stage.'

'I'll brief Carrington immediately after the meeting,' Mason agreed.

With that the meeting closed.

Chapter Nineteen

South Shields town centre had a different character at lunchtime. It was school half-term, and the main shopping precinct was busy. Mums out shopping with kids, office workers scurrying to Subway, the place was alive and kicking. Tucked away in an upstairs room above King Street, and only if you knew where to find it, was Frankie's Diner. Nothing flash, the place was certainly popular. Sixties décor, hardback seats, plastic union jack tablecloths and decent sixties piped music. Frankie's was intentionally stuck in a time warp. The food was good too. Homemade mince pie, pork chops, liver and onion, chicken casserole, and not forgetting Mama's special spaghetti bolognaise.

Engrossed in a women's magazine, he found DC Carrington sitting in a window seat overlooking the main shopping precinct. Having stayed up half the night listening to ominous creaking noises coming through the rafters, David Carlisle had finally fallen asleep propped up in his favourite armchair. Not the most comfortable night, but at least he'd received no more text messages. The killer, whoever he was, certainly knew how to play psychological games with his mind and these past few days had been a living hell.

He checked his watch.

'You're late. I gave up on you an hour ago,' said DC Carrington, glancing up at him.

'I got held up,' Carlisle half apologised.

'This isn't how it works.'

He sensed the young detective's angst, but assumed it went with the territory. Not that it bothered him as he now had more important things on his mind. A killer was out there and threatening to tear his world apart.

Eyes like daggers, Carrington stared harshly back at him. 'Are you aware that I've been assigned as your personal protection officer?'

Carlisle feigned surprise. 'So it's not a rumour?'

'No it isn't!'

'Bugger!' he said out loud.

'Hasn't Jack Mason told you anything about what's happening?'

'Not to me he hasn't.'

'Well,' Carrington explained, 'I'm charged with your well-being, if that means anything to you.'

Stifling a yawn, Carlisle whistled through clenched teeth. The young detective had made her point, and it wasn't a good one at that. In hindsight he should have been more forceful, more open in his approach. He let her waffle on a while, before cutting her off mid-sentence.

'And what exactly are you protecting me from?' he asked.

'Someone out there has taken a gross disliking to you. Not that I can blame them.'

'A disliking—'

'Yes. Jack Mason wouldn't elaborate, but from now on you're to go nowhere without me knowing about it.'

Carlisle detected a hint of nervousness in Carrington's voice.

'And those were Jack Mason's instructions?'

'No, Acting Superintendent Sutherland's.'

'Blimey!'

Carrington wrinkled her nose. 'What's more, I've been instructed to pick you up every morning and drop you off at the end of my shift. Not that I'm happy about it, because I'm not. It's adding at least another two hours to my journey every day.'

He noticed the earpiece. Carrington was wired to a control centre somewhere. Another bad sign, he thought. If Acting Superintendent Sutherland was taking the killer's threats seriously, he would need to stay vigilant.

'Tell me, after you drop me off at the end of your shift, what if I want a pint?'

'That's not my problem.'

'But we're in this together, I presume?'

'You could say that, yes. As far as I'm concerned, this is a covert operation and no one else is to know about it.'

'Are you carrying a gun?' he whispered.

'No, just a Taser, so don't try anything stupid.'

Well at least that was over with, and Carrington knew nothing about the killer's recent threats. Sutherland had clearly withheld that vital information back from her, but why? There again there was something reassuring about the tone of the young detective's voice, as if she was taking her new role seriously. He'd been running on adrenaline and catnaps lately, and it couldn't go on indefinitely. One thing was for sure, if ever he was being followed he'd know it was an undercover police officer.

'Feeling peckish?' Carlisle asked.

'*What, here!*'

'Best food in town.' he replied, pointing to the stainless steel serving-counter tucked away in the back of the room. 'Take a look for yourself.'

Carrington burst out laughing. 'It's a bloody pensioners' café.'

'So what!' he frowned. 'This close protection malarkey isn't all it's cracked up to be. I've been there before, worn that T-shirt, so you better start getting used to it.'

'God help us if I'm being dragged down to your level.' Carrington sighed. 'What other surprises do you have in store for me?'

'Wouldn't you like to know?'

The young detective stared at him, huffed and put the magazine down.

That was it, no turning back. Ignoring her petulance, Carlisle pulled out a brand new notebook and wrote down some words on the very first page: *stay clear of Gateshead*. From his experience it was obvious the killer had stepped up his bitter campaign of hate against him. The trouble was there was something menacing about the killer's intent. Sometimes the mechanics of a murder investigation could be frightening, and the physiological strain quite draining. Yes, the killer had a sound knowledge of how the forensic systems worked, but anyone could read up on that. If there was a darker side involved, then who the hell was he?

A man sitting at the next table writing out a birthday card suddenly burst out laughing. It was the little things that Carlisle clung to most. When he was a kid, his father had told him always to go straight home after school. There are people out there, wicked people who gobble little boys up. There was a time, somewhere back in the mist of his childhood, when he didn't believe a word his father had said. Thirty years on, and never a truer word had been spoken. Life was cheap and murders an everyday occurrence. Catching the culprits was never easy, as all too often it meant weeks spent building up a mental picture of another person's broken life.

Carrington's eyes widened. 'Penny for your thoughts,' she said.

'I was trying to get my head around a murder, Sue.'

'And you're asking me out to lunch!'

'Yes, well—'

'Rubbish!' she remarked.

Carlisle stared at her for a moment. 'What if his latest victim had been held captive somewhere? At least it would account—'

'Account for what?' she insisted.

Carlisle thought quickly, not wanting to get involved. 'The killer's cunning.'

'Reading into other people's minds isn't my thing,' Carrington shrugged. 'Besides, it takes me all of my time to know when someone is lying to me.'

'That's easy, Sue. You can always tell by the way a person looks at you to know if they're lying. The eyes are the mirror of the soul. If they look to their left when they're talking to you, it usually means it's a lie. Look right, it's the truth.'

'That's fallacy.'

'But is it? It's a well-known fact that a stranger is more likely to lie to you in the first three-minutes of you meeting them. Even a baby will fake a cry when it wants to see who's around.' Carlisle drew back in his seat. 'Still not convinced?'

'No, it's utter codswallop,' Carrington insisted.

They talked a while, about everything and nothing. Carrington had a soft Geordie accent, lovely to listen to, he thought. Beneath the angelic charm there was an underlying tough streak – no doubt one of the fundamental requisites for close protection selection. In many ways, she reminded him of Jackie. Intelligent, incredibly quick witted, not to mention a slightly wry sense of humour that came with the territory.

'I've been thinking,' Carrington said, turning sharply to face him. 'If we're going to live in each other's pocket over the next few weeks, maybe we should set some ground rules.'

'Ground rules!'

Carrington stared at him looking deadly serious. 'Yes, you heard me—'

'Like what?'

'Well, for one,' she said, puffing her cheeks out. 'If you do decide to take off unexpectedly, I need to know where to find you. That way we stay close – keep in contact with one another.' She paused momentarily in thought. 'That means we always use my unmarked pool car, no buggering off in that stupid old Rover of yours. Oh, and one more thing. No Indian takeaways. I hate the smell that curries leave in a car.'

'Nothing unreasonable,' he shrugged, 'but you forgot to mention one thing.'

'Oh! What's that?'

'The weekends——'

'Is that a problem?'

'There could be, as I spend most of my free time with my ageing father. It's a man's thing. We go fishing together, and have done for as long as I can remember.'

Carrington sighed. 'Perhaps we can come to some arrangement.'

'Like what?'

'I'm always open to suggestions.'

Carlisle suddenly smelt a rat.

'You could prepare the maggots, of course.'

'Hold it,' Carrington said, putting her magazine down again. 'I'm trying to be diplomatic here. Besides, I doubt Acting Superintendent Sutherland would appreciate you swanning off without some sort of police protection.'

It was time to put his foot down.

'Listen, young lady, I warned you earlier about this close protection malarkey. It's not as good as people think.'

Carlisle's iPhone pinged. He checked the display and let it ring out.

'So what are your plans for the rest of day?'

'I haven't any. Why?'

'Good,' Carrington replied sagely, 'cos DCI Mason wants us to visit Cheryl Sawyer's husband in Redcar.'

'I thought he was cleared of any involvement in his wife's murder.'

'He was.'

Carlisle held her glances. 'So why visit him now?'

'Remember the barman at the Gold Medal pub? He thought that Caroline Harper's boyfriend had a Yorkshire accent.'

'And—'

'We know that Cheryl Sawyer was heavily into drugs and liked to go clubbing every night. The thing is did Caroline Harper follow in her footsteps.'

'I doubt it.'

'Well Jack Mason seems to think she did, and wants us to check it out.'

Still struggling to make the connection, Carlisle challenged her.

'Is Mason now saying that Caroline Harper's murder was drugs related?'

Carrington fluttered her eyelashes. 'We know they both grew up in the same part of Middlesbrough, so there could be a connection.'

'Old schoolmates, do you think?'

'Spoken like a true detective.'

'Cheeky sod—'

'Redcar it is then,' the young detective grinned.

Chapter Twenty

March 2013

Early morning Teesside was bathed in a low wintery sun as DC Carrington sped southbound over the A19 Tees flyover near Middlesbrough. David Carlisle could not recall the last time he'd travelled this route before. Marske-on-Sea rang a bell. The roads were extremely busy that morning, and the moment they pulled over and onto the eastbound slip road towards Saltburn he felt somewhat relieved. There were still plenty of juggernauts clogging up the lanes, and he hated them with a vengeance. Ugly big lumbering container wagons heading to and from Teesport container terminal seven days a week; it was utter madness. As the countryside opened up, the patchwork of green fields suddenly gave way to the Cleveland Hills. Dominating the skyline, the views from the top were spectacular. On a clear day you could see as far north as Hartlepool, and even further some days.

Carlisle had been listening to a JJ Cale CD on their journey south. Travel-Log, recorded between 1984 and 1989 at Capitol Studios. At times he found it difficult to concentrate. Now they'd escaped the rat-race, he was engrossed in one of his all-time favourite tracks 'End of the Line.' Three minutes and seven seconds of sheer bliss, JJ Cale at his best!

Still without a motive, more than fifty police officers were now engaged in the hunt for Caroline Harper's boyfriend. Despite all the public support, nothing had turned up so far. The thought that Richard Sloane had hired someone else to do his dirty work for him, had also crossed his mind that morning. It was possible, but highly unlikely, he thought. There again, had he done so then surely the Northumbria Police would have picked up on it.

Of all criminals, rogue coppers were hated most. Few and far between there were always some police officers, a good number senior in rank, whom the public would definitely be better off without. The trouble they caused and the impact to public confidence they exposed could be devastating. And that was the problem: Mason was adamant the killer was a rogue copper. According to him, serial killer Dennis Nilsen had served an eight-month stint as a member of the Metropolitan Police, before murdering and dismembering at least fifteen men during a five year period in London. That alone had sparked the Detective Chief Inspector into action, and he wasn't taking it lightly.

No, Carlisle thought, Mason had got it wrong as nobody on the team fitted that description. Sometimes it was easier to let things go. Concentrate on the big picture and not be distracted by details. One of the problems of tracking down some serial offenders was the women who'd slipped their net. Most were unwilling to come forward for fear of reprisals. The bizarre fantasies of a psychopath's mind didn't bear thinking about at times. The more organised a serial killer is, the more intelligent they likely are, and the less likely to raise the interests of others around them.

As the landscape flattened out towards the coast, they drove down a bumpy narrow lane until finally reaching their destination. Carrington pulled up in front of a pair of large wrought iron gates, and switched off the engine. Even though Bertram Sawyer had been cleared of any involvement in his wife's murder, that still didn't mean he was innocent. Nothing was being left to chance, and whatever it was that had drawn the killer's attention towards these women,

Carlisle was determined to find out.

Behind a high boundary wall he could just make out the house. Stately looking, with beautiful Georgian windows and an impressive facade overlooking formal gardens, Carlisle was notably impressed. Then, high up on the building roof his eye caught the security camera.

They were being watched.

Moments later Carrington pressed the gate intercom button, and spoke in a soft authoritative voice. 'Police,' she announced.

'What do you want?' an elderly man's voice crackled out through the gate speaker panel.

'We're here in connection with a young woman's disappearance. May we have a word?'

As the gates slid open, at the end of a long gravel path Carlisle caught his first real glimpse of the stately grandeur. The approach entrance was Baroque, Italian in design. Not that he was an expert or anything, but his visits to Florence had taught him that much. The garden was tiered like an amphitheatre, reminiscent of one half of a hippodrome racecourse. Surrounded by terraced lawns, a beautiful ornamental fountain topped with a replica statue of Neptune stood on a bed of shimmering moss. It was an awe-inspiring sight. There was no other word to describe it.

Meeting them at the top of a flight of steps, a tall man of Scottish descent, Bertram Sawyer looked much older than his sixty-seven years. He had sunken eyes, high cheekbones, and a heavily pockmarked face. Unsteady on his feet, in his left hand he carried a gnarled walking stick which he used to his best advantage. Not exactly a prime suspect, Sawyer looked more a victim of crime than any killer. After exchanging pleasantries they were ushered into a magnificent lounge with high ceilings, and plain emulsioned walls full of modern art. The furnishings looked expensive, a mixture of modern and old. In Carlisle's mind's eye this was his dream house. Oozing with charm, he could certainly imagine himself living here.

Squire Carlisle had a nice ring about it!

'Northumbria police,' Bertram Sawyer mumbled, as he stared down at Carrington's warrant card. 'You people are a bit off your beaten track. What is it you're after?'

'We're here in connection with your late wife, Mr Sawyer. We need to ask a few questions surrounding another case we're currently dealing with. It shouldn't take long.'

'Questions,' Sawyer began abruptly. 'I thought I'd finished with you people years ago.'

'Tell me,' the young detective said, returning her warrant card to her handbag. 'Does the name Caroline Harper mean anything to you at all?'

'No, I can't say as it does. Should it?'

'Perhaps this may help jog your memory.'

Carrington handed him a copy of Caroline Harper's driving licence.

'No. I've never seen her before – who is she?'

'Her name is Caroline Harper, and several months ago,' Carrington began, 'her husband reported her missing. Eight weeks later she was found dead in the front passenger seat of her car.'

Sawyer eyes softened and his voice had mellowed slightly.

'So that would explain your presence here.'

'Yes,' Carrington nodded. 'And that's the main purpose of our visit here today.'

'Car accident was it?'

'No, she'd been strangled.' Carrington bit her bottom lip as if waiting for Sawyer's response. When there wasn't one, the detective delivered her punchline. 'We believe she may have fallen foul of the same person who murdered your wife, Mr Sawyer.'

'Are you certain?'

'Yes, it would appear so,' Carrington confirmed.

There was bitterness in Sawyer's voice, anger, as if not quite believing. 'So what is it you people want from me?'

'Information,' she replied.

'What kind of information?'

They stood in silence for a moment, a television blasting in the background. A western movie, by the sound of things. Not that Carlisle was a movie buff, he wasn't, but he recognised the yelping of Indians and the sound of cavalry bugles. It had been ages since he'd last sat down and watched a decent movie. Not since Jackie's passing. Armed with a good bottle of wine, preferably white, they would often spend a night in together cuddled up in front of the TV screen. How times had changed, and how quickly the memories fade.

'Tell me, said Carrington awkwardly. 'Is anyone in your family in any way remotely connected with the police?'

'No. Not to my knowledge.'

'Are you sure?'

'Of course, why do you ask?'

Carrington puckered her lips. 'After your wife's disappearance, did you ever talk to anyone – a pushy journalist perhaps?'

'How would I know? The moment she buggered off, that was the last I saw of her.'

'I see.'

'What's going on?' Sawyer demanded.

'It's just that someone seemed to know an awful lot about your wife, that's all.'

Sawyer gave her a quizzical look. 'We're talking five or six years ago here. The only police officers I ever came into contact with were the ones at Seaham police station.'

'Think carefully, it's important to us,' Carlisle insisted.

'I am,' Sawyer replied, his demeanour conspicuously defensive. 'If I may say so, you people are asking some rather awkward questions.'

Carlisle held his glances as he spoke. 'These things are never straightforward I can assure you of that. Sometimes it's necessary to build up a family background. It's standard procedure, Mr Sawyer, the police need to explore every avenue open to them – scratch beneath the surface so to speak.'

'This young woman you talk of, where exactly did you find her?'

'Coldwell Lane, it's close to the Felling High Street. Do you know the area at all?'

'No I don't, but no doubt he took advantage of her as he did with my Cheryl?'

'I'm sorry,' said Carlisle.

The anger in Sawyer's eyes spoke volumes. 'They should bring back hanging, especially for sick bastards like him. Six years, how many more women has he killed in the meantime?'

Carlisle changed tack, knowing exactly where this was now heading.

'We understand you made several statements to the Seaham police about your wife's sudden disappearance. What can you tell us about them?'

'The police were never forthcoming with their information. They dilly-dallied around far too long in my opinion. It was an utter shambles.'

Carlisle felt the cutting edge of Sawyer's sharp tongue.

'After Cheryl left home, did she ever make contact with you at all?'

'No. Why?'

Carlisle turned. 'She'd been gone six months, hadn't she?'

'That's right,' Sawyer nodded.

'What about friends, did she ever make contact with them?'

'If she did, then they never let on to me about it.'

'How long were the two of you married, did you say?'

'Three years.' Sawyer's expression changed to one of resentment. 'Even now it's hard to understand why she walked out on me. Why leave a beautiful home like this, she never wanted for anything.'

'Some things are difficult to explain,' Carlisle shrugged.

'I suspect you've never lost anyone close to you, Mr Carlisle, so I doubt you understand what she put me and my family through. I'd thought I'd got over it, but I obviously haven't.'

Carlisle steadied himself, the hurt washing over him in waves.

'I too lost my wife under very tragic circumstances, Mr Sawyer. You can never bring them back, I'm afraid. We know that, and yet we still cling to the hope they will return one day. That's the thing; we all go through the same grieving process. Me, I hate the summer holidays, birthdays and Christmas — so please don't tell me that I know nothing of what you're going through.'

Sawyer shook his head, looking genuinely contrite. 'I'm sorry.'

Carrington's voice cut through the tension.

'After Cheryl left home, were you at all aware she was living in Wingate?'

'No. Not at the time, I wasn't.'

'When did you first find out?'

'It was the police. They told me she'd rented a property there. It was next to the village pub I believe.'

'What about friends, do you think they might have known about it at the time?'

'Probably, but they certainly never let on to me about it.'

'But you knew she was living somewhere?'

'Yes, of course,' Sawyer replied assertively. 'But surely that was a job for the police to find out, not me?'

Bertram Sawyer had known very little about his wife's disappearance, or so he would have them believe. A lot of water had passed under the bridge since then, and yet her murder still seemed fresh in his mind. Remarkable, he thought, six months was an awful long time for someone to go missing without ever making contact — any kind of contact. Sawyer was lying, and according to Kurt Gillespie — the Seaham drugs dealer — *everyone knew our Cheryl was living in Wingate.*

Carlisle suddenly turned his gaze to Sawyer.

'What strikes me as odd, is that before your wife's disappearance she'd transferred large sums of your money into her own personal bank account. Surely you must have known that?'

'Not at the time I didn't. The first I'd heard of it was when the police questioned me about it.'

'So you had no idea that she might be planning to leave you?'

'No, it never crossed my mind.' Sawyer lowered his head. 'Besides, these money transfers you talk of, they were done over a long period of time.'

'All the same she was transferring large sums of money, wasn't she?'

'Yes, but—'

'Are you telling me that never once did it cross your mind what she might be up to?'

'Cheryl had a drug problem, she—' Sawyer hesitated as if a painful memory had jogged him. 'Besides, I'd lost track of the money she'd spent on clothes and expensive jewellery. Cheryl was high-maintenance, I knew that. She was a very attractive young woman, but I had no reason to believe she was ever planning to leave me.'

'When you finally found out that she'd cheated on you, were you not angry?'

'No, why should I have been? Cheryl was a breath of fresh air. Besides, why would I want to stop her from looking beautiful?' It was Sawyer's turn to turn the tables on them. 'I know I'm not exactly prince charming; even so, money never entered my head.'

He was lying, and the old man's eyes were the giveaway.

'What about Cheryl's close friends, how would you describe them?'

'They were decent people, easy to get on with. Why do you ask?'

'Were they Cheryl's age?'

'No, they were a mixture.' Sawyer was clearly surprised by the question. 'I'd be a damn fool not to say my wife wasn't a very highly strung young woman, everyone knew that. Cheryl was a party animal, she was hyper, and certainly knew how to enjoy herself.'

'Yes, she did like to go night clubbing?' Carlisle smiled.

The old man's eyes frosted over. 'I know what you're thinking, but that never once crossed my mind. Age has its limitations, but sometimes you have to turn a blind eye to what's going on around you. Besides, I can't stand loud music – it always gives me a headache.'

'Were you ever jealous of your wife's late night jaunts?' asked Carrington.

'No. Not in the least.'

'And it never once crossed your mind what she might be up to—'

'No. Why should it?'

Carlisle put on a false smile.

'Even though you knew she was heavily involved in drugs?'

Now on the back foot, Sawyer had every reason to be angry. He'd been drawn down this avenue before, many times, and they were only digging up old wounds. Unfortunately, Carlisle wasn't the only one who felt Bertram Sawyer was innocent. The Cleveland police had thought so too. Desperate to find a connection, the profiler had to dig deep. If it wasn't sex or drugs that attracted the killer's attention towards Sawyer's wife, then it could only have been her money?

'I know this may sound awkward, but the other victim, she too came from Middlesbrough.' Carlisle paused to let his statement sink in. 'I was wondering if there might be a connection here – old school friends perhaps?'

Sawyer looked at each of them in turn, but said nothing.

They talked a while about his wife's high extravagant lifestyle, and her love for horse riding. God, thought Carlisle, how could anyone be so naïve? Sawyer was either living in cloud cuckoo land, or his brains were squarely between his legs.

'Cheryl's friends,' Carrington queried. 'Did you ever meet up with any of them?'

'Hold it,' Sawyer replied, arms folded across his chest in a defensive stance. 'I've been over this ground before. Why don't you contact the

Seaham police about that – find out what they have to say?'

'We have,' Carrington said brusquely. 'I was merely trying to establish a connection?'

Not the best of interviews, Carlisle thought as they left. A man of few words, Bertram Sawyer was completely blameless of his wife's death. It wasn't a coincidence she'd orchestrated her own disappearance, the money transfers, the rented accommodation in Wingate village and her drugs contacts in Seaham. They were all part and parcel of her cunning little scheme. Hers was a marriage contrived, and once the novelty had worn off she began to execute her own escape from it. Cleveland had seen its fair share of murder investigations over the years, but nothing compared with this. He'd been right all along. Cheryl Sawyer's sole intention had been to feather her own nest, but things had tragically gone wrong.

Carrington's unmarked pool car idled in front of the huge wrought iron gates. Stifling a yawn, the young detective seemed overawed by it all. As well she might have been, thought Carlisle. The house was a magnificent masterpiece of architectural beauty – something to be admired. But what had sparked Sawyer's wife to run away from such a luxurious setting to live in a small village. It didn't make sense, none of it did. There again, what if someone had helped plan her escape – won over her confidence before killing her?

Carrington turned sharply to face him.

'I felt sorry for the old man,' she said. 'He's certainly gone through the mill these past six years.'

'It wasn't the best of interviews, Sue.'

'And there's me telling him his wife's killer has struck again.'

'I hate to admit it, but we're probably looking for a serial killer.'

'Tell me you're joking—'

Ever since leaving Redcar it had never stopped raining. Windscreen wipers flapping like crazy, headlights on full beam, they skirted Middlesbrough in a hailstorm. Seconds later they hit gridlock. Carrington swore as she pulled up behind an old green double-decker bus with "NOT IN SERVICE" written across the back window.

'It's a funny old world,' she said, fumbling with the car's radio. 'Bertram Sawyer struck me as a really nice guy.'

'I got the same impression he knew nothing about his wife's disappearance, or that she'd spent months planning to leave him.'

Carrington shot him a glance. 'Attracted by his wealth, do you think?'

'That's some women for you, Sue. They'll fleece you of every penny you've got.'

The young detective scowled at him.

'Not all women are like that!'

His iPhone pinged and he checked the display.

It was him again!

Chapter
Twenty-One

DCI Jack Mason folded his hands behind the back of his head, and sighed. With Bertram Sawyer now out of the equation, the team had turned its attentions towards Richard Sloane. The pressure was mounting and if Sloane didn't kill his wife, then who did? Mason's biggest concern right now was Sloane's refusal to cooperate. Part of the reason, he knew, was Sloane's confession that he'd spent the majority of his time out in the Far East. Barely keeping his head above water, let alone worrying about his wife's disappearance, his business empire was in free-fall and domestic production in the Hong Kong fashion industry had fallen away dramatically over the past few years. As more and more manufacturing companies switched their operations to mainland China, rising manufacturing costs in the province were clearly squeezing Sloane's profit margins. Unable to pay his creditors, let alone his employees' wages, the man was facing financial ruin.

Increasingly uneasy over his recent business dealings with Lee Wong – a Chinese multi billionaire clothing tycoon from Kowloon – Sloane was trapped in a time warp. Wong was a rogue, a ruthless con-merchant who had duped dozens of unsuspecting buyers into making full or partial 'up front' payments for goods that Wong had no intention of ever supplying. Having placed his entire Far East operations in Wong's hands, Sloane was now wholly dependent on Wong providing him with the necessary manufacturing raw materials that would keep his business afloat. There was little chance of that, and Sloane knew it.

Mason also realised that doing business on the other side of the world was unquestionably fraught with dangers. Apart from the cultural differences, Sloane was never happier than when his Emirates flight finally touched down at Heathrow Airport. Even then he was highly suspicious of the Chinese race. There were far too many gangs, too many bad guys in town. Life was cheap and according to Richard Sloane, organised crime was alive and kicking in good old Great Britain. These past few days had certainly taken its toll. Now sat opposite him in the Gateshead police station interview room, Sloane wasn't the relaxed dude anymore. The man looked physically ill, agitated, and completely out of his depth.

Not good, Mason thought, as he took another huge bite of his KitKat. Now that DS Holt was in charge of the interview he could simply sit back and enjoy himself. Watching Sloane squirm as the sergeant dug his heels in, gave him more pleasure than sex.

'Like to tell me why you think a Chinese secret triad killed your wife?' asked Holt.

Sloane stared at the two of them in turn.

'Wong knows of my intentions to pull out of Hong Kong, and if I do go ahead as planned, he's threatened to get violent with me. That's how these people operate. Get on the wrong side of them and they make your life a misery.'

Mason sat intrigued as the sergeant tightened the screws.

'Are you telling me Lee Wong is the mastermind behind all of this?' Holt said.

'I'm positive.'

Sloane wiped the sweat from his brow, and shot him a wary glance. Despite the man's utter fear of reprisals, it seemed highly unlikely that a Chinese Triad had reached out to England to kill his wife. Besides, Mason smiled wistfully, why hold his wife captive for several months without administering some form of ransom note?

It didn't add up, none of it did.

'Tell me,' said Holt, looking decidedly pissed off. 'Why did your wife run off in the first place?'

'She'd obviously been threatened.'

'Threatened,' Holt repeated.

Sloane was on the edge of his seat. '*Yes, threatened!*'

'What's confusing me,' the sergeant acknowledged calmly, 'is that you certainly never mentioned anything about blackmail in any of your previous statements to the police. Had you done so, I doubt we'd be still sitting here.'

'That's how these people operate,' said Sloane. 'They're violent people to deal with and once they have you on their radar, they never let go.'

Holt chewed the end of his pen, and shook his head to show his disapproval.

'That may be so,' the sergeant replied, 'but there's nothing in your wife's bank statements to support such a claim. We know she had expensive tastes and lived an over indulgent lifestyle, but no ransom payments were ever paid out from her bank account.'

Sloane looked at Mason, then back at Holt.

'How do you account for the large sums of money she stole from me?'

'Well,' said Holt, thoughtfully stroking his chin. 'We had an interesting conversation with your wife's elder sister. They met in York apparently, a few days before your wife was murdered. According to Ms Harper, Caroline certainly never felt threatened in any way – quite the contrary, I'd say.'

'Perhaps someone followed her?'

'They apparently did, and that's when she was murdered.'

Sloane sat flushed with anger. 'This is absurd—'

'Never mind the bollocks,' said Holt. 'You grew tired of your wife's presence, didn't you? The novelty had worn off, and you just wanted rid of her. Isn't that the case?'

Sloane smiled thinly. 'Do you really believe that I would murder my wife?'

'It's not looking good,' the sergeant said staring across at him. 'The thing is I have it on good authority that you never got on with your wife in the first place. You were far too busy looking after your own personal interests to realise what she was getting up to in her spare time. You turned a blind eye, so to speak, buggered off to Hong Kong. The trouble with people who do that is that they always end up jealous. It's a man thing, unfortunately. We're very defensive creatures by nature, and we don't like it when someone else comes sniffing around our property. How to put a stop to it, that's the question?'

Sloane sounded irritable. 'What exactly are you getting at, Sergeant?'

'Well,' said Holt, as though he was beginning to enjoy himself. 'In my books it's called resentment, and that's when the shit hits the fan.' Holt drew breath. 'How am I doing, Mr Sloane? Does this all sound a bit familiar to you?'

Mason turned to his companion, and winked.

Sloane looked physically shaken, and well he might be. The sergeant's questioning was relentless.

'All right,' Sloane said nervously. 'Perhaps I was a little harsh on Caroline at times, but that doesn't mean I killed her. I've been under an awful lot of pressure lately and I'm desperate to sort things out.'

'Who said you killed her?' Holt shrugged. 'I was merely making a point.'

'But you inferred I killed her, and you were trying to put words into my mouth.'

'If you loved her so much,' said Holt, tapping the end of his pen on the desktop, 'then why the reluctance to make a formal identification when we asked you to do so? If that had been my wife lying flat on her back on a mortuary table, I would have been extremely upset about it.'

'I was suffering jetlag. I don't travel well.'

The sergeant stared at his note book, before turning to face him again.

'Why should I believe you?'

'It's the truth, goddammit.'

Mason, who had said very little up to now, watched as the Detective Sergeant took another sip of his coffee. He was playing around the edges and waiting to pounce at the slightest opportunity. With nowhere to hide, Interview Room One suddenly felt claustrophobic.

Time to cut to the chase, Mason thought.

'The truth is, Mr Sloane,' Mason said, 'I doubt you know the meaning of the word jetlag. When I put it to you on your arrival at Newcastle Airport why your wife had left home, you told me, and I quote: *I have absolutely no idea.*'

'But she *did* leave home, and I *did* report her missing to you people.'

Mason's eyes bore down on him. 'What I'm disputing, Mr Sloane, is you telling me that it was a Chinese triad who killed your wife. You're lying, and you're making a crap job of it.'

'But it's the truth, Chief Inspector. Lee Wong is responsible for all of this.'

Mason had calmed down.

'The trouble is,' DS Holt cut in, 'I tend to believe you.'

'Thank God,' said Sloane, head in hands.

'Not about Lee Wong, though. Whoever killed your wife was certainly known to her.' Holt stood for a moment before pointing a finger at Sloane. 'Now here's my problem. Who's to say that you didn't get someone else to do your dirty work for you? Let's face it, your business was in free-fall and you were under enormous pressure from your creditors, besides having difficulty in finding the money to pay your employees' wages. Then there's this little problem of your wife's uncontrollable spending. Whilst you're out in the Far East working your bollocks off, she's swanning around living the high-life. Not only that, she's withdrawing huge sums of money from your personal bank account.' Holt closed his notebook, as if that was end of the matter. 'This is all about trust, Mr Sloane. The minute you realised what your wife was up to, you wanted rid of her. She'd taken you for a ride, hadn't she?'

'That's not true!'

'But you can see where I'm coming from.'

'Yes, and you're clutching at straws,' Sloane replied. 'You should write a detective fiction novel, Sergeant. You'd make millions with an imagination like yours.'

'Do I detect a bitter streak?' Holt laughed.

'You're barking up the wrong tree, Sergeant.'

'But am I? A little bird tells me I'm very close to the truth,' Holt explained. 'I bet you never knew that your wife was seeing someone else whilst you were working out in Hong Kong?'

Sloane's face darkened. 'You're lying—'

'A guy from Gateshead, apparently.'

'Tell me you're lying.'

'That's odd. I thought you'd have known about it.' Holt shrugged. 'Surely you must have bumped into him at some stage or other. A tall guy, a bit of a charmer by all accounts. He drives expensive cars, and likes to flash his money about on all the pretty young ladies.'

'Why wasn't I informed of this?' Sloane insisted.

Clever, Mason thought. He never saw that one coming.

'How could we?' Holt frowned. 'You were far too busy out in Hong Kong.'

'You're lying! Caroline would never have done such a thing to me.'

'He's thirtyish, good looking, and has a bit of a Yorkshire twang.' Holt pushed his chair back and folded his hands behind the back of his head. 'He was one of her old school mates apparently and extremely good in bed by all accounts.'

Sloane swallowed hard. 'A Yorkshire accent, you say?'

Holt stiffened.

'Yeah, do you know the guy?'

'No I don't, and even if I did, I'd——'

'Ah. There's that nasty streak again,' Mason said. 'Didn't Caroline come from Teesside? The reason I ask is that another young woman of similar age and stature, was murdered under very similar circumstances. She too came from Teesside. Acklam if I'm not mistaken. Old school mates perhaps or did they work in the same estate agents. Who knows?'

Mason finished off the last of his KitKat.

Holt turned to Sloane. 'How long did you say the two of you were married?'

'Four years; why do you ask?'

'Was your wife ever friendly with a police officer?'

'No. Why?'

'The reason I ask is that she was seen drinking with one in Gateshead High Street.'

'No. It couldn't have been Caroline.'

'What a pity, I was rather hoping you knew him.' Holt stood and turned to face Mason. 'What do you think, boss? Should we lock him up and throw away the key?'

'Nah,' Mason shrugged. 'Let's leave it to this Lee Wong fella to sort out.'

Sloane remained silent for a moment.

'Take it from me, Inspector, when Caroline ran away from me I had absolutely no idea where she was, or what she was up to for that matter. As far as I was concerned, our marriage was over. Even my solicitors will confirm that.'

'Right then,' said Mason. 'In which case, you're free to go.'

Sloane glared at the two of them, annoyed he'd been duped.

Mason stood in the doorway and leaned casually against the jamb. He knew then that Sloane was innocent, but he was damned if he was going to tell him as much.

Let the bastard sweat, he thought.

Chapter Twenty-Two

Twenty minutes later, they'd found a little coffee shop across from Wetherspoons in Gateshead town centre. Carlisle ordered two lattes, and sat with his back to the wall, overlooking Jackson Street. Even if Sloane's story rang true, neither Lee Wong nor the Chinese triads had anything to do with his wife's death. Yes, these were ruthless people to deal with but Sloane was overreacting. Even so, Carlisle had always believed that Sloane's wife was partly responsible for her own death. Hers was a fake relationship, and it was a dangerous game she'd played.

Seated opposite him, Jack Mason was fiddling with his iPhone and trying to make a connection. Despite the pressures of work, the Detective Chief Inspector had managed to grab a quick bite to eat.

Carlisle stared at him bleakly. 'I guess that clears Sloane from your investigations.'

'This all comes down to where the bodies were found.' Mason tapped the side of his forehead with his index finger. 'Our man's local, I'm convinced of that.'

'What about motive?'

'Vulnerable women, easy targets,' Mason shrugged. 'There again, we're putting far too much emphasis on this satanic salute thing of yours. Let's face it, removing their fingers for twenty thousand quid's worth of sparklers sounds more feasible.'

'These women weren't randomly plucked off the streets, Jack.

They were carefully chosen. If we didn't know it then, we certainly know it now. It's my guess their husbands didn't have a clue what their wives were up to once they'd left home. Neither did the police, for that matter. No, he's grooming them and the control he has over them is mind boggling.'

'You make it sound so simple.'

Carlisle's expression darkened. 'You only have to reconstruct his fantasies to see why he's killing them. He's angry about something, and whatever it is that's been eating away at him all these years has finally caught up with him.'

'So what tipped him over the edge?'

'It was pure resentment.'

'How does that fit in with his second victim?'

'He probably saw in Caroline Harper what he saw in Cheryl Sawyer, but that's just my opinion.' Carlisle eased back in his seat and took another sip of his latte. 'Let's hope he's not evolving.'

'So why threaten you?'

'I can think of a thousand reasons and every one of them makes sense. Take a look around, any one of these people could be the killer. That's the scary thing; he has the ability to blend into society at will.'

'Yeah, but let's not get paranoid over it.'

'You're not in my shoes, though.'

Mason gave him a hapless look. 'True—'

Carlisle shuddered inwardly, but managed to maintain his composure. As the dangerous cat and mouse games continued to unfold, the innermost workings of a serial killer's mind became more apparent. Whoever he was, he was good at his game, and it was slowly tearing him apart.

'Sutherland's adamant he's targeting these women through the missing person files,' Mason said. 'She's called in the tech boys to see what they can do.'

Carlisle thought about it, but not for long.

'We need to take another look at Caroline Harper's flat. I'm convinced he's returned there.'

'You're clutching at straws, my friend. No one's been near the place in weeks. And even if they had, Tom Hedley's forensic team would certainly have picked up on it.'

Mason's was a typical off the cuff remark. Even so, he had a point and a good one at that. There was no mistaking the glaze in his eyes, firmly fixed ahead and staring into empty space. The Detective Chief Inspector's drinking problem didn't just manifest overnight. It wasn't an everyday thing. Jack Mason would go weeks without a drink and suddenly start up again. It was all about the pressure of work, and today he was having a bad day.

Something was wrong.

'I get the feeling we're being watched,' Carlisle said nervously. 'Every time someone stares at me, it sends a cold shiver down my spine. Let's hope the fantasies don't kick in and he starts looking for another target.'

'What, you think he will strike again?'

'It's an addiction with these people. Deep inside their twisted minds, they see themselves as the only person who can solve their innermost problems.'

The man at the service counter smiled at him, and caused him to sit up and take notice. He was tall, early thirties, wearing a lightweight parka jacket and red baseball cap pulled low over his brow. His mind running amok, Carlisle sat for a while without appearing obvious. Even in a crowded room he still felt vulnerable. His hands were shaking, and the lump in the back of his throat threatened to choke him.

Filled with indecision and the fabric of uncertainly, he decided to make his move. Before he had a chance to change his mind, he instinctively reached over and grabbed the stranger's arm. As the chair gave way beneath him, his shoulder caught the edge of the table opposite, sending him sprawling to the floor.

Get a grip, he cursed. You're a profiler and it's not supposed to happen like this. Embarrassed, it suddenly dawned on him that the man was just an innocent bystander. Feeling a right prat, he sheepishly apologised to those around him and brushed himself down.

'What the hell was that all about?' Mason said looking confused.

'I thought it was him.'

'Who—'

'The tall guy hovering over the service counter,' Carlisle replied.

Mason shot him an inquisitive glance. 'You need to relax, my friend. You're spooking the punters, and it's not good for business.'

Still shaking, Carlisle gathered his wits.

'It's time we put the cat amongst the pigeons,' he said.

'And do what?'

'Credit someone else with his murders. Say we have another suspect in mind. If nothing else it might bring out the Jekyll and Hyde in him, especially if he knows someone else is taking all the credit for his handy work.'

Looking like a kid in sweet shop, the grin on Mason's face broadened. 'What if it backfires and he decides to take it out on *you*?'

'The way I feel right now, I'm willing to take the risk.'

'Yeah, but will it work?'

'There's only one way to find out.'

Mason pondered his statement.

'Leave it with me. I'll run it past Sutherland and see what she has to say about it.'

Carlisle felt the knot in his stomach tighten. It was a hare-brained scheme, but he felt they were left with no other option.

Chapter
Twenty-Three

Mid-afternoon and Gateshead centre seemed darker than ever, thought David Carlisle, as he drove towards Sheriff Hill. Earlier that morning a strong media contingent had turned up at Gateshead Magistrates' Court to witness a local drug gang being sentenced. The scourge of modern society, it was headline breaking news. More drug gangs had been dismantled in the local courtrooms than anyone cared to remember. As soon as one gang had been taken off the streets though, another popped up in its place. The local drug barons' tentacles were spread throughout the whole of the North East, and as far south as Yorkshire. It was big business, and most of its profits were being pumped back into low affordable property. The irony was that many of its tenants were already hooked on drugs. It was a vicious circle and one the police were struggling to keep in check.

Things hadn't gone as planned, and Carlisle was running late. Having picked up a pile of case files from a local solicitor's office, shortly after lunch he pulled up opposite St Alban's church in Windy Nook village and switched off the car's engine. Of course it would have been an entirely different landscape the night Caroline Harper's body was discovered here. The commission of murder was swift, incisive, and carefully orchestrated. There were those who even argued the crash was never staged in the first place, believing the victim's car had simply broken down at the top of Coldwell

Lane. Whichever side of the fence you sat on, nothing seemed straightforward anymore.

Carlisle's instincts as a profiler had developed enough over the years to know that this was no accident. He also knew as he walked along Carr Hill road towards the crossroads with Coldwell Lane, why the killer had chosen this particular area. It was out-of-the-way, remote, isolated. Ideal for what he had in mind. He tried to picture the scene that night, to climb inside the killer's head and unravel his hidden secrets.

Standing at the top of Coldwell Lane, his victim's lifeless body sat motionless in the front passenger seat of her little red Volkswagen Polo, it would be time to rock and roll. Now minus two and with more heavy snow forecast, it would have been textbook conditions, thought Carlisle. It was dark in the lane that night. Plenty of cloud cover, very few people about. It was all about timing, and the killer would have known how crucial that would be. One final check before he would turn the ignition key to unlock the car's steering wheel, and gently release the handbrake.

Only the sound of the tyres crunching hard rock salt to be heard, nothing could stop him now. What the killer couldn't see, or maybe he could, was the blue transit van travelling in the opposite direction that night. With only its headlights visible, one final correction of the Polo's steering wheel and it would be time to abandon ship.

Perfect, he thought.

Well maybe it happened like that!

Wait a minute! Psychopaths were devious operators, so in which direction would he have run to that night. Not past the Bay Horse, he wagered. It was near closing time and far too risky. No, his best option would be to head west and back along Carr Hill Road towards his waiting getaway car. Windy Nook was no stranger to serial killers: Mary Elizabeth Wilson had trodden this very same route the night she poisoned her husband. Known as the Merry Widow of Windy Nook, Wilson was the last woman to be sentenced to death in Durham prison. Convicted of murdering two of her four husbands with beetle poison, the remains of her previous two husbands, John Knowles and John Russell, were later exhumed to reveal high levels of phosphorous.

Carlisle was so wrapped up in his inner thoughts that he'd momentarily forgotten what he was supposed to be doing. Now that Richard Sloane had been cleared of his wife's murder, the case was wide open to speculation. It was a large cast; and every white male professional between the ages of thirty to thirty five whose life was in crisis, was now a potential player. The problem, and he had no idea how to resolve it, how to unravel the chaos. In a way, though, Carlisle felt he already knew his subject's thought processes. Having amassed a sizeable chunk of her husband's money, Caroline Harper was about to enter into a whole new phase in her life. But things had gone tragically wrong, and she'd paid the ultimate price for her sins. Not the easiest of cases to solve, but there was still plenty to go on all the same.

He didn't know why, but Carlisle sensed he was being followed. A tall man, early forties, wearing a black hoody pulled over his head, was lurking in one of the side streets. He stood for a while without appearing obvious, and weighed up the situation. Prompted by the stranger's unnatural antics, Carlisle considered if he could take him out alone. He'd been in this kind of situation before, many times, and he was pretty sure he was up to no good.

Carlisle stood for a moment, the lump in the back of his throat threatening to choke him. Not forty feet away he could see his parked Rover, and he decided to make his move. He immediately thought about the jack lever he'd kept in the boot of his car.

Too far, he cursed.

The distance between them closing, he reached into his pocket for his iPhone. Determined to capture the stranger's image, he searched the display and quickly pressed the tiny camera icon. The moment he fired off a shot, the stranger had already turned tail and disappeared into the warren of back streets. Then he heard a motorbike revving up.

Who are you?

Three exits, two possibilities, but which one? He pointed his iPhone in the general direction of the second entrance, and waited. Then, just when he thought his luck was about to change, the roar of the motorbike engine grew fainter.

Shit, he cursed.

Whoever he was, he certainly wasn't hanging round.

Chapter
Twenty-Four

The traffic in Gateshead wasn't too bad when Carlisle finally pulled up outside Caroline Harper's flat on Prince Consort Road. He sat for a while aimlessly staring out through the windscreen. They would find him soon enough, there was plenty of CCTV coverage around Windy Nook. Then it would be down to the driver and vehicle licensing agency to weed him out, and they were extremely good at that. Even so, there were still no guarantees. Besides, the motorbike was probably nicked.

His iPhone rang.

The voice on the other end of the line sounded strained. 'I thought we had an arrangement?'

'We do. Where are you, Sue?'

'Sat opposite you across the street,' DC Carrington protested.

His iPhone went dead.

The young detective approached the driver's side. 'What the hell is going on?' she said, peering in through the open door. 'You're supposed to keep me informed of your movements.'

'Problem?' he asked.

Carrington stared at him stony-faced. 'The next time you go swanning off on your own, you're to let me know about it. OK?'

Sometimes it was best to take it on the chin, say nothing. The main reason he was here was to get inside the killer's head, not to get into an argument. Still numb with shock from the stranger's antics, he entered the building with trepidation. It always felt strange returning to a victim's home, as if the occupant had never seen their own death coming. It was clear that forensics had been here. The living room curtains were closed, white powder dust everywhere, and the floor in need of a vacuum. He didn't know why, but he suddenly felt on edge. Offenders who staged crime scenes usually made mistakes. They arranged a scene to resemble what they believed it should look like, and not as it actually was. If the killer had returned to her flat, it wasn't noticeably obvious? Following a cold trail was never easy. He preferred the adrenaline rush, where he was hot on the heels of his suspect and closing in for the kill. This felt different, though, as if the killer was constantly watching over him.

Gripped by uncertainty, he slowly began to strip away the physical evidence. It was then he caught his own reflection in the hallway mirror. Unshaven, his hair was unkempt, and his eyes were sunken into their sockets giving his face a ghostlike appearance. God he looked dreadful. Unnerved by the killer's mind games, sleep did not come easy nowadays. He preferred catnaps in a chair, as his brain had a nasty habit of playing tricks with him in the middle of the night. The motives for murder were never quite so obvious, but the reasoning behind them unnerving.

The fact that all the windows were shut gave the place a musty smell. He'd smelt worse, but this was overpowering. Reaching the top of the landing stairs, he saw that the bedroom door was slightly ajar. He didn't know why, but he felt he was entering into an actor's dressing room. Carlisle cherished the quieter moments, when he had a building all to himself. He knew also that most offenders would go out of their way to ensure they left the same signature at each of their crime scenes. It was part of their make-up, their so called signature. This felt different, though, untidy and yet remarkably controlled. It was then he spotted the morning after-pills tucked away in among many of cosmetics containers. How bizarre, he thought. What had prevented life couldn't prevent death.

Wait a minute! If Caroline Harper had been sleeping with her new boyfriend, then surely they must have had regular sex together. And yet, according to Gillian King's post-mortem report it had shown completely the opposite. There was so much information to digest, so much detail to take in, it felt like he was driving through dense fog.

'Where are you?' Carrington shouted up from the hallway.

'I'm in the front bedroom, Sue.'

'No funny business,' she replied climbing the creaky staircase. 'Remember I'm wired to control.'

'Oh! And here's me thinking you were looking after my well-being.'

'Like hell I am.'

It was weird the notions that sometimes came into Carlisle's head. Maybe it was sitting up late into the night watching horror movies that had caused him to think as he did.

'What are you up to?' Carrington asked, poking her head round the bedroom door.

'I get the feeling we're being watched,' he said, thinking out aloud.

'Tell me you're joking?'

'There's no limit to what these people can get up to, Sue.'

'Well,' she said her voice devoid of its usual enthusiasm. 'If she never returned here after leaving York, then where the hell did she go?'

'Good question!'

A memory tugged at him. It was one of those mad cases he'd been studying back in his university days, a guy called Harvey Glatman. Known in the media as "The Lonely Hearts Killer", Glatman was definitely a bit of an odd-ball. He would contact his victims with offers for pulp fiction work, and then lure them back to his apartment. After he'd tied them up, he would sexually assault them, taking pictures of everything he did. After strangling them he dumped their bodies in the desert.

Carlisle leaned back against the bedroom wall and began to consider his options. Now wasn't the time for thoughts of perverted fantasy, and he quickly dispensed them from his mind.

'What's on your mind,' Carrington quizzed.

'I was being followed back there.'

'You were what!'

'A tall guy, he was wearing a hoody.'

'Did you get a good look at him?'

His pulse quickened. 'Not really, he was long gone before I could get a close look at him.'

'You should have informed me earlier – I could have done something about it?'

They made their way back downstairs.

Carrington's inquisitive mind had set him thinking again. Whoever it was they were dealing with, his soul was fuelled by pure fantasy. Despite all that was going on inside Carlisle's head, the killer's mind games were beginning to get him down.

How much more could he take?

'I'm almost done here,' he said leafing through a small bookcase crammed full of old books and magazines.

'Thinking of taking up cooking, are we?'

'No, but take a look at this,' he said nervously holding up a well-thumbed recipe book.

'So what? She probably liked cooking.'

'That's my point,' he replied. 'She detested it according to her husband.'

Carrington gave him a quizzical look. 'Sometimes I wonder what goes on inside that head of yours.' The young detective teased back the window blinds as if to check on the outside world. 'Anyway, what's wrong with having a couple of Paul Hollywood books on your bookshelf? He's rather dishy if you ask me.'

Carlisle refused to be drawn in; he had more important things on his mind.

He flipped through the well-thumbed pages of the book, and found what he was looking for – a slip containing an estate agent's address along with several telephone numbers. The handwriting was shaky, as though written in a hurry. He tucked it into an inside pocket and continued about his business.

It was the mind games he feared most. They scared the living daylights out of him. How much longer they could go on before the killer finally struck again was anyone's guess.

He shivered, the knot tightening in his stomach.

Chapter Twenty-Five

Anticipating a cold reception that morning, Carlisle had found the Acting Superintendent in a surprisingly buoyant mood. Jack Mason's overnight stake-out in the hunt for the Alpaca thieves had finally paid dividends. Caught red handed in the early hours, two Irish travellers, Bodgit and Scarper, were now detained in police custody. Now back in Sutherland's good books, if nothing else the big cheesy grin on Jack Mason's face told him everything he needed to know.

Carlisle glanced down at the pile of paperwork cluttering Sutherland's desk, and cringed. Four months into a murder investigation the position of a senior police officer wasn't all that it was cracked up to be. Surrounded by mountains of witness statements, search warrants and forms for just about everything under the sun, the sheer volume alone was mind-boggling. Having spoken earlier that morning with Jack Mason, Carlisle felt the DCI was too full of his own achievements to take any of it in. A few loose ends had been tied up, a couple of fresh leads to investigate, other than that nothing.

He watched as the Acting Superintendent chewed the end of her pen as she pondered over her next statement. 'Could he be operating from a safe house, do you think?'

'He probably is, ma'am.' Carlisle glanced at Hedley, then at Mason, and finally back at Sutherland. 'Somewhere out of the way, I suspect.'

Sutherland's eyebrows raised a fraction. She was no fool.

'Umm, that certainly puts a different slant on things.' Sutherland turned to Mason. 'Looking at the case files, Jack, that doesn't surprise me.'

'It's feasible, ma'am.' Mason nodded.

'If he *did* abduct these women, it means he's targeting the vulnerable. It's not surprising when you think about it. Coming from opulent, secure surroundings as they did, they end up in cheap rented accommodation.' Sutherland's attention was wandering. 'It's not exactly a fairy tale ending, is it?'

'That's true, but what follows is an all too familiar pattern in my experience. Psychopaths are ruthless manipulators and have the striking ability to deceive.' Carlisle flipped through a few pages of notes. 'This one's no different, it seems. He's undoubtedly a social predator, someone who is show-boating his narcissistic charm to win his victims over.'

Sutherland cocked her head to one side, pen poised. She seemed to be concentrating more on the bigger picture and less on the minor detail, which was encouraging.

'You mentioned he could be incapable of performing,' she said. 'If he wasn't having regular sex with these women, then why bother to groom them in the first place?'

Carlisle looked at her. 'He's enticing them, and once they've taken the bait, he's using them for his own self-gratification. If he did hold Caroline Harper captive, the question remains, was he eroticising his power over her?'

The Acting Superintendent shuddered. 'I was rather hoping you weren't going to say that.' She paused to drink some water as if mentally taken aback by it all. 'Let's push those notions to one side for a moment. You mentioned a family figure. Is he married, or living with a partner, do you suspect?'

All eyes were on him.

'He's a loner, ma'am, so he's more likely to be single.'

'If I may say so,' Mason interrupted, 'this fits in rather nicely with a police officer's role. Out on the job every night, long hours spent away from home. Whoever he is, he had all the time in the world to execute whatever plans he had in mind.'

'That's true,' Sutherland acknowledged. 'Who would question a police officer in the line of duty, especially if he comes home late at night?'

Tom Hedley, who had said very little so far, shuffled awkwardly in his seat. 'Well he certainly knows a thing or two about how the forensic system works.'

Sutherland rounded on Carlisle. 'Still not convinced he's a police officer?'

'No, I'm not.'

'And what makes you say that?'

Well, he thought. In for a penny in for a pound, it was time to say it as it was.

'It's not uncommon for some young women to marry rich old men twice their age. Many live happily ever after of course, but not all women marry for love. There is a very small select group of women who see rich husbands as easy pickings, and they're in it for what they can get. There have been numerous high-profile cases where women have been awarded generous settlements and maintenance in the courts.'

'The notion that a wife can get half of the joint assets after even a short, childless marriage is a fallacy,' Sutherland explained. 'I'll admit the issue of divorce and family law is a hot political potato and that the law hasn't kept up with changes in society. But I still can't see the point you're trying to make.'

'Well, ma'am,' Carlisle replied, 'the reality is their husbands are very powerful people in their own right and will stop at nothing to protect their assets. That's why they invariably employ top barristers to defend their corners. The mental strain of going through a divorce settlement is never a straightforward affair at the best of times, and that's why some women resort to blackmail.'

'Blackmail...'

There was a long silence.

'Yes ma'am, blackmail. Threaten to publish their autobiographies, or sell their husbands' sordid stories to the national newspapers. It's not uncommon, and they certainly know how to hit back. Strange as it may seem, some women even believe they're the real victims in all of this.'

'I can agree with that,' Mason said as though speaking from his own bitter experience. 'It's not exactly a match made in heaven, it's a bloody death wish if you ask me.'

'That's my point,' Carlisle replied.

'Nah, I've gone off the idea of Richard Sloane getting someone else to do his dirty work for him. Besides, it doesn't account for Cheryl Sawyer's death.'

'I'm thinking more about the women's vulnerability,' Carlisle replied.

Sutherland raised her hand as if to make her point. 'Are you suggesting the killer could be offering these women an alternative solution to their problems? Is that how he's winning them over?'

'It's possible. We know he's extremely manipulative, someone who has a good grasp of other people's emotions and vulnerabilities.'

'It's an awful lot to take in,' Hedley acknowledged. 'If it is true, then he's a cunning old fox.'

'He is, Tom,' Carlisle replied. 'Wealth is the core of these women's relationships. It's all about them. What better if our killer can dress up his own image? Hire expensive cars, take them out to flash restaurants and spend lavishly on them.'

Sutherland took a deep breath, and then exhaled. 'Yes, but surely not on a police officer's wages. Who on earth on the team could afford that sort of money?'

'That's my point, and that's why I doubt he's a police officer, ma'am.'

Sutherland threw her arms up in the air.

'So why is he using the police missing person files to select his targets?'

'Maybe he's not,' said Hedley pensively. 'But I do like the idea that he's hiring expensive cars and booking into flash hotels to act out the part.'

Mason considered Hedley's statement for a moment, and then said, 'You may have a point, Tom. I can think of half a dozen ex-coppers who've done very well for themselves after leaving the force.'

'Let's not go jumping to conclusions,' Sutherland insisted. 'We need to think this through carefully.'

Carlisle pushed back in his seat. 'Psychopaths always view their victims as their possessions. They own them in their eyes. After the excitement of the kill, they're more likely to sink into depression again. In order to preserve their fantasy they collect their victims' possessions. Clothes, body parts, even photographs of their dead victims. Ian Brady, the Moors murderer, was a prime example of that.'

'He's unquestionably egotistic.' Hedley agreed. 'I suppose it's a bit like a game hunter sticking stuffed animal heads on his living room walls. It's utter madness to you and me, but to them it's a show of power. Tell me, what is he trying to achieve?'

All eyes turned towards Sutherland.

'What are your thoughts, Jack?' she said. 'If he's not operating from inside this building, where's he getting his information from?'

Mason despondently shook his head. 'I've no idea, but if drugs *are* the bottom line, then I rest my case. Find these women's diamond engagement rings and we're half way to finding our killer.'

'He's too well informed,' Sutherland retorted. 'Whatever's driving him into doing these things, he's managing to stay ahead of the game.'

'Which begs the question,' Mason said, anxious to make his point, 'who beyond these four walls is capable of murder?'

Sutherland looked down at her notepad again.

'If he did abduct Caroline Harper, where did he hold her?'

Mason sighed. 'Bloody good question.'

All eyes now strained towards the whiteboard at the back of Sutherland's desk.

'This idea of goading the killer out into the open,' she said turning to Mason. 'Could it work?'

Mason looked at Carlisle, then back at Sutherland. 'That's more David's department. But whatever we do, we'll need to make some kind of formal statement to the press. Outline our progress, eliminate people's fears, and suggest we have our suspect in custody.'

'That could be tricky; the press aren't stupid,' Sutherland replied.

'Not if we don't tell them which police station our suspect is being held in.'

'And what do we hope to achieve from that?'

'He's narcissistic, ma'am,' Carlisle cut in. 'He's proud of his achievements so he'll not warm to the idea of someone else in the limelight.'

Sutherland thought a moment. 'It's far too risky. What if he decides to step up his hate campaign against you?'

Carlisle slumped back in his seat again.

Ch✦pter
Twenty-Six

Within hours of the police releasing their bulletin of an imaginary suspect's arrest, it was headline breaking news. Even the local radio stations were running hourly bulletins on the suspect's possible identity. And there were plenty. Not twenty-feet away, DC Carrington, looked distinctly ill at ease in her new role. These were perilous times, and Carlisle hated uncertainty at the best of times. News travelled fast, and if the killer was to strike again, now was the perfect time. Get it right, and everything else would fade into insignificance. Get it wrong, and Acting Superintendent Sutherland could soon find herself with another dead body on her hands. He knew that vultures could sniff out their next meal over a mile away, the media even further. It was all about timing, and Carlisle was having second thoughts about it all.

Reaching over, he grabbed a handful of runner beans from the yellow plastic tray, and popped them into his basket. A young man opposite in trainers and tracksuit bottoms, with 'FREEDOM' written across the front of his t-shirt, gave him the cold-eye stare. The fruit and veg shop on King Street in South Shields was busy. It was late afternoon, and Carlisle was working on a side dish he'd discovered in a Keith Floyd recipe book he'd found in Caroline Harper's flat. Nothing adventurous, but its freshness appealed to him.

His iPhone rang, and he immediately switched to voice mail.

Kurt Gillespie had never once let him down, and the drug dealer seemed eager to make contact. Earlier that morning, his informant had texted him with information regarding Cheryl Sawyer's close friends. One man in particular, a white male in his mid-thirties was definitely of interest to Carlisle. According to Gillespie, the person in mind had driven a high-end car at the time of Cheryl Sawyer's murder.

A silver one at that!

Twenty minutes later, DC Carrington pulled up outside the little corner shop in Whitburn village and switched off the undercover pool car's engine.

'Same time tomorrow?' she said.

'It's Saturday, Sue. I'm going fishing with my father?'

'Awkward,' she replied. 'Jack Mason's instructions are that I'm to stick to my task at all costs.'

'That's bloody ridiculous.'

'Why?'

'Cos the minute you drop me off, what happens to my close protection then?'

'That's Mason's call, not mine. He's the one who's calling the shots.'

'This is getting out of hand, I'm—'

Carrington held her hands up as in surrender. 'Like it or lump it, those are my orders.'

Carlisle thought about it, long enough to form his answer.

'OK, right then, pick me up at five o'clock tomorrow morning.'

'*Five o'clock!*'

'If you're that keen to go fishing, that's the time we're leaving.'

Carrington's face was a picture.

'I'll need to run it past my boss first. Let's see what he has to say.'

Carlisle grinned, knowing Jack Mason didn't do sympathy.

Chapter
Twenty-Seven

It was Friday night, and he was determined to send the profiler another text message. There was always something that could go wrong, no matter how well you planned things. Shit happened. Now that someone else had taken all the credit for his handy work, he was more than annoyed with the press. It was time to put the record books straight, and have a little fun in the process. The police weren't stupid. He'd learnt that much over the years. Even so, he would still need to tread softly just in case.

He checked his rear mirror and slid in behind a DAF truck with Edinburgh Haulage written across its rear doors. The A1 north was busy – red tail lights trailing into the distance as far as the eye could see. A mile further on and he was drawn towards the bright lights of Newcastle. The town would be bouncing this time of night, plenty of pretty girls to choose from. He smiled gloatingly to himself, and licked his lips in anticipation of things yet to come. These were old hunting grounds, and he loved every minute of it.

At the next junction he swung north over the Redheugh Bridge, passing a number of buildings to his right. Sticking rigidly to the speed limit, he caught the blue flashing lights as a speeding police car tore past from the opposite direction. Relieved, he kept a watchful eye on his wing mirror, just as a precautionary measure.

It was fast approaching midnight when he finally pulled into his favourite parking bay overlooking the Quayside. He'd used this spot before, on several occasions. Strictly speaking, this area was a designated taxi pick up point, but he couldn't have cared less. It was always lively this time of night, and full of possibilities. He would need to keep an eye on the CCTV cameras. It was that kind of area; nothing could be taken for granted round here anymore.

He decided against texting at the moment. That would come later, when he had something more concrete to report. Reaching over he grabbed another handful of mobile phones from the glove compartment, his fingers working the buttons. It was a job lot he'd purchased from the local charity shop, and they were cheap. And, as he always did, he loaded a new SIM card into the back of one before snapping the plastic cover shut.

He checked the display.

Then, just when he was about to pull away, she started to walk towards where he was parked. This one was a looker, long legs and nice thighs, a little more mature.

Even better, he thought.

His mind all over the place, excitement gripped him and he could barely breathe let alone think straight anymore. Alone, he watched as she stooped down beside his door and poked her head in through the open window. It was then he caught the whiff of her perfume, and could hardly believe his luck.

'Taxi—' she slurred.

'Yes, where to, sweetheart?'

'Durham,' she giggled.

His heart raced as she slid into the back seat, and slammed the passenger door shut behind her. Seconds later he pulled away from the curb.

Chapter Twenty-Eight

Not the best of arrangements, but at least a sensible compromise had been reached. Had it not, then his weekend's fishing trip with his ageing father would have been called off. Mixing business and pleasure had its practical benefits, but having a close protection police officer trailing in your wake all weekend would be a pain in the arse, Carlisle thought.

When all of their fishing tackle had been safely crammed into the boot of his old Rover P4 100, they joined the steady stream of traffic heading north. The weather forecast looked good too. Despite a few rain clouds threatening to spoil things, the prospects of a day's good fishing excited him. Not everything in the garden was rosy of course. There was one fish, a gigantic sea trout his father had spent a lifetime trying to catch, that had taken precedence over everything else that morning. Sometimes he wondered whether fish had emotions. If not, then his father was certainly making up for it.

'I know Herman doesn't swim in this stretch of water, but we're here by invitation. Just be grateful that our weekend hasn't been cancelled.'

'It's very kind of them, I know, but it's still not the same, son.'

'I'm sure you'll make up for it. There are plenty of other big fish to be caught in this stretch of water.'

'I doubt it,' the old man replied bluntly.

Carlisle didn't answer.

Now in his late-seventies, his father still had a good head of hair. It ran in the family, passed down through the generations from father to son. Sometimes he could be as nice as nine-pence, others a grumpy old sod. Today wasn't one of his better days.

It was mid-morning when they finally reached their destination. At the far end of a long row of stone terraced cottages stood the Anglers Arms, a large white impressive building overlooking Weldon Bridge. The pub certainly had appeal. With its own private stretch of the River Coquet available to guests, according to the brochure this small stretch of water offered anglers some of the best fishing in the county. It certainly was a stunning location, and set in some of Northumberland's most picturesque countryside.

At the rear of the building Carlisle found a suitable parking space, and switched off the car's engine. Still trying to distance himself from his father's moaning, he grabbed their bags from the back seat of the car and stood for a moment. He could hear the river tinkling, but could not see it. Guarded by tall trees, it was hidden from view at the bottom of a steep embankment.

With a beat of excitement Carlisle squeezed in through the pub door. The bar was 'L' shaped, with low black ceiling beams from which hung an array of copper cooking pans. The walls, decked out in fishing memorabilia and paintings of local castles gave the place a cosy atmosphere. To one side stood an imposing grandfather clock, and nearby stood an old leather sofa. Taking centre stage, its mantelpiece filled with a glut of antique Staffordshire cats, was a roaring log fire.

It was then he caught the landlady's eye.

Late fifties, with a ruddy complexion and long silver hair swept back at the sides and tied back, she was serving another customer whilst apologising for the lack of hot meals.

'What can I get you two gentlemen?' she said.

'The name is David Carlisle; we're booked in for two nights.'

There followed a moment of hesitation, a checking of the

computer screen.

'Ah yes, we have you both down as fishing guests.' The landlady fingered the collar of her polka dot blouse and forced a wry smile. 'We do have a few rules which you need to be aware of, but I can see you're experienced anglers. Everything you need to know is set out in your information pack, and you'll find that in your bedroom.' She smiled, and handed him their room keys with the flourish of an actor playing out her last grand performance. 'Can I get you gentlemen anything to drink?'

'Later, perhaps,' Carlisle replied.

'Yes, of course,' she smiled. 'Just ask when you need anything.'

The bedroom was tidy and functional, just as the brochure had described. Rectangular in shape, it had two single beds with matching coloured bedspreads. A sliding wardrobe occupied the back wall, along with a small bedside table filled with tea and coffee making facilities. It was perfect, he thought. Dumping their bags down in the corner of the room, they returned to the bar together. Out of habit, Carlisle ordered two pints of Timothy Taylor's Landlord and found a quiet window seat overlooking the stone bridge. It had just turned ten-thirty, and there was little sign of trade.

Then, from a backroom annex, a stranger appeared. He was a tall man, medium build, balding, with large ears sticking out beneath a well-worn black woollen hat. As soon as the stranger moved towards the corner of the bar, Carlisle spotted the half-empty beer glass.

'Passing through?' the stranger asked.

'No, we're here for the fishing,' his father replied abruptly.

'Are you regulars?'

'No, and I'm not pinning my hopes on catching anything either. Not around here, I'm not.'

The stranger almost laughed. 'You never can tell. Only last week someone pulled a whopping great five-pound brown trout out of the river – not forty metres from the bridge. According to the locals he had a hell of a struggle trying to land it by all accounts.'

His father's eyes lit up. 'That's a big fish.'

'You should see some of the salmon they're pulling out of these waters. I've never caught one myself. Not around here, I haven't. The pub runs a catch and release policy, which means you must return everything back to the river. That aside there's been some whopping big fish pulled out of the river lately. Mind, I did hear a man say he'd caught a twenty-five pound trout here last year – if you catch my drift.'

True, Carlisle thought. His father always did have a vivid imagination when it came to sizing up a fish. Never short of spinning a good yarn, it seemed the stranger had finally met his match. At least his father had quietened down and things were beginning to look up.

★

It was shortly after eight when Carlisle's alarm clock woke the two of them on the second morning. After a comfortable night's sleep, he showered, got dressed, and just before nine they ambled downstairs for breakfast. Feeling quite peckish, Carlisle ordered full English with black pudding and two slices of thick brown toast. He was right. His father insisted they sat at the same window seat that morning. Old habits die hard, and the old man was a stickler for keeping to a routine.

Many years of memories had been crammed into their conversation that weekend. They'd talked of old times, of when he was a young lad and growing up at school. Those were his fondest memories, stories he'd never heard before. With no more talk of Herman, a gigantic fish that neither was Perch, Bream, Pike nor Roach. Herman was purely a figment of his father's imagination, a nemesis that would live to fight another day. It was a great tale, and one his father would no doubt take to his grave with him.

They'd dined in the A la Carte Pullman Railway Carriage that previous evening, a retired railway carriage attached to the side of the building. Tastefully decorated, it gave the impression that you were eating your meal on a railway journey. It was an unforgettable experience, and the meal was cooked to perfection. Fresh salmon, with lemon butter sauce, and served with a side dish of piping hot fresh vegetables. When the desserts arrived, steamed chocolate pudding covered in lashings of fresh cream, he thought his stomach was going to explode. The thing that surprised Carlisle most was how much his father could eat. Every plate he returned was empty. Not that it bothered him, of course. The night had simply flown by and every hour seemed as though it had been compressed into a single minute. Unfortunately the old man was a bit of a rail buff and complained to everyone present that it wasn't actually a Pullman Coach at all, just an ordinary MK1British Railways carriage. If nothing else, it had brought some good humoured banter to the surrounding tables and the old man had thoroughly enjoyed himself.

As the last of sausage slid into the corner of Carlisle's mouth, he wiped his hands on his napkin and began to take in the views. It was a beautiful day, with just a sprinkling of white cotton-wool clouds racing across clear blue skies. After breakfast, and still with a few hours to spare, they strolled along the river bank together. Only when they'd walked for quite some distance, did his father stop to gather his breath. He was in pretty good shape for his age, a little stiff in his movements perhaps, but still remarkably agile nevertheless. Sadly his mind wasn't all it was cracked up to be nowadays, and occasionally he could be very forgetful. There were times when his father's recollections of places, people and incidents were all jumbled up as one. He blamed it on his tablets, the Statins, to reduce his high-cholesterol. It wasn't just that of course; the old man was fast approaching his twilight years and his memory was slowly beginning to fade.

The pub car park was full when they returned and the atmosphere lively. Some were ready to go fishing, others saying their goodbyes.

He watched as an overweight man in a green threadbare jumper took a huge bite out of the last of his bacon sandwich. He wore an old fisherman's hat, baggy corduroy trousers, and a jacket three sizes too small. His eyes were heavily glazed over, but he didn't appear to have a hangover. Moments later, he climbed back into an old beaten up Mercedes truck and disappeared from view back over the narrow road bridge.

The weekend had flown by, Carlisle thought. They'd caught a few fish, done some digging around, and generally had a great time together. The Anglers Arms had certainly lived up to its expectations that weekend. It had a great atmosphere, served a great pint and the bar staff were extremely friendly. After settling their account they made themselves comfortable in the tiny bar snug, eating biscuits and drinking black coffee.

'Home time?' the stranger said.

'Ten more minutes,' his father replied.

Carlisle recognised the tall man now installed at the bar. They'd spent the previous evening together chatting over the Border Wars and wars of Scottish Independence. The man was a natural storyteller, and had everyone on the edge of their seats.

'Tell me,' the stranger said, 'did this stretch of water live up to your expectations?'

'It was OK, I suppose,' his father replied half-heartedly. 'There's much bigger fish to be caught a mile further up river.'

'Brown Trout?' the stranger said as he peered over the top of his beer glass.

'Oh, yes. Brown Trout the size of Dolphins,' his father bragged.

'What kind of weights are we looking at?'

The old man stretched his arms out as far apart as they would go. 'These are whoppers.'

The stranger shook his head in bewilderment.

'Bugger me. That is a big fish.'

Well, Carlisle thought, if the stranger thought he was going to talk

a minnow into a whale he'd definitely met his match. He watched as
the old man buried his head inside his morning paper and prepared
for the stranger's next onslaught. It never came. Dressed in a blue
checked shirt, brown corduroy trousers, and wearing a black baseball
cap, if nothing else he certainly looked the part. Unlike his mother,
who was a strong-willed, god-fearing woman, his father could be an
extremely cantankerous old sod at times. It used to drive him mad.
Not anymore – he'd somehow learned to live with it. How he had
no idea.

His iPhone pinged, and he checked the display screen:

I know where you are.

Not you again, he cursed.

Fear gripped him like never before, and he felt the knot in his
stomach tighten. Thrown into confusion, he watched as a black
Peugeot 208 pulled up alongside the pub's front door. Its engine still
ticking over, the driver's face was in shadow but he sensed he was
being watched.

Who was he?

Then, before he realised what was happening, the Peugeot sped
off again. Surely he couldn't have known where they were that
weekend. Impossible, he thought. As the pieces of the jigsaw began
to fall into place, so did his imagination. If the killer wasn't a copper,
then how had he gained access to such classified information?

He had the upper hand, of course. He realised that. But he still felt
vulnerable all the same. Perhaps he should have gone with the flow,
listened to DC Carrington in the first place. He hadn't, and now he
felt threatened by a maniac hell-bent on tearing his world apart. No
doubt Jack Mason would have something to say about it, and Acting
Superintendent Sutherland for that matter. One thing was for sure,
after looking round, he hadn't a clue what he was looking for.

The man opposite playing the gaming machine, smiled at him.
He too seemed to be running out on his luck. The problem was,
and there was no getting away from it, nothing was black and white

anymore.

His iPhone pinged again.

Isaiah 10.3…

Carlisle's heart sank.

The day of reckoning!

Chapter
Twenty-Nine

It was mid-morning when David Carlisle finally drew up outside the "The Ship Inn" in Front Street, Benton. Not the greatest start to his day. Ever since receiving the killer's latest batch of threatening text-messages, his nerves had been on edge. On the face of it, his weekend fishing trip now seemed a million light-years away and there was no simple answer to uncovering the killer's identity. Whoever he was, he certainly knew how to keep a low profile. This latest attack, crude as it was, had certainly put the cat among the pigeons. Now the centre of attention, Carlisle felt totally exposed.

As it happened Carlisle found Jack Mason in buoyant mood that morning. Not that he was giving anything away, because he wasn't.

'Well,' Mason said, pint in hand. 'You certainly know how to dent this bastard's ego.'

'At least he's declared his intentions, Jack.'

Mason raised an eyebrow. 'The minute we relaxed our guard, he was onto it like a flash. Whoever he is, he's got to be close to the action.'

'It could be a coincidence, of course.'

'Bollocks,' Mason scoffed. 'He's one of us. He's a copper. What's more, Sutherland is spoiling for a fight and has asked me to get to the bottom of it.'

'I'd guessed as much.'

'Well, then!'

'Let's be honest, Jack, he probably didn't have a clue where I was at the weekend. Besides, there's nothing in his text-messages to suggest otherwise.'

Mason grabbed his arm.

'Oh. Yeah. Well he certainly knows where you live, my friend.'

Carlisle had never thought about that before, and it completely threw him off balance. Not the greatest strategist in the world, for once Jack Mason was thinking positively and not running around like a headless chicken.

'It seems the killer is blaming you for these latest events,' Mason said.

'Isn't that what we set out to do?'

'Yeah, but it's taken everyone by surprise.'

'But why me?'

Mason made a little sweeping hand gesture as if that was the end of the matter.

'I know I'm right, goddammit.' The DCI looked at him, and released the grip on his arm. 'About a year ago, I attended a university training seminar along with twenty other senior police officers. We were asked to write down the names of five serial killers, and five Chancellors of the Exchequer who'd served in government office over the past fifty years. Nineteen of us got the five serial killers' names right, only one person managed to write down more than three Chancellors' names. Doesn't that tell you anything about the man we're up against?'

'Notoriety, that's what these people thrive on unfortunately.'

Mason frowned, 'Yeah, but how do I put a stop to it. That's my biggest concern.'

'With difficulty, I suspect.'

Mason cocked his head to one side, and Carlisle was waiting for another knee-jerk reaction. It never came.

'Any ideas?' asked Mason.

'Our strongest lead is Caroline Harper's boyfriend. The question is how many other people in the Northumberland force talk with a Yorkshire accent? Not many, I'd wager.'

'It's nineteen according to Sutherland.'

'God, she's quick,' Carlisle acknowledged.

Mason cradled his empty pint glass, intrigued by the number of punters suddenly gravitating towards the bar. There were times when he looked mean, unapproachable. Though he wasn't a tall man, what he lacked in height he certainly made up for in stature.

'These latest text messages were traced to Low Fell,' Mason said thoughtfully, 'and it isn't a stone's throw from Caroline Harper's old flat. Now we have a fix on the area, Sutherland wants me to apply some pressure.'

'Is she still convinced he's local?'

'And tell me why not?'

Carlisle stood his ground.

'Everything points towards Gateshead, but I wouldn't hang my hat on it if I were you.'

'Care to tell me why?'

'There are plenty of good reasons.'

'OK, then. Give me one.'

'With all the CCTV coverage available to us, it's strange that we still haven't picked up any more sightings of Caroline Harper after she left the B&S Supermarket in Houghton-le-Spring. Unless, of course—'

Mason eyed him suspiciously. 'Unless what?'

'She never left the area in the first place.'

Mason just stared at him, his lower jaw hanging.

'What! You think she was holed up in Houghton-le-Spring?'

'It's possible!'

'That's ridiculous.'

'Not really. We're placing far too much emphasis on Gateshead,' Carlisle insisted. 'We need to expand our horizons, concentrate more on the geographical locations.'

The landlady stared inquisitively towards the corner of the bar, where two middle-aged men with huge beer bellies now stood. The smaller man, with HATE tattooed across his right knuckles and barely a courteous word in his vocabulary, ordered two fresh pints.

'Ready for another?' the landlady said, turning to face them.

'Better not, Helen,' Mason shrugged.

They talked a while before getting back to the real business in hand.

'Come to think of it,' Mason said spreading his hands on the bar top and yawning, 'you could have a point. The victim was last seen leaving the B&S Supermarket car park. If she never made it back to Gateshead, it's possible she——'

More thought.

'It's a twenty-mile round trip from Houghton-le-Spring to Gateshead,' Carlisle said. 'I know because I've driven it. And another thing, Middlesbrough is within easy spitting distance.'

'What about Wingate village?'

'That's ten miles to the south, just off the A19.'

'And Seaham——'

'It's barely a dozen miles east where Cheryl Sawyer was murdered.'

Mason stroked two day stubble. 'It's pretty central, I guess. We know Cheryl Sawyer ended up in a rubbish skip near Seaham Harbour. But why take Caroline Harper to Coldwell Lane of all places?'

'Does his work take him there?'

'Hold on!' Mason said. 'This so-called safe house, what if it was near Houghton-le-Spring?'

Finally the penny had dropped.

'It would need to be a long term rental, of course.'

'That's what I'd be doing if I were him.'

'There's also the possibility that he——'

Mason habitually grabbed his arm. 'If he was grooming them, then someone must surely have spotted them together.'

Carlisle took another deep breath. 'You would have thought so. There again, we still haven't established where Harper ate her last pizza that night.'

'True. Maybe we need to get the local police force involved. In the meantime I'll get the DVLA to run a few discreet checks over the local car rental companies.'

Carlisle's iPhone buzzed in his pocket. Thinking it was DC Carrington, he pressed the unlock button and viewed his new text-message.

His heart sank.

Delivery – Chester-le-Street railway station. LOL

Mason was onto to it like a flash.

Chapter Thirty

Blue lights flashing, Mason at the wheel, the unmarked pool car hurtled south in three lanes of heavy traffic. Carlisle checked the speedometer and could hardly believe his eyes – 110mph and climbing. As the A1 (M) Washington Services flashed past in a haze, the traffic began to pull over. Taking the next exit junction, towards Park Road North roundabout, they turned left towards Chester-le-Street. On entering the town, Mason braked hard. Ahead he could see the red traffic lights. Narrowly missing a post office delivery van in the process, he swung left and up into Front Street. Not the greatest manoeuvre in the book, but effective nevertheless.

It had taken less than twenty-five minutes to reach Chester-le-Street station, and barely two seconds for Mason to swing into action. 'Right then,' the DCI said, staring across at the station taxi rank. 'Let's see what all the fuss is about.'

Still badly shaken, Carlisle climbed out of the undercover pool car just as an InterCity Express train approached. Warning horn blaring, he felt the sudden rush of cold air on his face as the train thundered southbound. It was then he saw the small knot of people surrounding the body. First priority on his mental checklist was the victim. Bolt upright on one of the station bench seats, from a distance her face bore that all too familiar look that only death could bring. She wore a pink flowery dress, black chiffon scarf, and a blue Panama hat.

Mason's approach was hurried.

'Who is she?'

A plump community police support officer wearing a bright yellow high-visibility jacket turned sharply to face them. 'And who the fuck are you?'

'Detective Chief Inspector Jack Mason, Northumbria Police,' Mason said, flashing his warrant under the CPSO's nose. 'Did you report this?'

'Yes, sir.'

Mason nodded. 'What do you know?'

'Some prankster has super glued her to the seat.'

'Is she dead?'

'Hardly, it's a life-size mannequin.'

Clearly embarrassed, Mason took a closer look.

'Who found her?'

'It was a local taxi driver, sir.'

'What time was this?'

'Five o'clock this morning. Everyone thought it a joke until your people raised the alarm.'

'OK. Right then,' Mason said. 'Let's run a check on the station's CCTV, before—'

'It's already been carried out,' the CPSO replied. 'Unfortunately the cameras don't cover that section of the station.'

'What about the car park?'

'I'm afraid not.'

They stood for a moment as a northbound Trans-Pennine express train pulled into the platform opposite. Engines throbbing, Carlisle watched as a few passengers exited the carriages and climbed the bridge stairs to the other side of the station. Seconds later, the train continued north again.

They were joined by the duty Scene of Crime manager. A dour man a few inches shorter than Carlisle, Stan Bowles bore the look of an undertaker. Capable enough, despite his outward appearance, Bowles was a man of few words.

Mason's jaw was set tight, and the muscles in his neck twitched.

'What are we doing about the outlying area, Stan?'

'Uniforms are on it,' Bowles replied. 'I've instructed them to take down the details of every car parked within a hundred metres radius of the station.'

Mason cocked his head. 'What the hell for?'

'People park their cars in the nearby streets before catching the train to work. It's cheaper than paying the city parking fees apparently.'

There followed an awkward silence, before Mason's serious side began to surface again. 'What do we know about the station – is it manned?'

'Apart from the taxi office, there's a daytime rail ticket office, a passenger waiting room, but nothing on the northbound platform.'

'Did anyone report seeing anything?'

'Not to my knowledge,' Bowles replied.

'Right,' said Mason, jotting down some notes. 'What time does the first train to Newcastle stop here in the morning?'

Subdued, Bowles spoke in a whisper. 'Weekdays, there's the six-fifteen southbound to Liverpool, and a six forty-five northbound to Newcastle.'

'And the mannequin was first spotted around five, you say?' Mason said, pencil poised at the ready.

'Yes, a local taxi driver. He's already made a full statement to that effect.'

'Good man.'

They moved towards the end of the southbound platform and away from prying ears. Then there was the dress worn by the mannequin, thought Carlisle. It was expensive looking. Not the kind you'd expect to find in one of your usual high street retail shops. With any luck, it may even have been an exclusive designer label – traceable, right back to a credit card. But that would come later, after forensics had completed their initial findings.

'You look puzzled,' Mason said, breaking Carlisle's thoughts.

'Why here; what's he telling us?'

'Let's not jump to conclusions. If it is him, then he certainly doesn't hang about.' Mason, both hands in pockets stared aimlessly down towards Chester-le-Street railway viaduct. 'Let's hope uniforms don't find a real body in one of the backstreets.'

Carlisle hesitated – a gathering of thoughts.

'He's posing us the question, Jack. To him it's a game. Let's hope he hasn't kicked off again.'

'Don't tell me this was planned?'

Carlisle held Mason's glances. 'That's what you get for crediting someone else with his handiwork. He's angry, and feels let down by it all. It's his way of letting us know he's still around.'

The DCI was first to spot the newspaper reporter.

'Shit!' Mason cursed. 'Look who's just arrived.'

Even though the immediate crime scene had been taped off and a constable posted at the entrance to the station car park, Christopher Sykes, a local sleazebag journalist, had somehow managed to blag his way into the inner security ring. Sykes was weird, he was not to be trusted, and had a nasty habit of rubbing people up the wrong way and twisting their words to suit a good storyline.

'Well I'll be damned, if it isn't Jack Mason of all people,' said Sykes. 'Fancy bumping into you here. This is a strange place to be holding a fashion show, don't you think?'

'What brings you to this neck of the woods?' Mason groaned.

'A little bird tells me we may have another stiff on our hands.'

'Well, well, chance would be a fine thing,' Mason replied. 'What gave you that idea?'

'You know me, Jack. I like to keep my ears to the ground.' Sykes' lips were on the verge of that nasty little superior smile that Carlisle was all too accustomed to seeing. The reporter took out his notebook and fumbled around in his pockets for a pen. 'It would help if I knew what all the excitement was about?' said Sykes.

Mason shrugged. 'Some prankster having a good night out, I suspect.'

'I wonder if it has anything to do with this recent murder case.'

'What gave you that impression?' Mason replied bluntly.

'You know me, Jack.'

'You're wrong, mate. We already have someone banged up for that.'

Sykes eyed them with suspicion, as he brushed the flecks of dandruff from a badly creased jacket. 'If you don't mind me saying so, it's a big turnout for such a small fashion show.'

Mason gave him a cold smile. 'No doubt you'll find plenty to write about.'

'That's right, Jack. You know how I like to keep my readers informed.'

'In which case I'll not keep you any longer,' Mason nodded.

The reporter stopped dead in his tracks and turned sharply to face them again.

'Anywhere out of bounds?' said Sykes, sarcastically.

'I'd stay well clear of the tracks if I were you.'

Sykes bottom lip quivered. 'Now *that* would make one hell of a headline story.'

'Glad to be of assistance,' Mason chuckled.

They remained silent, but Carlisle sensed a reaction as Sykes sauntered towards the platform waiting room.

'Scumbag,' Mason muttered through clenched teeth.

Chapter
Thirty-One

The weather forecast was abysmal. The lid of grey-clouds that had hung over the coastline that morning had turned everything monochrome. Two minutes to eight, and the steady stream of traffic crawling through the village of Whitburn that morning had finally ground to a halt. Gridlocked at the traffic lights again! It was the same damn place every time. Whoever had designed such chaos needed their heads examining, thought Carlisle.

Stood waiting for DC Carrington to return to the undercover pool car, Carlisle's mind was all over the place. The expensive dress, the one found on the mannequin on Chester-le Street station, had turned out to be an exclusive designer label. With only five purchased throughout the whole of the north-east of England, the tech boys had done a fantastic job in tracing every single one of them. All that remained now was to check on the owners.

With several people to interview, the day ahead looked a long one. One of the dresses had been purchased on a joint bank account belonging to a George and Mary Fowler. Unable to contact Mary Fowler, DC Carrington had made arrangements to meet with her husband at Slaley Hall Hotel in Northumberland.

There was a definite purpose in DC Carrington's stride as she stepped out of the bakery that morning. Dressed in a smart blue coat, black trousers and matching shoes, she heaved her bag over her shoulder and zapped the undercover pool car's automatic unlocking system.

'Monday morning sucks,' the young detective announced. 'What about you?'

Carlisle faltered before climbing in beside her.

'Give me Saturday any day of the week.'

She gave him a frosty look. 'Don't tell me you're a boring football fan?'

'I could be, why?'

'Let's not go there. I can't stand football at the best of times. The game's full of overpaid, deluded prima donnas who hate getting their strip tops dirty.' The young detective fiddled with the car radio before picking up on their conversation again. 'Sunday's the only day of the week I seem to have any free-time on my hands these days.'

Carlisle bit his bottom lip as he glanced uneasily at the distant tree-line. He hated to admit it, but he was spending far too much time with his ageing father lately. Now in his twilight years, the old man was becoming more and more dependent on him each passing day. What with their Friday night shopping trips, and sorting out his father's household bills, it was trying to fit everything in that was the problem.

'What's so special about Sundays?' he asked.

'I treasure my sleep-ins.'

Carlisle felt a conflicting surge of emotions, as he listened to her story. 'It's funny you should mention sleep,' he said. 'I've been getting these recurring nightmares lately.'

'Nothing serious I hope?'

'It's not him, it's Jackie this time.'

Carrington turned to face him. 'And—'

His thoughts elsewhere, he pretended to fiddle with his mobile still unsure that he wanted to talk about it. 'It's always the same weird dream,' said Carlisle. 'It's Jackie, and she's lying face down in the water and her body is drifting slowly towards me.'

'That's creepy,' she shuddered. 'What happens next?'

'I reach out to her and pull her into the river bank.' Carlisle swallowed hard, annoyed with himself for having dared to even think about sharing his intimate thoughts with the young detective. But the look on Carrington's face and the sympathy in her eyes, seemed to force him to continue. 'After dragging her out of the water, I keep shaking her but she doesn't respond. Then, out of nowhere this Hindu holy man appears.'

'A holy man—'

'Yes, and his whole body is covered with ash and his forehead painted bright yellow. It's the look on his face that puts the fear of God in me. It's as if he's already dead.' He waited for a reaction, but it never came. 'I know it sounds stupid, but he reaches out to her and brushes me aside. All the while he keeps chanting this recital in a dead monotone.'

'Don't tell me she opens her eyes.'

Carlisle turned to face her. 'No. That's when I wake up sweating.'

'How long has this been going on?'

'Several weeks—'

Carrington reddened, as though she'd touched another raw nerve with her. 'It's weird how your mind can play tricks with you. When I was a young girl, I used to get these awful nightmares where I couldn't run fast enough to get away from danger. My mother always used to tell me that a traumatic event in your life can trigger bad dreams.'

'That's scary,' he said trying to humour her.

'Not half,' she sighed.

The young detective nodded, her eyes peeled on the road ahead.

Carlisle turned his attentions to the day ahead, but the killer was never far from his mind. And another thing, there was something about Alexander Moore that had got Jack Mason's back up. Although he had to agree, Moore was definitely a bit of an odd-ball and could be extremely anti-social at times. Whether the temporary SOC photographer was capable of murder was another matter, but Mason seemed to think so. There again, trying to convince Jack Mason that it wasn't a copper they were looking for was like talking to a brick wall.

'How's Peter Davenport doing nowadays?' Carlisle asked casually.

'I've not seen him since he returned back to work. Why?'

'Just curious, that's all. I've been thinking about his replacement.'

'Oh. What about him?' Carrington replied.

'What's Alexander Moore's background?'

'I've no idea.'

'He comes from Middlesbrough, doesn't he?'

Carrington seemed taken aback. 'Yes, Acklam, I believe.'

'Doesn't that strike you as odd?'

'No. Why should it?' Carrington shrugged. 'Moore was only here on temporary assignment. Now that Peter Davenport's returned to work, I guess Moore's gone back to his old post in Middlesbrough.'

'That makes sense.'

'Why do you ask? Has Jack Mason mentioned something to you about him?'

'No, not to me he hasn't. Why?'

'It's just that he's been making a few enquiries about him lately.

'What, Alexander Moore!'

'Yes.' Carrington frowned. 'Everyone's looking over their shoulders nowadays. It's as if we're all under suspicion.'

Carlisle feigned surprise. 'Thankfully I'm not involved in internal politics anymore.'

'You're lucky. Things have moved on since you left the force,' Carrington said, 'Me, I try to steer well clear of the backstabbers on the team – they always give me the jitters.'

Wise move, he thought. He made a mental note of it.

'Have you ever stood in a crowd and said to yourself the person standing next to you works as an insurance broker?'

'This isn't another one of your stupid brain games, is it?'

'No.'

'Then the answer is yes, many times,' she replied.

'It's called extrasensory perception, a sixth sense. Call it what you will, but there was something about Moore that caused you to think that way. Not that I disliked the guy, but he did have a peculiar way of interacting with people.'

Carrington wrinkled her nose. 'What can I say? You're the so-called mind expert around here. I'm just the general dogsbody who chauffeurs you around everywhere.'

'Don't push it.'

As the undercover pool car sped north towards Consett, midday County Durham suddenly seemed a darker place than ever. Plagued by a serial killer who seemed hell bent on destroying his mental wellbeing, Carlisle didn't hold out much hope of ever catching him. Not at the moment, he didn't. There again, he thought, had the team dismissed the killer's spiritual text messages too readily. Not a religious man himself, the concept of God was something that Carlisle had never quite got to grips with. With so much killing in the world, he was beginning to doubt if God really existed at all. And, if he did, why had he allowed such evil to happen in the first place? The more he thought about it, the more he argued with himself. Surely Satan was the driving force behind so much unprovoked slaughter in the world. If not, then who else was responsible? Either way, the question of God rested heavily on Carlisle's mind and he still hadn't reached a final decision over the matter.

Not yet he hadn't.

Chapter Thirty-Two

A steady drizzle had turned into a sudden downpour when they finally reached Slaley Hall in Northumberland. Set in its own grounds, according to the brochure this striking Edwardian mansion boasted 142 hotel rooms, two golf courses, a gym, swimming pool and a spa with five treatment rooms. Oh, and not forgetting laser clay pigeon shooting. Not that Carlisle was into pigeon shooting, he wasn't. But the thrill of shooting at flying discs and watching them explode into a million fragments somewhat appealed to him.

Carlisle was stepping out of the car when a sudden flash of inspiration struck him. What if the killer was a foreigner who had hired an expensive yacht to show off his imaginary wealth? It seemed a perfect cover. There again, he knew that every port in the country was now under renewed scrutiny with the Border Patrol. Even so, Mason was desperately short of manpower and his team were overstretched. Things were slipping under the radar, even he could see that. The fact that not much progress had been made in determining Caroline Harper's last known movements backed this theory up.

At the reception desk they were directed to the Claret Jug, where they identified themselves to George Fowler. Everything about the man oozed wealth, and his appearance was distinctly old Etonian. He had a posh accent and spoke through his nose.

'How can I help you?' Fowler asked as he stood to face them.

'We'd like to speak with your wife, if we may,' DC Carrington said.

'Oh, perhaps I can help?'

The young detective showed him her warrant card, and stepped back a pace. 'No, sir, we need to talk to your wife about a dress she recently purchased on a joint bank account.'

'A dress,' Fowler said, looking somewhat bemused. 'That's not possible, I'm afraid. Mary's away at the moment.'

Carlisle and Carrington exchanged glances.

'Where can she be contacted?' Carrington asked.

'I'm afraid I really can't help you with that either.'

'What about telephone contact details?'

'She does have an iPhone, but she refuses to answer it.'

'Any reason why?'

'The silly woman has buggered off again, and I've absolutely no idea where she is at the moment.'

'I take it she's left home, sir?'

'Yes, if you must know.'

'Have you reported this to the police?'

'Good God, no, this isn't the first time that Mary's left home.' Fowler sighed. 'It happens regularly, I'm afraid. When you marry someone who can't make her mind up what a normal healthy marriage relationship is there's not much you can do about it.'

'Oh!' Carrington said, trying her best not to laugh.

Fowler folded his arms. 'When the stupid woman finally comes round to her senses again, no doubt she'll return home.'

Carlisle suddenly felt the hairs on the back of his neck stand on end.

'I'm afraid it's not that simple,' Carrington explained. 'We believe your wife may be involved with a man who isn't exactly the nicest person to be going around with at the moment.'

'Another man—'

Carrington slid a photograph out of her handbag and handed it to him.

'Do you recognise this dress?'

'No, I don't,' Fowler retorted.

'Take another look,' she insisted. 'We believe your wife may have purchased it from an exclusive department store in Newcastle.'

Fowler paused in a display of indignation, and gave Carrington another withering look. 'How do you expect me to know that? Mary's wardrobes are crammed full of the stuff. I've lost track of the number of dresses she's bought over the years.'

At least he'd given her an honest answer, thought Carlisle.

'Have you any idea as to where your wife might be at the moment?'

Fowler shrugged, as though full of resentment. 'That's pretty obvious isn't it?'

'Oh, so *you do* know where Mary is?'

'Well not exactly, but I do know she has a little terraced house in Durham.'

For some reason Fowler was trembling, as though Carrington had struck a raw nerve with him. Carlisle made a mental note and turned to face him again.

'And where might that be?' he asked.

'Claypath, it's close to the city centre.' Fowler smiled resignedly to himself. 'The reason I know is that the last time she skedaddled off, I hired a private detective to look into the matter. That's when he found out where she was living.'

Life was full of little surprises.

'I presume Mary rents this so called property,' said Carlisle.

'Good God, no.' Fowler composed himself. 'She owns it outright. Mary's a highly talented woman, she's intelligent, but every now and then she likes to get away from it all.'

'Get away from what exactly—'

Fowler cut him off mid-sentence. 'She's reached a midlife crisis and thinks she's twenty-one again. I know my limitations, Mr

Carlisle, but there's not a damn thing I can do about it. We're very fond of one another's company, and like to travel abroad when we can. Mind, I find it difficult at times. I just don't seem to have the energy to keep up with her nowadays.'

Carrington's eye's narrowed. 'Tell me about Mary, how would you best describe her?'

'You only need to look at her photographs to see what an attractive woman she really is.' Fowler tugged at his watch strap. 'Like everyone, she has her moments and can be very belligerent at times.'

Oh dear, Carlisle thought. Here we go again.

'How old did you say your wife was?' Carlisle asked.

'She'll be coming up to forty-two next month.'

The profiler did a quick mental calculation. 'If I'm not mistaken that makes you fifty something?'

Fowler nodded, but refused to be sucked in.

What made this case so decidedly different was their smaller age difference. It didn't look good. If his wife had fallen under the killer's spell, then how had he selected her? Thinking of this, it wouldn't have been difficult for a good social predator to spot a pretty woman in difficulties. You only had to look in the right places for that, and the night clubs, of course.

Carlisle finished his drink and sat for a moment staring blindly into space. Who were the most likely candidates, he wondered. Who on the team could he trust least?

'So why would your wife purchase a property in Durham City?' Carlisle asked.

Fowler sat flabbergasted. 'That's where she grew up. She went to Art College there.'

Carlisle noticed some uneasiness in Fowler's voice. Sitting directly opposite him, his mannerisms reminded him of a meerkat. A commodities trader in his past, Fowler had made a shed load of money out of selling energy to India. There again, it wasn't his wealth that attracted his errant wife towards him, it was something else.

Clearly an attractive woman, why had she gone to all the trouble of marrying a man she had no intention of living with all of the time? Something was wrong. Unlike the others who had regarded their husbands as mere pawns in the grand scheme of things, Mary Fowler seemed more mature. It didn't add up. None of it did, and Carlisle was floundering.

'Tell me about your wife, where did she grow up?'

Fowler swallowed hard. 'After she left school, Mary studied creative art at Durham New College. Friends used to compliment her on her creative interior home designs, and that's when she began to take on free-lance contracts. Despite a lack of formal training, her talents soon began to become recognised. That's when she expanded into commercial contracts.'

Carlisle nodded.

'My wife is a very talented woman, Mr Carlisle. She knows how to deal with other people's high standards and demands. After several years of hard work, that's when she set up her own interior design business – *Creative Design*.'

'How did the two of you meet?' Carlisle asked.

'I was in need of some interior design work in new office blocks, and Mary came highly recommended through a friend. That's when he introduced me to her, and we first became good friends.'

Fowler's voice was drowned out by laughter coming from another part of the room. Carlisle caught the gist of what he was saying, but didn't press the matter further.

'How long has your wife been missing, did you say?' Carrington asked.

'Five weeks, it could be more. I seem to have lost all track of time lately.'

'And she's never once made contact with you since leaving home?'

'No.'

'Not so much as a text message?'

'No.' Fowler cradled his glass. 'She seemingly goes into complete hibernation and cuts herself off from the rest of the world.'

Carlisle paused before answering.

'I find that very hard to believe, Mr Fowler. Is your wife involved in drugs at all?'

'Good God, no, she's never touched the stuff.'

Not as far you know, Carlisle mused.

Fowler stared at them, as if waiting for the next question to come.

'Why didn't you report this to the police?' Carrington asked firmly.

'Why would I? This isn't the first time that Mary's buggered off from me.'

'You don't sound very convincing, any reason why not?'

Fowler lowered his head. 'I grew out of the loud music and disco clubs that my wife still likes to visit, many years ago. Don't get me wrong, but some of the places the younger generation frequent these days I wouldn't be seen dead in.'

Too damn right, Carlisle thought.

The room had cleared somewhat. Now two o'clock, most of the club members had left for an afternoon round of golf. Having finally made up his mind there was nothing more to gain from the interview, Carlisle stood to leave. It was then he noticed the young detective had also begun to gather her belongings together.

'I don't wish to sound alarmist,' Carrington said, 'but there are some very nasty people out there whose intentions aren't quite as honourable as yours. May I suggest that on your way home, you call in at your local police station and report your wife missing?'

'Yes, I will.'

'In which case we'll not keep you any longer,' Carrington confirmed.

Had they missed something, Carlisle wondered.

They left the building into bright sunshine with more questions than answers. How someone could turn a blind eye to someone who appeared to have the morals of an Amsterdam alley cat, was beyond him. But George Fowler had, and that was the crux of the matter. This wasn't a marriage involving money matters; this was a marriage contrived. The difference was Mary Fowler was a very wealthy woman in her own right. She was a creative interior home designer who seemed to have a good business head on her shoulders. Above all, she sounded articulate and knew how to handle extremely difficult clients. Fortunately there was no offspring involved in their marriage. A future divorce settlement perhaps, but no children thankfully.

Chapter
Thirty-Three

Detective Chief Inspector Mason loved uncertainty; the not knowing what was coming next. Lurking in the shadows in Leazes Place, he watched as a team of police officers drawn from the operations team moved into position. Barely a stone's throw from Durham Market Place, close to Elvet Riverside, Mary Fowler's terraced house appeared shrouded in secrecy. Located on three levels, the curtains were closed, no light seeping round the edge of the windows. The trouble was, hidden amongst them could be a potential killer. Who, Mason had no idea, but he was determined to find that out.

Under the cover of darkness, and in what was now a well-kept secret, he finally gave the order. Tooled up and ready to go, a dozen police officers drawn from the Tactical Firearms Unit emerged from the shadows. Dressed in their familiar black combat jackets, black balaclavas and boots, they were difficult to pick out in the murky dawn light.

Mason checked his watch. It was coming up to 4.00am.

So far so good, he thought, pointing towards the occupant's front door. Seconds later a burly police officer dressed in a short sleeved black shirt and carrying a battering ram in his left hand stepped from the shadows. As the door flew inwards at the third attempt, the rest of the team piled in.

'Touch nothing,' Mason shouted.

There was always the off chance he might catch his killer red-handed. Not today, unfortunately. Despite his meticulous planning the occupants had long gone. Feeling the knot in the pit of his stomach, all kinds of emotions were raging through Mason's head. There was still plenty of work to do, and given the recent turn in events, he was pinning his hopes on forensics coming up trumps.

Apart from a small team of hand-picked officers, the remainder of the men were stood down. Even so, the search for clues was relentless. Squeezed between the sofa and an old reclining armchair, he watched as the Senior Forensic Scientist peered down at the heavily stained coffee table and made a few notes.

'This shouldn't take long,' Tom Hedley said.

'Keep your eyes peeled,' Mason whispered. 'If we are dealing with a bent copper here, he may want to try and remove something.'

'I'll get Davenport to run a video camera over the premises,' Hedley acknowledged.

Alexander Moore, Peter Davenport's replacement. Now there was a name that conjured up whole bunch of possibilities, Mason thought. Apart from Moore, there wasn't another police officer on the team that he could readily point a finger at. Not at the moment, he couldn't. He'd been over this ground before, many times in fact, and he still couldn't fathom it out. The problem was, and it had been eating away at him for days now, the killer had remarkable guile. And, needless to say, he was extremely good at it.

Harry Manley shook his head in total dismay, and stood in silence for a minute. Married with three teenage sons, Manley certainly wasn't a killer. A muscular man, early forties, he didn't have an ounce of hatred in his body. The joker in the pack, the Detective Constable was the least of Jack Mason's worries. No, he thought. It had to be someone else, someone with a bitter hate campaign against rapacious women. Looking around there was any number of officers to choose from, but none of them fitted the bill. Not at the moment, they didn't.

'Anything in particular we're looking for?' Manley asked.

Mason's radio crackled. He turned the volume down. 'Check upstairs, Harry. I'm looking for anything that points us towards the occupant's whereabouts.'

'There's nothing up here,' said George Holt, making his way back down the rickety staircase. 'No sign of a mobile phone, no laptop computer, nothing.'

'She obviously left in a hurry?' Mason acknowledged with a nod.

'It would seem so, boss.'

'Any indications as to how long she may have been gone?'

The Detective Sergeant scratched the side of his cheek. 'Hard to say; forensics might give us a better idea.'

True, Mason thought, but it wasn't the answer he was looking for. Things were slipping away from him and if he didn't catch his killer soon, the press would be all over him like a rash. God, what a mess!

Mason steadied himself as he stared at the shattered front door frame again.

'Anyone bothered to check the kitchen?' he asked.

'I'm on it, boss,' DS Miller replied, poking his head round the open kitchen doorway.

'Before you touch anything, check with Tom Hedley first.'

'Will do, boss.'

Mason stood for a while, and searched for a moment of inspiration. Something would turn up; it usually did. Having mentally cleared Vic Miller from his checklist of potential candidates, the Detective Sergeant was far too trusting to pose him a threat. Besides, from what he could recall of their social nights out together, Miller wasn't a woman hater. No, the sergeant's only grudge in life was his long overdue promotion. Recent government cutbacks had undoubtedly put paid to many a man's career advancement lately. It was a major bone of contention, and there wasn't a damn thing that anyone could do about it.

Close to the hallway he heard the distinct whirr from Peter Davenport's digital camera. Unquestionably a bit of an oddball,

Davenport wasn't a killer. A slightly built man, of average height, he had huge inquisitive eyes that protruded from their sockets like a bubble eyed fish. Although Davenport was untidily dressed, Mason envied his artistic talents. The SOC photographer certainly had a keen eye for detail and a sound knowledge of how the forensic system worked. Apart from that, he knew very little about the man's social background. Davenport's role was to photograph a crime scene, a means of cataloguing evidence, a blueprint for reconstructing a scene at a later stage.

Mason knew his team, but these were mere amateur players in the grand scheme of things. All bar one, that is – Alexander Moore. Now there was a name to conjure up his imagination if ever there was one. Moore wasn't a team player, and Mason had picked up on it. Not only that, Moore's enthusiasm for photographing a murder scene was unnatural. As if he thrived on the victim's misfortunes. And another thing, the night he'd attended the Coldwell Lane murder scene he recalled the notable swelling to the side of Moore's face. What's more, there were deep scratch marks to the back of his hands which the stand-in SOC photographer had put down to walking into a glass door. But it wasn't that kind of injury, everyone knew that. It was as if Moore had been caught up in a fight.

But there it was. Unless he could come up with something more concrete, there was nothing he could do about it. Perhaps it was time he ran a cursory check over Alexander Moore's background. Find out what made the SOC photographer tick – what he got up to in his spare time. Yes, there was scant evidence to link him to the first murder and very little to pin on him for the second. But Moore had a darker side, and one that Mason was determined to get to the bottom of.

'Find anything of interest?' he asked.

Tom Hedley held up a large plastic forensic evidence bag full of silver cutlery. 'Sutherland's asked me to check these out.'

'Damn fingerprints,' the DCI cursed, his voice in a low hypnotic monotone.

'I'm just following orders, Jack.'

'Sometimes I wonder if—' Mason checked himself mid-sentence.

'It's really not a bad idea when you stop to think about it.'

'The woman's fixated, Tom.'

The forensic scientist leaned back against the doorframe, and shook his head. 'I hate to admit it, but whoever lived here has turned their back on the place. There's nothing in the fridge, dust everywhere, even the seven-day carriage clock spring is fully unwound.'

Mason stared at him. 'Just when I thought we had him in our grasp, he slips through the net again.'

'Chance would be a fine thing,' Hedley went on. 'The more I think about it, the more I can agree with David Carlisle's theory. He's grooming them, Jack, and if I'm perfectly honest with you, this place bears all the hallmarks of Caroline Harper's flat.'

'The bastard's too well informed for my liking,' Mason shrugged.

They talked a while, the dim street lighting casting long eerie shadows down into Elvet. As daylight began to filter through the clouds, so the temperature began to rise.

Mason pointed to the letterbox.

'Miller,' he shouted. 'Anyone picked up the post?'

'Not to my knowledge.'

'Check around, see what you can find out, and—'

'I doubt she's been receiving mail,' Hedley cut in.

'What. Not even junk mail?'

Hedley uncharacteristically swore.

Mason pursed his lips, taking his time before continuing. 'Who's the mole in the organisation, Tom? That's what I want to know.'

'I've no idea, but it certainly looks like another professional clean up.'

Suddenly everything had been turned on its head again.

Chapter Thirty-Four

Detective Constable Carrington wrinkled her nose as she peeped in through the Estate Agent's office window. It was lunchtime, and Sunderland's city centre was now in full swing. Carlisle could think of a thousand reasons to feel frustrated, and most of them involved legwork. What's more, Jack Mason's recent house search of Mary Fowler's property had thrown up very little in the way of fresh leads. A few items of interest had been bagged; apart from that, nothing. It was then he noticed the middle-aged woman peering over the top of a pair of green tinted kaleidoscope coloured glasses. She gave them a – *we're open for business smile* – and beckoned them inside. It was moments like these that Carlisle felt a glimmer of hope. If there was a downside in all of this, it was that neither of them genuinely looked like house-hunters.

'How can I help you?' the woman asked.

'Police,' Carrington said, closing the door behind her.

'Oh. It wouldn't be about the trouble in Dukes Street, would it? We've—'

'No.' Carrington flashed her warrant card in front of the woman's hard-done-by face. 'We're looking for information regarding a rented property in Prince Consort Road in Gateshead.'

'I'm sorry, pet. We don't deal with that area. We're a family-run business, we deal mainly with low rental properties in and around the Sunderland area.'

Carrington hesitated. 'It's—'

'I can put you in touch with someone who may be able to help you?'

'No. That won't be necessary.'

'May I ask what this is in connection with?'

'A young woman found murdered in Gateshead,' Carrington replied. 'We're making a few enquiries as to her last known movements.'

The middle-aged woman threw her a cynical smile, picked up the telephone receiver and tapped a three-digit number into the keypad. 'Sharon, pet,' she whispered, loud enough for both of them to hear. 'There are two police officers down here from Gateshead, they'd like a word with you about CH,' the woman put the receiver down and turned to face them again. 'I presume this is about Caroline Harper, isn't it?'

'It could be—' Carrington acknowledged.

'My boss was a good friend of hers – known her for years. What a terrible tragedy; who would have thought such a thing could happen in the centre of Gateshead?' There followed an awkward silence. 'She'll be down in a jiffy. Can I get you people anything to drink?'

They both plumped for coffee, which came in huge pink mugs – the estate agent's name emblazoned around the sides. Looking round, pictures of available properties lined every wall. Mainly cheap terraced property, some Carlisle wouldn't let a rat live in, let alone human beings. Some things never change, he cursed. The problem was Sunderland had one of the worst unemployment statistics in the country. The number of people registered unemployed and out of work was rising not falling as recent Government statistics suggested. Money was tight round here, and most homeowners had to make do and mend.

Sharon Nash was a slim, fair complexioned, forty-something. Similar in height to him, she had alert dark blue eyes, short cropped brown hair, and a high intelligent-looking forehead. Dressed in a smart two-piece business suit, white cotton blouse and matching high heeled shoes, she approached them with an air of uncertainty. The minute she held out her hand, Carlisle felt genuine warmth.

'How can I help?' the estate agent manager asked.

Detective Carrington retrieved a copy of Caroline Harper's photograph from her handbag, and handed it to her. 'Do you recognise this lady?'

'Yes, that's Caroline Harper.' There followed a gathering of thoughts before Nash spoke again. 'What a terrible tragedy. Who could have done such a thing?'

'When was the last time you saw her?' asked Carrington.

Nash made a little show of emotion, and the tone in her voice had softened. 'A few weeks ago we had coffee together in a little café in Gateshead High Street. It's opposite Wetherspoons. Do you know it at all?'

Carrington acknowledged with a nod. 'Yes I do, I sometimes go there at lunchtime. They make a nice latté there.' The young detective shuffled awkwardly. 'I realise this must be awkward for you, but how would you describe Caroline. What was she like as a friend?'

As her story began to unfold, Carlisle got the distinct impression that things hadn't quite turned out as Caroline Harper thought they would. After leaving home, according to the estate agent manager, she'd struggled to make ends meet. But that wasn't all, there was more, and they both sat gobsmacked as her story began to unfold.

'This new boyfriend you talk of,' asked Carrington. 'Did you meet with him at all?'

'No, it was just what Caroline had told me about him.'

Notebook in hand, pen poised, Carrington looked at her hard.

'And what exactly did she tell you?'

'Just that he was incredibly rich, and he was over here on an important business trip. He lived in Spain apparently, Marbella I believe. According to Caroline, he had a large yacht and owned several exclusive properties there. She seemed quite excited about it all, and was looking forward to joining him in Spain after he'd finished his business here.'

'It sounds like he was a very wealthy man,' Carrington sighed, making a few notes. 'Did she mention his name to you at all?'

'No, not to me she didn't, but she did show me a photograph of him.'

Carrington and Carlisle's eyes met.

'How would you describe him?'

'He was tall, swarthy looking with dark swept back hair and big round dark eyes.'

'Mediterranean looking, would you say?'

'No, more Asian. European Indian if there is such a thing.'

A telephone warbled in the office and the middle-aged woman answered it. Having eavesdropped on their conversation, the look of disgust on her face said it all. Seconds later she slammed the receiver back down and feigned she was busy again.

'How old would he be?' Carlisle asked.

Nash's shoulders slumped. 'Fortyish – but I'm not very good with ages. He had a chiselled face and a slightly pointed chin as I remember.'

'What else did Caroline tell you about him?'

Nash folded her arms, a defensive pose. 'She was definitely besotted by him, and couldn't stop talking about the numerous properties he owned in Spain. But that was Caroline, of course, in for a penny, in for a pound.' Nash rolled her eyes. 'In a lot of ways Caroline was very materialistically driven. She adored fast cars, expensive clothes, and exotic holidays in faraway places. They were like gods to her.'

'High maintenance would you say?' Carrington said, cocking her head to one side.

'Yes, very. She certainly knew how to spend other people's money if that's what you mean.'

'Did she mention where this boyfriend of hers was stopping? A hotel perhaps—'

'No. As far as I could make out, and please don't quote me on this, I believe his family lived in Middlesbrough.'

'*Middlesbrough*—'

'I'm positive.' Nash replied defensively.

'What makes you say that?'

'Well,' said Nash, 'Caroline thought it funny that he should have all that money and still retain a broad Cleveland accent.'

'I see,' Carlisle muttered softly. 'Do you have any idea whereabouts?'

'No. She never mentioned it.'

'What about his family, did she mention them at all?'

'I'm sorry,' Nash insisted. 'I'm not used to this kind of questioning, and you're making me feel nervous.'

Carrington chewed the end of her pen, as she checked through her notes again. 'We know you're not involved in any way, but this is extremely important to us. Tell me,' said Carrington, her voice barely a whisper, 'this work her boyfriend was doing here in Newcastle. Do you happen to know what line of business he was working in?'

'I've no idea. As far as I recollect she'd only just met up with him.' Nash threw her head back and sighed. 'But that was Caroline, of course. She lived on the edge most of the time. Don't get me wrong, I wasn't jealous or anything, but she could be extremely boring at times. If I'm brutally honest with you, she seldom talked about the ordinary day to day things that you and I would talk about. It wasn't her thing. Caroline was far too materialistically driven for that.'

'And you have no idea what her boyfriend was doing here?'

'No, just that he was here in the North-East on business.' Nash made a little sweeping hand gesture. 'As I recall, he had one or two business connections here.'

'I see.'

Nash stared at the heavens again. 'Caroline liked to tell you things like that.'

The young detective nodded, as if to concur with her statement.

'I'm sorry for being a nuisance,' Carrington went on. 'But this expensive car her boyfriend was driving, did she happen to mention what make it was?'

'It was a McLaren and incredibly fast according to Caroline.'

Slowly the pieces of the jigsaw were coming together.

'You don't have to answer my next question,' Carlisle said leaning closer, 'but were they sleeping together?'

'I don't think so, but no doubt Caroline would have been working on it.'

'Oh!'

'That's how she liked to operate.'

'Did she ever brag about her conquests to you at all?'

'Caroline was always the first on the dance floor if that's what you're meaning. The trouble was, and I don't wish to sound envious, she enjoyed being the centre of attention.'

Carlisle said nothing.

'If I'm brutally honest,' Nash went on, 'as much as I liked Caroline she could be a bit of a Diva at times. You can only listen to so much, after that it all becomes incredibly boring.'

'What about her husband, Richard Sloane? Did his name ever crop up in your conversation at all?'

'No hardly ever. I knew he worked overseas somewhere and had something to do with children's clothing.' Nash gave him a tiny smile. 'Other than that, she never mentioned his name much.'

'After she left home, did she say where she was living?' Carlisle asked.

'Yes, but I got the distinct impression she wasn't happy there. Reading through the lines she seemed to be struggling to make ends meet.'

Carlisle's mind was racing. Not the best situations to be in under the circumstances, especially if her new boyfriend happened to be a serial killer. Wait a minute, what about the money she'd stolen from her husband?

Carrington had picked up on it too, and was the first to react to it. 'When did the two of you first meet?' the young detective asked.

'After I left school, I worked at an estate agent's office in Middlesbrough. That's when Caroline joined the team.'

'How long ago was this?'

'Goodness me, I would need to think about that one.'

'Six months, a couple of years—'

'At least ten, I'd say,' Nash replied looking flustered.

Carlisle knew there was nothing more to be gained from questioning her further, not today at least. That would come later. All in all, it had been a good morning's work. They'd made some good progress, opened up a few more leads, which was more than either of them had anticipated.

His iPhone pinged in his pocket, and he checked the display:

Meeting tomorrow, 9:30am Sutherland's office!

Chapter
Thirty-Five

The whiff of perfume was stronger than ever that morning. It played on David Carlisle's nostrils, causing him to sneeze. And another thing, glancing around, what the hell was DC Carrington doing in Sutherland's office. Something was afoot, and whatever it was, the young detective's presence had spooked him. He realised she couldn't go on indefinitely being excluded from Sutherland's inner circle. She was far too close to the action for that. There again, it had always been the Acting Superintendent's intentions to keep a tight lid on things. So why the sudden change in policy?

Now pinned to the corkboard behind Sutherland's desk was the artist's impression of the man the police wanted to speak to. The thing was, and it was a delicate issue here, it bore little or no resemblance to Alexander Moore. Just how Jack Mason would deal with it was anyone's guess. No doubt he would have something to say – he usually did. There again, he was the official Senior Investigating Officer appointed to the case and had every right to do so. No, Carlisle thought. He'd been right all along. Moore wasn't the killer and the proof was now staring them in the face.

'I've had a rather interesting conversation with the Head of Crime at Cleveland Police,' Sutherland explained. 'I was informed that Alexander Moore still hasn't reported back for work at the Middlesbrough office.'

Mason's grin broadened as if he'd been thrown an unexpected

lifeline.

'That is an interesting new development, ma'am.'

'Yes, Jack, it struck me as rather odd too.'

Carlisle sensed, rather than saw, that something big was bubbling under the surface. He'd always felt that Moore was a bit of an odd-ball, but never considered him to be the killer. Not so in Mason's case. The SOC photographer had been the Detective Chief Inspector's number one target for weeks now, and he was itching to get his claws into him.

'Well, ma'am,' said Mason. 'I realise the artist's impression bears little or no resemblance to Alexander Moore, but it's not an exact science.'

'True,' Tom Hedley agreed.

'Before we go making irrational decisions, let's be sure we have all the facts at our disposal.' Sutherland looked at Mason, who nodded for her to continue. 'Any accusations aimed at a fellow police officer, particularly one from another force, must be handled with extreme care. Do I make myself clear on that?'

Nods of approval all round.

'If I may make a suggestion,' Mason went on. 'This might be as good place as any to bring DC Carrington up to speed on the latest developments.'

'Thank you, Jack,' Sutherland acknowledged. 'I'm sure we can deal with it later. There's a lot to get through, and we're running short on time.'

The room fell silent again.

One thing was for sure, Carrington could be trusted to keep her mouth shut. As for reading into police politics, that was a different matter.

'Right, then,' said Sutherland. 'It's time we jogged a few memories.' She turned and pointed towards the corkboard. 'This police artist's impression of Caroline Harper's new boyfriend, I want it to go public. Anyone bearing the slightest resemblance to this man must be brought in for questioning.'

Mason raised an eyebrow. 'Everyone, ma'am?'

'Yes, Jack, everyone.' The Acting Superintendent wrote something down in her notebook, and turned to face them again. 'What are we doing about these latest text messages?'

'The tech boys are currently dealing with it,' Mason muttered.

'Good. At least we seem to be doing something right.'

Carlisle was tempted to say something, but he refrained from doing so. It was DC Carrington who broke the tension.

'Sorry to interrupt, ma'am,' the young detective said, 'but at yesterday's interview with the Sunderland estate agent manager, I was informed her boyfriend was driving a McLaren.'

'Yes. I was already aware of that, thank you.'

'I've been doing some digging around,' the young detective went on. 'Sixty-four McLarens were taken out on national hire on the day Caroline Harper was murdered.'

'Wait a minute,' Sutherland said, pushing back in her seat. 'Didn't the barman at the Gold Medal say his car was silver?'

'Yes, he did.'

'We need to look into it, Jack. Let's get the DVLA involved on this one.'

'Leave it with me,' Mason said begrudgingly.

Tom Hedley raised a hand as if to speak. The Forensic scientist, who had said very little throughout the meeting that morning, looked decidedly ill. For weeks now he'd complained about stomach pains. Not the best of situations, thought Carlisle. He should never have attended the meeting in the first place.

'Perhaps we should give Moore the benefit of the doubt,' Hedley said. 'There may be a simple explanation as to why he hasn't shown up for work.'

'True,' Sutherland replied, 'but highly unlikely don't you think?'

'Even so, someone should give him a phone call all the same.'

'What, and take away the element of surprise,' Mason scoffed.

'But we don't have anything to pin on him, Jack.'

'Not yet, we don't,' Mason interrupted.

'Jack's right,' said Sutherland. 'It does look very suspicious.'

Hedley paused in thought. 'But there's nothing to charge him with. It's pure speculation.'

'Perhaps we should obtain a search warrant.' Sutherland corrected herself. 'No Goddammit. He needs to be brought in for questioning.'

Hedley shook his head. 'It's a bit over the top in my opinion. Let's see what this latest artist's impression throws up before we go charging into a fellow police officer's property.'

Sutherland cautioned him with a raised hand. 'We're running out of time, Tom. Besides, this latest incident involving the Chester-le-Station mannequin is causing us another major headache. We know where and when Mary Fowler purchased the designer dress. What we don't know, not even you, is where the hell she is.'

Hedley's head dropped. God he looked awful. He was sweating profusely and continually wincing in pain.

Hedley struggled on. 'We found nothing in Mary Fowler's property that links Moore to these murders, so what has suddenly changed?'

Mason looked sympathetically across at Hedley. 'What about these latest text messages, Tom. We know they were sent locally.'

'Yes, I know, but nothing links them to Alexander Moore.'

'How do you know he hasn't got hold of Caroline's Harper's iPhone?'

'Oh, come on. It's highly unlikely, don't you think?'

Mason put his pen down on top of his notebook, and let out a long sigh. 'But is it? We both checked her flat and agreed a professional clean-up was done on the place. Whoever he is, he knows a hell of a lot about forensics.'

Hedley shook his head. 'But there's nothing to link Moore to any of this. Besides, Mary Fowler's lifestyle doesn't match that of the other two murder victims.'

Mason thought for a moment. 'He's a copper, Tom. Mark my words.'

Carlisle made an entry in his notebook, and circled it with his pen.

He's holding her captive!

'Let's not get carried away,' Sutherland said turning to face Mason. 'This safe house theory, how much water does it hold?'

The Detective Chief Inspector pointed to the police artist's impression again. 'With all due respect, ma'am, I'd like to see what the public's reaction is first. With any luck this new evidence might jog a few memories.'

'What are your views, David?'

Carlisle gave Sutherland a wan smile. 'Whoever he is, Mary Fowler doesn't fit his selection criteria.' Carlisle felt the skin on the back of his neck tighten. 'I've also been giving these text messages a lot of thought lately, and I'm convinced the killer is making a statement.'

'What kind of statement?'

Annoyed that no one had bothered to apply a bit of imagination, Carlisle shuffled awkwardly. 'He seems to be quoting Isaiah 10.3 a lot lately—'

'Yes, I'm well aware of that, but the world is littered with religious fanatics.'

'Tell me,' said Mason. 'What's so special about Isaiah 10.3?'

'What will you do, asks Isaiah, on the day of reckoning, when disaster comes from afar? To whom will you run for help? Where will you leave your riches?'

Sutherland shuddered. 'Yes, that's all well and good, but it still doesn't get us any closer to finding out this young woman's whereabouts.'

Hedley turned sharply to face Sutherland. 'Unless it's a threat, and it does sound as if he's trying to tell us something.'

'He is, Tom,' Carlisle insisted. 'And wasn't that what we set out to do in the first place — crush his ego and force him out into the open?'

'We did indeed.'

'Let's not get carried away here,' the Acting Superintendent interrupted. 'These text messages are all part of his mind games in my opinion.'

'I agree,' said Hedley, 'but why is he channelling them all towards David?'

Carlisle drew in an intake of air. He'd heard enough.

'He's posing me the question, Tom. 'Do I have this woman, or not?'

'Find Alexander Moore and we find Mary Fowler,' Mason insisted.

The inner circle was wobbling.

Sutherland closed her notebook, and leaned back heavily in her seat. The Acting Superintendent was no fool, and understood the situation perfectly. Well, so be it. There was a lot to think about, and so many avenues to investigate. The longer this went on the more they were playing into the killer's hands. Even Sutherland knew that much.

'It's a tough call,' the Acting Superintendent said thoughtfully. 'Which begs the question, if it isn't Alexander Moore, then we've grossly underestimated the killer's cunning.'

Mason glanced at the others for reassurance. 'Let's face it, Moore's a SOC photographer and close to the action in every respect. What better job to be in if you wanted to capture your handiwork on camera?'

'That's a very salient point,' said Hedley.

'I know this latest police artist's impression bears little or no resemblance to Moore,' Mason went on, 'but what if this estate agent manager has got it wrong?'

Sutherland cocked her head to one side, an inquisitive look.

'At least that's an honest answer, Jack.'

Wrong person to ask, thought Carlisle.

'You've said all along we need all the facts at our disposal, ma'am.'

Sutherland smiled, her ego enhanced. 'Very true, Jack.'

'It's not Moore,' Carlisle interrupted, 'but I can agree with Jack's sentiments. If we do bring Moore in for questioning, we'll need to retain the element of surprise.'

Sutherland thought for a moment.

'We'll need search warrants, of course.'

Mason's expression suddenly brightened. 'Leave that with me, ma'am.'

Sutherland consulted her notes before turning to face Carlisle again. 'This informant you've reached out to. Is he trustworthy?'

'You mean the Seaham drug dealer, ma'am.'

'Yes,' Sutherland nodded.

Carlisle thought for a moment. 'His information is usually pretty reliable, yes. But I'll need to do some digging around first.'

'Apart from Detective Carrington, is there anything else we can assist you with?'

'There is one other thing, ma'am.' Carlisle said nervously clearing his throat. 'It's my understanding the Peterlee police currently have my contact under surveillance for drugs trafficking. I realise the implications, but what are the chances of them easing off over the next couple of days?'

'What!' Mason shrieked. 'And trust a scumbag drugs dealer.'

Sutherland's eyebrows raised a fraction. 'Remind me of your informant's connection with the Sawyer case?'

'Up until the time of Cheryl Sawyer's murder, he was looking after her welfare. He knew the people she mixed with, her contacts, her friends, and the places she regularly frequented.'

'In other words, he was providing her with drugs,' Sutherland frowned.

'Yes, ma'am, he was.'

'Is he a reliable source, or is he just another drugs pusher looking for favours?'

'No, ma'am, my informant's information is usually pretty reliable.'

'We're running out of time I fear, and I'm left with no other options.' Sutherland thought for a moment, but not for long. 'I can't promise you anything, but I'll see what I can do. If as you say your source of information is reliable, I may be able to pull a few strings. There again, if it's not Alexander Moore and Mary Fowler's still out there, I can't see them refusing us a second crack of the whip. Tell me,' Sutherland said. 'How many more days do you need?'

'I'll have my answer by tomorrow afternoon, ma'am.'

Carlisle braced himself, as he caught the look of determination on Jack Mason's face.

Oh dear, he thought, could he trust Kurt Gillespie?

Ch⋄pter Thirty-Six

There were no other cars in sight when DC Carrington pulled her unmarked pool car onto the kerb that evening – except one, a blue Audi A4.

'We're being followed,' Carrington said, staring anxiously into her rear mirror.

'Can you be sure?'

'Unless I'm mistaken, a blue Audi has been tailing us ever since leaving Boldon Colliery.'

Carlisle's heart sank as he spotted a faint plume of smoke coming from the stationary Audi's exhaust. Its driver, masked by the car's sun visor and not more than thirty feet away, sat motionless at the wheel.

'Head towards the Souter Lighthouse and let's see what develops,' Carlisle insisted.

They were not alone when Carrington drove north along the coast road towards South Shields. Sure enough, the blue Audi was fast gaining distance. On reaching Marsden Primary School, Carrington put her foot down and Carlisle felt his head hit the headrest. He checked the speedometer – ninety-six and climbing. No matter how much the young detective altered her speed, the blue Audi continued to keep up with them. Suddenly the unmarked pool car screeched to a halt on the slippery tarmac.

Still there!

Fingers of one hand drumming the steering wheel, Carrington

used the other to punch the Audi's registration number to the Motor Insurance database (MIT). Whoever was shadowing them had surely blown their cover. Of that much he was certain. Seconds later the display screen lit up informing them the blue Audi A4 was registered with the Northumbria Police force.

'Let's not rush it,' Carlisle said, pointing the way ahead. 'Just before Gypsies Green there's a sharp right turn-off which leads to a car park overlooking the promenade. If this is who I suspect it is, we'll soon find out.'

'I know it,' Carrington nervously replied.

Now at a snail's pace, the young detective glanced over her shoulder as if to check her surroundings. Not twenty metres away, the blue Audi still seemed reluctant to budge. Could this be the killer? Part of him hoped it could. Then, just as the road dropped away from them, he saw a white wisp of smoke from the Audi's exhaust.

It was on the move again.

Who are you? Carlisle whispered to himself.

From where he now sat, Carlisle had clear unobstructed views of the approach road. The seafront was empty. Not many cars in the car park either. This was getting harder, he thought. Working undercover had its rewards, but this was an entirely new ball game. A serial killer was at large and hell-bent on making his life a misery. He'd been in some tight corners before, but nothing compared to this. The only thing in his favour, if there was such a thing, was that Carrington was wired to central control.

Despite the warm comfort of the undercover pool car, the wait seemed to go on forever. Then, just as they'd both given up on it, the blue Audi reappeared. It was clear they weren't dealing with a criminal genius here, but the stranger seemed to have all the advantages.

'What now?' Carrington said, as a hand appeared out through the Audi's side window and grabbed a ticket from the machine. Seconds later the car slid effortlessly into one of the parking spaces opposite.

'Let's not rush into it.'

'Anything but this,' Carrington shuddered.

The moment the profiler stepped out onto the car park, the ground underfoot made a crunching sound. Covered in a fine layer of sand, it felt as though he was walking on icing sugar. This wasn't something that came often in his line of work, but he had a bad feeling about all of this. Even the steely North Sea seemed angry.

What to do next?

Fear of the dark was one thing, but posting your victim's severed finger through your letterbox another. If that wasn't bad enough, his nerves had reached saturation point with all the text-messages he'd received lately. How much more could he take? Where would it all end? Then, out of the corner of his eye he caught movement. It wasn't much, but it was enough to send his heart racing again. From where he now stood the blue Audi's side window had opened slightly, just enough to see inside. Wearing dark sunglasses across a predatory face, the occupant was a dead ringer for one of his favourite film actors, Harvey Keitel.

'What now?' Carrington asked in a faltering voice.

'Do you recognise him?'

'No. I've never seen him before.'

'I can't be sure, but his face looks familiar.'

Carrington sighed. 'That's a relief. So it's you and not me he's after.'

'How did you work that one out?'

'Cos,' Carrington shrugged, 'I'm the only police woman around here.'

Carlisle felt a sudden adrenalin surge. Not the best of situations to be in, but he'd been in much worse. Don't rush it, he thought. Whoever he was, he was making a bad job of it.

Then, just as a young couple out walking their dog returned to their car, the stranger made his move. Sometimes it was safer to keep your distance, bide your time and wait for the right moment.

'Let's walk,' Carlisle said, pointing the way ahead.

'And where to for Christ's sake!'

'Civilisation—'

The Sand Dancer, a popular bar with mixed reviews, wasn't exactly at its busiest this time of day. After ordering drinks they found a quiet corner seat close to the exit door. At least they felt safe here, even if things looked pretty grim.

They did not have to wait long. Sure enough the stranger appeared in the doorway. Dressed in a black bomber jacket, scuffed trainers, and a pair of black corduroy trousers, his eyes scoured the room as a predator seeking its next meal. Then, as if to attract attention towards him he tossed a red beanie hat onto the nearest table and scooted up a seat. Of course, Carlisle gasped. It was the man with the sticky-out ears – the tall stranger his father had got into conversation with during their weekend fishing trip in Northumberland. The question was, and it wasn't a hard one at that, which side of the fence was he sitting on?

'What now?' Carrington asked.

'I need a pee—'

'Don't be long,' she replied anxiously.

His nerves all on edge he made a bee-line for the toilet door. Once inside, he found an empty cubical and locked the door behind him. He heard a tap running, followed by the hum of the hand dryer machine.

'You in there, Carlisle?' the stranger's voice boomed out.

'Who are you?'

'No names,' the stranger replied. 'I'm working for Jack Mason, and that's as much as you need to know.'

Carlisle gathered his wits. 'Yeah, but who are you?'

'Stay alert, you're being followed.'

He heard the main toilet door slam shut behind him, then silence.

Moments later, Carlisle stared down at the stranger's half-finished

coffee and blew out a long sigh of relief. It had been years since
he felt this traumatised. His hands were shaking, and his legs felt as
though they were about to give way on him at any moment.

'You all right,' asked Carrington.

'I think so. Where is he?'

'He left a few minutes ago,' she replied. 'Who the hell was he?'

'He was one of Jack Mason's cronies apparently.'

'Christ! He scared the living daylights out of me.'

'Me too,' Carlisle admitted.

Carrington fiddled with her earpiece. 'Are you sure you're all
right?'

'Yeah, a little shaken that's all.'

'You look like you've seen a ghost.'

'I thought I had back there.'

Carrington's eyes narrowed, the look of concern still showing.
'Whoever he was he looked a real nasty piece of work.'

Carlisle reflected for a moment. 'You never mentioned anything
to me about a round-the-clock protection team. I thought it was
just you and me?'

'Spare me a thought,' she sighed. 'I'm a police officer with secrets.'

Carlisle forced a grin.

'One man's darkness is another man's daylight, I guess.'

'What the hell are you on about now,' she groaned. 'This close
protection malarkey has got me all on edge.'

'I thought you were wired?'

Carrington swallowed hard.

'I am.'

'Well then!'

There followed a moment of hesitation, a gathering of wits.
'The truth is I haven't the foggiest when to activate the *'Push to
Talk'* button on my communications headset. Apart from relaying
my movements, the last thing we need is to bombard control with
unnecessary panic.'

He really liked her. Not long out of close protection training, Carrington had a bright future ahead of her. That aside, they got on well together even though his freedom had been severely compromised. When the moment of danger arose, no doubt the young detective would react accordingly. It wasn't the healthiest of situations to be in, he knew that, but at least he felt some comfort in her presence.

'Right then, what now?'

Carrington puffed out her cheeks and stared at him in bemusement. 'I've no idea. You're the one who's calling all the shots.'

Not true, he thought.

Ch.pter Thirty-Seven

It was Sunday morning. David Carlisle was relaxing at home reading the sports supplement and checking up on Saturday's football results – a favourite *JJ Cale* track playing in the background. Carlisle's home was his fortress nowadays, and once inside he felt safe. An awful lot of water had passed under the bridge since the severed finger incident and with it a lot of apprehension. The thought that a serial killer was able to move in and out of his life at will, had unsettled him. Yes, he felt angry by it all, but there wasn't a lot he could do about it. It was the not knowing he feared most, the not knowing what was lurking in the shadows.

He heard the front doorbell ring, but chose to ignore it. Probably another door-to-door salesman, he thought. Curious, he peered through the chink in the window blinds and out on the street. No it couldn't be, surely not. What the hell was George Fowler doing standing on his front doorstep at nine o'clock in the morning? This was no social call; the anxious look on this face told him that.

Seconds later, he opened the front door.

'I thought we might have a chat,' said Fowler.

'It's Sunday, it's my day off. If this is about your wife, you really must to talk to the police about it.'

'I know it's inconvenient, but you really need to hear me out.'

The size-nine shoe already planted over the door threshold told him the matter was already decided. Fowler was desperate, and whatever it was that was eating away at him at nine o'clock that morning, he was surely about to find out.

'What the hell do you want?' Carlisle demanded.

'It's the police, I can't trust them anymore.'

'Meaning?'

'I'm convinced they've tapped into my private telephone calls. Not only that,' Fowler protested, 'whenever I leave the house I'm convinced I'm being followed.'

'Look,' said Carlisle, furious at caving in so readily and allowing him to penetrate his defences, 'I've absolutely no idea what you're talking about. Besides, everyone's a suspect until they've been cleared from a murder investigation. That's the law of the land, I'm afraid.'

Carlisle removed some magazines from one of the armchairs, and Fowler sat down. They talked a while, about his wife's disappearance along with a few other grievances that Fowler felt necessary to discuss. By the time they'd finished talking, the profiler was still none the wiser. But what was the real purpose of Fowler's visit here today? What was he up to? Then it began to dawn on him: what if he was implicated in his wife's disappearance? He could have been, and nobody had said he wasn't.

His iPhone buzzed in his pocket, and he nervously switched the thing off.

'So what are your concerns?'

'It's Jack Mason. The man's an utter arsehole.'

Nothing changed there then, thought Carlisle.

'And what makes you say that?'

'Let's not go there,' Fowler said jabbing a finger in the air. 'I have a rather interesting proposition to put to you.'

'Oh! And what might that be?'

'Ever thought of working for me?'

'What? Me?'

'I've never been more serious.'

Carlisle hesitated, taken aback. 'And do what exactly?'

'Name your price.'

'It's not about money. It's more about the principle.'

Carlisle gripped his mug of coffee in both hands, and sat dumbfounded for a moment. Not a good move, he thought. Even Fowler knew he couldn't switch his allegiances at the drop of a hat. So, he asked, what the hell is he playing at? Besides, unsolved missing person files were never closed. Not until they'd been resolved that is. He would need to tread carefully, find out what Fowler was really up to.

'I hear you've put up a reward for information leading to your wife's safe return.'

Fowler nodded glumly. 'I was merely trying to heighten public awareness.'

'But isn't that a job for the police?'

'To hell with the police,' Fowler insisted.

'Is that a wise move, do you think? By you going public it's making it a lot harder for them to carry out their investigations.'

'What, those fools?' Fowler scoffed, in his plummy, posh accent. 'Publicity is a powerful tool, Mr Carlisle. It gets you into places where other people can't go. Besides, the press have been extremely helpful towards my cause.'

No doubt, Carlisle thought. *It's what sells newspapers.*

'But it's not the right way to go about it.'

'Something has to be done.'

'True, but that's a job for DCI Mason, surely—'

'*Mason!*' Fowler shrieked. 'The man's a blackguard. The longer this goes on, the less chance we have of getting my Mary back.'

Indeed, Jack Mason was a bully, and a good one at that. What's more, he certainly knew how to rub people up the wrong way. Maybe there was a hint of truth in what Fowler was telling him after all. There again, maybe not. The trouble was, and he wasn't treating it lightly, what if Fowler's wife had already fallen foul of the killer?

'These things take time, it's—'

'I can't just sit around all day twiddling my thumbs,' Fowler interrupted. 'We're running out of time, everyone knows that.'

Carlisle eased back in his seat and tried to get his head round it all.

'The police suspect your wife may have fallen into the hands of a very dangerous predator, Mr Fowler. By you going public and offering a reward for your wife's safe return, you've now put a price on her head. If it is the same man I'm thinking of, he may feel insulted by the meagre sum of money you're offering. What then? These are extremely dangerous people to deal with, and they thrive on the publicity it brings.'

'If I didn't have a sense of humour, I would probably burst out crying,' Fowler laughed. 'Besides, how can you be certain Mary is being held captive? It's pure speculation – another red herring put there by the police to suit their incompetence.'

'Really, and you expect me to believe that too?'

'Well,' Fowler muttered, 'that's what my lawyers are advising.'

'Let's hope your wife isn't being held by the same narcissistic maniac who killed Cheryl Sawyer and Caroline Harper. If she is, then he likes nothing more than to read about his exploits in the daily tabloids. Your wife's safe return needs to be handled very carefully, especially if we're to stave off the inevitable.'

Fowler's head suddenly dropped.

'Do you really believe she's being held captive?'

Carlisle mulled over the facts. This conversation was going nowhere, and he needed to put a stop to it. He could understand Fowler's frustrations, but this was ridiculous.

'We're all afraid of the dark. You only have to look out of your windows at night to wonder who's out there. It's the not knowing we fear most. And yet, the moment we draw the curtains shut we suddenly feel safe again.'

Carlisle put his mug down, and leaned over to turn the music down.

'But here we are, Mr Carlisle, left facing another day.'

'But nightfall fast approaches and soon it will be dark again.' Carlisle paused for effect. 'That's my point. By you going public you may have stirred up a whole lot of trouble for yourself.'

He caught the reluctant nod of acceptance.

'Will he kill her, do you think?'

'I'm not God. And, may I add, neither am I the police.'

'But you're a profiler, goddammit. Isn't that what you're supposed to do – read into other people's minds?' Fowler was desperate, and he caught the look of fear in his eyes. 'Tell me,' Fowler insisted, 'where is she?'

Good question. If only Fowler knew what being threatened by a serial killer was really like, perhaps he may have worded his statement differently. Somewhere in the confused haze lay the truth, but there was still a great deal to digest.

'This so called bolthole your wife regularly escapes to in Durham. Who are her friends?'

'I'm, umm—'

'Just answer my question, Mr Fowler.'

'I've never met them. Why do you want to know?'

Carlisle's next question was more direct. 'Tell me about this private detective you hired. Does he have a name?'

'I couldn't possibly tell you that, and you know it.'

'Oh, come on.' Carlisle nearly burst out laughing. 'He must have told you something, surely.'

'If you must know, Mary was seeing another man at the time.' Fowler's face suddenly darkened. 'He was younger than me by all accounts.'

That certainly never came across in Fowler's interview.

'Does he happen to drive an expensive car?'

'How did you know that?'

'Is it silver by any chance?'

'Yes. Why?'

'You see, Mr Fowler, we know more about your wife's disappearance than we care to let on.'

Fowler looked at him dubiously, and gave him a *forget-it* look.

'I have a good network of people working for me, people in high places. They tell me things. But you being a private investigator will understand the implications of sharing such information with anyone.'

Carlisle dug his heels in.

'Here's my problem. Jack Mason's a copper, the man in charge of a murder investigation. For me to come and work for you would be a total conflict of interests. Do you see where I'm coming from?'

There followed an awkward exchange of glances.

'I'm desperate, Mr Carlisle, and I'm willing to pay good money for your services.'

'It's not that straightforward.'

'But—'

'I appreciate your concerns, but two people have already been murdered and now your wife has gone missing. It's not looking good, is it?'

'No, not when you put it like that.'

Carlisle put his hands up in mock surrender. 'Now you understand my dilemma.'

'Perhaps a fifty grand deposit might change your mind?'

Carlisle stopped dead in his tracks.

In a novel way, he felt sorry for the man. He should have been more forceful, done things differently. He hadn't, and now Carlisle was desperate to get rid of him. Fowler couldn't be trusted, he was capricious and that was the crux of the matter.

When he did eventually leave, only after much persuasion, he'd barely turned the corner before Carlisle rang Jack Mason.

Chapter Thirty-Eight

After endless hours spent trudging the streets of Middlesbrough, the team's focus of attention had now shifted to North Yorkshire. Including Jack Mason, there were four detectives assembled in Briefing Room 2 that morning. Working on a tip off, they had every reason to believe that Alexander Moore had recently booked into a B & B near York city centre. What he was doing there, and why, they had no idea. The fact that he'd chosen York, of all places, had sent shockwaves amongst the backroom senior staff.

Mason stood hunched in front of the whiteboard gathering his thoughts. Shoulder to shoulder his three most trusted detectives were running back over their final preparations. Earlier that morning, having contacted the North Yorkshire Police, they learned that two teams, armed with search warrants, had carried out simultaneous raids on nearby properties. Nothing had come of it.

It wasn't a great plan, but Jack Mason had decided to travel south to York in two unmarked pool cars that morning. It was moments like these, and there had been many in his long distinguished career, when he wished he'd taken a desk job. Plenty of other officers of his rank had, and had gone on to live cushy lifestyles by all accounts. Some had regretted it though, saying hands-on policing wasn't the same anymore. Sat behind a desk pushing paperwork around all day wasn't Mason's idea of policing. He preferred to get involved, down at street level, in amongst the real hardened criminals.

'OK,' said Mason, eager to get going. 'The day before Caroline Harper was murdered she checks out of the Nova Hotel in York, and was last seen leaving the B & S Supermarket in Houghton-le-Spring. Forensics has thrown up little in the way of clues. We know he wore rubber gloves and some sort of protective overalls that night, so there's little in the way of DNA or fingerprints. If she never returned to her Gateshead flat, there's every possibility he was holding her here somewhere.' Mason pointed to a large map of Durham now covered with dozens of marker pins and post-it notes. 'The distance between Houghton-le-Spring and Windy Nook is thirteen miles and fewer than thirty to Middlesbrough.'

DS Savage, a tall man, with a thick Geordie accent, was eager to make his point. 'We know Moore was one of the first to arrive at the crime scene that night, so he had plenty of time to get rid of any evidence he may have felt necessary.'

'Rob's right,' said DS Holt. 'SOC photographers are no different from the rest of the team. Had he contaminated the Coldwell Lane crime scene in any way, he would have automatically been eliminated from our enquiries.'

Mason made a little grimace. 'In other words, he had a free role that night.'

'Best of both worlds, eh,' DC Manley shrugged.

The four detectives stood motionless, staring at the timeline chart.

'Let's put that to one side for a moment and spend a few more minutes on the corner shop CCTV footage,' Mason continued. 'We know the quality's crap, but it fits Moore's description perfectly – same height, same build, and same nonchalant swagger in his step. What else do we know about him?'

'He knew exactly where to find David Carlisle's house,' DS Holt acknowledged.

Manley annoyingly popped another humbug into his mouth, but Mason let it go. Wearing his trademark brown corduroy jacket, fawn shirt and green flowery patterned tie, it was obvious why

Harry Manley had never progressed further in the ranks. Not that it bothered him. Manley was a plodder, a down to earth copper who cared far more about his wife and kids than he did any promotion.

'This police artist's impression is a bit of a bummer, boss.'

'It's all we have to work with, Harry. I certainly wouldn't hang my hat on it.'

'Yeah, but it looks nowt like Alexander Moore.'

The Detective Constable gave the artist's impression of Caroline Harper's boyfriend a second glance. 'What about the barman at the Gold Medal pub, how did he describe him?'

Mason checked his notes before turning to face them again. 'Tall skinny chap, with long swept back black hair. Described as thirtyish, a professional of some sorts and not short of a bob or two by all accounts.'

'Yeah, but Moore doesn't have that kind of money,' Manley shrugged.

'I realise that, but he does have a Yorkshire accent.'

'That's true.'

'So what's he doing in York,' said Holt. 'Doesn't that strike you as odd, Harry?'

'Nah, not if he's from Middlesbrough it doesn't. York's just down the road from there. Mind, he could have something to do with this Mary Fowler's disappearance.'

'What makes you say that?' asked Holt.

Manley smiled thinly. 'It's my copper's instinct.'

'Right, then,' said Mason. 'What do we know about Cheryl Sawyer's last known movements?'

Savage looked down at his notepad. 'Six years ago, she buggered off from her husband in Redcar and set up a temporary home in Wingate. After a night out on the town, the following morning she was found dead in a skip overlooking Seaham Harbour.'

'What about witness statements?'

Holt stared at the map, and picked up on the story again. 'The last known sighting of her was outside a pub in Church Street. At eleven-thirty-eight, she was caught on CCTV camera talking to a white male. Described as medium build, six two, he was wearing a black hoodie, blue jeans and white Nike trainers. Before leaving he hands her a small package which was later found to be class 'A' drugs. Sawyer was a known addict, so the rest of the story kind of fits.'

'Who attended the crime scene that morning?' Mason asked.

Holt referred to his notes again. 'Alexander Moore,' the sergeant replied. 'He was down as the duty SOC photographer.'

'Yeah, and more drugs were found in her pockets,' said Savage.

'So he could have conveniently planted them on her,' Mason interrupted.

Savage stared at the timeline again, the cop inside him speaking. 'The Cleveland police always believed her death was drugs related. Forensic toxicology tests showed traces of heroin were found in her blood, enough to suggest she was spaced out of her mind that night. The guy who handed her the drugs, a local low life called Thomas Parker, was later remanded in custody. His alibi checked out, as did his DNA and clothing. In other words, they couldn't pin a damn thing on him.'

'Easy pickings,' Manley shrugged.

'At least heroin wasn't the cause of death, Harry.'

'What about alcohol?' Mason asked.

'Found present in her urine, boss,' Savage replied.

'Does it say how much?'

'Four or five drinks, not enough to cause her to pass out.'

'She was obviously still conscious before he struck her over the head?'

'Yeah, and we know she never put up a struggle,' Holt acknowledged.

Manley turned to face them. 'What if he's the squeamish type?'

Savage pointed to the timeline again. 'It's strange how the duty

SOC photographer happened to be Alexander Moore that morning – he couldn't have planned it any better had he tried.'

Mason smelt a rat. 'How far is the pub from where her body was found?'

'It's just over a quarter of a mile, boss.'

Savage ran an index finger along the route, as the others moved in closer.

'And yet both victims were killed by the same man,' said Mason thoughtfully. 'What are the chances of him not being a copper?'

'Now I see where you're coming from,' Savage said, shuffling awkwardly.

Manley screwed his face up. 'Hold on a minute, how come this wasn't picked up during Caroline Harper's murder investigation? Let's face it, the guy was a bit of an odd-ball and seldom mixed with any of us.'

'What are you suggesting, Harry?' said Savage.

'Well, didn't the profiler say the killer would be a loner who was familiar with both kill zones?'

'Yeah, but I still don't get where you're coming from.'

'Think about it,' said Manley sucking hard on another humbug. 'Moore comes from Middlesbrough and worked as a SOC photographer covering the Seaham area. Then, more by luck than judgement he moves up to Gateshead on temporary assignment. And guess where Caroline Harper's body turned up?'

Mason's face lit up. 'And first to attend both crime scenes may I add!'

'It's got to be him,' said Savage.

'There's only one way to find out, let's bring him in and see what he has to say for himself.'

Chapter
Thirty-Nine

Twenty minutes later two unmarked pool cars sped south, towards York. It had rained off and on ever since leaving Gateshead that morning, and now it was absolutely chucking it down. Jack Mason and DS Holt in the lead vehicle, DS Savage and Harry Manley bringing up the rear; the roads were busy. Most of his journey was spent listening to Radio 3, Bach Concerto written for two violins, played by Nigel Kennedy and Fionnuala Hunt – whoever she was? Not that Mason was into classical music. He wasn't, but it seemed to suit his melancholy mood that morning.

As the countryside flashed by in a haze of lorry spray, Jack Mason began to muse over his daughter's latest business venture. It was funny how daft thoughts came into his head. Perhaps it was his cynicism. Selling personalised T-shirts on the internet wasn't exactly his idea of earning a living. At least she was making a go of it though, but he knew she was strapped for cash. Even so, who in their right mind would trawl through the internet looking for T-shirts when there were dozens of back street shops selling them at knock down prices? Still, if it kept his daughter occupied before the baby was due it wasn't a bad idea. T-shirts, he smiled. Only his daughter could have thought of that.

Clifton in York was busy. It was race week, and every B & B in town was full. Mason sat for a moment, soaking in the atmosphere and waiting for the traffic lights to change. Opposite, a nosy traffic warden, a tall woman, with a large mop of blonde hair crammed beneath a hat three sizes too small for her head, peered inquisitively across at them. He gave her the evil eye. Not that she knew who he was, but she'd obviously smelt trouble.

As the traffic lights turned green, they swung right and down into Bootham Terrace. Close to the River Ouse, this was prime bed and breakfast territory – soft cotton sheets, full English breakfasts, and double price during race week. It was ideal, Mason thought. On one side of the road stood a long row of terraced townhouses; the other was lined by tall trees behind which sat a large railway embankment.

'Not many vacancies, George,' Mason pointed out.

'Not during race week, it's very popular.'

'What time's kick-off?'

'First race is two o'clock.'

'You a racing man, George?'

'I like the odd punt on the Grand National now and then, but it's not my thing. What about you, boss?'

'Nah, gambling's a mug's game. I'd rather have a pint with the lads watching a good game of rugby. Mind, I still fancy the odd lottery ticket now and then.'

'Still living the dream,' Holt chuckled.

The moment they spotted the guest house, the Detective Sergeant pulled over and onto the kerb. A quick check in his mirror confirmed Harry Manley had done the same. Now stationary, the DC's undercover pool car was not more than twenty feet behind him.

'Right then,' Mason said, 'let's see if our man's at home.'

Stepping out of the pool car, Mason gazed at the buildings opposite. Built on four levels, the long row of terraced townhouses looked Victorian. Why anyone would want to run a bed and breakfast business was beyond him. Some people did though, and they were obviously making a good living out of it. He peered in through the glazed panel glass, and checked for signs of life. He could see the hallway ran the entire length of the building. To his left was a steep flight of stairs, and three doors in a row on his right. The first was obviously a reception room, the other two he took to be the kitchen and utility room. What the hell, he cursed. At this moment in time he had more important things to think about.

He rang the doorbell.

Wearing a crumpled checked white shirt, blue jeans and a battered pair of old slippers, the look of the man who answered was curiosity. 'Sorry gentlemen, we're full.'

'DCI Mason, Northumbria police. May we come in please?'

Now joined by DS Holt and DS Savage, the proprietor gave their warrant cards a cursory glance over and ushered them inside. Standing there, Mason swore he heard a pump running – a muffled noise coming from somewhere towards the back of the building.

'Do you have an Alexander Moore staying with you?' Mason asked.

'Yes. Room Two.'

'Is he in?'

'Yes. He has a taxi booked for twelve.'

Mason cocked his head to one side. 'And where to may I ask?'

'It's race week, Inspector. It's our busiest week of the year,' the proprietor insisted.

'I see—'

'Shall I get him for you?'

'No, that won't be necessary.' Mason showed him the search warrant, and pointed to the staircase. 'I'll speak to him myself.'

'Turn right at the top of the first landing, second door on your left.'

A short sharp rap on the bedroom door was enough. Even so, it still took an eternity before the occupant answered it. It was the surprised look on Alexander Moore's face that caught Mason's sense of humour. It was priceless.

'Jack Mason,' Moore grinned. 'It's nice to see you. What the hell are you doing here?'

'I'm certainly not here for the racing, my friend.'

'Oh?'

Mason held back for a moment and focused on the task in hand. 'We have every reason to believe that you were involved in the murder of Caroline Harper.'

'For God's sake, Jack. I'm in a hurry, just cut out the bullshit.'

'This isn't a wind-up.'

'Oh! What then?'

'You do not have to say anything. But, it may harm your defence if—'

'Tell me you're joking.'

'I've never been more serious,' Mason replied. 'If you'd care to accompany me downstairs, there's a pool car waiting to take you back to Gateshead police station.'

Moore protested, but knew he was wasting his time. Angry, he opened the wardrobe door and flung a few things on the bed.

'Mind if I pack?'

'Of course not, take your time, but I'll need your mobile phone first.'

Twenty minutes later and they were ready to head north again, back up the A19. Much as Mason hated escorting prisoners back to police stations, he was more than pleased with the end result. Sat in the back seat of DC Manley's unmarked pool car, his suspect's look was grim. Not everyone gave in that easily, some liked to put up a fight. Whatever Moore's reasons for killing these women were, the SOC photographer seemed resigned to his fate.

Mason's iPhone buzzed in his pocket, but he let it ring a few more seconds before answering it. Checking the display, Acting Superintendent Sutherland's name popped up on the screen. He switched to loud speaker.

'Where are you now?' Sutherland asked.

'We're on our way back to Gateshead, ma'am.'

'And Alexander Moore—'

'Handcuffed and sitting in the back of DC Manley's pool vehicle.' Sutherland's voice sounded unusually guarded.

'There's been a new development, Jack.'

'Oh!'

'May I ask if your suspect has used his mobile phone within the last five minutes... rang his solicitor?'

'No ma'am, he hasn't. I confiscated his mobile twenty minutes ago. It was the first thing I took away from him.'

'I'm sorry to inform you, but David Carlisle's just received another threatening text message from you know who.'

'Tell me you're joking!'

'Sorry, Jack.'

'What time was this?'

'Not more than five minutes ago.' There was another long pause. 'Carlisle's with DC Carrington as we speak.'

'I thought Caroline Harper's iPhone was crushed under a high-speed train after it had been superglued to the East Coast main line?'

'It was, but it seems he's using another pay as you go.'

'How do we know it's him?'

'Isaiah 10.3, only the inner circle would know he uses that!'

'Fucking typical,' Mason cursed, crashing his fist into the dash panel.

Chapter Forty

Fifty miles north, and accompanied by DC Carrington, David Carlisle's investigations had taken them to an accountant's office in Middlesbrough. Things hadn't gone according to plan, and Lance Wynn, the man they wanted to interview, was away on company business. At this stage in their investigations, whilst each and every lead was being dealt with separately, Carlisle was more interested in the geographical profile of their suspect. Understanding the killer's movements was critical in understanding where Mary Fowler might be being held.

The truth was, at nine o'clock that morning DC Carrington looked anything but an undercover detective involved in a major murder enquiry. Wearing a black knee length coat, black leather boots, and a black leather handbag slung loosely over her left shoulder, she was more turned out for a funeral than anything else. Not that it bothered him. If anything, Carlisle was more concerned about the backlog of new business that had suddenly built up back at his South Shields office. Although in regular contact with his business partner, Jane Collins, at least a dozen new case files were waiting for him. Never a dull moment, he cursed.

Sometimes, David Carlisle wondered where all the money came from. Inside a plush foyer with high ceilings, marble floors and walls covered in expensive oak panelling, he stood overwhelmed by it all. Directly opposite the glass entrance doors, above the reception desk, an elegant business sign read:

TIMOTHY EVANS CHARTERED ACCOUNTANTS

'A bit over the top, don't you think,' Carlisle shrugged.

Carrington fluttered her long eyelashes. 'I was thinking the same myself.'

'Tell me,' he asked. 'Has Lance Wynn got any previous?'

'Apart from a sus for domestic violence eight years ago, that's about all I'm afraid.'

'It sounds like he got into an argument with a girlfriend?'

The young detective gave him a quizzical look. 'He probably did as the charges were quickly dropped.'

The trouble was they were working on a tip off given by a man who didn't exactly have a credible CV himself. Although Kurt Gillespie could be irritating at times, his information was usually pretty reliable. In most cases police officers viewed informants as vermin, and refused to work with them at any cost. But Carlisle felt differently; besides, Mary Fowler's sudden disappearance had left them with little alternative. They were running out of time and leads by the sound of things.

The man who checked in at the reception desk was in his mid-fifties. He wasn't a tall man, but he exuded confidence from every pore in his skin. Impeccably dressed in an immaculate handmade blue pin-striped suit, white shirt, gold cufflinks, and red silk tie, he looked every bit the CEO of the organisation. Impressed with his professionalism, they were ushered into a side room and offered coffee and biscuits.

'So, you're here to see Lance Wynn?' Timothy Evans, the company CEO, asked.

'Yes we are, but we understand he's away on company business,' said Carrington.

'Lance has very serious family issues at the moment, I'm afraid.' Evans wrinkled his brow. 'It's his mother, I'm afraid. She suffers from chronic kidney disease, and he takes her for regular dialysis treatment every day.'

Carlisle just sat there and said nothing.

'Perhaps I can help?' said Evans.

'I'm afraid not,' Carrington replied. 'There are a number of important questions that we need to put to Mr Wynn. Do you know where he can be contacted?'

'I take it this is official?'

'Yes, it is.'

Carlisle slid his business card towards the CEO, and Evans picked it up.

'A private investigator – may I ask in what capacity you're working for the police?'

'This is a murder enquiry,' DC Carrington interrupted. 'Mr Carlisle is a Criminal Profiler and he's been drafted in to assist with our enquiries.'

There followed an awkward silence, a gathering of thoughts.

'Murder,' Evans replied as if somewhat taken aback. 'How can I be of assistance?'

'Lance Wynn, how would you best describe him?'

Coffee arrived, brought in on a small silver tray by a tall, blonde secretary with long legs and beautifully manicured fingernails. Not bad a looker either, Carlisle thought. It was then he caught the look of scorn on Carrington's face. She wasn't impressed.

Evans gently stroked a strong jawline, searching for things to say. 'What do we know about Lance? Well he's reliable and a very charming person to get along with. You would hardly notice he worked here at times, unlike some of the others who work here.'

'When did he first join your company?'

'Lance has been with us almost ten years now,' Evans fidgeted awkwardly. 'He's the conscientious type, quiet, unassuming, likes to keep himself to himself. Mind, he's never late for work and seldom takes time off.'

'Does he live local?'

'Acklam. It's very convenient. Not like some of us who have to travel miles to work every day.' Full of contradictions, Evans snapped his biscuit in half and popped it into his mouth. 'I believe he went to Acklam Grange School before studying at Teesside University. You could say he's a local boy made good.'

'What was he studying?'

'Forensic Science, more your line of business I would have thought.'

Carlisle nearly choked on his drink. *'Forensic science—'*

'Yes, but Lance is more into number crunching nowadays. He would never have made a chemist in my opinion.'

Carlisle noticed a hint of a smile pass over Evans's taciturn features.

'He's married, I presume?'

'No. Lance lives alone.'

'Is he in a relationship at all?'

'Definitely not. Lance is a keen photographer.' Evans began to elaborate. 'That's where he spends most of his spare time. The man's obsessed. If you don't mind me saying so, he has quite a talent for it. Not that I'm an expert or anything, but I've seen some of the stuff he's produced and it's extremely good.'

'What subjects does he photograph?' asked Carlisle casually.

'Ladies' fashion design, mannequin modelling, that sort of thing. He's built up quite a reputation for himself by all accounts, and his work is in high demand.'

Carrington frowned. 'Women's fashion magazines, did you say?'

'Yes, but I've absolutely no idea who he sells his photographs to. It's just what I've picked up around the office. But that's Lance for you, he likes to keep these things to himself.'

'What about work colleagues. Does he socialise at all?'

'No, Lance is very prudish when it comes to the opposite sex. Don't get me wrong, he's not a male chauvinist or anything like that, but he can be very patronising towards women.'

'Any particular reason why?'

Evans lowered his voice a tone. 'I've heard rumours, but it's mainly office gossip.'

'What kind of rumours?'

'That he was badly let down by another woman in the past. She left him for another man, apparently. It's a long story, and one he never likes to discuss with anyone. Not even with me.'

'Jilted, do you think?'

'I have absolutely no idea. Perhaps you should talk to Lance about that,' Evans smiled. 'Mind, I must warn you he can get rather tetchy when people approach him about it.'

In some ways, Evans had been quite conservative towards his assessment of Lance Wynn, which Carlisle found odd. Wynn came across as a rather dull person, an uninspiring man, a loner who seldom mixed with anyone. His utter resentment towards the opposite sex was like reading the opening lines in a book when you knew how the ending would pan out. Of all the suspects they'd interviewed so far, Wynn seemed the most likely candidate.

They sat for a while listening to Evans waffle on. Then, out of the corner of his eye, he noticed Carrington had opened her handbag and pulled out the police artist's impression of Caroline Harper's boyfriend...

'Does this bear any resemblance to Lance Wynn?' she said, handing it to Evans.

There was a short pause, but only for a second.

'Yes, definitely across the eyes. His face is a little thinner perhaps, and the jaw line a little more predominant. Otherwise, it does bear a remarkable likeness to Lance. Might I ask how you came by this?'

'It's an artist impression of an eyewitness's account of the man we're eager to question,' Carrington replied. 'It involves a recent murder which took place in Gateshead.'

'Goodness gracious me,' Evans said shaking his head. 'Lance would never do anything like that.'

'You sound surprised.'

'I am. Lance is such a quiet, unassuming man he's certainly not capable of murder. Perhaps you should talk to some of the other members of the staff and see what they have to say.' Evans paused in reflection. 'Mind, some of the tittle-tattle that goes on inside this office, it's—'

Carlisle cut him short by holding his hand up. 'This dialysis treatment his mother is receiving, do you happen to know which hospital she's attending?'

'Do you know what I have absolutely no idea. I can certainly ask around for you.'

'That would be good,' Carrington nodded. 'The quicker we get to the bottom of this the better.'

'What about contact details?' Carlisle quizzed. 'A home address, telephone numbers that sort of thing?'

'I'll get my secretary to give you that before you leave.'

Carrington shot him a withering glance. 'You do realise our conversation here today is strictly confidential, Mr Evans.'

'Yes, of course.'

'We're grateful,' Carrington said standing to leave. 'You've been most helpful.'

Carlisle couldn't think of anything else to say; not at the moment he couldn't. No doubt they would be back.

Chapter
Forty-One

Carlisle grabbed his leather jacket, locked the front door, and slid into the front passenger seat of DC Carrington's unmarked pool car. Not the best of starts, he thought, as he adjusted his seat belt. It was five in the morning, and as conversations edged on the weather of all things, he had every reason to feel miserable. Today was his father's birthday, and he'd promised to take him out to lunch. There seemed little chance of that now.

Wide awake and feeling mentally alert, by the time they'd reached Lance Wynn's house a full scale search operation was in place. Not all had gone to plan, of course. The lack of police intelligence had made certain of that. Even so, the next few hours would be critical if they were to uncover Wynn's whereabouts.

By now it was impossible to ignore the activity taking place. Set back in a small cul-de-sac, the house was in complete darkness. After ducking beneath the police cordon tape, he signed his name in the crime scene entry log sheet, and joined the rest of the throng gathered in front of the building. Several senior officers were present; many were unfamiliar faces. Standing alongside the Acting Superintendent was a tall gentleman who Carlisle took to be a police negotiator. She'd been well advised. Often working under a great deal of stress in hostage situations, these highly trained police officers had the ability to talk down agitated people and resolve critical incidents.

Carlisle cringed at the number of reporters hanging around the street. Never a dull moment, he thought. News travelled fast, and the press were quick off the mark these days. Where they got their information from was beyond him, but they were better informed than the police it seemed.

'Have you heard the news about Tom Hedley?' Sutherland whispered.

'No, ma'am, I haven't,' Carlisle replied.

'He was rushed into hospital late last night after collapsing in his bathroom.'

'Goodness! Is he all right?'

Sutherland raised an eyebrow. 'Suspected perforated ulcer – let's hope it's nothing serious.'

Well it had to happen. For days now Tom Hedley had complained about severe stomach pains. Far too much emphasis was being placed on national crime statistics nowadays. It's what Her Majesty's Inspectorate of Constabulary and the Home Office based its trust and confidence in the police on. It was a contentious issue, and one that was putting undue strain on far too many good senior officers. Get it wrong, and the findings of the official police watchdog committee would come down heavily on you. It wasn't good for morale, and everyone was well pissed off by it all.

Hedley's team had worked their socks off over the past twenty-four hours. Fingerprints and DNA particle fibres found at Wynn's workplace matched those recovered from Mary Fowler's terraced house. They now had their man, and it was just a matter of time before they caught up with him. Or so Sutherland would have everyone believe. There again if Mary Fowler was being held captive inside the property, a police negotiator would be a valuable tool in her armoury. It was a wise move.

Kitted out in his white hooded coveralls, Mason emerged from the shadows.

'Ready to go when you are, ma'am,' the DCI whispered.

'Is everyone in position, Jack?'

'All bar the dog handler teams.'

The DCI appeared clearly fazed by the tone of Sutherland's voice, but the steely look of determination was unquestionable. Sutherland could be very dismissive of Mason at times. Too dismissive if the truth was known. It was a dangerous game she was playing and one that could only end in disastrous consequences. Mason was a creature of habit, a no-nonsense copper who despised taking orders from anyone – especially senior officers.

'Don't rush it. Remember the element of surprise is critical here.'

'The men know what they're doing, ma'am.'

By now it was impossible to ignore the activity taking place. Swarming with police officers, the whole area was in lockdown. He watched as a dozen ghost-like figures moved towards the rear of the building and took up their positions. Jack Mason meanwhile, and what Carlisle took to be a master locksmith emerged from the shadows and had prepared to enter the front of building. It was a tense moment, and amidst the high pitched screams they were soon inside and moving down a narrow hallway.

Was this the home of the man who had terrorised him for weeks?

Then, just as arranged, three officers drawn from the Police Tactical Response Unit secured the upper level of the building. It was over in seconds, but the house was completely empty. Nothing could be touched, of course. Not until the SOC Photographer had run a camcorder over the place. Even then there would be a great a reluctance to touch or move anything for fear of contaminating crucial evidence.

It felt strange not working alongside Tom Hedley for once, but Lewis Harris was an experienced forensic scientist who knew how to handle a major crime scene. If there were clues to be found, then Harris would no doubt find them. The trouble was, and it was no mean task, it would take weeks to sift through all the evidence.

Mason adjusted his particle mask.

'What are your first impressions?'

'He's certainly got queer tastes,' Carlisle said pointing to a disturbing painting hanging above the fireplace. 'Satan Summoning his Legions isn't exactly my choice of painting.'

'Mine neither,' Mason admitted.

It soon became plainly obvious why Wynn had never connected with people. Wynn was different – very different. The bizarre workings of a serial killer's mind didn't bear thinking about at times. If nothing else the Middlesbrough accountant had certainly captured the team's imagination. As others might collect rare stamps or film memorabilia, Lance Wynn collected satanic paintings of mutilation and death. Every downstairs wall in the house was covered in the stuff – a gallery of pure evil.

As a mental picture began to unfold, it wasn't a good one at that. If there were clues to be found, then they weren't readily apparent. It was a fine balancing act, a game of cat and mouse played out by a disillusioned maniac who regarded himself as a Marxist crusader trying to put the record book straight. For that reason alone it wasn't too difficult to see how he'd managed to slip through the net. Not the most obvious of suspects to weed out, Wynn was a devious predator.

The kitchen was small and stank of decay. It played on the back of Carlisle's throat, causing him to retch. Wynn's was a typical bachelor's house, as no woman would ever have tolerated such disorder. And yet, thinking back, these murders were highly organised.

Tolerance! He would need plenty of that, but where to get it was the problem.

Spacious and rectangular in shape, the master bedroom was surprisingly orderly and not as Carlisle expected to find. The bed hadn't been slept in in days. The neatly folded overlay was the giveaway. As a car's headlights lit up the curtain windows, soon the property was crowded with police officers. Still searching for that elusive moment of inspiration, his eyes scanned the room. If Wynn had been holding her here, it wasn't noticeably obvious. The only thing, if it made any sense, was Wynn's sudden flight.

'Find anything of interest?' asked Sutherland.

'Nothing—'

'What the hell has he done with her?'

Mason was right. Unlike most of the other senior officers he knew, Sutherland liked to get involved. Dressed in a white hooded coverall, the Acting Superintendent was staring up at him through the bannister rails.

Her gaze caught his.

'If you don't mind me saying so,' Carlisle said, 'it's easy to be wise after the event.'

'He left in hurry I take it.'

'Yes, but his mind's in total control.'

'It's not what I'm seeing,' Sutherland replied brashly. 'It's completely the opposite, I'd say.'

'You need to take a closer look, ma'am.'

Sutherland ascended the last few stairs with trepidation. Poking her head round the open bedroom door, she stood in silence for a moment. 'What the hell's going on?'

'He's delusional, and he's fighting it.'

'But these walls are filled with religious icons,' she gasped.

'There seems to be no real explanation,' Carlisle replied. 'If we could bottle it we'd make a fortune from it, but we can't.'

'There should be plenty of DNA evidence, and fingerprints too.'

'That will come later, ma'am. There are more important issues at stake here.'

'I fear there are darker forces at work here,' Sutherland insisted.

'No doubt forensics will point us in that direction.'

'I know, but it takes time unfortunately, and we don't have a lot of it.' Sutherland shook her head. 'Let's hope the public can assist us in uncovering this monster's whereabouts.'

'What about soil samples?'

'It might throw something up, but I wouldn't count on it.'

Trying to convince Sutherland was never going to be easy. He realised that. The question was if Wynn had been taking his mother to hospital every day of the week then which one was he taking her to? Nobody could answer that!

'Wynn's cunning, but I doubt he's killed her. Not yet he hasn't.'

Sutherland sighed. 'First it was Richard Sloane, then Alexander Moore, and now it's Lance Wynn. We seem to have been jumping around an awful lot lately.'

'Find Wynn and we'll find Mary Fowler.'

'I hope you're right, but I have a bad feeling about this one.'

By the sound of things, the jury was already out. Now that the focus of attention had shifted squarely back on his shoulders, he was beginning to feel isolated again. Some things were impossible to explain. He knew that, but nobody was listening to him anymore.

God what a mess!

'These murders aren't crimes in Wynn's mind. To him they're organised accomplishments.'

Sutherland's face clouded over. 'I wouldn't say that Wynn was organised. Far from it – this place is a tip.'

Carlisle bit his bottom lip, as if there was an invisible barrier between them. Sometimes it was easier to say nothing. Answer the questions and keep your thoughts to yourself. The pressure was mounting and if the raid on Wynn's property turned out to be another disaster, the Area Commander would come down on Sutherland like a ton of hot bricks. It wasn't looking good.

He watched as a young forensic officer bagged and tagged another bin liner full of Wynn's discarded clothing. Trace evidence was an important part of the forensic armoury. It could yield a wealth of information. Apart from reconstructing an event, in some cases it could indicate where a person may have been. Now that Alexander Moore was out of the equation, things were starting to get personal. They'd chosen the wrong man, and now they were trying to hide from the fact.

Sutherland worried him too. His only mistake, if he could think of one, was that he'd played his trump card too early. Not only that, a highly respected forensic scientist and crucial player on the team even Tom Hedley had singled Alexander Moore out. But that didn't make him a killer, and all too often investigative psychology including criminal profiling was as much an art as a science. Even then it couldn't be considered as an exact science as humans are unpredictable by nature.

Carlisle had always worked on the principle that there were four areas of investigation that were important to psychological profiling. All were crucial in helping uncover the killer's identity. Each had its own merits, of course, but predominantly so in Wynn's case – it was the suspect's post-offence behaviour that concerned him most. Taunting the media after a murder had been committed was crucial to understanding the killer's mind-set. In his experience he'd come across dozens of instances where killers had openly talked to the media after killing their victims. Ian Huntley sprang to mind. And yet, thinking back, this case was no different. If not, then why post his victim's finger through his letter box? Why run the risk of sending him text-messages from his victim's iPhone? No one in their right mind would do that, unless they wanted to reach out to someone of course.

There was nothing in the suspect's property to suggest that Wynn was a serial killer. Not yet there wasn't. Yes there was chaos and disorder just as there had been in Alexander Moore's life. But Wynn had all the right ingredients. He was a loner, someone who could slip in and out of society at will. The problem was convincing the others that Mary Fowler was still alive.

Carlisle checked his watch, 11:30am.

'Where to now?' asked DC Carrington.

'Do you know where Amici's restaurant is in Forest Hall?'

'No, but I can Google it. Why?'

'I've promised to take my old man out to lunch, it's his birthday.'

The young detective gave him a quizzical look. Had he misread the signs, made the wrong decision and brought this upon himself? Everyone was tetchy nowadays, bad-tempered, with morale at an all-time low. He should have been more forceful, more direct.

It was too late for that now.

'That's the thing about my job,' Carrington grinned. 'You get to see how the other half reacts.'

'Tell me about it!'

'What if she's already dead?' Carrington questioned.

Oh, shit, he thought, embarrassed at the looks she was giving him.

'Why does everyone doubt me, Sue?'

'Most people trust your judgement; it's just that they can't make up their minds at the moment. After the Alexander Moore fiasco it's hard to see how anyone can stick their heads above the parapet these days. You're different. You understand what goes on inside these people's heads.'

'We are who we are, I'm afraid.'

The young detective checked her mirrors before turning left at the next roundabout and onto the A1M motorway slip road. There was another awkward exchange of glances between them, and then Carrington said, 'Let's face it, you've said all along the killer had a bad experience with another woman in his past. You were right all along. Wynn's good at blending into the background. Pinning him down's the problem.'

'He's definitely a cunning bastard.'

'Tell me about it,' Carrington shrugged, 'but who else do we have in the frame?'

Thank God for small mercies, Carlisle thought. He wasn't alone anymore.

'Fancy an old man's birthday party lunch?'

'Why not, I'm quite partial to Mediterranean cuisine,' she replied.

Carlisle wondered what his old man would make of it all.

What the hell.

Chapter Forty-Two

Eyes glued to the computer screen, he licked his lips in anticipation as another wave of excitement washed over him. His throat tightened, and he could barely breathe. The room was 'T' shaped, a cold damp claustrophobic structure completely isolated from the rest of the building. It was dark inside, only a flickering candle-light. Rotating the focus adjustment, a familiar emptiness returned to the pit of his stomach.

He breathed in her fear. This one was another looker, long legs, slim waist, small firm breasts and neat rounded buttocks. He liked them like that, and he knew how to hurt.

Ever so slowly he zoomed in on camera one.

Where are you, bitch!

Then, in the fading light, he found her. Curled in a tight ball, she was cowering in the corner. Hands gripped firmly behind her knees, head tilted forward, her mouth was slightly agape. Stripped of her expensive finery, to him she was now ordinary. Nothing flash, just another worthless piece of shit he'd taken off the streets. It wasn't the fear in her eyes that excited him, or the fact that she was chained to the water pipe. No. It was the control he had over her.

Never once did he take his eyes off the monitor screen.

Not even for a second.

He playfully fingered the keyboard again, and felt another surge of adrenaline through his veins. He liked them to suffer, the slower the better in his mind. If this bitch couldn't see her own death coming, it was her fault. And guess what, it was coming. Oh yes – an unstoppable nightmare of uncertainty that was drawing her ever closer towards the pit of eternal darkness.

Her ankle straps tightened, and his eyes rolled back in their sockets until only the whites were showing. He was transfixed.

Then, as he switched to camera three the banging flared up again. Much louder this time!

More intense!

Annoying—

He zoomed back to camera three again, and refused point-blank to be drawn in. Not that this bitch was going anywhere; she wasn't. Not until she'd paid for her sins.

And there were many.

He focused his eyes to another part of the room, a distant, dark, forbidden corner of uncertainty. This bitch's fate was already sealed, of that much he was certain. He knew how desperate she was and he was ready to make his move. Excitement gripped him, and his eyes rolled back in their sockets again. Oh, and her voice was so pathetic that it almost made him laugh.

Then the banging flared up again.

Hardly noticeable this time—

Fainter! Much fainter, until only the echoes of his mind could be heard.

Not much longer now, bitch!

Chapter
Forty-Three

DC Carrington pulled the unmarked pool car into the lay-by and switched off the engine. She sat for a while staring aimlessly out through the rain-lashed windscreen. It was late afternoon, and the drive from Washington had taken them a little under thirty minutes. From the outside the old watermill looked deserted, but Carlisle knew otherwise. Close to the river and surrounded on three sides by dense woodlands, the fast fading light gave the place an eerie presence. From the moment he'd first clapped eyes on the place he knew the property had potential. Built of solid sandstone and set in two hundred acres of unattended countryside, the only visible access, as far as he could see, was via a narrow country lane and that was a good half mile away.

The rain had eased.

'What do you think?' Carrington said looking pensive.

'Estate agents seldom forget a face, and the Sunderland manager was convinced the police artist's impression bore a striking likeness. I know it's a long-shot, and she may have got her wires crossed, but there's only one way to find out.'

The young detective shrugged and gave a wan smile.

'I don't like it. Just because someone rents a creepy old watermill doesn't make them a serial killer.'

'Maybe not, but my gut instincts tell me otherwise.'

'My God,' Carrington huffed, 'we're surely not here on a hunch.'

'That's the beauty of being a profiler, Sue.'

Carrington glared at him through frightened eyes. 'What if we spook him, raise his suspicions? I'd feel much happier returning tomorrow with a search warrant and backup.'

'Trust me,' Carlisle explained. 'We've checked out a dozen properties today and none of them a pick of bother. Besides, we can always pretend we were genuinely lost.'

'You're joking! We don't even look like frigging hitch-hikers.'

It was agreed. Carrington would wait in the unmarked police car, whilst Carlisle went on ahead. It was only one hundred metres away, but he felt it would take forever. Then, as the mill door slid partially open, he was confronted by the occupant. Slightly taller than he was, that's where the similarities ended. And yet, come to think of it, the person standing before him was a dead ringer for the police artist's impression. If this was the killer standing before him, he would need to tread carefully.

He took a step back, steadied himself, and tried to make it sound convincing.

'I'm looking for—'

'Looking for what?'

The occupant's face had remained expressionless throughout.

'I've been given the name Lance Wynn by one of the local estate agents. I presume you are Lance?'

Carlisle was surprised by his accent. He was half expecting some sort of Teesside dialect, not a refined Northern accent. Not surprisingly, the occupant's eyes glowered with malevolence and he was breathing heavily.

'I'm Wynn,' he said scanning the fields behind him as if there were spies hiding behind every blade of grass. 'So what is it you're after?'

'I was told this place was vacant.'

Wynn's voice was deep and deliberate. 'Well, it ain't.'

'Oh!'

'No. It's occupied.'

Taken aback, Carlisle's words had come out all of a jumble. The truth was, he thought Wynn was about to reach out and grab hold of him. He took another step back – purely a precautionary measure!

'Well I was definitely told it was vacant.'

'Do you have a key?'

Carlisle feigned exasperation. 'There must be some sort of mix-up.'

Wynn checked his surroundings like an abscess jetting its poison through his nerves.

'Who's that in the car with you?'

'My girlfriend—'

'Is she alone?'

'We came together if that's what you mean.'

Wynn's lecherous grin suddenly widened. 'Well, well, fate and circumstance have finally brought us to this moment.'

'Is it ok if I take a peep around?'

'No it's not.' Wynn's grip on the door handle tightened. 'If you must, I prefer you call back tomorrow.'

'Not a problem.'

'Be sure to bring the pretty lady with you.' Wynn began to laugh. 'Young women are greedy like that. They like to see what they're getting for their money.'

'By the way,' Carlisle said, taken aback by Wynn's latest outburst, 'what kind of heating does the place have?'

'We'll talk about it tomorrow.'

'And the local pubs, do they serve bar meals?'

'Tomorrow—'

'Right then,' Carlisle said, suddenly feeling anxious.

'Mind, it kind of gets lonely round these parts at night.'

Drizzle drifted down from the sky in lazy waves, causing him to squint. With his foot on the bottom step, Carlisle turned to face him again. He was looking for signs of weakness, any kind of weakness.

'Don't go telling my girlfriend that. I'd hate for you to spook her.'

'That's some women for you,' Wynn said, staring repugnantly across at the undercover pool vehicle again. 'You can never be too careful – there are some real nasty people out there.'

'You seem to have a good handle on these things.'

Wynn was gaining in confidence and the condescension dripping from his lips reminded him of bees' honey.

'Like I say, you can never be too careful.'

'What makes some people tick, eh?'

Wynn almost laughed. 'You're not a copper by any chance, are you?'

'No I'm not, why?'

'I seem to recognise your face from somewhere.'

'It has that effect on people,' Carlisle shrugged, 'common as muck.'

Wynn's eyes narrowed. 'How old is this young woman of yours?'

'She's ten years younger than me.'

'A professional are you?'

'Yeah, you say could say that I suppose.'

Cunning, thought Carlisle. Wynn had turned the tables on him having taken over control of the proceedings. To catch a psychopath threw up an awful lot of challenges. They were charming con men, excellent liars, well rounded individuals who could win over your trust at the drop of a hat. Wynn had caught him unawares, but was this the man who had made his life misery for weeks? He would need to find out more.

'I've often wondered what attracts young women to older men,' said Wynn, staring across at the pool car again. 'Is it a security thing, or are they just money grabbing bitches?'

'I've never given it much thought, Lance.'

'Rich man's pickings—'

It suddenly occurred to him that Wynn was probing for frailties. Carlisle's next question, when it came, was more direct. 'What about you, Lance. Do you prefer younger women?'

Wynn laughed at him.

'Charm is deceitful, and beauty vain, but a woman who fears the Lord is to be praised.'

'Proverbs, thirty-one,' Carlisle acknowledged.

'You surprise me – I never had you down as a religious man.'

'I'm not, but I'm working on it.'

Wynn's stare hardened. 'With so much evil surrounding this world it's hard to imagine how anyone can sleep at night.'

'See you tomorrow—'

'Ten o'clock!' said Wynn. 'Don't be late!'

'Ten o'clock it is.'

As the door slammed shut in his face, Carlisle felt a wiser man. His hunch had paid off. The Middlesbrough Accountant was everything he'd imagined him to be – a narcissistic psychopath too full of his own self-importance to realise he was now under suspicion. Wynn had shown his hand, and it wasn't a good one at that. All that remained now was to find out what other hidden secrets lay beyond closed doors.

Easier said than done, he thought.

In some ways Carlisle felt relieved, as he hated putting everything down on record. Police procedures were one thing, gut-feelings another. Wynn had been taunting him, trying his utmost to scramble his brain and uncover his innermost thoughts. The fact that he'd chosen a religious verse to spout off his egotistic charm, alarmed him. It wasn't the done thing. There again, this was the perfect location and Wynn the perfect candidate.

Carrington was fiddling with the car's radio buttons on his return.

'What did you find out?' she asked.

'You'll never believe who I've just bumped into.'

'Who?'

'Lance Wynn!'

The young detective's face dropped. 'Are you sure it was him?'

'Yes, and he was spouting off religious teachings.'

'What do you mean religious teachings?'

'Proverbs, thirty-one,' Carlisle replied.

Carrington froze.

Chapter
Forty-Four

The ground underfoot felt damp as David Carlisle stood on the crumbling edge of a formerly grand structure. Now picked out in his flash-light, the south-facing walls of the old watermill stood in faded forgotten silence. Surrounded on two sides by tall trees, a high dry stone wall ran parallel down one side of it, behind which a team of police offers now advanced. It was the perfect location, totally isolated, with nothing more than a wooden door barring their entry. Beyond the stone wall, close to civilisation, a cluster of outbuildings contoured against a skyline that hinted early dusk. Every now and then he could make out the glow of a farmhouse, its lights flickering through the low lying mist causing him to squint. It was then he heard the distant echoes of a slowly advancing freight train, as it trundled northbound towards Durham. Two short warning blasts on its horn, followed by the distinct rumble of heavy goods wagons told him its driver was fast approaching danger.

Then Silence. Only the tinkling of the river could be heard.

Now stood motionless, Mason gave the signal. Stepping from the shadows, two burly police officers drawn from the Police Tactical Response Unit took up their positions at the rear of the building. Dressed in their familiar black armoured vests, the shorter of the two carried with him an enforcer ram door opener. Once inside, the speed of execution in clearing the building was breathtaking.

Wynn was nowhere to be seen!

Twenty minutes later, Carlisle entered the building with mixed feelings. The air inside stank of ketones. It hung in the back of his throat, a bitter taste reminiscent of a police gas training exercise. Seconds later he entered through a narrow side door, and down a small flight of stone steps. Now cordoned off, he could see the basement was 'T' shaped − a windowless brick-construction with low ceilings and thick concrete floors. This cold, damp room had once played an important part in the making of flour. Not anymore. Two forensic officers were busily processing and documenting everything down in what was now a major crime scene.

He spotted the water-pipe.

At first he thought nothing of it, and pushed it to the back of his mind. Then, glancing up, his eyes caught the chains. These were no ordinary chains; these were fitted with ankle constraints. Sinister looking, grotesque! Not three feet away a young female forensic scientist began another systematic sweep of the basement floor. It was painstaking work, but important nevertheless. An image formed in his head − a young woman laid out on a table in front of him, with terror written across her face. Her hair was matted and her lips barely moved, but she was desperately trying to tell him something. He tried to focus his mind. Become as one, and unlock the inner secrets that were haunting her. Of course, he thought. The bruising to the victim's ankles and wrists, this is where he'd been holding them.

Carlisle shuddered and felt the skin on his neck tighten, as if something repulsive had touched him. His mind running amok, he could have sworn he heard a whooshing noise.

There it was again.

Much louder this time!

At first he thought it was the water pipe, but it wasn't that kind of noise. Nearby, an acne faced SOC photographer with close cropped hair and a mouth full of fillings pointed to the corner of the room.

'Rats,' he whispered.

Carlisle nodded. Whoever had been imprisoned here had certainly left their mark. Etched along the walls were the words: HELP ME!

Was this Mary Fowler's doing?

The only route of escape, as far as Carlisle could make out, was back up the steep stone staircase. He'd seen evil before. Not often, but he'd seen it nevertheless. One such case that sprang to mind involved a mentally deranged husband who, having imprisoned his wife in the cellar of their rented house, had subjected her to unimaginable torture. While she was starving to death and shackled to a makeshift bed, two floors up he was making passionate love to his daughter. The ending, when it came, sickened even the hardiest of coppers on the team. Some things didn't bear thinking about, and this case bore all the hallmarks of that.

'Cameras!' the young SOC photographer pointed out.

Carlisle's eyes followed the wires.

'I see them—'

'The bastard's been filming everything.'

Sick in the pit of his stomach and unable to move, the revulsion came in waves. Carlisle felt nothing but utter contempt towards a fear-fuelled psychopath who now had more than blood on his hands. In what was a deadly mixture of satanic menace, these vile acts of inhuman terror had shown little or no remorse towards his victims' suffering. Given the severity of the crimes, it wouldn't be long before the whole world would be exposed to such barbarity.

'You can almost smell the fear,' Mason said, now stood behind him.

'She'd been chained to the water pipe, Jack.'

'And there's fresh blood on the upstairs floor.'

'He must have carried her up there?'

'Disturbed, more like?'

'Probably.'

Mason shook his head feebly. 'This bastard needs stringing up.'

'Let's hope she's still alive.'

'I wouldn't gamble on that if I were you,' Mason muttered.

There were times when it paid to have frayed nerves. Being a profiler had its benefits, but it also had its pitfalls. He tried to picture the scene, reach out to the killer's way of thinking.

'Here!' the young SOC officer pointed out.

'What is it, Watkins?'

'Another blood trail, boss, but this one's not recent.'

Got him, Carlisle beamed. Was this how Caroline Harper had died? Chained to a water-pipe and knocked unconscious before he strangled her. His mind all over the place, the more he thought about it the more it made perfect sense. There again, what if the act of killing hadn't quite lived up to his expectations? What if he felt utterly let down by it all? What then? If Wynn had been filming everything, then surely he must be living out his fantasies. Carlisle loathed the dark side and all that it stood for. Sadistic killers usually got under his skin at the best of times. Now he had a clear understanding of how the killer was operating, the pieces were falling into place. The question was, and it was now on everyone's lips, where the hell had he taken her?

Twenty minutes later and he found Jack Mason slouched against the outer wall. Hands in pockets, head stooped slightly forward, his face bore a look of resignation. The long knives were out for him, and the recent accolades in catching the Alpaca thieves now seemed a million light-years away. People were demanding answers, and if that wasn't bad enough, Wynn was probably miles away by now.

'Is this Wynn's doing?' Mason shrugged.

'I believe so. The trouble is, this is unchartered territory to him and his head is probably in pieces.'

'Let's hope he doesn't panic and do something stupid.'

Carlisle's flash-lamp picked out the fresh lines of tyre tracks.

'Wynn drives a black Nissan pickup truck, doesn't he?' said Carlisle, as though acknowledging he'd heard Mason's words and had taken them in.

'He does, why?'

'Knowing Wynn, he'll probably head for familiar territory.'

'And—'

'If this is the only back road out of here, you'll need to get forensics involved.'

'That's all we need.' Mason stared down at the tyre tracks as he reached for his iPhone. 'Close to home do you think?'

'No, it's far too risky.'

'Where then—'

'Somewhere he feels safe.' Carlisle paused to let the implications sink in.

'If ever I needed your help, my friend, it's now.'

Carlisle nodded. 'If Mary Fowler is alive, she'll probably be in pretty bad shape.'

'Let's not go there,' Mason grunted.

No one paid a blind bit of notice to George Holt. No one except David Carlisle, that is. Face flushed, eyes peeled directly ahead, the Detective Sergeant was holding something up in a plastic evidence bag.

'I found this,' Holt smiled weakly.

'What is it, George?'

'A parking ticket for Middlesbrough city centre, boss.'

Mason stood silent a few moments as if trying to focus his mind. 'Where did you find it?'

'Close to the back gate,' Holt replied.

'Middlesbrough city centre, eh. What time's on the ticket?'

Holt picked it out in his flashlight beam. 'Nine o'clock.'

'Nine o'clock when?'

'A. M. Two days ago, boss.'

'Middlesbrough—'

As another back of a fag-packet plan slowly began to emerge, Carlisle caught a hint of excitement in Mason's glances. It was precious moments like these that he wished he could bottle for keepsake. If only, he smiled.

The Detective Chief Inspector flicked an annoying moth that had flown into his face.

'OK. Let's not pussy foot around, I want Wynn's house turned upside down. Brick by brick if needs be. He can't be far away and we know he operates locally. Find Wynn and we find the woman.'

Then, taking a couple of constables towards the back gate, Mason was making his presence felt. For the first time in weeks there was a new sense of urgency in the team's step. They'd made a few mistakes, blown a few good leads, but things were now back on track again. All it needed now was to uncover Mary Fowler's whereabouts, and the rest would fall into place.

Well, that was the theory at least.

Ch*pter
Forty-Five

Mist clung to the rooftops as DC Carrington's unmarked pool car pulled into the kerb outside Lance Wynn's semi-detached house that morning. Not more than twenty metres away, three detectives dressed in black overalls and wearing green wellington boots were busy digging up Wynn's rear garden. Using ground penetrating radar, the whole area had been cordoned off and mapped out in a grid pattern. In what looked like a mass grave, three burly police officers were taking it in turns to sift through the piles of rubble. It was painstaking work, and one which had revealed very little so far.

Carlisle stood in silence for moment and tried to get his head around it all. DNA trace evidence found inside the property had positively linked Wynn to at least two murders. The police had their man, and all that remained now was to establish the third victim's whereabouts. In what had become one of the largest coordinated man hunts since gunman Raoul Moat had gone on the run, the search for Lance Wynn was relentless. In an effort to drum up public support, the Northumbria Police had called on local residents to check out garages and outbuildings close to their properties. Things were moving at a pace, and as hundreds of volunteers braved heavy wind and rain in their effort to establish Mary Fowler's whereabouts, the net was closing in. Not everyone was optimistic about finding the missing forty year old woman alive; even the media had their doubts. It was a difficult call, and one that had kept everyone guessing for days now.

Then Carlisle caught movement from an upstairs window.

Despite his fearsome reputation as a no-nonsense copper, Jack Mason was keeping a very low profile these days. The humiliation of charging the wrong man for Caroline Harper's murder had certainly knocked the wind out of his sails. He wasn't alone, of course. There were others on the team with egg on their faces. Needless to say, it was a former Teesside university student who finally blew Wynn's cover – an unexpected phone call in the middle of the night. Described as an oddball, an introvert with problems, Wynn had few friends. When in 2009 Cheryl Sawyer had walked out on him to live with a wealthy property developer, a man twice his age, that's when it all started to go wrong. Hunted down like a wounded animal, it wasn't difficult to understand why Wynn had killed his ex-girlfriend as he did.

This was clearly dangerous territory that Carlisle was treading on, and he understandably felt uncomfortable about it. Wynn was a dangerous predator, a man whose threats had spiralled out of control. Serial killers were habitual; they targeted their victims when they least expected it. Police protection was one thing, but Wynn's disturbing mind games had finally caught up with him. The question was, and there was no other way of putting it, just how far was Wynn prepared to go? Unsettled, he felt for the pepper spray now tucked deep inside his trouser leg pocket. It wasn't much, he realised that, but at least it gave him some added protection.

He'd barely set foot inside Wynn's property before the Acting Superintendent gestured him over. 'We've run out of time,' she announced, 'and we're looking for a body.'

Carlisle was quick to react. 'I beg to differ, ma'am. Mary Fowler is still alive, I'm convinced of it.'

'Gut feeling or just a profiler's wishful thinking?'

'Neither, ma'am, Wynn's a creature of habit who likes nothing more than to be the centre of attention. Once the dust settles down, he'll work out what his next moves are.'

'You're clutching at straws I fear.'

Carlisle felt the need to explain. 'When a psychopath feels challenged they will always resort to control. That's the thing about them, they're predictable. Wynn's no different; he's so fuelled up by delusional fantasy he believes he's now answerable to God.'

'We're past that stage I fear. Mark my words, Mary Fowler's dead.'

Carlisle gestured towards the current excavations.

'If she is, then he's certainly keeping everyone guessing.'

'What makes you think she's alive?'

'To kill Mary Fowler now would be to take away his greatest possession, and he isn't going to do that. Not yet he isn't. Wynn's an exhibitionist who seeks maximum recognition for his crimes.'

'But his mental state is surely one of confusion and panic?'

Carlisle detected the tiniest hint of doubt in the Acting Superintendent's glances. Not much, but it was enough. 'Wynn's at the stage where he believes he has the divine right over life and death. He's a religious bigot who's convinced that God has spoken to him.'

Sutherland brushed his comments aside. 'That's utter nonsense... Wynn's irrational. What's to say he hasn't already killed her?'

'Wynn always blamed his father's passing for his recent behavioural change. The truth was very different, of course. His father has been dead for almost twenty years now, and that's a fact. He's violent alright, and yes, he probably inherited his father's hot headed genes.' Carlisle swallowed hard. 'When Wynn's childhood sweetheart ran off for a man with more money than he could ever dream of, it turned him to religion. Not your everyday religion. Not according to the local parish priest. Wynn took religion to another level.'

Sutherland was silent for a second, looking decidedly uncomfortable.

'You have a very specific way of profiling people,' she said. 'What puzzles me, is why he killed Caroline Harper six years after he'd murdered Cheryl Sawyer. It's a heck of a long time.'

'Other women's lives probably seem much better than his, hence his resentment towards them. Let's face it, Cheryl Sawyer's murder never gained the notoriety that Wynn was craving, as her death was always classed as drugs related.'

'Six years of hatred building up inside you—'

'You can't anticipate your dreams, but you block them out,' Carlisle said thoughtfully. 'No wonder he snapped as he did.'

Sutherland allowed herself a brief, smug smile. 'If you're right, then why bother to groom these women in the first place?'

'Who knows? Caroline Harper's death was the executioner's perfect murder as far as Wynn was concerned. What more could he ask for having gained maximum publicity, let alone the threats that were aimed at me? Wynn must have been ecstatic over his achievements.'

'So this is all about notoriety?'

Carlisle considered the question. 'Wynn took umbrage the minute the media went into print that we'd charged someone else with Caroline Harper's murder. No longer the centre of attention, how else was he going to demonstrate we'd charged the wrong man?'

'So he kidnaped, Mary Fowler.'

'Yes. Purely to gain back control and capture the public's imagination.'

'And that's why you believe she's still alive?'

'Wynn feeds off the oxygen of publicity the media gives him,' Carlisle replied. 'That's why he's been filming everything. If Mary Fowler was dead, he would have delivered her back to us by now. It's the mind-set of these people; their inter-personal dominance plays a major role in their thinking patterns.'

'So that's what makes Wynn tick?'

'Amongst other things, God is his main driving force.'

'This sounds more like Satan's beckoning—'

'Sometimes you get close to these people, ma'am. You eat and sleep at the same times as they do. The trouble is their minds go into dark places where ordinary people don't go.'

Sutherland rolled her eyes. 'When God stretches out a finger to you, don't take the whole hand.'

'True. But just because I think like they do doesn't make me insane.'

Sutherland smiled. 'I hope not.'

'These people look quite normal to you and me, but nobody knows what their trade is. Wynn has the striking ability to charm his victims over before killing them. He's manipulative, and revels in the attention he gains from it.' Carlisle held back to allow a female forensic scientist to squeeze past them. 'When Cheryl Sawyer abandoned Wynn for a man twice his age, she sealed her own fate.'

'That is interesting,' Sutherland said thoughtfully. 'So how did you know it wasn't Alexander Moore?'

'Intuition—'

'Is that a profiler thing?'

Carlisle nodded but refrained from saying it.

'Tell me,' she said thoughtfully. 'How much information did this Seaham contact of yours give you?'

Carlisle could hardly believe his ears.

'Not a great lot, why?'

'You're not telling me the truth,' Sutherland said outright. 'If you were, then how come ninety-nine per cent of the Force thought it was Alexander Moore?'

Carlisle smiled. 'Your words not mine, ma'am.'

'But you've not answered my question.'

I'm a profiler, he mused. *Isn't that what you hired me to do?*

Banging noises came from upstairs causing Sutherland to flinch.

'Let's hope you're right,' she said.

Well, he thought, at least that was off his chest and it had probably cost him a job because of it. Carlisle was in no mood for pussy-footing around anymore, and he certainly wasn't going to lose any sleep over it.

Throughout that morning Jack Mason's team were slowly pulling the building apart, brick by brick by the sound of things. Then, just as Sutherland was about to leave, the DCI appeared at the top of the stair head.

She eyed him with suspicion. 'What is it, Jack?'

'We found these hidden in the rafters, ma'am.'

'Found what?'

Proudly holding up a large plastic forensic evidence bag and wearing a thousand watt smile, Mason was making his presence felt. 'It's a black handbag and pink laptop computer, I do declare.'

Sutherland raised her eyebrows a fraction as she glanced across at Carlisle.

'Pink laptop—'

'Well it isn't Lance Wynn's, and he was definitely trying to hide it from someone.'

It was Carlisle who broke the silence.

'Any signs of a weekend bag— '

'No,' Mason shrugged, 'but I know where you're coming from, my friend. There is a bag full of women's clothes in the loft, along with a dozen mannequins.'

Sutherland swivelled to face Mason. 'The same as the one we found on Chester-le-Street station?'

'Yes ma'am. Wynn was into fashion photography apparently.'

'If any of these items belonged to Caroline Harper,' Sutherland said authoritatively, 'Wynn has an awful lot of explaining to do.'

At last, thought Carlisle. The missing pieces of the jigsaw puzzle. For the first time in weeks, they now had something concrete to work on. All it needed now was to uncover Mary Fowler's whereabouts. There had to be an easier way, but right now he couldn't think of one. He gazed at the calendar pinned to the back of the kitchen door. It looked cheap, like something found in a charity shop. The corners were frayed, and someone had scribbled something in one of the date boxes. Carlisle made a mental note of it, and moved back into the hallway again.

'Right then,' said Mason. 'I'll pop these into the forensic van.'

Although pleased with his findings, Mason's face didn't exactly exude joy anymore. Then, beyond the police cordon tape Carlisle caught sight of the Area Commander. Standing alongside him was a sprightly gentleman probably in his late fifties whom Carlisle had never seen before. Heads bent in serious discussion over matters of great importance, they appeared to demand attention.

Mason hung back.

'How come Wynn was never picked up on our radar?' Mason asked.

'It's easy in hindsight, Jack. On the surface these people are regular guys. And yet, beneath the mask of normality there's a psychopathic killer lurking. Catching them is one thing, getting them to talk another. Let's hope we can get to her first.'

'How would you propose we do that?'

Carlisle remained silent for a moment, and then said, 'The answer probably lies in the question. He'll to need to break surface at some stage.'

'And when he does,' Mason grinned, 'I'll be ready and waiting for him.'

If only!

Chapter
Forty-Six

The car park was busy when Jack Mason turned his collar against the rain that morning. It was 9:32am, and still no sign of Lance Wynn's black Nissan pickup truck showing. If Wynn was true to form, then he should have made an appearance by now.

Regular as clockwork, the security guard had told them.

Either way Mason had prepared for every eventuality. As the minutes ticked by, so did his patience. Now standing alongside an unmarked pool car, he heard the crackled response on his car radio and twiddled with the volume control. The operator's voice seemed strained, but he quickly picked up the gist of it. Wynn was travelling south with an unmarked pool car in tow, and heading straight into his trap. Got him, he grinned. All that remained now was for the killer to enter into the inner security cordon and the rest would fall into place.

There was something fishy going on. He couldn't be certain, but he suddenly felt uneasy about the two cars stood opposite. Then in the blink of eye, Mason caught the opening of the windows and rapid exchange of goods.

An organised drugs drop!

Caught in two minds, his iPhone buzzed in his pocket. He thought about it, but that's when the stationary unmarked police car opposite flashed its headlights. Seconds later he saw the lumbering black Nissan pickup truck as it trundled towards the ticket barrier.

Mason hated uncertainty, but refused to believe the world was run by a random chain of events. One small slip and it would all end in disaster.

An arm reached out through the glass tinted window, and the man at the ticket office saluted. The driver would be watching, of course, but hopefully hadn't spotted them. Then, just as Mason thought he would, Wynn squeezed his vehicle into the first available parking space.

Don't rush it!

As the team closed in on their target, Mason felt a sudden adrenaline rush.

'Lance Wynn,' he shouted pulling the startled occupant out onto the tarmac. 'You are wanted for questioning in connection with the disappearance of Mary Fowler. Anything you say—'

Eyes like frightened sparrows, mouth slightly agape, the Middlesbrough accountant glowered at him. 'Tell me you're joking.'

Mason stood his ground, time enough to allow two fully armed police officers to apply a set of hand-cuffs. So far so good!

'The keys to the truck,' the DCI demanded.

'Fuck you—'

'You should know the routine by now.' Mason flashed his warrant card under Wynn's nose and pushed the startled suspect up against the door stanchion. 'Piss me about, and I'll make your life a real misery?'

Mason tried to think clearly, as he carried out a quick body search.

'What are the charges?' said Wynn.

'Let's start with murder.'

'You're wasting your time,' Wynn laughed, as he struggled with his handcuffs.

Not to be deterred one of the arresting officers kept a tight grip of Wynn's arms, whilst the other checked inside the van – nothing. It was a tense standoff, but there could only be one winner.

Mason waited as a motorbike rumbled down one of the car parks central lanes, before he continued. 'Mary Fowler. Where is she?'

'Who the fuck's Mary Fowler—'

It was time to make his presence felt.

'Don't make this hard for yourself. I'm in no mood for time-wasters. Just tell me where she is, there's a good lad.'

Hyperventilating in panic, Wynn could barely contain himself. His face was bright red and his mouth full of venom. 'With a name like that she sounds a right slut to me.'

'Yeah, well, all right.'

'Having doubts are we, Inspector?'

The one thing he'd learnt about serial killers was never to underestimate their cunning. Just when you thought you had them in the palm of your hand, all they were doing was tormenting you. This time felt different, though, unlike a previous case when he was suspended from duty for the use of excessive force. The only way to win these people over, if there was such a thing, was to make them feel important. But that wasn't his style, and Mason knew it. His was more a forceful approach. More direct. Putting the fear of God into his suspect's mind gave him a sense of ascendancy and that's how he liked to deal with these people. It's what they deserved.

He was the senior investigating officer, of course, the man in charge of the situation. If Mary Fowler was still alive, then where the hell was Wynn keeping her? For one terrible moment Mason thought he was about to lose his rag. He didn't. There again, he now had enough evidence to lock him away for the rest of life. It was only a matter of time.

'Play it your way, my friend, but this could take all weekend,' Mason said.

Wynn stared at him, bewildered, like a hunted animal.

'So what's your problem, Inspector?'

Mason leaned forward and grabbed Wynn by the collar. 'What have you done with her, you little trumped up pervert?'

Wynn smirked. 'Wouldn't you like to know?'

'Take him away—'

Mason watched as they bundled Wynn into the back of a waiting patrol car, and he didn't look a happy bunny. The only positives, if there were any to be gained from it all, was that a disturbingly dangerous man had been taken off the streets.

Sometimes it felt good to be a copper, and today he was having a good day.

Chapter
Forty-Seven

It didn't take David Carlisle long to reach Gateshead Police station, thirty five-minutes at the most. News travelled fast, and the crowd of journalists was growing by the minute. Several outside broadcast vans were already parked up outside the Magistrates' court, their satellite dishes breaking the skyline. Whatever it was they were covering, it had to be something big.

Wearing his favourite frayed blue denim jeans, baggy T-shirt, and a pair of scruffy Nike trainers, Carlisle entered the building with mixed feelings that morning. He was about to go fishing with his father when the text message came through. As usual Jack Mason was giving nothing away. The last time Carlisle had set foot in Mason's office was five days ago and things had moved on since then.

Surprised to find Tom Hedley sitting with his feet under the table, he knew then that something was afoot.

'Coffee?' said Mason, his hand hovering over the telephone receiver.'

'Black, no sugar, please.'

Carlisle turned to Tom Hedley. 'Nice to see you're back in the fray, Tom. Patched up and ready to go are we?'

Hedley's face told him a different story.

'I've been told to take it easy over the next few weeks, so I thought I'd call by and pick up a few things.'

Not a good idea, Carlisle thought.

Mason shot him a look. 'Have you heard the news, Lance Wynn's in custody?'

'So that's what all the media hype is all about. When did this happen?'

'Ten o'clock this morning.'

'And Mary Fowler—'

'No. Nothing yet,' Mason sighed. 'Wynn's refusing to talk and denies all knowledge of her. He's a shrewd bastard all right, and getting him to cooperate is a nightmare.'

'I doubt he'll talk,' Carlisle shrugged.

'Why not, for God's sake. What's wrong with these people?'

'That's how they deal with it unfortunately.'

'I'm at the end of my tether with him. He's a right pain in the arse!'

'Narcissistic psychopaths usually are. To them it's a game. The trouble is they actually believe they own their victims and treat them as their personal possessions. It won't be easy, especially if Wynn thinks he can get one over on you.'

'That shit's way over my head,' Mason began. 'My biggest concern is Mary Fowler's whereabouts. What has he done with her?'

Coffee arrived along with a plate full of cheap gingersnaps – the buy one, get one free kind. He watched as the disgruntled Detective Chief Inspector shuffled a few papers around on a cluttered desk and tried to suppress his annoyance. Sometimes it was impossible to gauge how Mason would react, and the press weren't helping any either. His body language was the giveaway, as if his mind had turned against him and there was no one to help.

'What's the latest on forensics, Tom?' Carlisle asked.

Hedley seemed unprepared for the question. 'Oh, yes. There's still plenty of work to get through. It'll take weeks to catch up on the backlog.'

'Everything bagged and tagged?'

'Yes, and we've gathered enough evidence to put Wynn away for life. That's the main thing.' The forensic scientist looked sheepishly across at him. 'I got it sadly wrong about Alexander Moore. What an embarrassment.'

'What did we find out about Caroline Harper?' Carlisle asked.

Mason reached for his notebook. 'Early days, I'm afraid. We know he took out a six month lease on the old watermill property, so he was in for the long haul.'

Hedley placed his mug down and leaned back in some discomfort. 'I doubt she's alive, poor girl.'

'What about video footage?' Carlisle asked. 'There must be plenty of that?'

'That's the trouble. It'll take weeks to sift through, and we don't have that sort of time on our hands.'

'Do we know where she was murdered?'

'Not at the old watermill, I'm certain of that.' Mason raised his hands in mock submission. 'But don't quote me on that as we've found more blood trace evidence there.'

'And Wynn's still refusing to talk?'

Mason took a huge bite out of his biscuit. 'You could say that, yes.'

Now the facts were beginning to unfold, Carlisle began to wonder where Wynn's anger came from, and why he'd crossed the line from a scorned lover to a woman hater. The killer's mind was obviously in a state of perpetual hyper vigilance, like a car's engine revved up to maximum speed. Getting him to talk would be difficult, but unravelling the truth even harder. It was a tense stand-off, and if ever they were going to find this woman alive they would need to get him to talk.

Carlisle sat silent for a moment.

'It's not the actual murder that excites him,' Carlisle explained, 'it's more the control he has over his victims. That's why he's refusing to talk. He's savouring the moment, and that's what excites him.'

'Never mind the bollocks,' Mason shrugged. 'Where the hell is she?'

Carlisle eased back his seat, knowing all too well where this was heading. 'Wynn's predictable, and sticks rigidly to set plans. We need to break down the mental barriers, find out what's going on inside his head.'

Hedley shot him another painful glance. 'How do you propose to do that when he denies all knowledge of Mary Fowler?'

'Let me talk to him, Tom.'

'That's ridiculous!'

'I'm a profiler. I know how these things work.'

Hedley was feeling the strain, and Mason had picked up on it.

'He's right, Tom, anything's worth a try at this stage of the game.'

Hedley responded bitterly, 'Yes, but Wynn spent the best part of his time trying to get inside your head as I remember. It was this heartless sod who posted her finger through your letter box.'

'That's true,' Mason nodded.

Hedley had calmed down a tad.

'I doubt he'll listen to you anyway.'

Carlisle stared at them, unblinking. 'Is that what this is about?'

'No, but what are the chances she's still alive?' Mason queried.

Carlisle thought a moment. 'He's holding her somewhere local, I'd wager.'

'What if she's already dead?' said Mason. 'Sutherland believes she is.'

'Then she's wrong,' Carlisle replied. 'Wynn's far too predictable, and we caught him in the middle of his act. Before he kills these women he obviously likes to watch them suffer. That's how he gets his gratification, from filming everything. What follows is an anti-climax, and he probably feels let down by the final act of killing itself—'

'But surely he's broken the cycle with Mary Fowler?' Hedley interrupted.

'You're right,' Mason acknowledged. 'Unlike the others, she didn't marry her husband for his money as she was wealthy in her own right.'

Tom Hedley was uncharacteristically on his high horse. It had to be the medication, Carlisle reasoned. If not, then things were getting out of hand.

'If Mary Fowler was dead,' Carlisle went on, 'then he would have made pretty damn sure we'd have found her body by now. No. Wynn's holding her somewhere. Where, I have no idea. To him it's a game, and he's angry that we charged someone else with his crimes.'

'So Sutherland was right. This is about ego,' Mason shrugged.

'In a way, yes, but getting him to talk about it won't be easy.'

Hedley held his gaze, his eyes filled with genuine concern. 'In some ways this case reminds me of Ian Huntley when he taunted his victim's families in front of the TV cameras.'

Mason stared long and hard at Carlisle. 'Do you think you can get close to him?'

'Isn't that what I'm paid to do?'

'I know that, but there's a life at stake here.'

'I know.'

Mason looked at Hedley and shook his head. 'What other options do we have left open to us, Tom? Wynn's refusing to talk to any of us, and we're fast running out of time.'

'I'm still not convinced it's a good idea.'

'Tell me why not for heaven's sake.'

Hedley shrugged. 'If Wynn's a control freak, then we're playing into his hands.'

Carlisle pushed forward in his seat, pondering Hedley's statement. Tom had a point, and a good one at that. Would Wynn cooperate? Probably not, unless of course—

'If Wynn thinks I'm inferior to him then why not play him at his own game?'

'He's not going to do that now,' Hedley replied, 'not after he's spent months taunting you.'

'You're right,' Mason shrugged. 'But what other alternatives do we have?'

Hedley shifted awkwardly in his position. 'It's far too dangerous.'

Mason stared at him, and Carlisle stared back.

'What do you know about Lance Wynn's background?' Mason asked.

'Meaning?'

'What makes Wynn tick – what doesn't. You need to think it through carefully, my friend. This one's a hard nut to crack. All the same, there must be a chink in his armour somewhere.'

Carlisle acknowledged with a nod, and then said, 'If Wynn thinks he's in control, he'll not feel threatened in any way. It could work in our favour, Jack.'

Hedley remained unconvinced.

'OK,' Mason said as if the matter was already decided. 'It'll be days before your people come up with anything, Tom. Even then there's no guarantees we'll find anything. My problem is this.' Mason stood to face the forensic scientist. 'If Mary Fowler's alive, we'll need to move sooner than later.'

'And what if she's dead?'

'That's exactly my point. What the hell do we have to lose?'

Hedley looked ill. He should never have come here in the first place. Dedication to duty was one thing, but this was bordering on insanity.

'Right then,' said Mason after a while. 'Let's see if we can't get this canary to sing.'

Carlisle said nothing. Sometimes it was safer to stay well clear of police matters, particularly internal politics. Behind the killer's mask of deceit lay a darker side, a side difficult to comprehend. If there was a guardian angel overlooking Mary Fowler then they still had an awful lot of work to do. For Wynn to give up his secrets now would be tantamount to self-betrayal. He was never going to do that, not in a million years.

Mason broke out in a grin. 'I guess it's all down to you, my friend.'

Suddenly the room felt a lonely place.

Chapter
Forty-Eight

David Carlisle had always dreamt of such a moment. Face to face with a serial killer in a police interview room. He'd often wondered what it would be like, and whether it would live up to his expectations. Despite the heavy media coverage, the police were no further forward in establishing the victim's whereabouts. Many believed Mary Fowler was dead. Rotting in a field somewhere as part of Wynn's narcissistic control? Even after sixteen hours of intense cross-examination, the team had failed miserably. Any hope of finding her alive now rested firmly on the profiler's shoulders. It was a fine balancing act, a game of cat and mouse where there could only be one outcome.

DC Carrington activated the recording tape and announced the date, time, and those present. Wynn's demeanour was strained. His body language tense, eyes full of hate, and his pupils dilated.

Carlisle gauged the man's hesitation, before he spoke. 'When you were a little boy, did you always pull the legs off spiders so that they couldn't run away? Or were you the little boy who would pick up an injured sparrow and try to save its life? Tell me, Lance, which one was you?'

'Fuck you, Carlisle; you know nothing about my childhood.'

The room fell silent again – a gathering of wits.

'Tell me about your father, what kind of man was he?'

'Why should I?' Wynn shrugged.

'Did he encourage you as a child, or did he simply beat you senseless after arriving home from the pub every night? Is that the kind of man your father really was?'

Now on the defensive, Wynn's eyes were everywhere.

'Do you really want to know what it was like, lying awake listening for his footsteps every night? I remember the stairs used to creak, all the way to the top landing. I could never close my eyes until my father was asleep. Even then I was too scared to get out of bed for fear he would wake up in the middle of the night.'

'Tell me about your mother, Lance,' Carlisle said, 'Was she always kind to everyone?'

'You're asking too many questions, it's—'

'When I was looking through your rooms, I found a photograph album of her in a bedside cabinet. She seemed such a caring woman, motherly, the kind of person who would protect her children at all costs. What was she really like, Lance?'

Wynn drew back in his chair and clasped his hands on the table in front of him. He was fighting it, unsure of which way to turn. Deep down, Carlisle felt he was winning over his trust. At least he was talking, which was a lot more than many had anticipated. Even so, it still felt like he was treading in a minefield. One false move and it would all end in disaster.

'My mother means nothing to you, Carlisle.'

'How old were you when she died?'

Wynn hesitated. 'Fourteen—'

'I too feel your pain,' said Carlisle. I lost my mother when I was seventeen, but three years when you're a teenager can seem like a lifetime. I still miss her, even though she's been dead almost thirty years. There's never a day goes by that I don't think about her. It's funny how young men always stay close to their mothers. Is it because they are always there for you, or is your mother the only person in the world you can share your secrets with?' Carlisle eased forward in his seat, and caught Wynn's hurt. 'My mother and I were close. She would always make sure I stayed out of trouble. If ever I needed to talk to someone, it was always my mother I would turn to. How about you, what was your mother really like?'

Wynn's eyes lifted to the heavens, and he made the sign of the cross.

'We talked. Unlike the rest, I always felt I could trust her. She once asked me what I was doing with all of my pocket money,' said Wynn. 'She was concerned. A lot of the other kids on the estate were spending their pocket money on drugs. My mum was naturally suspicious. When I told her I'd been saving to buy a second-hand camera, she took me into Middlesbrough and bought me a brand new one.'

'You like photography, don't you, Lance?'

'Do I?'

'You're really good at it. I've seen some of your work. You have a natural talent and I like the way you see things. Your pictures are an art form, something to be admired.'

'So why ask?'

Carlisle shrugged. 'Tell me what you're looking for when you're stood in the middle of a murder scene. What excites you most? What are your thoughts?'

Wynn's gaze was intense, eyes cold and piercing. The problem was, Wynn could never have escaped his abusive childhood and that was the crux of the problem. Even though his violent tendencies were uncontrollable, Wynn's greatest asset was his intelligence. And yet, after his first murder had been committed the anger inside him just wouldn't go away. Not without a lot of medical intervention that is.

Wynn's eyes narrowed as he took another deep breath.

'Who said I murdered anyone?'

Carlisle explained. 'With me, it's always the finality – the calm after the storm. You sense it, from the minute you first set foot on the crime scene.' He paused for effect. 'Do you always feel excitement when you stare at your victims; is your heart racing? Is it the rage that attracts you towards these women, or is it simply the thrill of seeing what you've done to them? With me it's always the victim's eyes. It's the emptiness in their expression, as if they're searching for a reason as to why it had happened to them. Tell me, Lance, what do you feel?'

'Why should I?'

'I'm genuinely interested.'

'How I feel, and how I react is irrelevant. Death is a finality that all of us must endure at some stage in our lives. Even you must face up to that, Carlisle.' Wynn clicked his tongue. He was drooling now. 'There are those who will never take control of their own destinies. Evil bitches that get what's coming to them.'

'And you genuinely believe you have control over these women's lives?'

'Of course—'

'What makes you say that?'

'Some people create their own destinies; others bring it upon themselves. Me, I know how the game of life plays out – its rules – the little idiosyncrasies that can change a person's destiny.'

'And you are the judge in all of this?'

'We are all answerable to God, Carlisle. We're mere transients in this life. It's God who decides when our time is up. Not me or you.'

Carlisle thought about it, convinced that Wynn was driven by some kind of religious fanaticism. Sitting there he felt nothing but vile wickedness, as though he was being sucked into a large vortex – a black bottomless pit full of writhing snakes. You don't point a finger at a serial killer when they're cornered he kept telling himself, as they will always see themselves smarter than you.

'Was Caroline answerable to God?'

Wynn's smug laugh told him he was reliving a fantasy.

'I doubt you realise anything about God's work.'

'What makes you say that?'

'It is written, that those who desire to be rich fall into temptation, into a snare, into many senseless and harmful desires that plunge people into ruin and destruction.'

'Timothy Chapter Nine, verse six,' Carlisle smiled.

'You surprise me!'

'Was your mother a very religious woman, Lance?'

'She taught me right from wrong, why?'

'What else did she teach you?'

'Thou shalt not covet—'

'How fitting she should teach you the Ten Commandments. My mother used to read them to me, over and over again until I could recite them verbatim. She would ask me questions about them. Number eight she would say – though shalt not steal, I would reply.'

Wynn acknowledged with a nod. 'You are good, I'm impressed.'

'Young women who marry older men, how do they make you feel? Do you feel angry? Is that what this is all about?'

'Meaning?'

Carlisle smiled with hopeless malice watching Wynn's every facial twitch. His eyes were expressionless, cold, calculating, staring directly across at him. He leaned forward and gently tapped the table with his finger. 'I'll tell you what makes me angry about these two-faced selfish bitches, Lance. They're all top show and no knickers. Five star hotels, expensive cordon bleu restaurants, chauffeur driven cars that turn every punter's eye that happens to pass them by. That's what they like to brag about. When you really sit down and think about it, they're nothing but high-class prostitutes. Is that how you feel about them?'

'You have no idea how I feel.'

'How fitting, Lance.' Carlisle held his gaze for a second longer than he would have liked to. He was closer now, closer than ever before. 'Does God tell you to punish these women?'

'You are good, Carlisle. I'm impressed.'

'Like me, you hate these women don't you, Lance?'

'I never said I killed anyone.'

'And I never said you did,' he replied calmly.

Carlisle sat quietly as Wynn's eyes suddenly shot open; as if the nightmare wouldn't go away. Where did it all go wrong? He wondered. Wynn had been quick to point out he was innocent of any wrongdoing, but where did the anger come from? Was it love at first sight with Cheryl Sawyer? Had Wynn been keen to set up a family unit with his childhood sweetheart, something he could never have had with his drunken father? Yes, of course, once Cheryl Sawyer had broken that trust and run off to marry a man with more money than Wynn could ever dream of, it was only natural that jealousy would take over. And that's when the aggression surfaced. Wynn wasn't a pathological liar who lied compulsively. Wynn's lies had a definite goal – to paint himself as the victim.

'She was a bitch,' Wynn whispered.

'What makes you so angry about this young woman?' Carlisle insisted. 'Did you love her, Lance? Did she mean so much to you that you would have given your life to have her back in your arms again? Is that what makes you feel so angry?'

Carlisle caught an ice cold look in Wynn's glances. He was fighting it, and there was nothing he could do to stop it.

The muscles in Wynn's neck tightened.

'She got what was coming to her.'

'Did you feel let down by her?'

Wynn's glances had hardened, and Incident Room One suddenly felt a more eerie place – shallow, sinister, and vile. 'I feel your pain, Lance,' Carlisle whispered. 'Having someone taken away from you like that must have been the hardest thing in the world to come to terms with. I know what you're going through. I've felt its loss too. The intolerable hurt inside, alone in the dark with only your thoughts to comfort you. At two o'clock in the morning your mind plays evil tricks with you. It's a lonely place. Then, just when you think you can't take any more, you begin to think about what might have been. As the darkness closes in, you begin to question yourself. Where did this all go wrong? Was it my fault, you ask? With me, it's the loneliness that eats away at your soul. It feels like you're being suffocated. There's nowhere to hide, no one to talk it over with anymore. It's just you and your lonely inner thoughts. Is that how you feel, betrayed by a childhood sweetheart who didn't give a damn about your hurt? Does the loneliness scream out to you in the middle of night?'

Wynn was inconsolable now, tears rolling down his cheeks.

'No more!'

Carlisle pressed harder. 'That's the thing, Lance. She's now with this rich old guy and he's holding her tight in his arms. Your mind plays evil tricks with you and wanders into places you don't want it to go. She's there in front of you, and you can't stop his hands groping her soft tender thighs. He's not stopping, is he; further and further between her legs until he feels her inner warmth. Do you remember when it was you doing that to her, Lance?'

'Yes,' Wynn groaned.

'Did he steal her away from you, this greedy little slut who left you for another man's wealth? Is that what the hate is all about?'

Wynn was reliving the moment, gutted, inconsolable.

'Stop it!' Wynn screamed. 'No more!'

The anger still in him, Wynn wiped the tears from his eyes. His hands were shaking, and his face had turned a pallid colour.

'Cheryl was a selfish bitch, and she betrayed you, Lance?'

'I know,' Wynn sobbed,

'She deserved to die, didn't she?'

Distraught, Wynn punched the air with a clenched fist. Inconsolable, his knuckles were white and his pupils dilated. Never once had he shown remorse towards his victim – never once. His love for Cheryl Sawyer had turned into a deadly obsession which had escalated out of control. But what drove him to kill? Was it an intermittent explosive disorder that had caused him to snap, or simply an uncontrollable loss of temper?

He was close, but he needed to unlock the door to Wynn's inner mind.

'What have you done with Mary Fowler, Lance?

'I can't tell you that, I've—'

'Is she alive?'

'She's—' Wynn's voice slowly tailed away.

'Mary's not a slut. She's not like the other worthless pieces of shit.'

'Yes she is. They all deserve to die.'

'If she *is* alive, then you and I need to finish it. This isn't as bad as it seems. I've handled worse before, a lot worse.'

Carlisle was surprised he'd even come this far. Wynn was fighting it, and his hands were uncontrollable shaking with rage. It was time to hit hard.

'Tell me about Mary Fowler. What kind of woman is she?' Carlisle's voice had softened somewhat. 'Could her husband not perform anymore, was he incapable, or had she simply grown tired of his lacklustre performance in bed? Is that why she became desperate to get away from him? Was sex the problem?' Wynn's body language had changed. He'd hit a raw nerve and Wynn was taking it badly. 'She's not worth it, Lance. She's slowly destroying you and it's time to give her up. I know how to deal with these despicable sluts, and I know how their filthy minds work. First they offer you their bodies, and then they ditch you for someone else. To them you're just another worthless piece of shit!'

Wynn was at breaking point and the anger inside him resurfacing.

'It's just you and me against the rest of the world, Carlisle.'

'Why don't you let me finish it? I'd like to smash her skull in, wrap my grubby fingers around her scrawny little neck and squeeze until the last ounce of breath leaves her body.' Carlisle fell silent for a moment. 'How does that make you feel?'

'Better, much better.'

'Where is she, Lance, because we mustn't let her get away with it.'

'How should we finish it?' Wynn sobbed,

She's alive, thought Carlisle.

'Just the two of us, Lance, is that how it is? Tell me where she is and I'll make her go away for you.'

'Don't mess with me, Carlisle.'

Wynn was now fighting him every inch of the way.

'*Now will the ruler of this world be cast out,*' Carlisle cried out.

Wynn's face instantly lit up. 'I like that. You're good Carlisle, extremely good. I always knew there was something special about you that I admired. Now I know why.'

'Just tell me where is she?'

'You know I can't do that.' Wynn licked his lips. 'That's not part of the game.'

'It's not a game, Lance. She's slowly destroying you.'

Wynn's face contorted. Then, in the blink of an eye he suddenly exploded into religious verse again.

'My father's house has many rooms. If that were not so, would I have told you that I am going to prepare a place for you?'

Carlisle stiffened. This was the last thing he wanted to hear right now.

'She's close to God, isn't she, Lance?'

'Yes.'

'It feels as if I can almost reach out and touch her,' Carlisle said. 'Where will I find her, Lance?'

Wynn's stare suddenly hardened.

'Go to hell, Carlisle.'

Chapter
Forty-Nine

It wasn't the best start to his day, thought David Carlisle, at nine o'clock on Monday morning. Having returned to his office in Fowler Street after months spent working alongside the Northumbria Police, it felt good to get his feet back under the table again. Now strictly a police matter, the search for Mary Fowler had been significantly scaled down. In truth, he was extremely disappointed with the Acting Superintendent's recent handling of the case. He'd always thought she had her finger on the pulse, but he was wrong. It was a terrible risk she was taking, but she was adamant they were now searching for a body. It wasn't the kind of ending he'd hoped for, far from it. Carlisle hated unfinished business at the best of times as it always left a bitter taste in his mouth. Being a profiler had its benefits but sometimes it could be soul destroying work. Once the police had their killer behind bars, his part in the operations was over.

Now onto his second cup of coffee, Carlisle stared at his in-tray and wondered just where to begin. His mailbox was full, there were fifty-two unanswered e-mails showing on his monitor screen, and now the printer had packed in. Ever since setting foot in his office that morning, nothing had gone to plan.

There was something else, he suddenly remembered. He'd neglected to switch the slow cooker on before leaving home that morning and unless a miracle cropped up, it would be beans on toast again for tea.

'Your new girlfriend called in earlier,' said Jane Collins.

Normally chatty, his business partner had barely spoken a word to him all that morning. Whatever it was that was niggling away at her, he sure felt uncomfortable about it.

'What new girlfriend is this?' he answered casually.

'The young Detective Constable you've been working with.'

'You mean Sue.'

Jane bit her lip and reddened. 'Sue is it now? Whatever happened to DC Carrington?'

'Well, we're certainly not sleeping together if that's what you're thinking. Not at the moment we're not.'

Jane stared at him open-mouthed.

'I was joking, David.'

He thought about it, but refused to be drawn in. 'What time did she call?'

'Shortly after seven thirty. I was opening the office at the time.'

That's odd, he thought. Carrington lived in Newcastle. Unless—

'Alone was she?'

'Yes, and she's been taken off the case apparently and is now back at Gateshead Police Station.'

'And that was it?'

'Yes, were you expecting something else?'

No answer.

Jane rubbed her hands together and smiled awkwardly. 'This young woman that's gone missing, it's not looking good, is it?'

'What, Mary Fowler?'

'Yes. They still haven't found her according to the latest news bulletins.'

'Why, did Sue mention something about it to you?'

'Not to me she didn't. Mind the poor girl's probably dead by the sound of things.'

Carlisle filed a few papers away and brought Jane up to speed with what he already knew about the case. Wynn was leading the police a merry old dance by all accounts, and no doubt revelling in the considerable media attention he was gaining. The only consolation, if there was such a thing, is that he was now behind bars. Serial killers had a nasty habit of hiding the truth, and Wynn was a master at his game. If Mary Fowler was alive, and Carlisle firmly believed she was, it was only a matter of time before she would slip into a coma and die from hypothermia or dehydration. Either way, it wasn't looking good.

When Carlisle was finished with the rest of the story, Jane seemed to have calmed down. It didn't take much. Jane wasn't the confrontational type, not like some of the other women he knew. The thing was, and he still hadn't mentioned it to Jane, George Fowler's naivety had probably cost his wife dearly. Plucked off the streets by a man hell bent on making his mark, she was now in desperate trouble. Carlisle's main concern right now was convincing the others that she was still alive.

He put his mug down on the desk and thought about this. Despite his resolve to make a fresh start, he'd taken his guard down and somehow allowed the killer to crawl back inside his mind again.

'I hate to admit it,' Carlisle said, 'but the poor woman is still out there.'

'Is Wynn still refusing to cooperate?' asked Jane.

'According to the prison priest, he's shut himself off from the rest of the world and is refusing to speak to anyone. All except God, that is.'

'Oh dear,' Jane sighed. 'Don't tell me God's told him to kill these women.'

'That just about sums it up, I'm afraid.'

'So how did he win these women over in the first place?'

'Wynn used a range of persuasion tactics to lure his victims into a sense of false security. He feigned he was rich, hired expensive cars, and rented flash apartments, and generally splashed his money about on them. Once he'd won their trust over, that's when their troubles began.'

Jane seemed genuinely concerned, and was keen to press the matter further.

'So when did you realise it was Lance Wynn?'

'It's a long story,' Carlisle sighed.

'These women were obviously up for it, even I can see that.'

'Yes, but it sounds better coming from your lips.'

They shared a smile.

'Where the hell did Wynn get his money from?' asked Jane.

'Good question.'

Jane's jaw suddenly dropped. 'Hang on a minute, wasn't Wynn an Accountant?'

'Yes, but he didn't fiddle the books if that's what you're thinking. No, his mother had a large property portfolio which had been passed down to her from her father. When she finally passed away, Wynn was the sole beneficiary in her will.'

Jane answered another incoming call and wrote something down in her diary.

Carlisle had to admit, he'd missed the office banter these past few months. It was like catching up on old times. Jane was easy to get on with, not complicated like the rest.

'That's strange,' said Jane wrinkling her nose up again. 'I thought Mary Fowler had money in her own rights.'

'She has, but that wasn't the reason why Wynn snatched her off the streets. He was angry with the police at the time. They'd charged someone else with his crimes and Wynn just wanted to get back at them.'

'What, they charged the wrong man!'

'No. It was a con. The police had made up a cock-and-bull story to force Wynn out into the open again.'

'Goodness that was sly of them.'

Carlisle shrugged. 'Right place wrong time unfortunately, and she probably never saw it coming. Life is a lottery it seems.'

Mulling this over, it was then Carlisle remembered the calendar stuck on the back of Wynn's kitchen door. Pictures of Durham — churches of all things. Then the penny suddenly dropped. Why hadn't he thought of that before?

First Isaiah 10.3, now John 14.

Clever, he thought. These were cryptic clues, and Wynn was reaching out to him and trying to scramble up his brain. And that was the thing; it couldn't be treated lightly as there was now another person's life at stake.

'It has to be—' Carlisle suddenly announced.

'Has to be what?'

'Wynn's back to his old tricks again.'

Jane gave him a bemused look. 'What the hell are you waffling on about now?'

Carlisle reached for his iPhone, and punched in Jack Mason's number.

Chapter Fifty

Earlier that morning

It was dark outside, the street lights were on and the assembled operations team was now on to its third cup of coffee. Bleary-eyed and shabbily dressed, at six o'clock in the morning DCI Mason looked exhausted. Some murder cases were easy to solve, others took a lot longer. Not this one. Jack Mason had reached breaking point and it was beginning to get on top of him. The trouble was, his search for Mary Fowler had gone cold and he had to think on his feet. Staring at his notes, his next words when they came were met with another wall of silence.

'We're looking in all the wrong places,' Mason announced.

Still no one spoke.

Everyone present knew the case files off by heart. Imprinted in their brains, the team had lived with them continually for the past six months now and they were finally running out of steam – *and ideas it seemed*. It was a large catchment area, stretching from Gateshead and as far south as Yorkshire. Even the public's insatiable demand for answers had thrown up very little in the way of Mary Fowler's whereabouts.

In the warm cosy comfort of Briefing Room One, Acting Superintendent Sutherland had said very little so far. Sitting at the back of the briefing room in a smart two piece suit, white blouse, and a pair of flat, comfortable shoes, she'd been taking down copious notes. The truth was, she too had run out of ideas and had nothing further to contribute.

Mason cleared his throat.

'Based on my observations, some people can survive without water for a week and that's being generous. If the loss of water in the body is not replaced, the volume of body fluid can drastically fall causing the body's blood volume to drop. When we stop sweating our body temperatures rise, and due to the loss of blood circulation caused through a drop in blood volume, our blood pressure drops to levels that can be fatal.'

Mason sensed uneasiness. He could almost reach out and touch it.

'How long do we have?' said DS Savage.

'Three days at the most.'

'What's the feedback from Crimewatch, boss?' asked Holt.

'There's been a good response, George. So good in fact, we've set up a special hot room to deal with the sheer volume of new information we're receiving.'

'What about clairvoyants?' DS Savage cut in.

'Nah, they're an utter waste of time.'

'And special search teams?' queried Holt.

'There's been very little in the way of feedback so far. We've checked rivers, ponds, outlying buildings, and large swathes of countryside in and around the Houghton-le-Spring area, and still found nothing.' Mason's head dropped. 'I know we've been over this ground several times before, but tyre tracks leading from the old watermill suggest Wynn drove west that night – and not south as many of you have pointed out.'

DS Holt stared at his notes. 'I've been looking into that, boss. There is any number of isolated buildings where he could have hidden her.'

'I'm not rejecting the idea outright, but the last thing on Wynn's mind would have been to find another remote location. He left in a hurry, which means his first reaction would be to move back into familiar territory.'

'Middlesbrough—'

'No, George and here's my thinking.' Mason shuffled awkwardly as he stared at the large map pinned the back of the office wall. 'On the day of his arrest, Wynn was first picked up by a passing patrol car heading east along A689. At this point he joins the A177 and heads south towards Stockton. Twenty minutes later, at nine-fifty-three, he enters Middlesbrough's city centre car park. That's where we finally nabbed him.' Mason traced the route with the point of his pen. 'To me, that suggests he was holding her somewhere between Durham and Gateshead.'

'Could an accomplice be harbouring her?' DS Savage asked.

'Possible, Rob, but highly unlikely, don't you think? Especially with the sort of media coverage we're getting.'

'True—'

'The trouble was,' Mason went on, 'Wynn was able to move freely around by using false number plates.'

Savage made a little grimace. 'What about forensic soil samples found in the tyre treads?'

'Nothing has shown up so far. It was raining that night, so any soil sample would have mainly matched the watermill area and we know he never returned there again.'

Harry Manley drew breath as he sucked on a humbug.

'What's the latest on the police helicopter, boss?'

'I was coming to that, Harry,' Mason replied. 'Hawkeye's thermal imaging camera can cover a lot of ground, particularly in open countryside. Move into the towns and cities and it's like looking for a needle in a haystack. It's crap. We know Hawkeye's ideal in an aerial pursuit, but we now believe the victim's gone static.'

'What information do we have from the estate agents?' Manley queried.

'No other properties have been taken out by anyone remotely resembling Lance Wynn's new mug shot.'

'If he did leave the old watermill in a westerly direction that night, there should be plenty of CCTV coverage,' Holt suggested.

Mason's iPhone vibrated in his pocket. He pulled it out and checked the display.

It was David Carlisle, and he switched it to loud speaker.

'Hi, Jack,' Carlisle said in his usual cheery voice.

'Yes, mate. What can I do for you? I'm in the middle of a meeting at the moment.'

'You asked me to ring the moment I came up with anything.'

'Yes. Thank you.'

'I've been thinking back to my interview with Lance Wynn, and . it was something he said.'

'Oh!'

'Well, one of the things he came out with was John 14:2.'

'What about it?'

'It's a verse from the Bible,' Carlisle said jokingly.

'Yes, I know what a bloody bible is goddammit. It's nine o'clock in the morning and I've been up since four.'

'It may not sound much, but John 14:2 could be a cryptic clue?'

'A what?'

'Let me put it to you another way,' Carlisle said. 'John 14 states: My father's house has many rooms; if that were not so, would I have told you that I am going there to prepare a place for you?'

Mason stared at the others present. 'What the hell are you on about now?'

'Well, a few things spring to mind, but I think he's holding her in a church somewhere.'

The muscles in Mason's neck tightened. 'Where are you now?' he asked.

'I'm in my office. Why?'

There followed a short pause, but only a few seconds.

'I'll ring you back, I'm nearly done here.'

The phone connection went dead.

Chapter
Fifty-One

Jack Mason had been involved in another suspicious death that weekend, a known drug dealer who'd mysteriously fallen from the nineteenth floor of a tower block in the centre of Gateshead. His death bore all the hallmarks of foul play, but neither the police nor the Coroner's office were one-hundred per cent at this stage. Smacked out of his mind on cocaine, it was one of those cases of – was he pushed or did he jump? Having set up a small investigation team to deal with the matter, Mason's biggest concern was still Mary Fowler's whereabouts.

Something of a lost soul, Jack Mason's past made his job complicated. Divorced, he drank heavily and constantly broke the law himself in order to get things done. Not the easiest of people to get on with, he was inflexible, single-minded, and all too often he rubbed people up the wrong way. A veteran of trouble, Mason was old school whereas Carlisle was completely the opposite. The profiler was level-headed, approachable, and liked to work things out logically. Not ideally matched, together they formed a formidable partnership but apart they were just ordinary. And that, everyone believed, was their biggest drawback.

Having spent the past sixteen hours working their way through the possibilities, Carlisle felt terrible. Unable to get comfortable, he'd been on edge ever since leaving St John's in Middlesbrough that morning. Fast approaching the next roundabout, the Satnav instructed them to turn left at the next exit and follow the A693 towards Annfield Plain. Stanley was in semi-darkness and most of the house lights switched off. It was then he spotted movement – a stout man carrying a stack of empty baking trays towards the back of an open green transit van. Instantly his spirits soared, and at five in the morning they weren't alone anymore.

It was starting to get light, when DCI Mason pulled the unmarked Ford Focus estate onto a little grass verge opposite St John's church and switched the car's engine off. They sat for a while, peering aimlessly out through the mud spattered windscreen. Their plan, inasmuch as they had one, had been to investigate every St John's religious building within a twenty mile radius of County Durham. It was a hare brained scheme and Dipton their last port of call.

Carlisle had read somewhere that due to a falling congregation this one hundred and thirty year old parish church was now in jeopardy of closing. Not that he was interested, but at least he was well informed. Throughout their journey, Carlisle had continually recited John 14:2 to himself. Wynn's religious quotations spooked him, as they always had a double-edged meaning to them. The man was delusional, a classic psychopath who liked nothing more than to climb into other people's heads and scramble things up. If Mary Fowler was alive, this was the perfect place to be holding her.

'Last chance corral, my friend,' Mason said, stifling a yawn.

'I know.'

'Which is it to be first, church or outbuildings?'

'Let's check the church.'

The front door was locked, as was the rest of the building. How things had changed, he thought. Carlisle could remember when church doors were never locked – left open for people to pray at any time of day. Not anymore they couldn't. Opportunist thieves had stripped lead from their roofs, helped themselves to religious silverware, and stolen just about anything of value left lying around. Mainly low-life scum, they cared little for the rest of the decent folk in society.

A vast silence reigned over the land that morning, the pre-dawn mist still clinging to the graveyard and creating a ghostlike atmosphere amongst hundreds of headstones. At the rear of the building Mason had found an unlocked window. Or so he claimed he had. Carlisle had his suspicions, as he found a broken window latch lying on the ground. He could certain of one thing; there was never a dull moment when you were working with Jack Mason.

Just as the Detective Chief Inspector squeezed head-first in through the tiny opening, Carlisle glanced up. Not the most gracious of entries, he thought. Once inside he shone his torch at the altar screen. St John's was full of ominous surprises at five in the morning. Weird ghostlike figures that danced across whitewashed walls creating all kinds of paranormal shapes. The House of God could be an eerie place at times, the unknown even scarier. Some churches claimed the spirits of the dead hung around in their buildings at night. Mysterious noises, unexplained phenomena that persistently walked their grounds. It was moments like this, and there had been many over the years, when the souls of the dead scared the hell out of Carlisle.

'Nothing here,' Mason said, slamming the vestry door shut behind him.

'We're close, Jack. I can definitely feel a presence.'

'Well, she ain't in the building, my friend.'

Carlisle wasn't a religious man, but the soft dawn light now filtering through stain glass leaded windows and creating a kaleidoscope of colour, seemed to have a calming effect on him. If God was on their side, then he was certainly showing them signs. His mind running amok, Carlisle pictured the terrifying scenes that night. Chained to a water pipe in a room full of rats was enough to drive anyone mad. How long Mary Fowler had been held in captivity was anybody's guess. The question was in which direction had Wynn taken her that night? Thinking back, this seemed as good a place as any. Well off the beaten track, it was far enough away to throw the police off his scent.

Picked out in his flashlight beam, a memorial plaque flickered on the wall. Filled with endless names of young men taken from their villages and never to return again, it was a stark reminder of Dipton's dreadful past. This once thriving pit mining community had clearly suffered enormous human sacrifice during the Great War, but their names lived on.

Then, through a small gap in a window, Carlisle's attention was drawn to the building opposite. It wasn't a big gap, but it was enough.

'I think I know where he's holding her, Jack.'

'Try pulling the other leg,' Mason groaned. 'It's time we called it a day.'

'Not yet. I swear I'm onto something.'

Mason gave him a stern, cautioning look.

'Let's hope you're right, because I'm fast running out of patience, my friend.'

'Trust me, Jack.'

Chapter Fifty-Two

It was picture-perfect, thought David Carlisle. Surrounded on three sides by tall trees, the building was scarcely visible from the road. From the outside its construction spoke volumes about its past. Late Victorian, an old blacksmith's shop or something to do with horses, he guessed. Either way it seemed the ideal location. Constructed on two levels, it had six ground floor windows, a high timbered roof, and was built of solid stone. On closer inspection he could see the main entrance doors were secured with an old rusty chain and heavily padlocked. The only visible access, if he could call it that, was via a steep narrow footpath leading down from the rear of the graveyard. Carlisle had a bad feeling about this, even though it looked like any other building in the area.

Mason's eyes widened as he prised back one of the ground floor window panels and poked his rubber flashlight in through the tiny opening. His face looked pallid in the early morning sunlight, but his look of determination unquestionable.

'We need to cut the locks,' Mason suddenly announced. 'I'll be back in a jiffy.'

Carlisle watched him go. There was a new spring in the Detective Chief Inspector's step, as though life had suddenly taken on a whole new meaning again. A hundred yards on, after disappearing behind a high stone wall, he returned carrying a pair of long handled bolt cutters. Seconds later they were inside and fumbling around in the dark.

'Over here,' Mason whispered.

Dimly lit, the room was much longer than Carlisle had anticipated. At one end a bar, the other, a large central stage overlooking what he took to be a long wooden dance floor. There were tables and chairs down both sides, along with some other eerie shadows he couldn't quite make out.

Music began to play – extremely loud.

Hands cupped to his ears, Carlisle tried to block it out but it felt as though someone was working a jackhammer and drilling into concrete. Thrown into utter confusion, he could barely breathe let alone think straight anymore. It was pitch black inside the room, humid, and stank of decay. Disoriented, just when he thought he couldn't take any more, the music suddenly stopped. Then, as if by magic, the stage lights mysteriously came on. Not for long, though, but enough to realise he was standing in a room filled with mannequins. Hundreds of them – some in party clothes, others dressed as clowns. It was surreal, and he tried not to dwell on it too long. He'd seen evil before, but nothing compared with this. Only a deranged mind could have dreamt up such a bizarre setting, and only one person's name sprang to mind.

Lance Wynn!

No sooner had Mason's flashlight picked out the lounge bar, than Carlisle's heart sank. Like a thousand nightmares rolled into one, he could hardly believe his eyes. Dressed in outlandish religious regalia and each wearing a large wooden cross around their neck, a small group of mannequins sat huddled together in prayer. What their significance was he had no idea, but they sure scared the hell out of him.

'Did you hear that?' Mason nervously whispered.

'Hear what—'

'Like a small child!'

Flashlight in hand, Carlisle crept forward towards the foot of the stage. His watch told him it was 5.45am, but he'd lost all sense of time. Sweat pouring out of him and unable to focus properly, he found the stench of rotten flesh overpowering. He swallowed hard, and tried to put it to the back of his mind. He'd experienced its like before, a sickly smell, like an infected wound that just wouldn't heal. This was sheer madness, he thought. There had to be an easier way, but he sure couldn't think of one right now.

Then the stage curtains slid open.

No motors, only a swishing noise to be heard.

'There—' Mason called out.

Eyes glued centre stage, Carlisle adjusted to the light. Beneath the solitary spotlight, he saw what he took to be a bundle of rags. Then, deep inside the shadows he caught movement. Not much, but enough to draw his attention towards it. The next thing he noticed, when he finally focused his mind, was the terrified look on the woman's face. Scarcely alive, she pitifully clawed her way towards them. Her movements were sluggish, almost robotic, like something he'd seen in a horror movie. Arms outstretched and eyes open wide in fear, she slowly began to topple over.

This wasn't a game she was playing, this was for real and she was desperately trying to tell them something. It was then he saw the chains – she was shackled to a large central ring.

Mason held out his hand, and she gripped it.

'Try not to move,' the Detective Chief Inspector whispered.

Her mouth frozen open in a cry of revulsion, she pointed towards the ceiling. Thirty feet up, in amongst the complex stage backdrop pulley mechanisms, they saw what she was trying to tell them.

A gigantic timber block, precariously suspended from a solitary metal hook!

Carlisle sucked in the air as if his whole life suddenly depended on it. This wasn't right, this was pure evil – pantomime played out in a room full of mannequins.

'Who are you?' Mason asked.

She stared at them, bewildered, but the sound that came from her lips was barely audible.

Mason moved closer. 'Are you, Mary Fowler?'

Her face contorted, and she managed a faint smile.

Then, looking up, Carlisle thought he was imagining things. Attached to some sort of winding mechanism, the huge timber block was edging towards them. Slowly at first, he could definitely see movement. Panic gripped him, and the palms of his hands felt clammy. He tried moving his legs, but they were rooted to the spot.

Oh shit. Oh no.

From what he could make out, everything seemed to be operated by motion sensors. The slightest movement seemed to trigger another new untold danger. They were trapped, and there wasn't a damn thing they could do about it.

Making good use of the bolt cutters, in one swift movement Mason cut through the young woman's ankle constraints and dragged her to safety. It wasn't over yet, not by a long chalk. When he was a young lad Carlisle remembered being trapped inside his father's cement mixing machine. It was a terrifying ordeal, but he knew how to deal with it. This was totally different, though. This was pure evil – delusional pantomime played out by a psychopath who didn't give a damn how many people's lives he destroyed in the process.

But that wasn't all. There was something else, something more sinister in all of this – movement detectors! Unable to move for fear of sending the huge timber block into free-fall, Mason pointed towards the fuse box. Barely an arm's length away, it was just out of fingertip reach. He tried shuffling sideways, but the slightest movement caused the red sensor light on the back of the hoist hook to flicker.

No, no, no, he cursed.

Carlisle heard the two outer support beams groan under the enormous strain, and saw the masonry begin to crumble from the walls. It was then he realised the real danger they were in.

'Watch out!' Mason screamed.

The noise, when it came, was deafening.

BOOM!

The next thing Carlisle heard, as the floor beneath his feet shook violently, was the sound of crashing timbers. Panic gripped him, and the hairs on the back of his neck stood on end. He froze, unable to move for fear of being struck by falling masonry. Moments later, the stage rigging came crashing through the air, narrowly missing him by inches.

In an eerie silence that followed, he unquestionably thought he was dead.

As daylight poured in through a large gaping hole in the roof, dust particles danced, and twinkled like suspended diamonds. Trembling with fear, Carlisle felt the sudden rush of blood to his head. What had seemed to take a lifetime had barely lasted more than a few minutes. It was over, and they had come out of it unscathed.

Mason meanwhile was wiping dust from his eyes with the back of his hand. Moving slowly towards him, the Detective Chief Inspector looked physically dazed by it all. Barely three metres away, Carlisle could see the huge gaping hole where the huge timber block had smashed through the stage flooring and down into the basement below.

It was then he realised just how close to death they'd all come.

'You OK?' Mason asked.

Carlisle allowed himself the suggestion of a smile.

'I'm still in one piece, if that's what you mean.'

'That was bloody close.'

'Too close,' Carlisle nervously replied.

Within minutes backup arrived. First the duty SOC manager, followed by three uniformed police officers dressed in their distinct hi-vis yellow jackets. Suddenly the place was alive and buzzing with police officers. The moment the paramedics appeared in the doorway, Carlisle blew out a long sigh of relief. Not all had gone to plan, of course, but it was the end result that mattered.

Glancing round, Carlisle's eye caught the pair of secateurs that had undoubtedly been used to cut off the victims' fingers. They'd been casually thrown on an empty chair. If Mary Fowler hadn't died in the hands of the killer, then she would most certainly have died from dehydration. This was one of the cruellest acts he'd ever come across. It was inhuman, vile.

Mason glanced at his watch.

'I'll get one of the lads to run you home.'

'I'd appreciate that.'

'Tell me,' Mason said, his voice now in official mode, 'how the hell did you work this one out?'

'If you want to make God smile, best not tell him your plans.'

'What plans,' Mason shrugged.

Carlisle's part in the operation now over, there was little point in hanging around. The rest was police work, endless hours of paperwork before the CPS would finally present its findings to the courts. Jack Mason was right. Having spent the best part of twenty-four hours reconnoitring every St John's church in the county, he'd seen enough of God for one day.

Carlisle had scarcely turned the corner before the music started up again.

Deafening this time—

Not exactly his choice of music either. Not at six-thirty in the morning it wasn't. He'd have preferred a little JJ Cale, *a*nything but *Dancing Queen!*

He couldn't stand the band.

Chapter Fifty-Three

Thrilled with the final outcome, it was late afternoon when David Carlisle finally entered into Gateshead police station. Still smiling, he signalled his arrival to the desk sergeant and made his way towards the third floor of the building. As another chapter in his life was about to come to a close, Mary Fowler was making a remarkable recovery. And, if he was completely honest with himself, he was here to pick up a big fat pay cheque. It had been weeks since he'd last been paid, but it was enough money to pay off their creditors and wipe the slate clean for at least another six months. It was a great feeling, and Carlisle was looking forward to some quality time off with his ageing father.

Earlier that morning he'd arranged to take DC Carrington out to lunch. Nothing flash, but it was the least he could do for all the close protection she'd given him over the past few months. He'd thought about The Ship in Benton, but it was pretty much a man's pub. In the end they'd plumped for Amici Restaurant in Forest Hall again – besides the food was always good and they'd made a lot of new friends there.

As for Mr Smallman, the ninety year old flamboyant bachelor who claimed his ninety-two year old partner was now having it off with a hunky fitness instructor, things had warmed up a tad since their last meeting. It was an unbelievable story, and he couldn't wait for the next instalment to unravel.

'How are things with you?' the Acting Superintendent said chirpily.

'Good, thank you,' he replied.

'It seems we owe you an apology.'

Carlisle feigned surprise. 'Oh. What for, ma'am?'

'Without your persistence, I doubt Mary Fowler would still be alive today.'

Carlisle shuffled awkwardly. 'I understand she's making remarkable progress. What a difference a few days can make.'

'Indeed,' Sutherland smiled, 'and her husband can't stop singing enough of our praises nowadays.'

His eyes caught hers. 'And who will pick up the reward money, ma'am?'

'Look, David,' Sutherland said, her expression demanding attention. 'This Ma'am business is beginning to make me feel like an old woman. We need to change it.'

'And how should I address you in the future?'

'I really don't know. I'd thought about Guv, but it sounds like something out of one of those TV soap dramas. I'd rather liked Boss, but DCI Mason seems to have that one covered.'

'That's true, ma—'

Sutherland almost burst out laughing.

'Tell me,' she said the serious side surfacing. 'What's your take on Lance Wynn? What tipped him over the edge, do you think?'

'It was pretty straightforward really. When Wynn's childhood sweetheart ran off to marry a man with more money than sense, Wynn was inconsolable. The trouble was he suffered from impulsive control problems and once the jealously kicked in, it rapidly turned to hate. It's not uncommon, but serial killers seem to take it the extra mile.'

Sutherland opened her bottom drawer and took out a paper handkerchief.

'Was Cheryl Sawyer partially to blame, do you think?'

'If not, she certainly knew how to fire up other people's emotions. Wynn would have been furious the moment he found out she'd ran off to marry an older man, and that's when the Dr Jekyll and Mr Hyde personality kicked in. The thing is, he probably had no intentions of killing her in the first place and it possibly never crossed his mind.'

'And yet he still hunted her down,' Sutherland said.

Carlisle looked up. 'Wynn was a disaster waiting to happen, in my opinion. His mind was in turmoil and he was wildly out of control. Then, in a moment of utter madness he lashes out and strikes a massive blow to the back of her head.'

'Then finished her off by strangling her, might I add?'

Carlisle made a little sweeping hand gesture. 'Yes, and that's when the self-preservation instincts kicked in. He knew how to cover his tracks. It was easy for him, having studied forensic science at Teesside University. After he killed Cheryl Sawyer he would have been hyper-focused, and that's when he removed her cell phone and personal effects. Whilst he was at it, he made pretty damn certain that drugs were found on her body.'

Sutherland raised an eyebrow. 'Which is why the Cleveland police always believed her death to be drugs related?

'He'd obviously thought it through.'

'Planned and professionally executed, by the sounds of things?'

'Yes, to some degree I suppose it was,' Carlisle replied.

'Even so, that still doesn't explain why he removed his victims' fingers. What are your thoughts on that?' she asked.

'It's a difficult one. At this point his misogynistic tendencies had obviously lain dormant, but Wynn's intense hatred towards Cheryl Sawyer had never waned. When the act of killing hadn't quite lived up to his expectations, it tipped him over the edge. That's when the violent fantasies kicked in, and that's when he removed her fingers.'

'To make it look like her rings had been stolen—'

'No ma'am.' Carlisle held eye contact for a few seconds longer than he'd intended. 'In Wynn's mind, if he couldn't marry Cheryl Sawyer then no one else could?'

She turned sharply. 'What about this satanic salute theory of yours?'

'I've been having second thoughts about that.'

'It's plausible, but I'm still not convinced myself,' Sutherland said thoughtfully. 'Besides, we still haven't found any rings.'

'He probably disposed of them in a mad fit of temper.'

Sutherland reflected on his statement for a moment. 'This six-year cooling off period you often talk about, why wait that long between murders?'

'After he killed Cheryl Sawyer, he probably got a taste for it. Let's not forget that Wynn was once her lover and now he's her executioner.' Their eyes met. 'When God told him to kill these women, it would have allowed him to conveniently wipe his hands clean of any wrongdoing. Slipping back into his normal self again, he was able to blend back into society as if nothing had ever happened.'

'Umm, but what triggered him to kill Caroline Harper in the first place?'

'Not surprisingly when a relationship ends in humiliation, we always feel betrayed. Full of rejection and self-criticism, the normal reaction is to turn inwards on ourselves. Wynn was no different, except he suffered from explosive violent tendencies inherited from a hot-headed drunken father. If Wynn believed it was God who had told him to kill Cheryl Sawyer, then his conscience was clear. But there lay a problem. Wynn's mind was torn between fantasy and reality, and what followed was a bitter hate campaign against these women.'

'And that's when Caroline Harper enters the scene?'

'Wynn's head was so mixed up he probably couldn't make head nor tail of it. Wynn had snapped, and he probably saw in Caroline Harper what he saw in Cheryl Sawyer. After years of pent-up narcissistic make-believe, the misogynistic hatred inside him explodes. From then on no woman was ever safe from his clutches.'

'Well that certainly explains why Wynn did what he did.' Sutherland stroked her chin in thought. 'And there's me thinking he had access to the missing person files.'

'That's the thing with serial killers, they're predictable. Wynn was a social predator who toured the night clubs and bars in search of potential candidates. We know how long it took him to find Caroline Harper, but he got there in the end.'

Sutherland sat down in her seat again.

'This mannequin business,' she said, 'the one found on Chester-le-Street train station. Now we know more about Wynn's background, it was a bit of a giveaway, don't you think?'

'The minute we blamed someone else for Wynn's murders, it severely dented his ego. We knew the risks we were taking, what we didn't know was just how Wynn was going to react to it. Looking back it probably sparked off all kinds of anger inside his head. There again, how else was he going to prove to us we'd charged the wrong man?'

'And had we not,' said Sutherland pausing in reflection, 'God knows how many more women he might have killed.'

Carlisle felt the need to explain. 'To catch a serial killer you need to play them at their own games.'

Sutherland was about to speak when DCI Mason appeared in the doorway.

'Ah, Jack,' she said. 'What's the latest on our Alpaca thieves Bodgit and Scarper?'

'They've both been given four years, ma'am.'

Sutherland's face lit up. 'Well done. That'll teach them to go around stealing other people's property. What about compensation?'

'Nothing mentioned, ma'am. I suspect it was an out of court settlement.'

'I'm curious as to what they intended to do with these South American camelids?'

'They sold them on apparently. Somewhere down south, I believe.'

'Well at least they didn't eat them.'

Mason grinned quietly to himself.

'Will there be anything else, ma'am?'

'Not at the moment.' As if to draw attention towards it, Sutherland tapped her pen on her note pad. 'Just for the record, David and I are going back over Wynn's psychological background.'

'Right then, I'll leave the two of you to get on with it.'

'Oh! There is one other thing,' Sutherland said. 'I need to speak to you later about this suspicious death that took place over the weekend. Thinking it through, I'm still not convinced the gentleman accidentally fell out of a nineteenth story window. We know that drugs were involved, and I know your views on that.' Sutherland stared at him. 'I'm reliably informed the autopsy has since thrown up scratch abrasions to the victim's lower jaw.'

'A facial blow!'

'Yes. He may have been involved in a fight, and the abrasions suggest a ring injury.'

'I'll check with Dr King, ma'am.'

'Yes, please do.'

Mason turned sharply to face them. 'If anyone's interested we're having an end of case knees up – seven o'clock tomorrow night at the Ship Inn.'

'Sorry, Jack,' Sutherland frowned, 'but I've already made other arrangements for tomorrow night.'

'What about you?' Mason said, staring Carlisle directly in the eye.

'You can count me in.'

'Seven it is then.'

With that Mason took off down the corridor.

Ch*pter
Fifty-Four

Puddles from the late afternoon rain still hung around the footpath when Carlisle strode into the Ship Inn that evening. The bar was heaving and many of those present were police officers. Familiar faces, friends he'd worked alongside on *Operation Marco Polo*.

Jack Mason enjoyed springing surprises on people, and he was extremely good at it. It was match night, and many of the regulars were wearing their Newcastle United strip tops. In what was a mouth-watering pre-season fixture, the atmosphere was buzzing. The landlady seemed up for it too. Having laid on a fantastic food spread, everyone was tucking in. Not that Carlisle was hungry, but he still managed to grab a plateful of sandwiches all the same.

'Does the name Willem de Kooning ring any bells?' Mason said casually sidling up to him.

'Yes, he's a client of mine. Why?'

Mason threw an arm around Carlisle's shoulder and spilled beer all down the front of his new trousers. There was a long silence. 'It's a funny old world. Willem de Kooning used the same group of accountants that Lance Wynn worked for in Middlesbrough.'

'What – Timothy Evans!'

'That's the one. At some stage you must have done some work for Kooning.'

'Yes I did.'

Mason pulled a funny little facial expression. 'His tax returns were the giveaway, and that's how Wynn found out where you were living.'

'Well, I'll be damned. That certainly answers a few questions.'

'Lance Wynn had you under his radar from the very start, my friend.' Mason took another huge swig of his beer. 'But that's another story, I guess.'

'But why choose me of all people?'

'You're the criminal profiler. I thought you would have already sussed that one out.'

Just as Mason was about to say something, the landlady appeared carrying a tray full of freshly made sandwiches. As a dozen hands made a grab for them, the Detective Chief Inspector fell backwards against the bar. Looking decidedly the worse for wear, his shirt was hanging out and he was staggering on his feet like a drunken sailor.

'Mind,' Mason said, jabbing a finger into Carlisle's chest, 'Sutherland's none the wiser.'

'That woman has eyes in the back of her head, Jack.'

'Tell me about it.'

Carlisle found a quieter spot at the bar.

'So what happens to you now?' he asked.

'I'm already working another case,'

'Really——'

Mason jaw slackened, as his grip on the bar rail tightened. 'Yeah, some crackerjack fell to his death from nineteen floors at the weekend, and probably thought he could fly. If not, then someone wanted to see if he could. It's not exactly rocket science, but where drugs are involved it's always the usual suspects who first spring to mind.'

'Drugs, eh?'

'The guy was a born loser who refused to play by the rules.'

'So you think he was pushed?'

'If not, then his wings didn't fucking work.'

'Nineteen floors up... bloody hell!'

They talked a while, about everything and nothing.

Mason clinked glasses. 'If I'm brutally honest with you, without your assistance I would probably be out on the bare bones of my arse by now. After we caught the Alpaca thieves red-handed, I thought Sutherland would have given me some breathing space. Chance would be a fine thing. Those bastards upstairs are never satisfied; they'll always find something to complain about.'

'Big desks, big fat wages packet, the two go hand in hand I'm afraid.'

'You're probably right,' Mason shrugged.

As the evening wore on and with only a hard-core of police officers still standing, it was time to make tracks. He'd enjoyed himself immensely, and he was sorry to be leaving so many good friends behind. But that was a private investigator's role; it could be a very lonely life at times.

Before leaving, he caught up with Mason again.

'It's time I was off, mate.'

'Right, then,' Mason said, squinting down at his watch strap as if it wasn't supposed to be there. 'Pity you're leaving, you'll miss all the fun.'

'Another time perhaps—'

'Don't push it!' Mason grinned.

'I'll keep that in mind the next time you're desperately in need of some help.'

'Oh, there is one other thing. I've heard Sutherland may have something for you.'

'Did she say what?'

Mason suddenly shot sideways across the bar, but somehow managed to grab hold of the bar rail. Face flushed and barely managing to stay upright, he was in a right old state.

'Something to do with leather thongs and kinky high-heels—'

'Yeah, chance would be a fine thing.'

The Detective Chief Inspector grabbed him by the arm. 'Remind me again about this Kooning fella again. What sort of work did you do for him?'

Carlisle thought about that, and then said, 'He was an antiques dealer. His business partner had walked out on him carrying a boot full of antiques in a Mercedes-Benz C-Class he'd stolen, and he asked me to help.'

'And you think I'm fucking pissed!'

Drunk out of his mind, Mason staggered off towards to the gents' toilet knocking into every chair along the way. It was well past closing time, and yet another round of drinks had mysteriously appeared on the bar. When he was a young copper working in the Met, Carlisle would drink himself senseless at the end of every murder case. It was the done thing back then, but those days were behind him now. If ever he was going to make a complete arsehole of himself, he preferred doing it in the comfort of his own home.

He was saying his goodbyes when Rob Savage grabbed his coat sleeve. Slumped over the bar with his arm wrapped around a rather large buxom blonde with a hard done by face and blonde peroxide hair, the detective sergeant was well-served.

'Nice one, Davy,' the sergeant slurred. 'You did another fantastic job for us.'

'No thanks to you,' Carlisle replied. 'Keep in touch, and don't do anything silly.'

Savage broke out into song.

Carlisle had seen enough; it was time to head home.

Chapter Fifty-Five

Six weeks into the trial, and Lance Wynn had finally gained the notoriety he'd always craved. It was headline breaking news. After months spent scouring the North East countryside trying to establish where Caroline Harper had been murdered, the police were no further forward in their investigations. They had their suspicions, of course, but nothing was cast in stone. Just as his idol Ian Brady before him, Wynn was giving nothing away.

Throughout the trial there had been intense speculation as to just how many more women Lance Wynn had killed. The police believed it was four, but proving it was difficult, if not impossible without a body. And, even if Wynn had killed them, he certainly wasn't letting on about it.

As the focus of attention now shifted towards the jury's final verdict, Wynn was facing a lifetime in prison. And yet, standing before Leeds Crown Court, he looked nothing like a serial killer. But that was the thing: serial killers were manipulative social predators who had the striking ability to deceive, no matter what havoc they wreaked. Even Wynn's defence lawyers were outraged at the lack of remorse their client had shown throughout the trial. Not that Wynn cared. He didn't. It was his way of dealing with it, his way of refusing to accept responsibility for the heinous crimes he'd committed. The only positive, if you could call it that, was that a dangerous predator had finally been taken off the streets of Gateshead.

Late morning and the sun had appeared. Even so, there was still a stiff breeze blowing directly across the top of High Fell. It was strange how barely a month ago this place gave Carlisle the creeps. Not anymore. That had all changed, and he was beginning to enjoy the peace and tranquillity that Windy Nook offered. Up here on top of the world the views were spectacular. This was undoubtedly God's country, the nearest place to heaven you could get.

A memory tugged him!

It might be nothing, he thought, but what if Wynn had never intended to stage an accident in the first place? What if the victim's car had suddenly ran out of petrol that night, or broken down at the top of Coldwell Lane? It was feasible of course, another way of looking at things. There again, what if Wynn's intentions had always been to transport Caroline Harper's body to someplace else? *The same location as he'd dumped the other women's bodies.* He could have done, and it wasn't irrational thinking. Six-years between murders seemed an awful long time – too long if the truth was known. It wasn't a clear cut case either, and never had been. Wynn was a religious freak, a disturbing psychopath with more than just a vicious hate campaign against greedy women. His victims were easy prey, and Wynn was never going to give in easily.

'Is this an old Rover P4 100?' a man out walking his dog asked.

'Yes, it is,' Carlisle proudly replied.

'Great looking car, but I can image getting spare parts must be a nightmare.'

Typical, Carlisle cursed. If it ain't broke, why try to fix it.

THE END

You've turned the last page.
But it doesn't have to end there...

If you're looking for more action packed reading in the DCI Mason and David Carlisle crime thriller series, why not join me at **www.mike-foster.me** for news, behind the scene interviews, and the latest updates.

Angelica's Curse, the next DCI Mason and Carlisle crime thriller — is planned for publication in 2017. Catch up with you later...

THE WHARF BUTCHER

(Book 1) in the DCI Mason & Carlisle Crime Thriller series

A serial killer is stalking Tyneside. But there is a pattern to his killing, his choice of victims, and his method of slaughter. David Carlisle, a criminal profiler, is brought in to assist DCI Jack Mason with his task of identifying the killer and stopping him in his tracks.

The Wharf Butcher is a fast-paced thriller that shines a light on the dark forces within the corridors of power, in the boardroom and the police force itself. The clock is ticking to catch the monster that has been unleashed. But first Carlisle must get inside the killer's head...

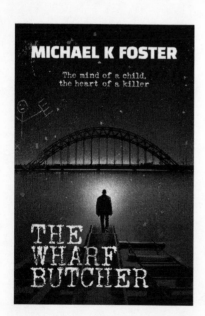

'Start to finish, the author hardly gives you time to catch your breath as horror piles on horror and the killer thumbs his nose at the pursuers.'

The Northern Echo